James Phelan is the bestselling and award-winning author of twenty-nine novels and one work of non-fiction. From his teens he wanted to be a novelist but first tried his hand at a real job, studying and working in architecture before turning to English literature, spending five years at a newspaper and obtaining an MA and PhD in literature.

The ex-CIA character of Jed Walker was first introduced in *The Spy*, which was followed by *The Hunted*, *Kill Switch*, *Dark Heart* and *The Agency*.

James has also written five titles in the Lachlan Fox thriller series, and the Alone trilogy of young adult post-apocalyptic novels. A full-time novelist since the age of twenty-five, he spends his time writing thrilling stories and travelling the world to talk about them.

To find out more about James and his books, visit
www.jamesphelan.com

Follow and interact with James
www.facebook.com/realjamesphelan
www.twitter.com/realjamesphelan
www.instagram.com/realjamesphelan
www.whosay.com/jamesphelan

ALSO BY JAMES PHELAN

The Jed Walker books

The Spy

Kill Switch

Dark Heart

The Lachlan Fox books

Fox Hunt

Patriot Act

Blood Oil

Liquid Gold

Red Ice

The Alone series

Chasers

Survivor

Quarantine

JAMES PHELAN

THE HUNTED

CONSTABLE • LONDON

CONSTABLE

First published in Australia and New Zealand in 2015 by Hachette Australia,
an imprint of Hachette Australia Pty Limited.

First published in Great Britain in 2018 by Constable

13 5 7 9 10 8 6 4 2

Copyright © James Phelan, 2015

The moral right of the author has been asserted.

A CIP catalogue record for this book
is available from the British Library.

ISBN: 978-1-47212-717-4

Typeset in Simoncini Garamond by Bookhouse, Sydney
Printed and bound in Great Britain by CPI Group (UK), Croydon CR0 4YY

Papers used by Constable are from well-managed forests
and other responsible sources.

MIX
Paper from
responsible sources
FSC® C104740
FSC
www.fsc.org

Constable
An imprint of
Little, Brown Book Group
Carmelite House
50 Victoria Embankment
London EC4Y 0DZ

An Hachette UK Company
www.hachette.co.uk

www.littlebrown.co.uk

In memory of Matt Richell,
a publishing champion and wonderful man.

Prologue

The gunshot sounded. Then another.

Walker looked up. Alert, not alarmed.

Nine-millimetre. Double-tap. Fired from an elevated position. A couple of blocks east, atop one of the multi-storey buildings. Fired downwards and at close range to the target, minimising the report.

No-one in the New York street seemed to notice. Just another sharp sound in a big city: a car backfiring or machinery clanging or something big and heavy hitting the deck.

But Walker knew. And the man seated in front of him knew. And the guy standing two yards away beside Walker's ex-wife knew.

'Somerville,' Bill McCorkell said from across the table. He shifted in his seat and added, 'Right on time, I'd say.'

Walker looked up at the rooftop and saw Somerville, five storeys up, a foot on the parapet, holstering her FBI-issued side-arm. He waved. She waved back.

Walker said, 'She wasn't shooting at birds, I take it.'

'Tying up a loose end,' McCorkell replied.

'Durant?'

McCorkell nodded.

Walker looked back up to the elevated position. She'd tracked Durant up there; it was a no-brainer what he'd been up to. Walker pictured the ex-CIA man's body sprawled next to a sniper's rifle. Walker wondered who would have been lined up in the scope first – him or McCorkell. On the street, a team of heavily armed NYPD uniformed officers appeared on foot from around a corner and entered the building. She'd planned it well. A good job all round.

'Thank Somerville for me,' Walker said, his eyes returning to McCorkell.

'You can thank her yourself,' the older man countered. He leaned forward on the table. 'This is the beginning of things, Walker, not the end.'

1

Walker paused for just a moment. 'This changes nothing.'

McCorkell sat there, silent, waiting.

'I'm not working for you,' Walker said. 'Just tell Somerville she and I are even.'

'You two will never be even.'

Walker didn't answer; instead he turned and walked the four paces to where the FBI man Andrew Hutchinson stood with Walker's former wife, Eve.

Separated. Then widowed. Grieving for more than a year, never knowing what really happened to her estranged husband who'd been listed dead by the CIA and State Department.

Now this.

The two of them, standing there, facing each other on the Manhattan street.

She was smaller than he remembered. A little older. Sadder. Beautiful.

Hutchinson stepped around Walker to join McCorkell at the cafe table. Walker could hear them talking, animatedly, but he blocked it out.

Eve.

Looking into Eve's eyes, he felt that it could have been yesterday he'd last seen her. A bunch of yesterdays ran through his mind. Most of them were firsts. Their first meeting, first kiss, first time they'd slept together, first time they'd fought. The last time they'd fought.

Standing before her, Walker was ready for war. For tears and fists. Anger. But if all that was there, it was coming later.

For now, Eve hugged him. Tight. Silent.

He'd always loved that about her: no matter what happened, she knew what to say, and what not to say. They stood together, embracing, until McCorkell tapped Walker on the shoulder.

'We've just had word,' McCorkell said, moving into Walker's line of sight over the top of Eve's head. 'We know where he is.'

From the tone, the poise, Walker knew what McCorkell meant before he elaborated.

'We've found your father.'

•

'He's in the UK,' Special Agent Hutchinson said to his boss, Bill McCorkell. 'That's David Walker, right there.'

Walker looked over the photographs.

The four of them – Walker, McCorkell, Hutchinson and Special Agent Fiona Somerville – sat in an office of the FBI's New York Field Office. Eve sat at a desk outside the glass-walled office, waiting. The Lower Manhattan office building was a shared federal government space, and staffers milled about, looking busy.

Fair enough, thought Walker. They'd almost lost a VP on their turf just a few days back. The same day that Walker had heard from his father.

'Near Hereford,' Hutchinson said, showing a map on his iPad. 'West Midlands, near the Welsh border.'

'I know the place,' Walker said. He looked at the long-lens shot of the man who had raised him. The man he hardly knew. 'I spoke at the SAS once. My father did too, several times.'

'So he had friends there,' Somerville said.

'Probably. None I recall, no names,' Walker said. He stared blankly, remembering the place. 'Hell, as a teenager I went with him on one of his trips and we fished the Wye together. How'd we get these photos?'

'British intel, about two weeks back,' Hutchinson said. The FBI man used a pencil to itch at his bandaged arm. 'They're investigating someone he was seen with.'

'Why?'

'We're not sure yet,' Hutchinson replied, as he brought up a satellite map on a large screen. 'The call that your father made to you at the New York Stock Exchange? It came from a location not far from the barracks.' He zoomed in on a dot on a tiny road at the centre of a cluster of small buildings. 'It came from a landline phone in this tavern.'

'That call was made three days ago,' Walker said. 'He won't still be in the area. The trail's long dead. He'll be gone. He's good at disappearing.'

'I've just run his image through TrapWire and Scotland Yard's

CCTV program,' Somerville said. 'He's come up four times over the past six months, all within fifty klicks of that tavern.'

Walker studied the images that Hutchinson had brought up on the screen. A couple were grainy and blurred, taken from ATM cameras. Another showed his father in the background of someone's Facebook photo. The last was a grab from a CCTV camera in a shop – in this last one the subject was looking directly up at it, as though he knew he'd been caught out.

'That last one,' Walker said. 'Where's that?'

'A gas station, just on the outskirts of Hereford on that same road headed to our tavern, soon after he called you,' Somerville said, checking the surveillance notes. 'Later that night it was robbed. All on-site stored footage was taken but this had been backed up off-site to the security company.'

'Does all that sound like the actions of a guy *leaving* the area?' McCorkell said to Walker. 'He's still there.'

'Covering his tracks . . .' Walker said, seeing his father's eyes for the first time in a long while. He looked over to Eve, silent, present, but not taking it in, as though the reappearance of yet another dead Walker was one revelation too many. 'You think he's been there for the last six months?'

'At least,' Hutchinson said.

'Seems he's made it something of a home base,' Somerville said. 'He could be running Zodiac from there.'

'We don't know his involvement in that,' McCorkell said.

'Yeah, well he *did* have contacts there,' Walker said. 'He had a hand in the psych training and debriefing of SAS guys, since at least the Falklands.'

'No-one you remember?' Hutchinson asked, cradling his bandaged arm. 'Anyone there particularly close to your father?'

'Nope,' Walker said, thinking back. 'But he had a few friends there, I'm sure. He'd go there every few years. They'd be drinking buddies and the like. Not close.'

'Close enough to work with,' Somerville said. 'Then, and now.'

Walker nodded.

'You got dates for those trips?' Somerville asked. 'I can get British Ministry of Defence personnel records to match, go through them.'

'Maybe,' Walker said, nodding. 'But this is the SAS we're talking about – whether serving or former, they're not going to lay out the red carpet for a group of outsiders to look into their people's whereabouts.'

'Worth a shot,' McCorkell said. 'Let's see where we can get.'

Somerville nodded.

'Why haven't we heard about this sooner?' Walker said. 'Why didn't his presence, plus the fact that MI5 are looking into him too, flag something months ago?'

'We're still waiting on answers to that too,' Hutchinson said. 'Brits are dragging their feet in cooperating – we don't know who they're surveilling, or why.'

'But we're working on it,' McCorkell said, looking to Walker as he spoke.

'I just can't imagine him being in a place like that,' Walker said, 'a place people might recognise him, when he's playing the dead man.'

'He's hiding in plain sight,' Somerville said. 'It worked for you for near-on a year.'

'Yeah, but I was trying to stop a terrorist attack,' Walker said, 'not playing a part in it.'

'You really think he's a part of this, don't you?' McCorkell said, matter-of-fact.

Walker remained silent.

'At any rate,' Somerville said, filling the silence, 'no-one's been looking for David Walker until now.'

'News travels fast, even over the pond,' Walker said. 'They'd have known he was supposed to be dead.'

'So, he's staying off the grid over there,' Hutchinson said. 'Maybe only a local friend or two know of his resurrection.'

Walker shook his head. 'It's not like him. He's too smart, and being over there seems too risky.'

'He's there because of something he needs,' Hutchinson said. 'Protection. Connections. Something.'

'Maybe he's retired there,' McCorkell said, leaning back and sipping a steaming tea. 'For the fishing.'

'Right,' Walker said, deadpan. 'You think he faked his death, had a hand in a terrorist attack on US soil, knew of an internal CIA takeover and an attempt on the Vice-President's life – all from a tavern in rural England?'

McCorkell shrugged.

'You're a pro at this, right?' Walker chided.

McCorkell feigned indifference. Walker looked from him to Hutchinson, then to Somerville. The three of them watched him. Waiting. For an answer. An answer they'd been waiting to hear for three days.

'Look, Walker, this, with your father. It's a lead,' Somerville said. 'The best lead we've got to break into the Zodiac terror network. And we're going to check it out. With or without you.'

'So tell us,' Hutchinson said. 'Are you in?'

Walker looked from the UN intelligence team to the larger office beyond the glass wall. Eve sat there. She was looking at him. Her eyes showed nothing.

Walker nodded. 'I'm in.'

'Nine years ago,' Walker said, looking through the car's windscreen at the English town. 'That's when I spoke here, after my first tour of Afghanistan.'

'For the CIA?' Somerville asked.

'No, before that,' Walker said.

'When you were Air Force?' Somerville asked.

Walker nodded.

'I still don't get how the Air Force has boots-on-the-ground frontline guys,' she said. 'Airplanes, airbases, the Pentagon, sure. But humping around in the mountains with SEALs and Delta?'

'Someone has to have the brains in those Special Forces teams,' Walker replied.

McCorkell and Hutchinson rode in the back of the hire car, a Land Rover Discovery. Bill McCorkell was not a field man. Never had been. Just past sixty, he'd spent a lifetime as an intelligence and international-affairs expert, rising to the post of National Security Advisor to presidents from both sides of politics. His current role was driving a specialist UN desk, from which he ran a small team of multinational investigators in the field and reported directly to the Secretary-General. The intelligence outfit was known simply as Room 360, named after its office number in the United Nations building in Vienna, and its members were sequestered from the world's best intelligence and law-enforcement agencies.

Walker watched the familiar streets slip by. On the flight here, plans had been made. He and Somerville would check out the tavern. McCorkell and Hutchinson would visit SAS headquarters, Hereford, to see if any old-timers had had contact with David Walker, the dead man.

Andrew Hutchinson was lead investigator and, like Somerville, was on loan to the UN from the FBI. Just a few days earlier, in the events leading up to the terrorist attack at the New York Stock Exchange, he'd been badly wounded. Walker glanced back at the guy. He had a lot to be thankful to him for – the lawman had saved Eve's life, and because of this his face was a mask of green and purple bruising, and his arm was in a sling.

Walker would not forget that.

And he would not forget Eve, who was now in temporary witness protection courtesy of the FBI. In Maine; that's all Walker knew.

The English town slipped by. The trees were losing the last of their leaves. The sky was one big cloud of grey.

Whatever happened here, there would be tomorrows with Eve. Maybe not like those yesterdays, but at the very least, there would be closure. Answers. Discussions. Decisions made. Progress. For more than a year he'd been thinking about it, about her, never finding the courage to make the first move, allowing her to believe he was dead, always justifying his actions as a form of protecting her while completing his mission.

'This is us,' McCorkell said from the back seat.

Somerville took the exit to the old RAF base, drove up to the guardhouse and stopped. The two men in the back got out.

'Keep in touch,' McCorkell said as he departed, Hutchinson close behind him.

Somerville nodded. Walker remained silent.

She drove back to town, tapping the sat-nav to take them to the tavern on the B-road.

•

The Boar and Thistle was some twenty minutes' drive west of Hereford.

There were four cars in the gravel car park: two rentals and a couple of locals.

Walker stood by their parked car and looked around. Twelve houses in view, all well-kept stone cottages. Dark stone, white-trimmed windows. Gardens set up with precision and allowed to overgrow just so. The road through was two-lane blacktop; cars, trucks and vans passed at an average rate of one every fifteen seconds or so. It was just after midday. The sky was darkening. A typical Midlands affair, the lot of it.

'You coming?' Somerville asked.

'That's what she said,' Walker replied, walking towards the FBI agent who stood waiting by the front door. 'Trading to thirsty travellers since 1514' was stencilled inside the entrance. Somerville had a hand on her hip, her jacket open, revealing where her side-arm would have been back in the US. Her bobbed blonde hair was tucked behind her ear against the wind. She dressed well, for a Fed.

Somerville said, 'What's what she said?'

'Joke.'

'Oh. I didn't know you had a sense of humour.'

'I don't,' Walker said, opening the door.

2

McCorkell looked across the desk at the SAS Squadron Commander, a Brigadier Smith.

'UN?' the Brigadier said, looking at McCorkell's card. 'Are you guys still around?'

'Our pay cheques say so,' Hutchinson replied. He and McCorkell were seated across the 1980s-era laminate desk.

'We need your help on finding this guy,' McCorkell said. They would have preferred to meet with the man at the top, a Major-General in charge of the regiment, but he was away. 'Never mess with the man in the middle', was one of McCorkell's mottos, and it had served him well in cutting through bureaucracy. He suspected that they would not get far here.

'And which guy would that be?' the Brigidier said.

'David Walker,' Hutchinson said, fumbling with his iPad with one hand as he showed the Brigadier the recent picture of David Walker. 'We checked records. You were here when he was.'

'Yes, I remember him. Walker. Yank. Intel expert, anti-terror specialist. Academic and policy man from DC.'

'That's right,' Hutchinson said. 'When did you last see him?'

'And where?' McCorkell said.

'Years ago. Here, on base.'

'What can you remember?' Hutchinson asked.

'Well, let's see. I was a lieutenant then, just over from the paras. He spoke to us during the first Gulf War, the week before we deployed, about what to expect to extract from prisoners – should we take any.'

'Right,' Hutchinson said. 'And you're sure you haven't seen him since?'

'Yes.' The Brigidier passed back the iPad. 'Why the interest?'

'He's dead and buried back home, full honours and mourning,'

McCorkell said. 'But he's been seen around here over the past few months.'

'Oh?' The Brigadier leaned back. 'You're sure?'

'Certain.' Hutchinson tapped on the iPad screen and brought up an image of the Boar and Thistle, which showed the front of the building and a couple of guys in the background, and passed it back.

The photo stirred something in the Brigadier. He stared at his desk, then said, 'Come with me. There's something I'd like to show you.'

•

Walker took in his surroundings within seconds.

The publican was a no-nonsense man who had served in the military. The publican saw Walker too and probably figured the same.

Three groups of people sat eating at tables; two were clearly tourists from the rental cars outside, and the other was locals.

Five people sat on stools at the bar, drinking. Three were inconsequential. Two were of interest. Also ex-military. Walker recognised one from the picture of his father taken here.

Walker ordered a pint of dark ale and turned to his colleague. 'Drink?'

Somerville paused a beat, then said, 'Cabernet.'

'And a glass of red,' Walker said to the publican, who went about the task with a laconic proficiency, placed the drinks on the mahogany bar and said, 'That all?'

'And a question,' Walker said, handing over a twenty and producing the photo of his father. 'Have you seen this guy in here?'

The publican's eyes shifted from Walker's to the pic and lingered a bit, then he said, 'Nope.'

Walker nodded.

The publican went back to his other patrons at the bar. The two ex-military types.

Walker picked up his drink, looked at Somerville and sipped.

'He's lying,' Somerville said, watching the publican keep busy.

'Yeah . . .' Walker said, placing his half-empty pint on the bar. 'That's all right. These boys will help us.'

Somerville looked up at him.

Walker felt a tap on his shoulder. He held Somerville's eye briefly and then turned. The two men from the bar. Each well on the other side of forty, each shorter than Walker but wiry with lean muscle. Former SAS men, or close to it. A lifetime of keeping fit the hard way, their former occupation's hazard writ large in their bones and joints and expressions and scars.

'We heard you're looking for someone,' the tapper said to Walker. He was the guy he recognised from the photo.

'Sure,' Walker said. He slid the photo of his father from the bar and held it next to his face. He was unsure whether the familial traits would be evident to the two guys. The first man stood two yards from him, the second just a yard behind his comrade's right shoulder, the bar to their left. Both wore khakis with flannel shirts and light jackets. Unshaven, hair a little unkempt, just as they would have looked back in their SAS regiment days.

'What's it to you?' he said, looking at Walker.

'I need to find him.'

'Well then, you got a problem, mate,' the tapper said to Walker.

'Oh?' Walker replied.

'That wasn't a question,' he said to Walker, and took half a pace forward. 'I said, you got a problem.'

'How you figure that?' Walker replied. He relaxed his shoulders, let his arms hang loose by his sides, kept his body weight at the front of his feet.

'You're in a tight community here, lad,' the guy behind the tapper said. He looked ten years older than Walker but showed no obvious sign of diminished skill in unarmed combat. 'We look after our friends, including that guy you're after – who, by the way, doesn't want to be disturbed. So, best you leave then.'

'On your way, mate.'

'Yeah,' Walker said, putting his drink down, his head tilted slightly to the left. 'About that . . .'

•

'Some time in the past six months we had a break-in, to our archival armoury,' the Brigadier explained as they walked across a green grass field, dotted with small hillocks. 'Though we didn't know it at the time.'

'Didn't know?' Hutchinson said.

'It gets audited just twice a year, so there's a six-month window.'

Hutchinson asked, 'When was the last audit?'

'Not four weeks ago. That's when this was reported as missing.' They stopped at a metal door where three uniformed soldiers were busily stacking crates inside the earth-covered storage bunker. He handed an inventory to the Brigadier.

McCorkell looked over the list, and Hutchinson read over his shoulder. Twelve Browning Hi Power pistols. Four MP5Ks. Two crates of ammunition totalling a thousand 9-millimetre rounds. And a box of thirty way-out-of-date flash-bang grenades.

'How do flash-bangs go out of date?' McCorkell asked.

'Corrosion,' the quartermaster replied with a shrug. 'It's rubbish, though. They work just fine for at least twenty years; I've seen it myself. The company just wants to sell more to the MoD, and we're not allowed to use the old ones in case one does go wrong.'

'This is enough firepower to start a war,' Hutchinson said.

'It certainly is,' the Brigadier replied. 'And there was a crate of C4 too, we think.'

'You *think*?'

'That stuff goes boom all the time; it's hard to keep track of exactly how much the lads use.'

'Someone broke in here?' Hutchinson said, looking around the armoury. Two corporals and a sergeant looked pissed at the two American suits poking around in their den.

'Not on your life,' the Brigidier replied. 'The archival storage is in another above-ground bunker the other side of the base. Reinforced concrete with a hundred tons of earth all around, dating back to the war. One door is made of three inches of hardened steel from when battleships were a thing. A modern combination lock that's got a whiz-bang security guarantee.'

'Inside job,' Hutchinson said.

The Brigadier nodded. 'It's happened before. Those pictures you showed me? There's another guy in one of them. In the background. He used to work here. Real bastard, or SOB as you might call him.'

'I'll need everything you know about him,' Hutchinson said.

'Right,' the Brigadier said.

McCorkell watched the three other soldiers keep themselves busy as their boss explained the theft, full of silent professional fury at whoever had committed the crime.

Hutchinson said, 'You don't change the locking code?'

'Not as often as we should have,' the Brigadier replied. 'Remedied, by the by.'

'What's the relevance for us?' McCorkell asked. 'There's no way our man had that combination.'

'That's right,' the Brigadier said. 'But if your man is up to no good around these parts, then he's had a hand in this.'

'How'd you figure?' Hutchinson asked.

'Because,' the Brigadier said, 'I know for a fact that the geezer who once stood in my shoes knew that man. And he's the one in that photo of yours.'

3

The previous commander of Hereford's Sabre Squadron HQ element didn't live long beyond his current incumbent's mention. Not because Walker wanted to kill him, but the fact was, when guys like this entered into combat, armed or not, it was for keeps.

He moved at Walker. Fast, for an older guy, but Walker didn't let him near. He was smaller than Walker, an in-fighter who wanted to move in close and negate Walker's advantages of size, reach and relative youth.

Stepping aside, Walker let the guy propel towards him but kept him at arm's distance.

The guy kept on his toes, a well-honed fighting stance, manoeuvrable. He lunged to the right for a grapple hold, which Walker twisted out of, grabbing a wrist. That was the first move of the fight. Time enough for the other man to react, to start moving. But Walker calculated he was a second from joining the fight.

And a second was all he needed.

And a second was all the former SAS man had.

Walker raised his boot and stamped down on the guy's kneecap. A swift stomping motion, the heel of his boot carrying a few g's of force. He heard rather than felt the cartilage crunching and bone breaking and ligaments sheering off. That was the first half of the movement, the first half-second.

As the guy reeled, rocking instinctively back and away from the pain as the leg gave out, Walker, with a vice-like grip on the man's wrist, twisted. Not to break bones in the arm or hand. To break his neck.

In two movements, Walker pivoted his opponent around so that his back was to Walker's chest, and he wrapped his free hand around the guy's neck and twisted. Like taking the top off a bottle. The man's head might not have pulled off, but the life fell from him before his body hit the floor.

Somerville was moving by Walker, a blur of motion.

Walker only had eyes for the threat ahead.

The other man had used those two seconds of mayhem to move a pace towards Walker while drawing a Browning Hi Power. The pistol was still being brought to aim as he flinched past his falling mate.

Somerville was still a blur at the edge of Walker's peripherals, moving fast to his aid, but he beat her to the action.

Walker's first movement was to control the gun-hand. Both his hands connected with it and the pistol went off. The Hi Power was chambered for the standard 9-millimetre round, but close up in the confines of the five-hundred-year-old stone tavern, it was loud.

The SAS man had the smarts to improvise and adapt on the fly. Now close in, he attempted to head-butt Walker, but because he was a good six inches shorter than Walker, the move was nullified when Walker rocked up on his toes and the blow landed on his chest rather than his bottom jaw. A hard head meeting dense pectorals. Call it a draw.

Holding the man's wrists in his large hands, Walker brought them down, pulling them together and raising his knee. On impact with the forearms, one elbow popped out of its joint, the wrist of the other arm snapping in two places. The pistol clattered to the floor. Somerville went for it. Walker let go and elbowed the guy in the face. The man was knocked backwards a step from the kinetic force of the blow reverberating through his body. Walker caught up with him as he charged. Walker went with the force and fell backwards, the guy's head in the crook of his arm. Walker fell flat on his back, restraining his opponent in a tight embrace. The sound of the top of the guy's head hitting the flagstone floor was like that of a coconut cracking.

Lights out.

Walker stood.

Somerville held the Browning loose in her hands and shook her head at the barman, who held a cricket bat in his hands.

She said out the corner of her mouth, 'Is he . . .'

'Unconscious,' Walker said.

The barman tried to say something to Walker but no words came out, just an opening and closing of his mouth as he attempted to process the few seconds of action he'd just witnessed.

'Let's go check their car,' Walker said, taking a set of Land Rover keys and stepping over the bodies.

•

'We've got news,' Hutchinson said, putting his cell phone on speaker for the benefit of McCorkell. 'Your old man's been under surveillance by MI5 as it's in connection with the activities of four former regiment members.'

'Three,' Walker corrected. 'One has left the scene, and another will be in a neck-brace for a few months.'

'What?'

'Tell your buddies at MI5 to check out the Boar and Thistle. Tell them there's no rush, and to bring a hearse big enough to carry a former regiment member, along with an ambulance for a guy with a busted head.'

McCorkell was silent.

'We're headed to you now,' Hutchinson said. 'Borrowed an MoD vehicle. We're thirty minutes out.'

Somerville asked, 'Why has Five been watching them?'

'Suspected theft of some military hardware, for a start,' Hutchinson said.

McCorkell added, 'Small arms.'

'Why would MI5 investigate something like that?' Somerville asked. 'It's a military police issue, surely.'

'The MPs got nowhere on it. And, well, it's Special Forces we're talking about. It's like, who watches the Watchmen?'

'What?' Somerville said.

'Comic-book reference,' Hutchinson said. 'It's like saying, who polices Batman? In this case, the MoD probably reached out to MI5 for help.'

Walker said, 'Did you tell them this might be connected to what went down in New York?'

'You bet,' McCorkell replied. 'That got us our audience.'

'I'm still unsure about the MI5 connection,' Somerville said. 'It's not right.'

'They deal with domestic security,' McCorkell said. 'They might be looking at these guys as an emerging terrorist outfit. Their Terrorist Act of 2000 gives them a lot of sway. At any rate, we'll know more soon.'

Somerville asked, 'Did they give you a location on these guys?'

'It's a farmhouse,' Hutchinson said. 'Welsh coast.'

'Burnley Drive,' Walker said.

After a brief pause, McCorkell asked, 'One of the guys at the tavern talked?'

'Field map in their car,' replied Walker. 'Along with a piece of mail.'

McCorkell paused. 'Walker, you can't operate like this. I can't protect you, legally, not like this.'

'They started it,' Walker said. 'I was just trying to enjoy a pint.'

'It's true,' Somerville said. 'Well, the *they started it* bit. They instigated the violence. One drew a firearm. It was us or them.'

'Walker, they're *well* armed,' Hutchinson warned. 'Don't approach this house alone. We can get a crew in. Liaise with MI5. Be there by nightfall.'

Walker remained silent.

'But Five aren't talking to you,' Somerville said.

'It's political,' McCorkell said. 'I'm pulling strings. We'll have answers within the hour.'

Silence fell between the four people in the two cars. Walker thought, *We won't have an hour – let alone nightfall. That publican will contact the farmhouse. If my father's there, he will be warned – and he'll be gone, and those other SAS guys will be lying in wait.*

'Whatever it is you find out,' Walker said, 'tell them to send another crew to that farmhouse. Tell them to bring a hearse. Biggest one they've got.'

4

Walker stood in the tree line, watching the farmhouse through the only worthwhile equipment taken from the SAS men's vehicle: a small set of binoculars, about as far removed from military spec as you could get. The sun was an hour off setting. The farmhouse had whitewashed stone walls, a grey slate roof, gabled windows. The building was elevated, open terrain dotted with sheep wrapping around the house for a good 450 yards, creating a killing field all around; might as well have been a moat around a castle. Neither Walker nor Somerville had weapons besides the Browning loaded with twelve 9-millimetre rounds – good for in-close use only. Walker surveilled the scene, slowly raking his binoculars from side to side. No strong tactical options appeared.

'You think they're in there?' asked Somerville.

'That's the place,' Walker said, staring hard at the house. *Had they received word? Was David Walker there?* In just under three days, Walker had thought of the man less and less as his father and more and more as an adversary. 'And someone's home.'

'What if your father's in there?'

'I hope he is.'

'What then?'

Walker paused, his hands tight on the binoculars. 'Then I'll talk to him.'

Somerville watched him for a moment before speaking. 'Just like that?'

Walker nodded.

'You have a plan?' she asked.

'You stay here,' Walker said, passing her the glasses. 'Observe, and report to McCorkell and Hutch when they get on scene.'

'And you?'

Walker looked to the south. Another farmhouse stood half a mile away, on an unsealed driveway off Burnley Drive. Smoke rose from the chimney. A time-weary tractor and a 1960s Land Rover short wheelbase were parked near a small iron-roofed barn.

Walker said, 'I'm going hunting.'

•

'Walker's reckless,' Hutchinson said as McCorkell drove. 'Too gung-ho. He should wait for back-up.'

'He's worked with the best operators in the world. Hell, he trained them. He knows what he's doing.'

'That was, what, ten years ago?'

'He wasn't exactly relaxing on a beach those ten years after the military. He spent them at CIA's pointy end.'

Hutchinson looked out the window but didn't notice the scenery. He was aware of the very real prospect of Walker heading into that farmhouse, alone, putting himself in a position where this – their only lead into the Zodiac program – would be lost. 'Look, Walker's been on the outer for over a year. He's not as capable as he – as *you* – think he is. He's not a surgical instrument anymore. He's a wrecking ball. We need these guys alive. *Especially* his father. We're talking about twelve major terrorist attacks that can be prevented, but only if we do this right.'

McCorkell thought for a moment, just the sound of the engine and tyre roar. 'You might be right, about Walker's capabilities. But these guys have been out a long time too. And this *is* his father we're talking about. Walker won't jeopardise the long-term mission.'

'You trust him too much.'

McCorkell was silent.

5

Walker followed the road at a slow jog. His boots loud on the crushed granite that formed the surface but the strong wind blew the noise away. The land here was green, the sky now a darker shade of grey, the sun all oranges and yellows where it broke through the horizon.

The neighbouring farmhouse was distinguishable for the work it did: sheep, hay, grains. To the west a field of knee-high barley whispered in the wind. A hundred yards out a dog barked. Walker hurdled the stone fence and quickened his step, moving low through the barley at a run. He approached with the sun at his back, not that it served any useful purpose of concealment in this moment. Gulls spooked and squawked as he hit the open ground towards the barn. He could smell the sea.

He stopped dead twenty yards from the barn. The dog was there, some kind of long-eared hound, but that wasn't what stopped him.

It was the shotgun that gave Walker pause. Double-barrel, over and under. Old but well maintained. Like the hands that held it.

The holder was a woman in her eighties. Short wiry grey hair, a face creased like a griddle pan, her frame maybe a hundred pounds when wet.

'Ma'am,' Walker said, standing to his full height and raising his open hands above his shoulders. The gun was steady in her hands, like she'd learned to hold it seventy years ago to take care of foxes and hares, and had not missed a day's shooting since. 'I don't mean to bother you.'

She looked at him, and heard him. The American accent made her waver. His black jeans and dark blue T-shirt. His tan. Not all of it foreign to these parts but the sum of it different enough to give her pause.

'What are you doing out here?' she asked. She looked up in the direction of the road, as though expecting to see a car.

'Looking,' Walker said, a smile forming to ease the moment. 'I'm a scout. For a film crew.'

'Film?' The gun lowered a little. 'Hollywood?'

'That's right,' Walker said, lowering his hands and taking a few steps towards the woman. 'Hollywood. They think this area could be the next Middle Earth. Or Narnia. I'm here to see for myself. I'll be on my way, though, if you like. No need to point guns and all.'

The woman looked at Walker for a long moment and then pointed the barrels to the ground.

'I suppose you can come in for a cuppa,' she said, and turned her stooped frame that had stood against many a gale and ushered Walker inside. 'I do like the movies.'

•

'He's gone to a neighbour's house,' Somerville said into her phone. 'Another farm that I can see from here.'

'What for?' McCorkell replied over his car's hands-free speaker system.

'He said he was hunting.'

There was a murmur that Somerville couldn't make out, then Hutchinson said aloud, 'He's after a weapon. A rifle. And maybe some intelligence on the target building.'

'How far out are you guys?' Somerville asked.

McCorkell said, 'Thirty minutes.'

Somerville said, 'Better hurry.'

Hutchinson said, 'You ain't kidding.'

Somerville lowered the binoculars, knowing the tone. 'What is it?'

'MI5,' McCorkell said. 'We just heard back, and they're not taking chances with us crashing their surveillance op. They're on their way with a team of heavy hitters to apprehend everyone there.'

'Did they give you any answers?' Somerville asked.

'Not yet. But Walker better either hurry or stay out of the way.'

'You're on the road, you'll be ahead of them,' Somerville said. 'We can help Walker when you get here.'

'No,' McCorkell said. 'The MI5 crew won't be taking the road.'

•

'Thanks,' Walker said, taking the chipped blue enamel mug of steaming tea. He sat in a chair opposite his host.

'So, you're American,' the woman said. Her name was Doris. She had a friendly face, when not sighted down the barrel of a gun. 'I do like Americans. We had some stationed here during the war. Army Air Corps. Fourteenth Ordnance Battalion. A couple of field hospitals.'

Walker smiled. Sharp mind. Doris wouldn't miss much.

'Many neighbours about?' he asked.

Doris paused, said, 'No, not for miles.'

'What about the house to the north?'

Doris looked a little uneasy. 'Best you leave that place be.'

'Haunted?'

Doris shook her head.

Walker looked around. Books neatly lined on the shelves. The newspaper open on the table, the crossword completed. By the window facing the farmhouse sat an old pair of field glasses, better than the tiny binoculars he'd used earlier. Old enough to have been passed out to militia during the war to search the skies and fields for Nazis.

'Bird watching?' Walker asked, seeing that Doris's gaze followed his around the room.

Doris didn't respond.

Walker, a little forward, asked, 'Who do you see out there?'

She looked at him. 'Who do you think I see?'

'Men. Five of them. In the neighbouring house.'

Doris nodded, said, 'Do you know them?'

'No. Well, one of them. Do *you* know them?'

'No.' She watched him silently, the only sounds the crackle of the wood stove, the wind in the eaves and window frame. 'Why don't you tell me why you're really here?'

Walker saw the look in Doris's eyes. Canny. Calculating. Cautious. 'I don't look like a movie guy?'

'No more than I look like Ava Gardner.'

'Maybe you did, twenty years ago.'

'Don't you be cute.' She looked deliberately to the shotgun leaning next to the front door.

Walker liked the old bird.

'You were a soldier,' she said. 'Just like those men next door. But you're not with them, are you?'

'No ma'am,' Walker said. 'But I am here because of them.'

Doris was silent, watchful.

'I think they're up to no good,' Walker said. 'What do you think?'

'I think the same.'

Walker sat forward, said, 'I came here, to your farm, because I was hoping I might be able to sneak in and borrow an old rifle.'

'But instead,' Doris said, pausing to sip her tea, her gaze not leaving his, 'you found an old bird.'

'Yep. And I bet I won the jackpot.'

•

MI5 had its own paramilitary wing, and they weren't using the road. Based just next to Heathrow, when they got the call to move, they moved. Fast.

Six men, armed with the latest generation Heckler & Koch UMP submachine guns, aboard a charcoal-coloured AgustaWestland A109 helicopter.

They headed south-west at a cruising speed of 155 miles per hour. Their orders were clear: capture and detain any and all that they found. They knew that the targets were armed and dangerous. Deadly force was authorised.

6

Doris turned out to be a goldmine of information.

The house had been empty for a decade, and when the new tenants arrived they came in a couple of Land Rovers, nothing more. No furniture-movers, no truck full of domestic necessities. Four men. Ex-soldiers, like the tough and lean types she'd seen around Hereford, only these four, who had become her neighbours, were all old sergeants or warrant officers who'd retired.

At first she thought the MoD might be setting up a top-secret post, some kind of off-the-books site that traded in specialist training. Or, maybe it was going to be one of those places that trained movie stars how to hold guns and roll around in the mud. But no-one else came. No-one, except, during one gale-force winter afternoon when she was repairing some missing slate tiles, one more man.

This man was different. He was older, not her age but splitting the difference between her and the initial four: call him mid-sixties. He was tall, with an athletic build that had softened over decades of office work. He wore a suit the day he arrived, but never since. He dressed differently from the others. He wore jeans; they wore khakis. He wore plain blue button-down cotton shirts; they wore prints and tartans. He stayed in or near the house, leaving perhaps once a month; they went out daily.

Walker showed Doris the same photo he'd shown at the pub. Doris looked at it, then at Walker, and made the connection.

'So, what do you want with your father?' she asked. Her eyes twinkled with cunning – this was the type of lady who'd finish the cryptic crossword while watching a BBC whodunit. 'Is this about the Army?'

'No,' Walker said. 'Not really. It's hard to explain.'

'But it's important that you go over there. With a rifle.'

'Vital.'

Doris nodded.

•

Hutchinson drove hard, the Army's Ford Focus bouncing across the country road as they raced towards the farmhouse.

'Say we do get there before the MI5 crew,' he said to his boss. 'Then what?'

'We take Walker Senior in,' replied McCorkell.

'How?'

McCorkell paused as he slowed for a tight corner, said, 'Put him in the boot, get to a safe place, question him.'

'Those ex-SAS guys are armed to the teeth.'

'Walker will have sourced a rifle or gun – you said so.'

'And, what, he's going to take out these other two SAS guys and grab his father in the next, oh, twenty minutes?'

'I doubt it,' McCorkell said, his voice hard. 'If Walker's already on the move, it'll start and finish well before we get there.'

•

Walker moved towards the whitewashed house in a crouched run. For a man measuring six foot three and 230 pounds, he moved fast and quiet. Training. And application. Nothing sharpened the training like application under fire, and Walker had been through plenty enough of it to know to keep his head down, to stay alert, to expect the unexpected.

He paused to listen. All quiet.

He continued on.

The Holland & Holland shotgun in his hands – 20-gauge, under-over, twin triggers – was well used and well maintained for a working gun from a farm. Snapping the breech open had revealed the mechanism to be smooth and oiled. The top shell would eject clear, while the bottom caught a little due to a gouge in the breech. A defect like that was important to know about because the removal of the spent bottom shell and subsequent reload would add a second to any engagement. Walker had twelve shells in his jacket pocket and two in the gun.

Up against two ex-SAS guys with automatic weapons.

Not ideal.

The tall grass from the road provided visual cover during his approach. Ahead, the white house had four windows at the front – two downstairs, two up top – and Walker noted lights on in the right-hand window on each level. The wind was behind him. Soon he would reach the clearing in front of the house, where he would be exposed for the final leg of his approach. He could do nothing about that. The longer he waited, the more chance the occupants would receive word from either their surviving compatriot at the Boar and Thistle or the publican that there was a guy out there asking about them.

The house was 150 yards away. Walker paused at a hundred; barely fifty yards of cover remained ahead. He spotted Somerville's position concealed behind the pines; she wasn't visible from the house but Walker could see a glint off the car's roof from his location, caught by the dull low sun.

He pushed on. Fifty yards. His cover ended. All low-cut grass and gravel drive from here.

The kill zone.

He stopped. Waited. Watched.

Still no movement in the house. The windows to Walker's right were still lit from inside. The front door looked old but sturdy, solid timber, weathered as grey as Doris's hair.

Movement – the bottom window, this time on the left. Another light came on. A curtain moved as someone brushed by it. A man. Not his father. One of the ex-SAS guys, moving slowly, no urgency.

Walker looked around a final time as he readied for the dash ahead. The sun was low; he had perhaps twenty minutes before it dipped below the line of pine trees to the west. There was no sound but the wind in the barley. Like a calm surf washing ashore.

Then, a noise. Loud, distinct, sudden. A pistol shot. To the east. The Browning. Somerville.

7

Walker ran for the white house.

Again he saw movement behind that downstairs curtain – the ex-SAS guy.

Walker shouldered the shotgun and let off two rounds through the window, maintaining his forward momentum and speed as he broke the breech and ejected the stuck round and reloaded two more.

BRRR BRRR.

Two triple taps from an MP5K rippled through the air by him. The sound of the six 9-millimetre rapid-fire bullets was terrifying to anyone on the other end of it, and Walker was no different. But his best option was to push on with the assault. He hit the front wall of the house, next to the door, and listened.

The submachine-gun fire had come from the upstairs window. Walker looked up just as the gunman leaned out to clock him. The fourth man.

Walker raised the shotgun, fired twice.

By the time the man had hit the ground, Walker had reloaded and tried the front door. Locked.

Walker let off a blast through the door's handle and lock. He kicked the timber in and rushed the room, shotgun training to the open space on the right. No-one there.

He rushed up the stairs, the shotgun leading, his eye trained down the barrel, a single round in the chamber. At the top of the stairs he came to a landing, a hallway running off in each direction. Four doors, two on each side, all open. He went right.

At the open doorway he waited.

'Jed?' a dead man's voice called. His father. 'Come on in, Jed.'

Walker hesitated.

He scanned back towards the stairs. No sign of that final man. That was a worry.

'I'm unarmed, Jed.' His father's voice was steady. 'I knew you'd come sooner or later. So let's talk.'

Walker broke the breech and turned the corner.

8

Walker looked at his father, the bloodied nose, and spoke. 'I'm not going to ask you again.'

Walker had dragged his father downstairs. Seated him in a chair. And the questioning had started. The bloodied nose came about when the older man had tried to chastise his son. Now, there was buzzing air between them, electric with possibility. Walker didn't know how far he'd go to get the truth. And David Walker had moved from defiant to stunned.

'Four. Five, including me,' David Walker said.

'How many in the house now?'

'Two.'

'Where's the other guy?'

'Other guy?'

'I got one at the upstairs window. There's no-one else upstairs. And there's no-one down here. Where would he go?'

'I – I don't know. But the other two will be back soon.'

'No,' Walker retorted. 'They won't be coming back.'

His father met his eyes. All kinds of questions were writ there: What have you done? How did we get here? Where does this end?

'That's right,' Walker said. 'So, tell me what I need to know. About Zodiac. New York, the Stock Exchange – you had prior knowledge. Do you know all twelve attacks? The triggers? What's next? Where?'

'I don't know.'

'Bullshit.'

'They're cut-out cells. Terrorists, criminals, rogue agents.'

'But you have a hand in it – you helped in creating it, right? This falls at *your* feet – this is on *your* head.'

David Walker dropped his eyes to the floor and let out a sigh. 'Jed . . . You don't want to know.'

'Who's running Zodiac?'

'No-one *runs* it, Jed. It's self-perpetuating. Like the sun – it's going to burn on and on until it's done.'

Walker paced, looked out the front window. The guy he'd clipped through the upstairs window had crawled halfway down the drive, a smear of blood in his wake, and collapsed. He turned to his father, said, 'Who started it?'

Silence. Walker waited for an answer. When a minute passed and none came, he said, 'You did?'

'No,' David Walker replied.

'But?'

'But it was an idea of mine. It came up in a think-tank, a working group, years ago. One of those Red Cell-type things; a whole range of different people together brainstorming worst-case and out-of-the-box scenarios so that the government and security agencies could form responses.'

'And, what? Someone there took that idea of linked cells, each activating the other, and ran with it, years later?'

Walker Snr shrugged. Deflated.

'Right,' Walker said. 'And then what? You had to fake your death to – to what? You didn't try to stop that attack in New York.'

'What makes you think I faked my death? It was listed as a heart attack at the White House, remember? You think I could have faked that, there?'

'I think you had your heart attack, went to Walter Reed as reported, and there you were given a chance. A chance to go work for someone, to get Zodiac rolling?'

David Walker shook his head.

'You were mad at your country, at the system,' Walker went on. He'd thought about this for days. It felt good to say it. 'They'd let you down. They'd busted me out of the Agency, but that was chicken feed. You knew *all* their secrets, *all* their lies, *all* the cover-ups and fuck-ups over the last forty years – and you finally snapped.'

'No.'

'Tell me otherwise. Set me straight.'

'You can't stop this,' David Walker said. 'That's what's so

terrifying about it. Each action initiates the next. There's no contact or communication between the cells, just the go signal.'

'The signal being an attack.'

'Or attempted attack – so long as it's reported as such. Whenever that signal is received, the next begins. And it all started in New York, last week.'

'And this was all your idea?'

'In a sense.'

'What are you doing here, with these guys?'

Walker Snr dropped his head.

'Trying to stop it?'

'Trying to survive,' David Walker said.

'I'm not buying.' Walker waited for his father to meet his gaze, then said, 'Why? Why you? Why like this?'

'When I learned that Zodiac was a go, I had to do what I did. They would have killed us all, don't you see? Me, your mother, you. All dead. I did what I had to do, to save the two of you.'

Walker held his father's gaze and said, 'How'd that turn out?'

David Walker was silent.

'After New York we got intel from the CIA guy. A date and a location. You know what it pointed to?'

David Walker remained silent.

'A town in Afghanistan. A US Navy SEAL safe house. Yesterday was the date. We got a warning through, but we were too late – it had happened earlier. Two SEALs were found there, killed. Assassinated,' Walker said. 'It was a secure compound, no-one knew they were there. And this morning, another SEAL was killed in Germany. Gunshot wound to the head, same as those in 'Stan. He was transferring home, had a couple days' R&R, found dead in his hotel. At the same time, another was killed in his home in Florida. Exact same MO.' Walker watched his father. He twitched. 'SEALs are being killed. All of them from Team Six, the crew that went into Abbottabad. Tell me about it. Tell me what you know.'

David Walker said, 'Sounds like an inside job to me.'

9

Walker said again, 'Tell me!'

'Maybe they're in the way,' David Walker said. 'Maybe it's reprisal. Who knows?'

'What do you know about these SEALs?'

Nothing.

Walker said, 'Is it because of what they did in Abbottabad? This a reprisal for bin Laden?'

Still nothing.

'Help me out.'

'Let this go. You can't stop it, Jed. And if you try, they *will* kill you.'

'Who's they?'

'I don't know.'

'Who's they!?'

'The same people who took me, unconscious, from Walter Reed and dumped me in an apartment near JFK with nothing but an IV in my arm, a new passport and a wad of cash. Don't you see? I'm not the puppet-master here, Jed. I'm a cog in the wheel, just like you.'

A minute passed as the two men watched each other in silence.

Then Walker spoke. 'Someone will get the truth out of you. You know that.'

Silence.

'The next guys to get here,' Walker said. 'MI5. They'll take you to a black site. You know how this works. It'll be some shit hole. They'll work it all out of you. Everything you know about this. They'll wait you out.'

His father shook his head.

'What?' Walker said. 'Time? Is that it? What's the timeframe here? When's the next Zodiac attack coming?'

Nothing.

'Is it the SEALs? Is this the next terror event in Zodiac? Wiping out the Team Six guys who killed bin Laden?'

Nothing.

'The rest of that crew are in protection,' Walker said. 'They won't be taken out like the others. Whoever's hunting them, they won't get to them.'

'It's not me, son.'

There was silence for a beat.

'Who? Who's doing this?'

Walker Snr leaned forward. 'Are you sure they're *all* protected?'

Walker saw it in his father's eyes. An answer. Observed, not explained. He backed away from him, a couple of paces.

'I think they're being taken out now because they've *seen* what's coming,' Walker said. 'They've seen it, but they don't *know* they've seen it.'

David Walker stayed silent.

Walker checked his watch. Looked out the windows. No sign of anyone. *Yet*.

'There was no reasoning behind the order of it,' Walker Snr said. 'Nor what attacks Zodiac chose.'

'Who's behind it?'

'I'm working on it.'

'Tell me.'

David Walker was silent.

'Look, Zodiac was a list, that's it,' David Walker said. When he spoke, he spoke with his face down. 'No rationale, no idealism, no maniacal endgame. Just targets, linked via the attacks. Nothing more. Most were ambiguous. We put together dozens of worst-case scenario attacks, each detrimental to the US and devastating in its own way. Each is carried out by a cut-out cell. The idea was that no-one has any idea about which cells have which targets.' He looked up to his son. 'That's the very terror of it, see? That's why it's a worst-case, doomsday-type series of attacks, because there's no way to stop them all.'

'*Someone* has an idea of how they're linked,' Walker said. 'Someone sold this. Someone started it.'

Walker Snr shrugged.

'What are you doing here?' Walker sat on the edge of a table. Watched his father.

'Surviving,' David replied. 'The CIA guys, Bellamy and all of them, they were in on this – they started it, I'm sure.'

'They're out of the picture now.'

'It's self-perpetuating, remember?'

'You worked with them.'

'Only when they reached out to me. And when I realised what they were doing, in kick-starting Zodiac, I knew what I had to do.'

'Die.'

'Yes. Someone gave me a chance – an opportunity to get out. I took it. As you did. Work off the grid, to save lives.'

'Is that what you're doing here? Trying to save lives?'

'I'm looking for answers, like you –'

'Bullshit. You're hiding out, surviving. What are you really up to?'

'It doesn't matter if you believe me or not. You can't stop this. Twelve attacks have been set in motion.'

'I can catch up.'

'No,' David Walker said to his son, shaking his head, 'you really can't.'

10

McCorkell sped south-west as Hutchinson spoke on the phone.

'Just buy us some time,' McCorkell said.

'I can't,' Hutchinson replied, ending the call. 'MI5 are pissed. They've heard what happened at the tavern. They're headed into this farmhouse hot and, well, I get the sense that none of us should get in their way.'

'The sense?'

'They've stopped taking my calls. Oh, and they said, "Don't get in the way."'

'Tell Somerville,' McCorkell said. 'Warn her – warn Walker. Get them out.'

Hutchinson dialled, tapping fingers impatiently against the passenger door as he waited. 'She's not answering.'

'Keep trying,' McCorkell said, pushing the car faster.

•

'Is all that true?' a voice said behind Walker.

He tensed and looked behind.

The fourth guy, the one who'd earlier been downstairs. He was small and lean, with edginess in his eyes and an MP5K at the ready. Walker started running through options to get to the guy and subdue him, none of them appealing with the submachine gun in the game.

'Are you really part of some terrorist scheme?' he asked David Walker.

'Terry, it's not that simple.'

'I heard everything you said,' Terry replied. 'You've been feeding me and the boys lies this whole time. You said this was an opportunity. About settling some old scores, against forces that we knew. IRA and all that. Getting paid well to right some old wrongs. Hmm? Lies?'

'Not lies, Terry, but there's more to it,' David said. 'I needed you guys.'

Terry shook his head, his hands still firmly gripping his weapon. 'Nope. This is all new. You said we'd be well paid, looked after, working inside the system but apart from it. But what – this is about some genie you let out of a bottle back in the States?'

Walker watched his father and Terry eye each other off in silence. The dangerous end of the MP5K was just a few paces away, but he was seated. Not ideal.

'All that I told you, Terry, was true. You can see that. We have a mission.'

'We? This fucker killed Brian – with a fifty-year-old shotgun.' Terry nodded towards Walker without taking his eyes off the older man. 'And we've not heard from the others.'

'You won't,' Walker said, standing up. He was a head taller than Terry, but he was unarmed and going up against a 9-millimetre killing machine. There was a reason the SAS termed the MP5K the 'Room Broom': its high rate of fire meant it was capable of clearing a room in seconds. 'Why don't you join us and talk this through?'

'I'm out,' Terry said, looking from Walker to his father. 'You get that? You pay me, and I'm out. I'm going straight to bloody MoD and coming clean and making a deal – and you're gonna be hauled through the ringer for what you are – a bloody terrorist.'

Walker took a step closer to Terry. The ex-SAS man tensed and focused on him, the MP5K trained at Walker's chest.

'You have a choice here, Terry,' Walker said. 'You can help me stop a terrorist attack, or you can walk away now and let me do what I need to here.'

'You sure they're the only two choices?' Terry said. 'Brian was a good friend of mine. He's owed blood, mate. Get it?'

'Then I sure hope you're a better shot than he was,' Walker said. 'Because if you're not, the only blood that's paid will be yours.'

Terry's eyes narrowed. Walker moved right. The barrel of the MP5K followed. David Walker shouted, 'No!'

A gunshot rang out. Walker was splattered with warm blood. Another shot. Walker tensed as Terry fell forward, against him. In the doorway behind stood Somerville, breathless, the Browning pistol in her hands, the barrel smoking.

'I tried to warn you, Walker,' she said. 'I saw him in the field – I fired a warning shot. He came looking for me.'

Walker laid the body on the floor, then turned to his father. 'The Navy SEALs,' Walker said. He didn't bother to wipe the blood spatter from his face. He just stared down at the man who'd raised him. 'They've seen what's coming, right? That's why they're being hit. They've seen it but they don't know that they've seen it. Otherwise, whatever the attack is would have been prevented by now, right?'

'You need to look closer at them,' David Walker said, his head lowered, his gaze focused on his hands in his lap. 'What they have in common. I think you'll find the answer there.'

A noise cut through the silence. A helicopter, coming in fast.

11

'Next right,' Hutchinson said.

McCorkell eased off the gas and started to brake, making the turn as quickly as he dared. The road became unsealed gravel. He pushed the Ford hard. Traction control kicked in. They straightened up, McCorkell with his right foot planted hard.

'Two more miles,' Hutchinson said. 'Just beyond the pines up there.'

•

Walker didn't wait for the party to come to him. He escorted his father outside, Somerville close behind them.

The helicopter was dark, unmarked. The MI5 men were dressed the same as paramilitary guys all over the world. Black clothing. Kevlar armour. Silenced firearms.

'Sorry,' Walker said to his father. 'They're going to take it from here, at least for a while.'

David Walker looked at the two armed men rushing towards them and then back to his son.

'Stopping this isn't an option,' Walker Snr said. 'Zodiac, I mean.'

'I know what you meant,' Walker said. 'And I don't understand it.'

David Walker smiled as the black-clad men took him by the arms. 'It's all about chaos and anarchy – that's what the attacks are supposed to achieve. And out of that, after it, order will be restored.'

'Order?'

David Walker nodded. 'If you can keep up, you will save lives. But you have to stop them at the very last moment, to activate the next cell. Understand? Let Zodiac run, and dismantle each as it rises. It's the only way.'

Walker remained silent as he processed the information.

No words were spoken in the handover to the MI5 crew. None were needed. The paramilitary guys in black ski masks led David Walker away, while another crouched in a cover-fire position in the clearing. Walker knew he'd lost this battle, but he would get the chance to question his father again soon enough. McCorkell would get him access. The UN might be damned and maligned, but Bill McCorkell represented US intelligence, and that trumped the UK intel community; the Brits may have thought of themselves as the brains in the alliance, but the US had what they needed: money.

Walker watched as his father was loaded aboard the unmarked Bell 412, the four-blade main rotor speeding up with the characteristic whomp-whomp-whomp of the Huey family of aircraft. One MI5 paramilitary operator paused before climbing aboard, looking back at Walker and Somerville. Walker saw his father say something, and the guy turned and climbed aboard, sliding the side door shut. The rotors spooled up and the pilot turned the nose into the wind as they climbed, heading out towards the sea.

•

'That's it, end of that lane,' Hutchinson said.

McCorkell drove the Ford along the unpaved road and took the corner at speed. The white farmhouse grew bigger. They drove by a body on the ground. McCorkell pulled to a hard stop.

McCorkell and Hutchinson made their way towards Walker and Somerville, who stood together, their body language tense as a new sound emerged. A helicopter, approaching from the north-west in a big sweeping arc. Walker identified it as an AgustaWestland. As it made its way closer, he saw the charcoal paint scheme, the fine white MoD stencilling on the tail.

'Who's that?' Somerville said.

'MI5,' McCorkell replied. 'I'm surprised we beat them.'

'What?' Somerville said. She looked to Walker.

He watched as the helo came in to hover over the clearing and six guys in paramilitary outfits fast-roped out the open side doors. They hit the ground running, Heckler & Koch UMPs raised, shouting for Walker, Somerville, McCorkell and Hutchinson to drop to their knees.

'Son of a bitch . . .' Walker said, looking west, the Bell Huey no longer visible in the afternoon sky.

12

Walker stopped the car to look at the clock tower in Hereford. It was inscribed with the names of dead SAS officers; many had been added since he'd last seen it. He stood, silent, reading the names, then closed his eyes. The events of the previous day ran through his mind. His father's words and actions. McCorkell's pulling in of favours to have him and Somerville freed and cleared. The manhunt for his father underway. He opened his eyes. A new day to battle, to reconcile.

'Is this place how you remember it?' Somerville asked.

Walker shook his head and looked around. 'Ever notice that progress looks more like destruction?'

'Yeah . . . Chaos leads to order. That's what your father said, right?'

'Something like that.'

'It sounds like some new-world-order kind of mumbo jumbo.'

'Yeah.'

They stood in silence, each lost in their own thoughts. McCorkell and Hutchinson were back at the SAS headquarters, squaring away the stolen gear recovered from the farmhouse, liaising with the MI5 team, working with the DoD to track the unmarked helicopter. Walker knew it would be up to his father whether he'd be found again.

'Walker,' Somerville said, 'I don't know who I thought you were, but right now I don't even think *you* know who you are – or who you were.'

'Being dead changes a guy.'

'Talking about you or your father?'

'Both.'

'Change as in progress?'

'Progress? Destruction.'

'Right. And your father? How has he changed?'

'Same as me.'

'As in?'

41

Walker shrugged. It was easier seen and felt than explained. Doris got that. Walker had seen it, when something had resolved in her to help him. He'd recognised the same thing in his father. Resolution. Decisions made a long time ago. Would he ever understand why – why his father had left the family, faked his own death, had foreknowledge of terrorist attacks and not prevented them? *Maybe. Maybe not.*

'You're not your father.'

'I know.'

'You won't become him.'

'Probably not.'

'Come on. Let's go,' Somerville said eventually. 'We've got a flight to make.'

Walker remained silent, unmoving. At the clock tower time stood still. No progress, no regression. A moment in time, when all he had were his thoughts and a world to figure out.

Somerville said, 'You're coming back stateside, right?'

Walker looked up and down the street. 'Maybe.'

'Fuck you maybe.' Somerville pushed him in the chest. He looked at her. 'We *need* you working on this. You're a *part* of it, as much as your father. *You* can stop this, if you just come back, if you get to work.'

'Look—'

'No. Don't say another fucking word.' Somerville looked away, then back at him as she took the car keys from his hand. 'You know what? Do what you want. Go, disappear for another year. Leave these terrorists up to us. Leave Eve to remain in the dark, alone. Leave the rest of the SEALs to whatever fate decides. Leave it all and walk away. It's easier, right? To just keep looking back. Hanging with the dead. Going nowhere.'

Somerville left without a backwards glance.

Walker looked at the shrine. The names of dead men, inscribed in stone. Not a fake among them. He made his decision. Resolved it. A long time ago.

He could never let go. Never stand by, when he knew he could make a difference.

Walker followed Somerville.

13

Walker sat at the bar, ordered a beer, and waited.

The beer was fine. American, cold. The glasses were clean, as though they had only ever served American beer, cold. Most of the men were drinking whisky, or a clear liquor that looked like some kind of local brew not far beyond bathtub moonshine. The prohibition hadn't much touched these parts, but they'd made their own supply regardless, before and after; that's what these people were good at: they got by, on their own, no outside help needed or wanted.

He had spent almost a week asking around, while McCorkell and his team were working from desks, checking phone records and databases. All of them looking for a SEAL who didn't want to be found – the one unaccounted-for member from the Abbottabad raid that had killed bin Laden. Which was why Walker elected to be here, on the ground, searching for this SEAL. Needle in a haystack? He had fifty bucks against Somerville and Hutchinson that he'd beat them to finding the guy.

Thing was, how do you find a highly trained operator who doesn't want to be found? When the hunter becomes the hunted, the hunter turns pro. And this was the SEAL's backyard – if he didn't want to be found, he was going to stay that way.

And that reality was starting to wear away at Walker.

The bar was in a squat building sitting in the middle of a paved car park on the highway that cut through town. It was confederate grey on the outside, union blue on the inside. The patrons were old and young, nothing in-between. Thirty-four people. The women drank beer. None sat alone; each with a man. Of the twenty-two men, six looked like they would be more than capable in a bar fight – though, Walker thought, who knew what a capable man looked like in these parts? Hatred ran deep here, wariness was a second language, and near-on everyone was armed.

It felt like a closed community because it was, as closed as a place could be without barbed-wire-topped walls. Those compounds in the Middle East that protected Westerners and local big shots had nothing on these people. The folk here were kin. They didn't need walls to keep unwanted people out; didn't need locks on their doors, nor their cars.

The fact was, Walker knew, if you messed with someone here, they, and their family – considerable in size and spread wide in geography – would see to it that before you managed to reach a county or state line, you'd never trouble anyone again.

Another thing he noticed was that the outside world could end and little here would change.

Self-sufficient didn't begin to describe these folk.

Walker settled in, watching and listening. The hubbub was inconsequential but he listened hard. Every time he sipped, he watched the scene around him in the mirror behind the bar. When he wasn't looking up, he was looking at his beer bottle, eyes down, like they did in these parts.

The same went for interference, Walker knew. Meddling. Messing. The town welcome signs might as well have read 'Ya'll not welcome. Turn around'.

The empty streets outside were louder than this bar. No music played, the conversations were hushed, the occasional laugh or snort was brief and muffled, the loudest noise being the bang of the bathroom door – flimsy plywood into a battered and warped timber frame.

Walker finished his drink and glanced up and down the bar, a side-to-side sweep. The mirror above the bar had a patina of rust eating at it from the aeons of damp that clung in the valleys here until noon. Everyone wore denim of some sort, and a mix of T-shirts and cotton checked flannels, leather jackets and parkas. Heavier coats hung on the wall near the door.

Not even winter and the cold was cutting and dank.

Walker liked the place.

'Another beer,' Walker said, sliding his empty bottle forward. The guy behind the bar popped another, handed it over and took the money from Walker's previous change of a twenty. All in silence.

He returned to the end of the bar, to Walker's left, where he spoke with three young men.

There were two empty bar stools and then a couple of old guys between Walker and the three boys. The latter were young, early twenties, but Walker counted them among the six capable guys in the room, along with another wiry young guy sitting with a girl at a table directly behind him, and a couple of older men sitting about fifteen feet away by a stack of firewood. Immediately to Walker's right at the bar was a couple in their late fifties.

They were why he'd chosen this spot to sit, after standing at the bar and ordering a beer from a bartender who Walker had quickly realised would not be forthcoming with information. The couple next to him had just finished their dinner; roast beef, boiled vegetables, gravy, biscuit. The woman, on the stool beside Walker's, was drinking a glass of light red wine. Her husband was a local; her clothes and make-up and jewellery told Walker she was either a transplant or was trying her best to look like one. Maybe that meant she'd be friendlier, more forthcoming.

'Excuse me,' Walker said to her, his tone that of one outsider to another.

Nothing. Her back was half-turned to him, her bar stool pointed thirty degrees towards her husband.

Walker leaned back a little, watching the husband drain the last of the clear stuff from a lowball, and forced his way into the older man's eye-line.

'Hey,' Walker said, friendly. 'My name's Jed. Jed Walker. I'm just passing through.'

The husband almost nodded. He looked over Walker's shoulder, then back to the bar in front, not making eye contact again.

'I'm just wondering,' Walker continued, 'if you've heard of a friend of mine? Lives around here. I'm trying to find him. We served together in Afghanistan. Charles Murphy? Ex-Navy. Good guy.'

The guy didn't look at Walker, but he shook his head.

'Ah, damn,' Walker said, looking at the bar and seeing the husband's eyes watching him in the mirror. 'We served together, see. Just trying to reconnect.'

Walker sold the lie convincingly, but the husband wasn't buying into the conversation. His mouth was shut tight. The wife, however, had turned front on, and she was now eyeing Walker in the faded and rusted old mirror above the liquor bottles.

Neither of them said anything, but Walker could tell that Charles Murphy was a name they'd heard. So, they either knew him or knew of him. Sure, there'd be a lot of Murphys around here, but this one they knew of.

'You see,' Walker said, straight at the mirror. 'I owe him. And I've been lookin' for him for four days already, in every little speck of a town around here, every bar and diner.'

'Maybe he doesn't live around here,' the wife said. Her accent was local. Her lips pursed when she finished speaking. Her lipstick was an orange shade of red. She was older than Walker first thought, or maybe it was just this climate, sucking the life out of her bones, forcing her face into a squint of cracks and creases.

'You got the wrong place, wrong name, maybe both,' she said, and the husband looked down to stare at his plate. 'No-one by Charles Murphy around here. You best move on, go lookin' someplace else.'

Walker noted the tone. It wasn't a suggestion to leave. And yet, it was an invitation. He was getting nowhere talking like this. But the fact that she was closing the door to this town on him? Well, that suggested he'd found the right place. It was in her eyes – she *knew* Murphy. And she was smart enough to know that Walker knew that she knew. The woman looked all the world like she was up for a challenge by some stranger pressing her for answers, and knew that she had all the advantages and then some.

Walker liked a challenge. And the realisation that he was closer to Murphy just gave him the right amount of adrenaline to pursue the matter. 'It's the right name, ma'am,' he said to her. 'I'd never forget it. He saved my life in Afghanistan. You don't forget a man's name when he does something like that. You don't forget where he's from.'

Her eyes remained fixed on his, in the mirror's reflection. 'You were in the Navy?'

'Air Force,' Walker replied, telling the truth.

She seemed a little disappointed.

'Special Operations, like Murphy,' he added, sipping his beer. 'Side-by-side stuff, in the trenches together more than once.'

'They call it Special Forces, don't they?'

'Only the Army.'

Her eye twitched. She was someone not used to being corrected, let alone outright challenged.

'Trenches . . . I dunno,' she said, as though the term 'trenches' was more silly than outdated. 'Look, Walker? There's no Murphy here. Certainly no Charles Murphy. Maybe your memory's at fault.' She turned to look directly at him. 'Too many concussions in 'em trenches?'

Her eyes were as grey as the outside of the bar. Her face was angular and much harder than the blurred and patinaed mirror had suggested. She had a high hairline and pale wrinkled skin. There was a line around her face where the make-up stopped, paler than pale.

'Maybe you misheard me,' Walker said, holding her gaze, sensing something as battle-hardened as many Afghani women of her age he had encountered. 'I need to find Murphy, because I owe him. I *owe* him, and right now *he* needs *my* help. So, I'm here to pay that debt, see?'

The woman held Walker's eye for another two seconds, then looked over his shoulder and gave the slightest nod. She then lifted her glass for a moment, placed it back down. By the time the barkeep had refilled it from a bottle with a cork, Walker sensed movement behind him.

Walker turned around on his seat, watching the mirror as he did so.

The three guys from the end of the bar.

They moved before he could adequately react. He could have enacted several options, most of them lethal, but he let them win the first round while he evaluated and reassessed based on their actions.

Two of the guys grabbed Walker by the arms, pinning him where he sat, his back now to the bar.

The third man stood before him, arms hanging by his side, fists clenched.

Walker smelled alcohol coming from the three of them. More pros than cons, that fact. They'd have slower reaction times. Be less precise in their movements. Bleed more.

'I'm guessing the three of you are brothers,' Walker said, and the guy out front nodded with a grin. 'And I'm assuming your parents were cousins. No, wait – brother and sister?'

The guys who pinned Walker had grips that made forged bench vices seem like paperclips.

'The three of you married to each other?' Walker said. 'They allow that in these parts, right?'

Someone in the bar sniggered. Someone else shushed that person quick smart.

The man out front flushed red, wound up for his punch, said, 'Welcome to the Ozarks, bitch.'

14

'Rachel Levine,' she said into her phone, seeing that the call was coming from NCIS headquarters in Quantico, Virginia.

'We have a lead on your Chief Petty Officer Charles Murphy,' Agent Brewster said to her. From the hum in the background Levine guessed he was in The Pen, a large open-plan room full of hot desks to which agents were delegated on a situational-needs basis. Sometimes that room was full, three shifts a day, around the clock. Sometimes it didn't have half the staff for half the time. Today it was full, and it was set to remain that way for the foreseeable future.

'Go.' She wrote down the details and hung up before turning to her partner, Special Agent Tom Woods. 'We're rolling.'

'We just ordered.' He looked at the barbecue, the ribs slow-cooking, steaks on a grill, a rotisserie of chickens being basted. It was someone's front yard, in Memphis, Tennessee, and the smoke pouring from the three purpose-built cooking rigs smelled of myriad melting fats and charcoaled chicory. A result of the GFC, people like these had been booted out of places they used to rent as diners and started plying their trade from their front yards instead. Woods loved them. Levine too. But this was her case, and it was getting further away from them, and she knew that time was not on their side.

'Yeah, well, take whatever's ready in the car, Tom,' Levine said, headed for their government-issue Taurus, a dark metallic grey with a V6 under the hood and more plastic than the Barbie Dream House her little sister used to have. Levine sat behind the wheel and plotted the course in the sat-nav, ready to roll by the time Woods climbed into the car with two heavy foil bags, a handful of napkins and bottles of iced tea.

He asked, 'Big drive?'

'We'll be there by nightfall.'

'Nice. The road trip continues.'

Levine looked sideways at him. He was genuinely happy to be out of the office and on the road. He didn't look Navy, though she supposed she didn't either. His hair was long, well over his collar. Hers was cropped short and tight, but there was the hint of a tattoo at the base of her neck that showed when she wasn't wearing a collared shirt.

'Where we headed?' he asked, buckling up as she took off.

'Calico Rock, Arkansas.'

'Ah, Ozarks,' Woods said, starting in on his smoked-brisket sub. 'My kinda people.'

•

Walker ducked, the big guy's first punch flying high and wide.

The follow-up left landed in Walker's guts, then was followed by an elbow to the back of the ribs that knocked the air out of him.

'Round one is yours, boys,' Walker managed to say. 'Enjoy it.'

He let them have that, to allow himself to take in what was what and who was who. They weren't about to seriously damage him. Not unarmed like this. They weren't fighters – big, angry, a little drunk, sure, but these were guys who had regular jobs, for these parts; eating meat they hunted themselves was about as adventurous as they got. They were not men who lived on ration packs and hunted and killed other men for a living, always under the constant threat that the next step into enemy territory would be their last. Walker had spent more than half his life as the latter. It gave him confidence, knowing what he knew, having done what he'd done.

Fact was, this situation was a world away from the Boar and Thistle and the two ex-SAS men who had confronted him.

Walker still liked this bar. Which was probably evident in his smile.

'He's got a big smart mouth on 'im,' the guy to Walker's left said. 'Hit 'im again, Seabass!'

Seabass was the big slab of beef in front, the action man with the mangled anvil fists. He did as he was goaded, and went in with a right hook.

Walker didn't give them this one.

He had played no resistance to the two at his arms. So far. This time Walker rocked his back against the bar, pivoting his body where the timber edge met the base of his spine, and dragged his left arm across his body. It was a fast jab, one that not only hit the guy to his right on the tip of the chin, but also dragged the man holding his left forearm across his body – just in time to meet Seabass's heavy blow as it landed.

TAP – WHACK.

First, the guy tapped on the chin fell to the floor. Walker knew a lot about the dense nerve cluster there, and that when hit just right, it's lights out. Boxers train for hundreds of hours to hit that sweet spot and rarely get it as accurately as Walker managed.

Second, the guy who had taken Seabass's blow to the side of the head slid down Walker's front and fell at Seabass's feet, squirming and twitching. He'd collected the heavy punch to the temple, and as big as he was, the skull was thin there, weak. He might be permanently brain damaged. Or it might have smarted him up. Whatever.

Walker stood tall, his full six feet three inches, eye to eye with Seabass. He saw the latter's mind working to compute and catch up with what had just happened. Whether the alcohol intake had slowed that brain, Walker was unsure, but the fact was, he was on the clock, and it seemed as though Seabass was going to stand there with his mouth open like that until next Tuesday.

'Kill him!' the face-painted woman yelled.

Seabass looked from his fallen friends to her, then to Walker – and then he grinned. He reached behind his belt and drew a large hunting knife.

Walker looked at it and decided that it was the last time this guy would ever pull a knife on a man.

'Enough!' A small voice cut through the air. Young, forceful, female.

15

The voice belonged to the girl who had been seated behind Walker –
so now she was behind Seabass. Walker watched her get to her feet.
She was young – late teens, maybe twenty – and had been sitting with
a guy about her age, both of them on some quiet and uncomfortable
date up until now. Conflict, or defusing it, seemed more her speed;
romance be damned. She was five feet nothing, finely featured with
a heart-shaped face, and with shoulder-length brown hair pulled into
a loose ponytail.

She was moving, all 120 pounds of her, her little fists up and each
with a pointed index finger, and she approached Walker from her
table. She stepped around Seabass and placed herself between them
and the wife, in the centre of a triangle.

'It's *my* cousin he's asking about,' she said, pointing at Seabass,
'and *I'll* take care of this!'

Silence in the air. Walker kept his eyes on Seabass and the knife. He
was holding it in a forehand grip, which wasn't what military training
dictated, but with the size of the blade, and the serrated back edge
of it, grip technique was academic. In this space, especially with the
young woman now crowded next to him and the bar against his back,
Walker knew it'd be hard to dodge the first attack without sending
the knife arcing through the air at her or someone else. The pale old
woman he didn't much care about, but this girl, with her fists and her
Moses-like voice that cut through the room and the family connection
to Murphy? Her, he liked. A lot. She had spirit. Spunk. Fight.

'This is *my* business,' the girl said to the woman. 'Not yours. My
family business. I never get into your business, Barb, never have,
never will, right? So, let me deal with this.'

Walker sensed that the pale old woman, Barb, still seated at the
bar, was weighing up that statement. Finally, her pack-a-day smoke-
riddled voice cut the air like a diesel train passing by: 'He leaves
town. Right now.'

'Fine.' The young woman turned and faced Walker. 'Come with me.'

Walker nodded.

'Wait,' Barb said, chuckling a dry laugh. 'Susie, you ain't going nowhere *with* him. You and I got our *own* business now. He leaves? You stay. You owe me for this, now. See? Unless you want to change your mind about this stranger's fate tonight?'

The young woman called Susie turned and looked at Barb, then Walker, then back to the woman and said, 'I owe you nothing. *See*?'

Silence.

Let it go, kid. Just walk out of here with me . . .

'You don't think I can handle him, is that it?' Susie said to Barb, her tone now turning sing-song while remaining self-assured – Walker had helped train many a CIA operative to talk just like that: to be persuasive, to talk someone into your bidding. She turned to Walker, looked him up and down, said, 'He's nothing, this guy. Look at him. He's big, but he's soft. Some east-coast city guy, I bet. Air Force? Who the hell joins the Air Force? Fags. That's who. You don't think I can handle a soft city fag like this?' Someone sniggered. Someone shushed. The bar was silent, waiting for the next person to talk. 'Remember what I did to your boy here? Last summer?'

She motioned with a kick of her boot to the butt of the wiry guy who'd held Walker's left arm, the one who was now twitching on the worn timber floor.

'Fine,' Barb said. 'You'll keep, Susie. I got my eyes on you, you know that? So go, get. Get him outta here now. Right the hell away from here, outta my space, outta my town.' She turned to Walker, her eyes almost lost in craggy, creased, chalky white skin. 'And you? *Walker*? You come here again, this town? You're in the ground. Get!'

Walker took a step towards Seabass, who continued to hold the knife out. He looked comfortable, like he used it on a regular basis, skinning and gutting animals. And it was steady, as if he'd had opportunity and reason to use it on a man before.

'You really shouldn't bring a knife to a civilised little dust-up like this,' Walker said to him. 'One day it might do the talking for you, and they'll be words you can't take back.'

Seabass looked confused.

'Come on, mister,' Susie said to Walker, stepping between the two men and giving Walker a shove in the arm. 'We're leaving.'

16

'You didn't have to help me out back there,' Walker said.

Susie was silent in the dark damp cold. They stood in the gravel car park outside the bar amid a few bikes and a bunch of pick-ups. Walker saw his hire car and knew he wouldn't be driving out of town in a hurry.

'You got a car?' Susie asked.

Walker pointed to it – its tyres slashed. 'Easy to make friends around here,' he said, tossing his keys onto the bonnet. 'How'd they expect me to bug out of town fast without a car? Idiots.'

'Follow me,' Susie said, headed for a pick-up. Old. The colour of the earth, rust mostly. Made back when the only panelling was made of steel, and all components were made in America.

It was unlocked; it didn't even have working locks. Walker's end of the cracked vinyl seat was wet – his window wouldn't go all the way up.

'Susie—'

'Susan,' she said, starting the engine, the choke out full. She turned the headlights on. 'My name is Susan.'

'They don't call you Susie?'

'No-one with brains calls me Susie,' she said, giving the engine a little gas with a few light pumps of the accelerator.

'My name's—'

'Walker. I heard you, mister, in the bar, remember? I was there. I was the one who saved your bacon.'

'Yeah, well, like I said—'

'Yes, I did have to do that,' she said.

'You think they would have killed me?'

'Maybe. I doubt it, though. Not there, not like that.'

'Well, let me tell you, that knife never would have got close to me.'

'Regardless. I'm not doing this for you.'

'Oh?'

'Nope. Right now, you might be the only way I can find my cousin.'

'This is Charles Murphy we're talking about?'

Susan nodded. 'I think he's in trouble. I know it. But . . . I need to find him, to be sure.'

'What kind of trouble do you think he's in?' Walker asked.

Susan looked at Walker as though he should know the answer to his own question; as though it was obvious, given that he'd stated that he was there because Murphy was in trouble; as though it had not occurred to her that there was trouble and then there was Trouble with a capital T.

The engine started to settle. Susan eased the choke on the old pick-up, feathering it to half-open.

Walker watched the bar. No-one came out. He figured they were listening to the car, waiting for it to drive off before settling back down. Between the rusted exhaust and loose fan belt he figured they could hear them all the way to the next county line.

'Do your friends call you Susan?'

'No.'

'What do they call you?'

Silence.

The car idling. Feathering the choke again. The heater starting up as the engine warmed. The smell of oil burning in the cylinders. Nearly ready for take-off. The thing was older than the girl – older than Walker, maybe – created back when cars were made out of heavy sheets of metal and the dye presses did little more than push a simple curve or fold here and there. When everything was functional and had a purpose and could be fixed in a backyard garage. She dropped the stick selector into drive and took off, the back tyres spinning on gravel. The tyres were chunky and loud on the coarse asphalt road. The engine was loose and pinging as it built up speed.

'Squeaker.'

'Squeaker?' Walker repeated.

She nodded.

'Well then, Squeaker,' Walker said, 'you don't know where your cousin is, but you're worried about him? Because of some trouble?'

She didn't answer, but she did push the car harder. Heading out of town, the way that Walker had come into it. She drove like that for two minutes, then started to ease off the gas. Walker saw signs up ahead. An intersection. A sign pointing to the next interstate.

Squeaker eased to a stop, the engine thrumming at the empty black intersection in the middle of nowhere, no cars or lights in any direction.

'You should get out here,' she said.

17

Squeaker's hands were tight on the steering wheel. Her gaze fixed straight ahead.

Walker said, 'You want me to walk from here?'

'Eight miles west there's a town,' Squeaker said. 'You could walk there. Stay the night. Take the first bus out in the morning. Seems sensible.'

'Sensible?'

Squeaker nodded.

'Or?' Walker said.

'No *or*. You should leave this be. My cousin's tough. Wherever he is, he'll be all right. Besides, you've got Barb's threat back there to think about. It ain't idle. She'll get you if you stick around here.'

'But you're worried about Murphy too,' Walker said.

'They're my worries, not his. He'll be all right. It's me – this town. It's falling to pieces. I want to talk to him about options before I bug out myself. Maybe I could live with him a while. Babysit for them. Live in?'

Walker remained silent. He looked from Susan to the empty roads and back to her. Silence, but for the thrumming idle of the old cast-iron block V8 ticking away.

Eventually he said, 'Leave what be?'

'My cousin. This place. All of it.'

'Why?'

'No good will come of it.'

'I beg to differ.'

'Huh?' She looked at Walker.

He could see that this escape route she was providing was given not in earnest, but as an easy out for him. It was like she wanted him to stay, as though her little challenge here was to test him, his bona fides in how far he was willing to go to help out her cousin. 'Susan – Squeaker – I have to find your cousin. It's bigger than just his safety.

There's something big going down, soon, and Murphy has a tiny part in it – an integral part, but just a part. See? If I don't find him, look out for him, get to talk to him, well – well, then, some serious shit's going to go down.'

She nodded. 'Is this about his service?'

'Yes.'

She nodded again. Her hands were tight on the wheel, her pale knuckles bright in the moonlight through the windshield.

'I'm going nowhere,' Walker said, looking forward, the grimy old headlights bathing the road in yellow light. 'With or without your help, I'll find your cousin. He's around here someplace.'

'Hm,' Susan said with a smile, putting the Dodge back into gear and taking off dead ahead. 'I'd like to see you try finding him.'

'But . . .' Walker checked over his shoulder at the intersection. 'You're going to help me?'

Susan nodded, said, 'I'll tell you what I know, Walker. But you should also know some other stuff before.'

'Okay.'

She glanced at him when she said, 'You've been warned. I warned you, right? Gave you a chance to leave, just before?'

Walker nodded. 'You wanted to ditch me back there with the wolves and bears in the middle of the road, between butt-crack and nowhere.'

Squeaker looked ahead and drove.

'I've been to war,' Walker said, looking out his side window. 'A few times. Whatever's going on here, with Barb and all them, I think I can handle it. We can handle it.'

'You may have been to what you *think* is war, Walker.'

'Jed.'

'That doesn't sound right – I like Walker more.'

'Okay.'

'Walker, you ain't seen nothin' yet. This is God's own country, and he's got a hornet so far up his ass that he's got everyone who's anyone at war with one another. It's been that way for too long, and you coming here ain't going to do nothing about it.'

'I just want to talk to your cousin. Warn him. See that he knows what's coming after him. See what he knows.'

'They all do. And they all don't. Want to talk to him, I mean. You gotta be careful about what you wish for, Walker,' Squeaker said, braking and taking a tight turn from the road, now headed north-east along a single-lane blacktop. 'Some things? Hell, some things should never be done up, you get that?' They were quiet a while, just the sound of the engine and the creak of the springs in the bench seat as they travelled over bumps. 'Sometimes you just gotta say nothin' to no-one. You have to hang your head and walk away, forget what you saw and heard, for nothing good will ever come of it.'

18

'Yep?' the man called Menzil said into his phone. The phone was nothing fancy, a throw-away, and he had a bag full of them. Menzil was a man of precautions, of keeping a distance, an arm's length deniability. He'd learned how to do that through a lifetime of chasing and busting crooks. He was in a rented warehouse, in St Louis. There was nothing inside but their two vehicles, one of which would be staying here for the next stage of the op, and two trestle tables with a heavy tarp covering the contents. His team of operatives was close by. Their gear was under the tarps. They would be ready to move at a moment's notice. Menzil was sure of it.

'We've had a complication,' the voice on the phone replied. 'There's someone getting close to Murphy.'

Menzil asked, 'How do you know this?'

There was a pause, and the voice said, 'All you need to know is that there's a guy tracking Murphy.'

'A guy?'

'Named Walker. Ex-Air Force and Agency guy who now seems to be doing some freelance contract work.'

'For who?'

'We don't know.'

'Wait – *Walker*?' Menzil said. 'That the guy from the news – from the thing in the New York Stock Exchange?'

'Yeah, that's him.'

'Okay.'

'Okay?'

'Okay. He's a guy. It's interesting.'

'It's troubling.'

'So, he's tracking Murphy – why?'

'No idea.'

'Has he made us? The op?'

'No. He doesn't know what he's looking into. No clue. He's just got the end of the string and he's tugging. But with his skill set he just might achieve what we couldn't these past couple of weeks.'

'Find Murphy.'

'Yep.'

'You had three separate PIs down there scratching around and they got squat. What makes you think Walker will get the job done before us?'

'Instinct. Mine, and his. Just remain contactable and I'll update you.'

'Is he ahead of us?'

'Call it even.'

'Great.'

'Have you got this?'

'Got it.' Menzil ended the call and headed out to get the four guys in his team. This Walker guy seemed like a challenge. Menzil enjoyed challenges.

•

'Murphy hasn't been seen or heard of,' Squeaker said as the car cruised through a small town. Past the bar, closed for the night. Past the general store. Past the gas station, lit up like a star in the sky. Past the few roads that split off the two-lane highway, each headed to houses on small plots in the woods. 'Near-on a year. No word from him. No sign of his whereabouts.'

'Missing?'

'No-one goes missing around here. You're either alive, or dead.'

Walker weighed that up. *Dead?* Another name added to the list? If so, where'd they get him – out here, or while he was still deployed overseas? The Navy had him listed as discharged, straight after the operation to kill bin Laden in Abbottabad . . .

'He's alive, if that's what you're thinking,' she said. The headlights of the pick-up bathed the way ahead with the dull yellow light on his side, a brighter shade on hers.

'You're sure?' Walker said.

Squeaker nodded.

'But you've not had word from him,' Walker said. 'Nothing.'

'That's right,' she said, following the highway, the tired old engine topping out around fifty-five. 'But he's alive. He has to be. He's got family. He's protecting them, you see?'

'He's in hiding?' Walker said, tapping his side window at the tall spruce and hickory pine trees. 'Out here, somewhere?'

'Nah,' she said, slowing and making a turn to the left, the mismatched tyres doing better on the gravel road than on the highway blacktop. She pointed ahead. 'Out there. Way out there.'

19

Squeaker's cabin was a double-width trailer, placed on cinderblocks in the 1980s and never moved. Paint seemed to hold the walls together, while grass in the roof joints tried to break it apart. The lot was a clearing in the forest, and a dozen similar trailers were ringed around about half an acre of gravel. The hum of a generator came from a tin shack at the top of the slope, and the smell of diesel exhaust hung in the air.

Inside the trailer was a world of whimsy. Fairy lights were the only lighting, hundreds of tiny bulbs plugged into linked power-board sockets, each light wrapped in orange or pink or yellow plastic stars from some long-ago Christmas decoration. The result was a cosy space. Two worn armchairs. A small television on a timber crate. A couple of side tables stacked with messes of newspapers. Worn carpet underfoot, the same colour as the worn pick-up truck outside. Walker left his boots on the mat inside the door, as Squeaker had done. It was warm, care of a small cast-iron stove that had been jemmied into place against a wall and flued out the ceiling. She went to it and used an oven mitt to open the steel handle, then took a split log from a steel bucket and placed it on the coals.

'You're not worried about me?' Walker said, waiting by the open door. 'Being a stranger and all, in your home?'

Squeaker looked at him like she'd never considered the notion of a stranger in her home being dangerous, and the ramifications of what might go wrong for her in such an eventuality. Walker saw something in her then that he'd not noticed before. She was scared. Deep down. Behind her eyes. They betrayed her. She was maybe twenty years old, living a hard-scrabble life, eking out an existence somehow, far from any government handouts. A survivor.

'You want nothing with me, mister,' she said, her eyes leaving his and going to the fire, which she poked and settled before adding a second piece of wood. 'And I can handle myself, besides. Close the door.'

'I believe it.' Walker closed the door behind him, the flimsy aluminium siding rattling shut.

'So you should.'

'Who's out here?' Walker asked, motioning out the window to the glowing lights in the other trailers in the clearing.

'People. Real Americans. If *you'd* call us that.'

'If I'd call you that?'

'Where you from?'

'Texas, as a kid. Then Philly, as a teen.'

'Right. So what'd you think of us?'

'Nothing. Never thought about you.'

She was silent.

'Look,' Walker said. 'Your cousin isn't here. But what did you mean before – that he's way out here, in the forest or mountains?'

'Probably.'

'Probably?'

'Yep. Probably. The probability being that he is out there, further, somewhere, in the forest and mountains. Coffee?'

'Sure.'

Squeaker put the kettle on a small gas-bottle stove. The ceiling above it was discoloured, but the rest of the trailer was neat, clean, but for the newspapers and a makeshift bookshelf made up of side-stacked cardboard boxes. She kept her front door locked too, he noticed. Only a dozen or so others around here in the clearing and she couldn't trust them?

'One of my neighbours,' she said, watching him.

'Sorry?'

'The lock, on my door,' she said, nodding towards the place he had just looked. 'It's new. Two years, since not long after I moved in here. One of my neighbours used to come in while I was away. Go through my underwear.'

'Charming.'

'Right? Anyway, each to their own. I think he still comes in here. Somehow.'

'You know who it is?'

'Maybe. Yeah. I do.'

Walker sat on a hard chair at a small table, facing the flimsy door. He watched her put ground coffee into a French press.

'I like good coffee,' she said.

'I can see that.'

'I have a job, at a motel, couple towns west.'

'Okay.'

'They serve this stuff. I got hooked. And using this press is cheaper than getting filter papers.'

'Fair enough.'

'Are you really in the Air Force?'

'Was. Once upon a time.'

She looked at him. 'Did you know my cousin?'

'No.'

'You said you did.'

'I said that to idiots.'

'They're not idiots,' she said, taking a couple of small tubs of long-life milk from a cupboard above the sink, the type they stocked in motels. 'They're hard.'

'Hard in the head maybe,' Walker said. 'Live hard lives, I don't doubt.'

'They're rich,' she said, putting mugs and milk and motel packets of sugar on the table. 'So, they can't be that hard in the head.'

'How'd they get that way?'

Squeaker was silent. The aluminium kettle started to whistle, so she turned off the gas and poured the water over the coffee grinds. The smell filled the room. She took the pot and sat opposite Walker.

'What danger is my cousin in?'

'That's a tough one.'

'Try me.'

'Okay. Well, what do you know about Osama bin Laden?'

'Our president?'

'No.'

'I'm joking. Just testing to see your reaction.'

'I really don't think that *all* people in the Ozarks are backwards hicks.'

'Okay.' She pressed the coffee down and poured it. 'Okay. So, he was the bad guy, the terrorist, the former CIA employee, killed by SEALs like my cousin in some Pakistani town a few years too late.' Walker looked at her, the surprise clearly evident on his face because she said, 'I went to school. And I read newspapers I bring home from work. So, what about him?'

'Well, let me tell you that bin Laden wasn't killed by SEALs *like* your cousin.' Walker picked up his coffee mug, held it between his hands. 'Your cousin was there, in the house in that Pakistani town, on that mission. He was one of the Team Six guys who did the job.'

It was Squeaker's turn to be surprised. Confusion, for a second, then a beaming smile for her heroic cousin.

She said, 'Seriously?'

Walker nodded.

'He's a hero – and he never said nothing about it!'

'Those guys tend to be quiet,' Walker said.

'Why?' she asked, then followed up with her own animated answer: 'Because it's all secret stuff.'

'Partly that's the reason,' Walker said. 'But ultimately it's about the missions. They fail more often than not. If you boast about the successes, you can't help but have all those failures working away at you. They're a closed bunch. They can talk about it together, because they know what it's like – to get the bad guys, and to lose the good ones.'

Squeaker nodded. 'Chuck's always been like that. Always quiet. He comes from a loud family. Brothers. All of them around here.'

'Have they seen him?'

'Nope. Maybe. I doubt it.'

'You asked them?'

She nodded.

Walker sipped his coffee. It wasn't great, some generic blend bought in ten-pound packs for roadside motels, but it was strong.

'What's his trouble?' she asked. 'Seriously.'

Walker looked at her slowly, carefully. 'Someone wants to kill him.'

She leaned back a little from the table.

'Not me,' Walker said. 'I want him to know that he's in danger.'

'He can take care of himself.'

'I'm sure he can,' Walker said. 'All the SEALs can, right? But the thing is, eight have already been killed.'

'Eight SEALS dead?'

'From that mission.'

'How? In Afghanistan?'

'All over. Murdered.'

'By who?'

'I don't know. Not yet.'

'Terrorists?'

'Of some sort.'

Squeaker leaned forward, said, 'Who *are* you?'

'I told you.'

'I mean, *why* you? Why aren't the police here? Or the Navy's police?'

'They will be. I'm ahead of them. There're others working this. There're others who are protecting the rest of the SEALs from that op.'

'How is it that you're ahead of them?'

'Because . . .' Walker looked into his coffee cup. 'This is a part of something that I've been working on for a while. And there's a good team behind me.'

'Working on, with a team? So, you're still in the military?'

'No. It's complicated.'

'Try me. I went to school.'

'And read newspapers.'

She nodded.

'I'm here as part of a special UN investigations team.'

'UN?'

Walker nodded.

'Cool.'

Walker asked, 'What can you tell me about your cousin?'

Susan took her time replying. 'Angry. As a kid. He's older than me – I'm twenty-three. He's, what, thirty-four? Yeah, that'd be right. He and his sister used to babysit me sometimes, when Mum used to have to work. It was just her – her and me. And Chuck, he used to . . . he'd always be fighting, with the other kids around. Always bigger than him – he's not a big guy, nothing like you, and even as a kid he was small. But his anger . . . I saw him once – I would have been five or six – I saw him beat two grown men, big guys, like you and then some, near to death, for saying something about his sister.'

'Where's his sister?'

'Albuquerque, last I heard,' she replied.

Walker nodded. That was the information he had too; she was listed in DoD records as Murphy's next of kin. But she'd been a dead end. As soon as Walker had called her and started to explain things, she'd hung up on him. As soon as Walker had shown up at her door and started to talk, she'd closed it on him.

Walker asked, 'What about parents?'

'His?'

Walker nodded.

'His father's dead. His mother's in a state place, in Jonesboro. Lost her mind at least ten years ago. They were old parents when they had Charles – unexpected, my ma used to say about it. Anyway, Marg Murphy, his mother, must be near-on eighty now. Alzheimer's got her brain all rewired.'

Then came a knock at Squeaker's front door. Urgent. Incessant. Then the door was flung open.

20

'Really?' NCIS Special Agent Levine said, turning the volume down. The highway stretched out ahead, and there was plenty of listening time between now and their destination.

'It's James Levine returning at the Met for *Cosi Fan Tutte*,' her partner, Tom Woods, said. 'Don't suppose he's a relative of yours?'

'No. And I don't like it.'

'It's Mozart. Who doesn't like Mozart?'

'Mozart? I thought that was beneath you.'

'He's a little tame. A genius, sure, but give me a Russian any day.'

'I worry about you.'

'Hmph,' he replied, looking out his window. 'I suppose I should listen to that LA soft-rock stuff you like.'

'It sounds like this singer is strangling a cat,' Levine said. 'Did Mozart hate cats?'

'It's a soprano, singing the role of Despina,' he said, turning it back up. 'This is her main aria.'

Levine moved to turn it down again, saying, 'She can stick her aria up her—'

The phone cut in over the Bluetooth and Levine hit answer. 'Special Agent Levine.'

'It's Grant,' the Assistant Director for Investigations said from his San Diego office. 'We have a complication.'

'What is it?' Levine asked.

'Someone else is looking into this.'

Levine said, 'Who?'

'A former Air Force guy. Jed Walker.'

'Air Force?' Levine said, pulling onto the shoulder so that she could give the call her undivided attention. 'What do they want with this?'

Her boss was silent on the phone. Levine looked to Woods, who merely shrugged. They sat there, on the side of the interstate, just the hum of the Taurus ticking over.

'We're still waiting on details on this guy,' Assistant Director Grant said.

'Will it be a problem?'

'I'll keep you posted,' Grant replied. 'In the meantime, you have to get to Murphy as quickly as you can.'

'We're working on it,' Levine said. She checked her mirrors and then over her shoulder and pulled back onto the dark highway. 'Anything else on the other SEALs?'

'I can confirm that they are all now in protection,' her boss said. 'The last couple didn't want it, but they got it, courtesy of the Secretary of the Navy. Get to Murphy. Debrief him just as we're doing with the others.'

The line went dead. Mozart resumed over the sound system.

Levine looked to Woods and then concentrated on the road ahead as he placed a call to the San Diego office.

Brewster, the tech wizard, answered on the first ring.

'Working late?' Levine said.

'No rest around here,' Brewster replied. 'Grant's got everyone he can find tasked on this SEAL thing – and here was I thinking they rounded them all up quick and easy.'

'Well, this last guy, Murphy, has no fixed address,' Woods said, 'so it's not that easy.'

Levine said, 'In this day and age, they could get a cell-phone fix or facial recognition image.'

'Nope.' They could hear Brewster's fingers tapping at a keyboard. 'This guy's off the grid.'

Levine said, 'Define off the grid.'

'In the boonies, in the stowage,' Brewster said. 'This guy ain't just a SEAL who don't want to be found. He's a born-and-bred mountain man from the Ozarks. He could be anywhere there. Probably has solar cells for power, a sat phone tucked away somewhere for emergency, gas by the bottle, water from the sky or nearby stream. I'm talking Off. The. Grid.'

Woods said, 'You're talking thousands of square miles of forest.'

'Yep,' Brewster said, ''fraid so.'

'Narrow it,' Levine ordered.

'On it,' Brewster replied. 'Got a whole team working on it.'

'Keep on it. We'll contact you again in an hour.'

Woods waited until the call disconnected and then asked, 'Why do you suppose this ex-Air Force guy is looking for Murphy?'

'Jed Walker?' Levine said. 'No idea. But I want to know. I want to know who he is and why he's doing this. Then I'm going to arrest him for getting in the way of Federal Agents.'

'Badass.' Woods turned up the Mozart. Levine turned it off and drove faster.

●

'You gotta get!' the woman said, standing in Squeaker's open doorway. 'Seabass is at the turn-off, his car and another, and they're planning somethin'. We just heard what happened in town. Now *get!*'

Squeaker didn't need to be told again. She darted into her room and out again, a backpack over her shoulder, a scoped rifle in her hands, and said to Walker, 'Come on!'

He followed her outside to the clearing.

The neighbour said to Walker, 'You a cop?'

'No,' Walker replied. She'd come from the trailer opposite, her door wide open, the light and heat spilling out. She was in her nightclothes and mud-splattered rubber boots.

'You look like a cop,' she said. 'Cut him loose, Squeak. Let this thing be. Before those boys get up here and do somethin'.'

'He's my worry, Deb,' Squeaker said, tossing the pack in the back of her pick-up and putting the rifle into a holder inside the cab. 'I took him on. I'll get him out.'

Deb didn't push it. Just watched. There were other faces about, all of them inside their trailers, not dumb enough to go outside and get involved. Walker got that. Then Deb got it too – headlights were coming up the drive, down at the twist through the trees. Deb was at her trailer before the first car made it to the clearing.

21

By the time the second car pulled up, Squeaker had her rifle out. Marlin, 30-30 Winchester. Cheap – less than four hundred bucks at Walmart the last Walker checked – but reliable. It looked well maintained for an amateur's weapon.

As Seabass stepped out of his car, Squeaker had the rifle cocked and aimed at his chest. He raised his hands.

'No,' he said to her. 'Uh-uh. Think about it now, girl.'

Walker noted two guys behind Seabass – older guys, from the bar, nothing of note. He looked over to the other car, another pick-up, this one a new black Chevy Tahoe that Walker had seen back at the bar. Barb's husband was at the wheel. He stayed inside, but two men, unfamiliar, climbed out.

Five guys. With Barb's husband there were six.

'Now,' Seabass said, 'we didn't bring guns along.'

'You're on my land,' Squeaker said in a loud voice that carried in the air. 'And this is my guest. Be on your way.'

'Now, now,' Seabass said, taking his hands down. '*Whose* land?'

'Mine. And my ma's before me.'

'I think you'll find all this belongs to Barb,' Seabass said, then pointed over to Barb's husband. 'And Gus.'

'They don't own shit – she takes and bullies, and we're not standing for it!' Squeaker kept the rifle steady.

'We?' Seabass said, his arms out. 'Who's we?'

He looked around the cabins and trailers. Heads disappeared behind windows.

'Who's we!?' he yelled.

Squeaker was silent but she held the rifle firm.

'I got this,' Walker said to her, moving between her and Seabass, his eyes on the guys in front of him.

'You were told to leave this place,' Seabass said. He stood up straight and tall. He'd had some coffees and a stern talking to since

Walker had encountered him last. 'You hard of hearing or just plain dumb?'

'See,' Walker said, 'that's the problem.'

Seabass said, 'How so?'

'We don't want you here,' Walker said. 'You heard the lady.'

Seabass smiled. 'We? *Lady*?'

'Me. Susan. That's two.' Walker looked at him and lowered his voice as though he was about to whisper an embarrassing question. 'Seabass, you *can* count to two, right?'

'You had your chance, Walker, when she saved you back at the bar,' Seabass said, red in the face as he flushed with anger. 'And you screwed it. Now we're gonna fix you good, hear? And then we're gonna screw this little lady thing, see if she really does squeak.'

Walker twitched involuntarily as he felt the surge of adrenaline.

'Thanks,' he said, taking a couple of steps towards Seabass. His leather steel-capped boots were steady in the mud. His well-worn jeans had plenty of stretch and movement. His T-shirt, flannel shirt and lined leather jacket were all loose enough for the action that was coming.

Seabass looked behind him, grinning to his cohorts, then turned back to Walker.

'Thanks?' Seabass said. His grin remained. 'For what's coming? We're gonna *burn* you both in that shit trailer, you know that? You be thankful then, city boy?'

Walker smiled.

'You bring that shiny knife with you again, bub?' he said, taking another step into what was now arm's reach of Seabass.

The guy grinned again as he brought the knife out. The blade caught the lights of the trailers, which glinted off scratches from the wear and tear of grinding and sharpening on steel and stone.

Seabass's smile lasted for just one more second.

In the moment that followed, the knife was pushed up through his Adam's apple, through the cartilage of the oesophagus, through the vertebrae and out the back of his neck. He fell to the ground, Walker's hands already moving with him to his right, to the next closest guy, who was still looking at his falling leader. Walker kicked him square in the groin. On his way down the guy's head connected with Walker's quickly rising knee. Lights out.

The other older guy turned and ran for Seabass's car as Walker set upon the two younger ring-ins. They both rushed him as they realised he was coming at them, the shock of seeing their comrade with a knife through his neck overtaken by a primal do-or-die urge to fight.

Walker wasn't planning on doing any more killing tonight. Not these young guys. There was no reason to. They were big, muscled by hard work, maybe spending their days clearing forests and eating plenty of basic protein, but they'd been called into something they knew nothing about. They weren't armed, they were merely there to be counted. Background. A wall of beef, to intimidate the outsider. Unlike Seabass, who'd drawn a knife against a well-trained killer. If you drew a knife in a fight, you had to expect consequences, but these boys were just attendees.

Walker kept them at arm's length. The two of them matched him in height and weight but what these guys didn't have in equal measures with Walker was a decade of hardened combat training and experience. One had served in the Marines, Walker soon saw from his stance and fight moves, so he was dealt with first.

Walker halted the ex-Marine's advance by stomping on his foot. The forward momentum carried the guy into Walker, and while he was quick, Walker was quicker. Walker parried the flailing arms out of the way, then elbowed the other guy – who had advanced into their space – before dealing a devastating uppercut into the sternum of the Marine. It was probably Walker's favourite move of incapacitation; his signature move, if he had to pick one. A fast and hard blow to the point where nerves cluster. Not so hard as to leave permanent damage, but enough to shut things down for a day or two. The guy was down in a foetal position by the time his comrade fell over him, a quick three-punch combo to the face knocking him out cold.

A gunshot rang out.

Squeaker, with the rifle. She'd shot the driver's-side mirror off Gus's gleaming pick-up and now stood, rifle tucked into her shoulder, eye at the scope. It had been a deliberate shot, and she was ready for more. Then Walker saw why.

Barb's husband had a pistol in his hand. A shiny snub-nosed .357 revolver was now aimed clear out the open driver's window, a finger hooked through the trigger guard.

The other older guy stopped at Seabass's car, clearly realising that the keys were on a corpse in the mud by Walker's feet.

'How good are you with that thing?' Walker asked Squeaker, not taking his eyes off the men ahead.

'Better than most,' she replied, the rifle steady in her hands.

'Keep on them.'

'Yep.'

Walker approached Barb's husband, Gus. 'You want to harm Susan?' he asked him.

The older man was silent. His eyes darted from Walker to Squeaker to Walker again.

Walker took the out-held pistol from him, breaking three of Gus's fingers in the process. Gus screamed, and Walker used the heavy pistol to smash his nose, pulverising the cartilage. Gus shut up, stunned into silence, the shock taking over, and blood began to pour.

Walker opened the car door and dragged him out, landing him on his hands and knees in the mud, then pushed him over onto his back with his boot.

'Don't . . . shoot . . .' Gus said.

'Hold your nose with your good hand,' Walker said to him. Then he turned to the older guy by the other truck and called him over. 'You came here to kill. You're lucky this is all you're getting. Clear?'

Gus nodded.

'You help your pal here back to town, or wherever it is that you people call home,' Walker ordered. 'You walk. The whole way there. Got it?'

Gus nodded.

Walker kneeled down to Gus and spoke quietly. 'You see me?'

Gus nodded, pinching his nose, blood pumping over his mouth and chin.

'You mess with Susan here, or anyone on this plot,' Walker said, 'and I'll come for you. Got that?'

Gus nodded again.

'Right.' Walker put a heavy hand on Gus's chest, applying more and more pressure. 'Charles Murphy. Tell me what you know.'

'Noth-nothing,' Gus replied, all nasally. 'He's out there, somewhere. That's all I know.'

'Bullshit. Barb wouldn't get so riled up and send you idiots out like this if it were nothing.'

Gus was silent, until Walker cocked the revolver, a big mechanical clonk that echoed in the quiet night.

'He's trouble for us,' Gus said, 'or he was. Was trouble.'

Walker said, 'What's that mean?'

'He tried to stop us. Shut us down. Couple years back, when – when he got home. Barb worked something out with him.'

'What was that?'

'We left him alone – we don't go into his area no more, and he leaves us alone.'

'He wanted to shut you down on what?'

'Crystal.'

'Crystal?'

'Meth,' Squeaker said, standing next to Walker, the rifle loose in her grip. 'These idiots run it around here. Murph took to them after they messed up the lives of a couple of childhood friends of his.'

'That's right – and it's all I know. He's gone,' Gus said. 'Over a year, not a word. Hell, he might have moved right away, interstate. I don't know!'

Walker turned to Squeaker. 'Go get our bags from your truck – we've got a new ride.'

Gus said, 'No, you can't—'

'What?' Walker looked down to Barb's husband. 'Your old lady gonna breathe fire at you?'

Gus was silent.

'That's what I thought,' Walker said. He eased off the hammer on the pistol and lifted Gus by the lapels of his jacket as though he were as light as air, and said close to his face, 'You remember everything I said.'

Gus nodded once again.

Squeaker tossed their packs into the cab of the Tahoe, and Walker got into the driver's seat and buzzed the seat adjustment button all the way back. Every trailer in the clearing had their lights on inside, and heads were at the windows, looking through curtains at the night's show.

'And tell Barb,' Walker said out the window as he selected drive and heard Squeaker crash into the seat next to him and shut her door. 'If I hear she's making a fuss, I'll be back, and I'll use your butt to wipe that shit she calls make-up right off her face.'

22

'Where should we be headed?' Walker said as he drove. They were back on the B-road that had led up to the clearing. The Tahoe rode fast and smooth, and the headlights' bright white beams cut the night. He kept to the speed limit and headed east.

Squeaker said, 'North. Take the next major exit and head north where it hits Highway 63.'

'What's north?'

'Missouri.'

'Right.'

'That, and a whole bunch of stuff. They won't come looking for us to the north.'

'They?'

'Barb and Gus.'

'I don't think they'll be looking for us in a hurry.'

'You don't know them, Walker.' Squeaker looked out her side window for a stretch. 'People around here don't soon forget.'

They drove to the two-lane highway, then cut through a low forest either side and headed up into the hills. A low fog was rolling into the valleys but they were soon out of it.

When they passed a sign that said 'Salem, 10 miles', Walker asked, 'How far?'

'Through Salem,' Squeaker replied. 'Keep going. Thayer is over the border. Route 63 cuts right through it. Probably another twenty, twenty-five miles past Salem.' She leaned across and looked at the dash. 'You can stop there and gas up. Then keep north.'

'North. You seem specific.'

Squeaker watched him for a moment and then sighed. 'Okay,' she said. 'Murphy was seen in Willow Springs by another cousin of ours. In town for supplies, he'd said.'

'So, he might be near there,' Walker said.

'He might.' Squeaker paused, watching out the window, then said, 'Is that what you'd do, if you were him, hiding away with your family?'

'Do what?'

'Go to the nearest town for supplies.'

Walker smiled. 'Probably not.'

'Right. But people there might know him.'

'They might. It's worth a shot.'

'And we can stay there the night. We'll be fine there.'

'You're sure?'

'I've been there once. And besides, what Gus, Barb's husband, said back there, about meth and Murphy? They no longer peddle their crystal across the border. I'm pretty sure Murphy had a hand in that.'

'How would Murphy have got them to do that?'

'Ah, let me check in my butt,' Squeaker said, making a show of putting her hand on the back of her jeans. 'Nope, no answers there.'

Walker smiled. He liked Squeaker more and more with each mile. And he got the sense that he'd like Murphy just the same.

'He tried to shut them down,' Squeaker said. 'Barb and Gus. After he got out of the Navy and found his two best friends on the pipe, in some crack den. He busted the legs of a few local dealers. Then Barb and all, they came after him, like they did with you tonight. Only Murphy was at it for months, and they were at him for months, hunting him through the woods. He's got a family, you know? Young'uns, two of them. Maybe three by now – at least that's what I heard from that last sighting.'

'His file didn't mention kids. Or a wife.'

'Murphy's real private. Like, *real* private. Anyhow, he tried to run Barb and her crew out, and he failed, and in the end he made a deal with the devil.'

Walker looked at her.

'Another group now controls things up there over the border. With the meth. Murph had a hand in them heading south to the border as their new demarcation line, and he brought them in, worked to get them established as . . . well, muscle, I guess.'

'Hence Barb's not his biggest fan,' Walker said, slowing as the bright white lights of the expensive pick-up highlighted a deer and her fawn ahead.

'Good eatin',' Squeaker said, as the animals sauntered across the road. The rifle was between her legs, the butt on the floor and the danger end pointed straight up.

'I'm sure we'll find a burger joint on the road.'

'What – you're a pacifist now?'

'Nope,' Walker said, easing on the gas and going around the mother and child. 'You never saw *Bambi*?'

Squeaker gave a muted little laugh, deep for a person her size. After a moment she spoke, all trace of laughter gone. 'You had to kill him, right?'

'Seabass?'

Squeaker grunted.

'Right,' Walker said. 'I had to. A guy like that, doing a show like that with a big knife. He had it coming.'

'No-one will ever say nothin' about it,' Squeaker said. 'To the law, I mean. Be sure of that. It's all a law unto itself round here.'

'I get that,' Walker said, and up ahead the Arkansas town of Salem appeared with an all-night truck stop on the highway leading in, and beyond, a row of old street lights bathing the main street in yellow. It was after midnight and most of the houses on the side streets were dark. 'Hungry?'

'We should push on.'

'Quick stop,' Walker said. 'Besides, Gus and his buddies have the night's walk ahead of them all the way in the dark.'

Squeaker stifled a laugh, then said, 'Okay. I'm always hungry. I forgot to pack my wallet, though.'

Walker grinned as he pulled into the truck stop and parked next to a big empty logging rig. He killed the V8 engine via the push button on the dash.

'It's on me,' Walker said. 'Come on, let's fuel ourselves up, debrief and plan what's ahead. Then we gas up the car and head north.'

'Plan?' she said, leaving the rifle in the footwell and zipping up her parka as they headed into the night. 'Hell, that doesn't sound fun.'

'It's an important step,' Walker said, scraping the mud off his boots on a metal bar put by the front door for just that purpose. 'You should try it sometime.'

'You should try living in the Ozarks sometime,' Squeaker countered, opening the door and holding it for Walker to go through first. 'You'll soon find, no matter how prepared you are, things go upside-down, fast.'

23

Walker had a hamburger, fries, onion rings, a banana split and coffee.

Squeaker ordered scrambled eggs, mushrooms, pancakes with syrup, and a bottomless glass of seltzer.

'All that talk about eating that baby deer,' Walker said, finishing the last mouthful of his burger, 'and you didn't order meat. And you've not eaten half your food.'

'Yeah . . .' She looked to where she'd pushed her food around with her fork, then up at Walker, holding his gaze.

There was that fragility again, Walker thought. It was there, not very far from the surface, but usually well hidden, pushed not deep down but aside, as she'd somehow learned, probably the hard way, that it needed to be.

'I've . . .' She looked around. Just the one trucker at a table, another guy at a counter paying for gas, and the two owner–operators. All out of earshot but she spoke in a hushed tone anyway. 'I've never seen a man killed before. Dead, sure. Accidents and all. But not killed.'

'Oh,' Walker said, pushing his empty plate to the side. 'Right. Sorry. Do you need to talk about it?'

She shook her head. 'I'm trying to forget it.'

'It was him or me. And if it was me, then it was going to be you.'

'I know that. I get that. It's just . . .' Squeaker's gaze drifted, middle-distance, to Walker's sternum. He looked down. There was blood there, a splash of it, from where he'd nicked Seabass's carotid artery. He pulled his leather jacket together nearer to the neck to hide it from view.

'It ain't the how or why, Walker,' she said, looking at him. 'He had it comin' and then some. It's just the sight of it. Up close. So quick. So easy.'

'It gets easier,' Walker said. 'The sight, I mean. As cold as that sounds. When it's do or die, and when there's no other choice, and when you know you're in the right, it gets easier.'

'Will you do it again?'

'Probably.'

'Soon?'

'I hope not.'

'Don't. Not while I'm around. Okay?'

Walker looked at her. Her sweet face. Young, but tough. Knowing, but worth protecting from knowing too much. 'Okay.'

She nodded.

Walker got up and paid the bill at the counter. He bought a bag of snacks and drinks to take with them. Squeaker joined him and asked the counter-hand for a quart of whisky. Walker didn't comment, just added the bottle to the bag for her alongside the snacks.

'We should find a place to rest,' Walker said, pushing open the aluminium-framed glass door. He did his jacket up as the cold cut around his neck. It was an odd cold, this. Damp. He'd been in far colder climates, but this chill made his knees ache.

'Yep,' she said, holding her hands out for the car key. Walker passed it over. 'I know a place.'

•

The place turned out to be a motel on the western edge of Thayer, just north of the border. Even with the windows shut the sounds of the interstate could be heard, tyres speeding by on coarse bitumen.

The room was tired. Oatmeal-coloured carpet worn and stained, ingrained with cigarette ash over a decade or two. The twin beds had mismatched floral quilts, the mattresses were lumpy and the pillows thin and cold. The heater worked, though, an electric thing blowing out hot dusty air, and Walker turned it to full while Squeaker sat back on her bed and ate crisps and sipped whisky from a chipped mug while watching a late-night chat show on television.

'Nice place,' Walker said.

'I came here after a date once,' she replied. 'When my ma was still alive – we lived together, her and I, back at the clearing, so I had no decent place to go after the date. I mean, I didn't want to use the car, and we'd been further up in Missouri headed back – so we stopped here.' She stopped herself, looked at her mug of liquor like it was some kind of truth serum. She took another sip. 'The rooms with the big beds are nicer.'

'Can't be much worse,' Walker said, picking up his pack. 'I'm gonna take a shower.'

'Okay,' she said, not taking her eyes off the television. 'Then we plan, right? For tomorrow.'

'Right,' Walker said, smiling, and she shot him a mischievous grin with her lips moving to her drink.

Walker went into the bathroom and closed the flimsy door, the warped plywood not shutting right in its jamb. He set the shower on hot and waited for it to steam while he stripped off, rinsing his bloodstained shirt out under cold water in the basin, scrubbing it with the pitifully tiny bar of soap. Once it was clean and wrung out, he hung it over the rail that held the torn shower curtain. He adjusted the shower and stepped in. As the water rained down, he washed the specks of blood from his neck, where it had splattered. Washed the cold out of his hair. Scrubbed at his stubble, getting rid of what he imagined were minute specks of Seabass's last stand.

The bathroom door opened. He looked out under his hanging shirt.

Squeaker stood in the doorway, naked, and came right on into the shower, her hands up over her chest against the cold. She stood in the shower and pushed her body against Walker's, nuzzling under the streaming hot water.

'Look—'

'Sh,' she said, wrapping her arms around his waist, her feet between his.

'Susan—'

'Squeaker.'

'I'm an old man next to you.'

'How old are you?' she asked, looking up into his eyes.

'At least thirty-nine.'

'That's not old. I'm twenty-three.' She smiled.

'Still. You're too small – I'm throwing you back into the ocean.'

Squeaker looked up at him. Walker looked down at her.

'Fine. Just let me hold you awhile,' she said, turning her head and resting it on his chest. 'Hold me too.'

Walker rested his chin on her head, let out a breath and wrapped his arms around her. He felt her smile against him.

•

'We have a problem,' Menzil said to his crew.

The four of them looked at him, silent, waiting.

'The final target, Murphy,' Menzil said, looking at his guys. 'He's hot. There are Feds on his tail.'

The tallest of the four said, 'You sure?'

Menzil gave him a look, like questioning him was not a good idea.

'What kind of Feds?' another guy asked.

'NCIS,' Menzil said.

A couple of the guys snorted, but they stopped when they realised their boss, Menzil, wasn't pleased and didn't think any of it was joke-worthy.

'So, what's the problem?' the first questioner asked.

'They have resources. And from what I hear, they're ahead of us on this target.'

'We *have* been busy.'

Menzil shot the speaker another look that silenced him. These men had known his brother, and respected him before he was blown to pieces by an IED on patrol in Afghanistan with these men. And Menzil had become their friend, and later, their meal ticket. A big, fat meal ticket. They knew he'd been a cop, a detective in Detroit, but that was it. They didn't know who he was working for, and they didn't care. For them, a big payday while sticking it to Uncle Sam and the DoD trumped all else, and he was their conduit to that.

'This is the final target we have to get to,' Menzil said.

'There're others, under protection,' one of the team piped up.

'Their protection list is compromised,' Menzil replied, reminding himself of the lie he'd told these men. 'And anyway, that's not our concern. This is the last target for us.'

'How long have we got?'

'Until 5.30 tomorrow, before the demonstration. We gotta get this last guy and then back here onto our objective.'

A couple of the guys shared looks.

'Too hard for you?' he asked them.

'No.'

'No, sir.'

'Right. Now, pack your gear. All of it. We're headed south. Within a couple of days you'll all be on some sunny beach someplace, getting drunk and having your brains screwed out or whatever it is that you're after.'

The men left without a sound but the look on each one's face was that of a soldier finally getting to complete the mission for which he had trained long and hard. Menzil remembered what that felt like, remembered his first kill as an undercover cop. Remembered the rush he'd experienced when, later, he'd taken down some serious gangbangers on his own, six guys, all jacked up on ice, and he'd smoked them with his Glock in one hand and his badge in the other. His Glock and his badge had been handed in. But a silenced 9-millimetre Sig was now strapped to his thigh, and his team of four ex-Army personnel were tooled up to the eyeballs.

And in a couple of days for Menzil, hell . . . it'd feel . . . it would be like winning the Super Bowl.

24

Walker woke up and saw that Susan – Squeaker – was asleep sideways across her single bed, the quilt wrapped around her, a bare leg hanging off the edge.

It was still dark outside. The digital alarm clock cut the darkness in the room with red numerals: 03.23.

Zero-Dark-Thirty. A military term, for an unspecific time in the early morning. The time when shit went down. In Afghanistan it was a time of work for men like Walker and Murphy. Spec Ops teams would go hunting, the darkness their friend. All kinds of optical equipment would aid them in the field, making day of night. The enemy wasn't nearly as well equipped or prepared. Tactical safety for the well-stocked attacker.

It was also a time when the human physiology was at its lowest ebb. In the full dark the pineal glands of those who slept released high levels of melatonin into their brains. They'd slow. Deep REM sleep. Tactical advantage for the attacker.

So, Walker was awake, alert. Old habits. He'd slept for three hours. He listened. Silence but for the trucks heading north or south on the 63, and the occasional and far quieter car. He again looked over at Squeaker, at her skin blue–white in the neon light that streamed through the gap in the curtains. He thought of Eve, asleep somewhere, protected. Then he thought of his father.

Asleep somewhere? Protected?

Part of this? Or perpetrator?

03.29

Walker closed his eyes. Rest, but not sleep. He listened to Squeaker's breathing, rhythmic and deep. He couldn't recall a time when he had ever slept that soundly.

•

At 04.30, near-on two hundred road miles north-north-east of Walker's position, Charles Murphy, Chief Petty Officer US Navy, Ret., opened his eyes. He woke without an alarm, as he rose around that time every morning.

It was hunting time.

He left his warm bed, where his wife slept soundly. His infant son lay in a crib at the foot of their bed, sleeping deeply and snoring through his tiny nose. Murphy checked on his two daughters, each in a single bed at opposite sides of their shared room. He smiled while looking them over. He pulled the quilt over his eldest, a four year old. The little girl squirmed and Murphy settled her with a hand on the chest. The ex-SEAL smiled again, remembering those weeks of leave he'd enjoyed when his first child was born. He'd missed that contact time with his second child, while he'd been working afar. With his eldest he'd had the chance to watch her as she stared into his eyes, slowly, day by day, week by week, focusing.

Murphy dressed in the laundry that doubled as a mud room at the back of the house. He pulled on combat boots, took a rifle from the tall metal cupboard by the back door and ammunition from a locked box on the shelf.

He went out the back door and locked it behind him. The squat log cabin was in the middle of the woods, twenty difficult miles from the nearest house, sixty from the closest town, but he locked the door, and the key was around his neck on the same chain that held his old dog-tags. He walked off the porch of the log cabin, which he had built with two friends a year ago, from rough-hewn green logs. The windows were laminated three-quarter-inch glass, bought from a pawn shop that had gone broke and the wooden walls fitted around them. The ventilation in the eaves was set in quarter-inch steel grates, surplus things he'd got from his cousin at the junkyard. The roof was corrugated iron, fixed with double the screws necessary, paid for with what was left of his Navy salary after purchasing the rights to this freehold. The cavity between it and the cement-sheet ceiling was full of un-spun lamb's wool that he'd swapped a truckload of in return for setting up a professional-grade rifle range for a farmer-turned-tourist-rancher over in Tennessee. All of it built by his hand, doused with his sweat and blood.

Murphy looked at his house, locked up tight in the middle of nowhere. He set off at a jog, light on his feet, his rifle over his shoulder, his daypack on his back. He took to his favoured trail, headed east, towards a rise some twenty minutes' hike away. He'd stop there, check for tracks and signs, then find a perch and settle in to wait for a deer to amble through the morning sunlight as it ate at the dewy undergrowth. He did that most days, trading anything beyond what his family needed. Twice in the past spring he'd come back with boar; they were still eating the jerky. As Murphy moved, he thought about what the morning's hunt might bring.

25

'He's with a young local woman,' Woods said, climbing back into the car after exiting the Sheriff's office. He pulled a small notebook from his jacket pocket. 'Named Susan Orlean.'

Levine said, 'Who's she?'

'She's Murphy's cousin.'

'Shit.'

'I know.'

'How's he know Walker was with her?' Levine said, nodding towards the office.

'Last night, near midnight. Walker made a ruckus at a local bar.'

'Nice. Cops involved?'

'Didn't say. Just said Walker was with this young woman.'

'Well, in her he found a lead to get to Murphy,' Levine said. 'You think he's taken her hostage?'

'Sheriff just said he was *with* her,' Woods replied. 'Like they were friendly; he didn't seem concerned about her whereabouts or wellbeing.'

'Not that he said so, specifically.'

'Yeah, I suppose. But he'd have said if she was hostage, right?'

'Did you get an address for her?'

'Her mother's address, but she passed a few years back and the bills are still being paid.'

'Then she's at that address.'

'That's what the Sheriff figured,' Woods said, punching the address into the sat-nav.

'Fifteen minutes from here,' Levine said, putting the Ford in gear.

'The way you drive, it'll be half an hour – maybe more.'

'Oh?' Levine tore out of the Sheriff's car park with wheels spinning on gravel. She saw the Sheriff in her rear-view mirror, walking to his car and talking on his hand-held radio, watching them depart.

•

'Why didn't you wake me?' Squeaker said, sitting up in bed and rubbing sleep from her eyes as she saw Walker standing beside her, dressed and his bed made long ago.

'You looked like you needed sleep,' Walker said, putting a paper-wrapped egg-and-bacon roll next to her, along with a tall coffee in a styrofoam cup.

'What time is it?'

'Six am.'

'Six am!' she said. 'Why did you wake me?'

Walker chuckled.

'God, what am I doing here?' Squeaker said, lying back down in bed and putting her hands over her face. Then she sat bolt upright. 'And – and what did we do last night?'

'Do?'

'I mean . . .' She looked down. She was wearing his T-shirt, huge and oversized on her, and nothing else.

'Nothing.'

'Nothing?'

'You sound disappointed,' Walker said with a grin, sipping his own tall cup of strong coffee from the diner across the street. 'Surely you'd remember it if something happened.'

It took a moment for Squeaker to speak. When she did, it was matter-of-fact, the same tone he'd first heard in that bar, though quiet.

'I came into your shower. You held me. It was warm, and safe. I remember that.' She put a hand to her head. 'And whisky. I remember whisky.'

'And that was that.'

'That was what?'

Walker smiled, said, 'We showered, Squeaker, that was it. We stood there, and then we each went to our separate beds.'

'Oh. Right.'

'Yep.'

'Why?'

'*Why?*'

'Why – why didn't we do anything?' Squeaker opened her breakfast and paused and then looked up at him. 'You don't find me . . .'

'You asked me that last night,' Walker said. 'Look, you're great, pretty, cute and tough – all at the same time. Which is awesome. But I've got a mission I need to focus on. Stuff going on.'

'To find my cousin. Save him and save the day. And stuff.'

'That's about it.' Walker sipped his coffee. He was aware that they should be moving, on the road by now.

'Sorry. I was tired, last night. Maybe a little drunk from the bar. And then the whisky . . . God, what do they say? Whisky after beer, never fear?'

'I think it's beer before whisky always risky.'

'Oh. Right.'

'You shot well, for a drunk girl. Unless you were aiming for Gus's head.'

'Ha. Well, you should see me sober,' she said, then sat up, sipped her coffee. 'Turn around.'

'Huh?'

'I need to get dressed.'

Walker paused, said, 'You know, I've seen you naked.'

'That was last night. Last night was insane. Last night is history, gone, disappeared.'

'Like your cousin.'

'Would you just turn around already?'

'Okay.' Walker turned around and smiled again and drank more coffee. He really liked the girl – she had spunk and then some. And he felt good about the day.

26

Walker drove while Squeaker navigated and ate her breakfast, then finished her coffee, then told stories about her upbringing and her cousin. They were headed north, slightly to the east, the road not quite a highway and not quite a rural road. Some places were dead straight, and he'd wind the Tahoe out to sixty-five, and next thing there'd be a blind intersection or bend in the road and he'd have to slow to a crawl.

Outside the trees were tall and spindly, mostly pines and spruce upturned to the cold and ready for snow. They passed a couple of general stores that sold gas and supplies, but they'd filled up and the Tahoe still had half a tank by the time they passed a sign welcoming them to a town: West Plains, Missouri, population 12,000. It looked about the same as Thayer but maybe double the size. Same rows of grocery stores, barber shops, post office, pizza joints, liquor stores, gun stores, sport stores – just double the number of them.

'I haven't been here since I was a kid,' Squeaker said. 'And this is the last place anyone I know saw Murphy.'

'Where do we start?' Walker asked, slowing to thirty as he turned right onto the main street. It was full of pick-ups and four-by-fours, old and new, lined with squat one- and two-storey buildings either side of the wide street. His pick would be a bar again. He figured, towns this small, barmen knew most people's business. Plus, Walker knew, most military personnel liked bars. So, of all the places to check, there was a high probability that they'd get some information there. But it was too early; they were still shut up.

'Casey's,' Squeaker said.

'Is that a bar?'

'Nope. That's another cousin of ours.'

'Is everyone related out here?'

'Everyone out here's related to someone,' Squeaker replied, deadpan as she watched out her side window.

'Right,' Walker said through a grin. 'Where is she?'

'*He's* way through town, left at the sign that points to the garbage dump.'

'Got it,' Walker said.

They passed a small police station, two cruisers parked out front. Probably not much for them to do around here. He kept on the gas.

'So,' he said, 'this is some other family's meth territory?'

'Yep,' Squeaker replied. 'This isn't just a clash of two families over drug turf, though. It goes waaay back before that. That's recent news. There's a bigger story in this. It's really about the battle for America.'

'Oh?'

'One side's rooted in traditional ways. And another side, up here in Missouri, they want progress and things to change. It's been going on forever, a never-ending battle, and that's what this is really about. Not drugs. Well, it is now, but only because there's stupid money to be made. Really it's about power, a struggle between the families, real deep-seated. On one side is Barbwire Barb and her crew – you've met *them*.' Squeaker looked sideways at Walker.

'Charming lady.'

'Yep. Some people here reckon she's an outlaw, but others think she's a generous and hard-working churchgoer. But one thing is certain, she wants to keep doing things the way they've always been done, and she won't stand for any form of progress or change.

'And then there's Derek Copper, who heads up the Copper household; these days they run the meth business this side of the border. Funny, all these hundreds of years the state borders meant jack, and now that there's drug money on the table, they're respected.'

'Money changes things.'

'Yep. I've seen it change plenty of people. But not Murphy. He could have been an enforcer for Copper – or a sergeant-at-arms on either side, I suppose, earning crazy drug money – but he chose to go get lost instead.'

'He sounds like a decent guy.'

'The best.'

'But it sounds like he's going to be hard to turn around.'

'No,' Squeaker said, 'not really.'

'How'd you figure that?'

'You've got *me*.'

Walker looked sideways at her, said, 'I've got you?'

'I'm coming with you.'

Walker paused. 'It could be dangerous.'

'Oh, *please*.'

Walker smiled. 'You're a good egg, kiddo.'

'Kiddo?'

'Yep.'

'Hmph. Don't know about "kiddo".' Squeaker leaned back in her seat. 'The last thing Murphy said to me, before he disappeared, was that he was going to bug out, to the forest some place. He said that not a hundred years ago you could live self-sufficiently off the land and it was a good life, but with all the taxes and rules and regulations nowadays, it's all but impossible. You can live off the land if you have someone else subsidising it for you. He said that's what's wrong with America today.'

'That we don't take care of ourselves anymore?' Walker said.

Squeaker nodded. 'Instead, we expect others to.'

'I hear you,' Walker said. 'But sometimes, even smart and hard guys like your cousin need a helping hand.'

27

'Makes you wonder, right?' Woods said, sitting back, flicking through Murphy's file as Levine drove north. 'How is it that *eight* SEALs get themselves murdered, all within a few days? How's that happen? I mean, these guys are the best, right?'

Levine replied in a flat tone, 'Best fighters in the Navy.'

'What – you think there's better, in another service?'

'Sure. Delta. They're the pinnacle. The benchmark.'

'Says who?'

'Says people who know.' Levine looked to him. 'Says me.'

'You think? You really believe that? Have you seen *Black Hawk Down*?'

'Shit, Tom, you're clutching now. And how weren't they the best in that engagement?'

'Yeah, well, is this just because your dad and pappy were Army?'

'Nope. But the SEALs? They're only as good as the individual. Yeah, they're good, and yeah, they've seen plenty of action for a good decade. But who's to say that they're the best of what we've got in the armoury? I mean, think of Delta – they're the best *the Army has*. And how many soldiers does the Army have?'

'A lot.'

'I do believe that's the technical amount. And how many shooters does the Navy have?'

'A handful?'

'Compared to the Army, yes. So, okay, call it, what, two hundred thousand full-time fighting troops in the Army at any given time – out of over a million Army serving, guard and reservists? That's a pool of two hundred thousand men and women trained in the art of killing for our country.'

'The art of defending the country.'

'Perspective. They're trained to kill, not defend, right?'

'I suppose you're right.'

'Right. So, Delta? They're the *best* of all those. It's like saying that the Army represents every kid playing football across the country in any given year – they're training to play. Right? And the NFL, they're Delta – training to decimate. Got it?'

Woods looked out his window, said, 'Yeah, I guess so.'

'Hell, for all we know,' she said, 'there's better than Delta out there. The best of the best of the best. Guys pulled out because they're so good, they're needed in areas that no-one even knows exists.'

'Government,' Woods said, still looking out his side window and rubbing sleep from his eyes. 'Can't trust them. Can't . . . whatever.'

•

The garbage dump was just a few miles up the road, a corrugated gravel track worn into disrepair by heavy trucks driving fast.

Walker heard the gunfire before he saw the shooter. He looked at the Ruger revolver in the door pocket, loaded with six semi-wadcutters, a box of fifty rounds in the centre console.

'That's him,' Squeaker said. 'That's Casey. Loves shooting trash and talking about government conspiracies that come through our TVs and are put into our chicken nuggets.'

'Nuggets, you say?'

'*He* says. He's smart, too. One of the smartest in the family, my mammy always used to say.'

'This is Casey, I take it,' Walker said, letting the engine idle, watching the scene in comic disbelief. 'Not Murphy, your skilled-up Navy SEAL cousin.'

'Yep. That's Casey all right.'

'You sure your ma didn't say he was special in a different kind of way?'

'How do you mean?'

'Oh, nothing . . .' Walker watched the guy shoot with a sawn-off pump-action shotgun. He was obliterating televisions and washing machines and fridges and microwaves. He had what Walker regarded as an impressive mullet hairdo: all business up front, with shoulder-length tails out back, covered with a well-worn trucker's hat. He wore an open flannel shirt with a stained tank-top underneath. He was seated in a cast-iron bathtub in the middle of the junkyard, as though it offered him ballistic protection from ricochets and at the same time would shield him from the evil government agents broadcasting from the TVs he was blasting to smithereens. 'What did white goods and electronics ever do to him?'

'Well,' Squeaker said, watching her cousin pump and shoot and laugh and pump and shoot and laugh. 'Ma did say that he used to sit too close to the television.'

'Maybe the government agents tinkered with his brain.'

Squeaker laughed, said, 'Maybe . . .'

'And he can help us *how*?'

'He's the most northerly family Murphy and I've got in common,' Squeaker said. 'Come on, let's get our weird on.'

•

It took Levine and Woods twenty minutes to find the clearing in the woods. Susan's trailer door was open. They entered, wary, Sig pistols drawn. Empty; nothing showing inside but two mugs on the coffee table.

Outside, Levine looked around at the faces at the windows of the other trailers.

'They probably think we're FBI,' Woods said. 'In their eyes we're worse than cops; we're the government, here to interfere.'

Levine crouched down in the mud, picked up a broken side mirror. 'Big,' she said, examining it. 'From a pick-up or SUV. Modern. A fancy vehicle. And it didn't fall off by accident. See?'

Levine pointed at the entry point of the bullet, a large jagged hole in shiny black plastic.

She looked back towards Susan's trailer and pointed at the ground. Woods went over to the spot, crouched and used his pen to pick up a brass object.

'Shell casing,' Woods said. 'Rifle. 30-30 Winchester.'

'Short-range shot.'

'A shootout? Susan or Walker defending themselves – from who?'

'There was more than one car here,' Levine said, looking at the tracks in the gravel and mud.

'Everyone here has a car.' Woods went to the old Dodge. 'This one's Susan's. And its gun rack in the back's empty. There's a couple of 30-30 shells in the side pocket of the door.'

'Is she registered for a firearm?'

'No-one's registered for a firearm around here.'

'Then we should talk to everyone.'

Woods looked doubtful.

Levine walked to the nearest trailer, then turned and pointed to the far one. 'You start over there,' she said. 'Tell them we're here to check firearm licences, that if they don't comply, we'll come back with paperwork and fifty agents. Tell them that if they tell us what went down, and who was here last night, we'll go away in the next five minutes.'

28

Walker killed the engine and followed Squeaker out. Casey let fly with what was left in the 12-gauge, and a 1980s television set was reduced to shards of plastic and glass. He climbed out of the bathtub and eyeballed the arrivals. First the car, which seemed to impress him, and then the two of them, standing there, not twenty yards away. His eyes were drawn first to Walker, the bigger of the two, and then to Squeaker. He stared at her a while, then tilted his hat back and whooped.

'Pipsqueak! That you?'

Squeaker smiled. 'It's me.'

'Damn, girl, as I live and breathe!' He loped over. The two of them hugged it out, then spoke some rapid-fire catch-up about however long it'd been and who'd been doing what and what life had been up to.

Walker remained silent for the couple of minutes it took. He learned that Casey was the owner and manager of the part of the junkyard that collated all the electrical appliances and white goods and broke them down to their constituent parts to then on-sell for repairs and scrap materials. What was near-on worthless became fodder for his hobby: shoot'n' shit.

'I call her my recycler,' Casey said, hefting the sawn-off shotgun. 'Good for disposing of varmints and junk all the same.'

Squeaker said, 'We're passing through here to see about Murphy.'

'Murphy?'

'Our cousin. Chuck?'

'I know who you mean. But damn, ain't seen him in a year or more. What's up?'

Squeaker said, 'You been hearing anything about him?'

'Nothing more than you would have.' Casey eyed Walker suspiciously. 'You government?'

He said it like *gov-mint*.

'Nope,' Walker said.

'Fooled me.'

'I need to help Murphy out,' Walker said. 'Soldier to soldier. He's got trouble headed his way, if it hasn't caught up with him already.'

'Hmph,' Casey said, then started guffawing. 'Trouble – headed Murphy's way? Shit, man. That trouble will be damned – damned to hell! Murphy is the toughest customer any place he's at. Devil himself couldn't rattle Murph's bones. Even the sun's afraid to shine on him. Right, Squeak?'

Squeaker was silent, long enough for the smile to start to fade on Casey's face as he watched her.

'This trouble ain't like what's around here,' she said to Casey. 'This isn't anything to do with what went down back home, the drugs and all. This is terrorist stuff.'

'Terrorists?'

He said it like *terr-ists*.

'Yep. It's bad, Casey, real bad. And we gotta at least warn him about it.'

'Shit. Shit. Okay. Right. Let us think now.' Casey walked around, the shotgun over his shoulder as he paced, looking at the mud and detritus underfoot. 'Okay. Okay. You know, I did hear that he had some help getting logs out there.'

'Out where?' Squeaker asked.

Casey gave a vague wave to the north. 'Way up in the hills some place. The forests.'

Walker looked in that direction. He'd call them mountains but supposed hills would do. Forest, rocks, fog and cloud. And height.

Walker asked, 'Who helped him?'

'Yeah, right . . .' Casey paced, looked up as though he'd got it, then down again and paced some more. 'Nope. Never did hear that much. Just that someone who knows someone went up there and delivered it with a truck. Full load. That's maybe thirty trees. Call it at least a ton a tree. Had it hauled and dropped and he did the rest himself, the guy supposed. That's why I heard about it – some crazy guy getting trees dropped off in the forest some place the end of the road. And some roofin' iron too. That's right. Roofin' iron. Shit, darn nearly forgot that. Well, gotta be to build a house, right? Ain't no other need for so much lumber and iron.'

'Where was this?' Walker asked.

Casey thumbed in the general direction over his shoulder to the north again.

'That it?' Squeaker asked.

''Fraid so. Sorry, Pipsqueak.'

Squeaker nodded.

'Where'd you hear it from?' Walker asked, and frowned as he found himself starting to talk like this guy. 'Think.'

'General talk. You know, chatter. Nothing doing. Just in conversation. Can't for my life remember who said it. One of them truckers, I s'pose.'

'These conversations,' Walker said, looking at Casey. 'Where'd you have them?'

'Ah, um . . .' He scratched his head and looked at his hut – one of those temporary buildings sometimes used as school classrooms, but this one had sat here for decades – then at his yard, then down the empty road leading into town and then to the east. 'Yeah – yeah. It was in town. That's where. Some trucker bar, in town.'

'Trucker bar?' Walker said.

'Yeah, trucker bar. You know,' Casey said, 'one of them ones on the highway, no good for nothing but gassing up nearby and drinkin'.'

'This place have a name?'

Casey scratched his head again, said, 'They was talking about some crazy man in the forest . . .'

'Where?' Walker asked. 'Where in town was this trucker place?'

'The *only* place to drink,' Casey said, leaning back on his boots and grinning with tobacco-stained teeth. 'O'Halloran's.'

29

O'Halloran's wasn't an Irish bar – there was nothing Irish about it, Walker saw, inside or out. It was made of cinder blocks, unpainted, the only window being the one set into the plain front door. Inside wasn't much more decorated, the tables adding a little colour with their dull red tops and the bulbs in the bar lighting the place not much beyond dark. A jukebox played classic rock. It was just on ten o'clock in the morning, yet the place was already half full with heavy drinkers. Walker liked it.

'Chester's track is down. Mudslide. No work for none of us next two days,' Walker heard one of the patrons say as he and Squeaker made their way to a table near one of two open fires that heated the space.

'What's the go?' Squeaker asked, her voice barely audible over the hubbub and background music.

'I'll talk to the barman.'

There were two people behind the bar, an older guy, presumably the owner, and a young woman in a short skirt and tattooed suspenders on pale legs who was kept busy reaching up for the top shelf by the clientele.

'Drink?'

'Coke.'

Walker headed for the bar. The barman was the other side of sixty. Short and squat, arms bulging at the biceps in a T-shirt branded with an American beer. His beard was one of dedication.

'Coke,' Walker said. 'And a beer.'

The barman served the drinks, both in bottles. Walker paid with a fifty, left the change on the bar and said, 'If I was looking for someone, would you be the right guy to ask?'

The barman looked at the change, shrugged.

'Someone I used to serve with.' Walker nodded to the anchor on the guy's arm, a pretty 1950s-style pin-up perched upon it. 'Navy?'

'Nam. *Forrestal* and *Leary*. Five tours.'

Walker nodded. Five tours was a lot. Both ships saw plenty of action, especially the *Forrestal*, notorious for its 1967 fire that killed or wounded near-on 300 sailors on board.

'You in Iraq?' the barman said.

'And Afghanistan,' Walker said. 'And some other places.'

The barman smiled. 'New world, right? Different wars nowadays.'

'It's still just as hard to see the enemy,' Walker said, leaning on the bar. 'Not like those before us had, all those Germans and Japanese ahead of them. Point and shoot. Or duck and cover because the Russians have hit the button.'

'Right. Who's your friend?' He motioned to Squeaker who was approaching.

'Local guide,' Walker said, then he paused so that the barman would look at him. 'I'm looking for a Charles Murphy. Known probably just as Murphy, or Murph. Maybe even Chuck. Ex-Navy. SEAL. He's somewhere north of here. He needs my help.'

'Yeah? And why'd that be?'

'Someone out there's going to hunt him down.'

The barman was stoic in his silence.

'I'm Murphy's cousin,' Squeaker said. 'He don't know it yet, but he really does need our help, and fast.'

Finally, the barman said, 'Sorry. Never heard of him.' He walked away to the crisps section and turned his back and busied himself with restocking the rack.

Walker took the drinks over to Squeaker.

'We're getting attention,' Squeaker said, sipping at her bottle and giving the slightest gesture to the far wall, near the back, where a group of big guys sat by what must have been the rear exit.

'They must be wondering how an old warhorse like me got a hot young babe like you out on a date,' Walker said, sipping his beer and eyeballing the guys.

Squeaker smiled.

The bar owner came over to their table and dropped off a basket full of crisps and left without a word.

'Thanks,' Squeaker said to Walker, munching through a mouthful.

'I didn't order them,' Walker said, seeing that the lining was a white napkin with something on it. Words, written in thick pen.

Old Pelts Road. See Dylan.

•

Menzil was in the passenger seat of the Jeep.

'This Murphy,' said the driver, one of the ex-Army guys. 'He doesn't want to be found. So, what are we gonna do?'

'We find him.'

'You think?'

'Bet your ass,' Menzil replied, looking out his window as they sped south. 'These NCIS agents will lead us right to him. And I tell you boys what: twenty-grand bonus to the guy who caps either Murphy or this Walker dude.'

30

'Nope. Uh-uh,' Squeaker said. 'No way.'

They sat in Gus's Tahoe. The engine was running and the heat was on low. The leather seats were warmed too, a button that Walker had found in the dash and subsequently thought someone deserved a Nobel for inventing. They were parked just down the road from O'Halloran's, having gassed up the tank to full.

'This place,' Squeaker said, tapping the map. 'It's just beyond a hornets' nest that you don't want to disturb.'

'The northern crew,' Walker said. 'The guys that Murphy cut some kind of deal with?'

Squeaker nodded and ate a strap of truck-stop jerky.

Walker glanced at the map and drove off. Out of town, onto another sealed road that was too narrow for modern American SUVs. It held no painted lines, just headed north, towards a sign that said: Mountain View, 24 miles.

'I never said he cut a deal with these folk,' Squeaker said defensively. 'It's just that it was counter to what Barb was running. So, it could just be by default, see, that he's having to live up there? It could just be that he had to move north.'

'And it could be that he *did* make a deal with these guys up here,' Walker said. 'I mean, if *I* were some meth operator, or running a crew of guys, cooking meth and selling it on, and I heard about a guy like Murphy – an ex-SEAL who had issues with those meth runners bordering on my business interests interstate – *I'd* go out of my way to get him onside. A guy like him would be an asset too good to let pass.'

'It's not that simple here,' Squeaker said. 'It's not like business-is-business, like it might be in the cities. Round here, it's blood all the way. At least, it's blood until you've pushed it too far – then you might as well not be a blood relation at all.'

'Right. Well, we'll soon see,' Walker said, picking up the vehicle's speed once they'd cleared town. 'Hopefully.'

They drove in silence for nearly twenty minutes, just the sounds of the car and Squeaker sucking and chewing her jerky.

'Walker . . .'

'Squeaker . . .'

'Do you really think they'll kill Murph? These guys you told me about?'

Walker checked his rear-view mirror. 'Yes. I do.'

'Not just rough him up or somethin'?'

'Nope. The crew that's targeting him – they've already killed eight SEALs. Eight, Squeaker. That's no mean feat – tracking them down, killing them. I mean, SEALS are good, yeah? They're among the best-trained hardened killers on the planet, yet eight of them are dead.'

'But he'll be okay out here.'

'No, he won't. They'll find him. If we can find him by asking, this crew can find him by being even more persuasive.'

'Huh?'

'They'll demand rather than ask. Maybe torture the family members; it's more effective. When they're here – and we must be ahead of them, or we'd have heard by now – things will happen fast. *They'll* be fast. They'll catch up. It'll be ugly.'

'Okay.' She was quiet for a while, then said, 'And if we don't get to Murphy first, and save him – there's no chance that we can stop a big terrorist attack from occurring, right?'

'Right.'

'Okay. Shit. Okay. And here's me – I just wanted to see his stupid face, and his wife and kids, to say hi, because it had been too long since I'd heard from them, and because of what I'd heard,' about him having to move out of our area, because I worry. But I had nothing to worry about, right?'

'Squeaker,' Walker said, gripping the wheel and staring straight ahead, 'we've all got our worries.'

31

'Tell me,' Director of the United Nation's Special Investigations Unit Bill McCorkell said. 'Tell me what you're worried about.'

'Well,' FBI Special Agent Fiona Somerville replied. 'Where to start . . . It all started when I was nine and realised that Santa wasn't real and that unicorns were extinct.'

McCorkell cracked a smile. He was in New York. Meetings. Updates. Reports.

Somerville and fellow Special Agent Andrew Hutchinson were in San Diego.

'We've got nowhere on those SEALs,' Hutchinson said. 'I checked with old buddies, we tried back channels, cash changed hands, we've travelled some two thousand miles by air and road. Nothing. Nada.'

'Then they're well protected,' McCorkell said. 'That's good news, right?'

'Well,' Somerville said. 'That's what we thought too.'

'But? I sense a big hairy "but" around the corner.'

'I'm concerned – we're concerned,' Somerville said, 'about how tight this is.'

'They've been hidden by the NCIS,' McCorkell said. 'They could be on the beach playing volleyball in Diego Garcia for all we know. Whatever – they're safe.'

'That's what we thought too,' Somerville repeated. 'But then we checked with the families again.'

'And?' McCorkell said.

'And we're not the only ones checking on them,' Somerville replied.

'Who?'

'We're not sure. But they had visitors.'

'Last week,' Hutchinson added. 'All of them. They were told it was a routine security audit of the protection. Whoever it was said they were from the Secret Service. Two guys. From the description it sounds like we're dealing with military types.'

'We compared the times of the visits,' Somerville said. 'Fourteen families, all covered in one day.'

'And all of them asking at some point about Charles Murphy . . . Any news from Walker?'

'Yesterday morning,' McCorkell said. 'He feels that he's getting closer.'

'Bill, there's no way those audit guys were Secret Service,' Somerville said. 'Right?'

'Right,' McCorkell said.

'Right,' Hutchinson said. 'I checked, because you never know. And it definitely wasn't them.'

'But it's a big crew, at least four guys, maybe more,' Somerville said. 'Well resourced, well trained, good at coordinating a mission.'

'Military.'

'Serving, or ex,' Hutchinson said.

'Right,' McCorkell said. 'Did you meet with Navy?'

'Just about to,' Somerville said. 'We're outside NCIS.'

'Do it,' McCorkell said. 'Then you go to Walker. And Hutch, you head back to DC and stick with me. We'll start rattling some cages in Washington and see what we can find out about this Murphy's whereabouts.'

32

'Why are you doing this?' Squeaker asked. She used one of Gus's pens to pick the dried mud from her boots. The legs of her tight jeans were soiled halfway up the shins. Her long-sleeve top was loose and puffy. Her coat was balled under her arm.

'You just wondering that now?' Walker said, driving the Tahoe. It was crap through the bends, at speed at least. The back end was too light, the front and engine too heavy, and the back tyres where all that power transferred through slid out at the bends on the wet road. Everything seemed wetter and damper the higher they climbed. He knew once he got out of the car and its heat his knees would ache, thanks to all those years of high-school and college and Air Force Academy football.

'I've wondered it since I first heard you asking about Murphy in the bar last night,' Squeaker said. He could tell that she was watching him. 'But I didn't think to ask until now.'

'Why?'

'Because I trust you.'

'Why?'

'Because you seem trustworthy.'

'Yeah, well, score one for you. But be careful who you trust.'

'Are you my dad now?'

Walker smiled, said, 'You say that to the guy you startled half to death by coming into the shower all naked?'

'Right,' Squeaker replied, looking away with a smile. 'Score one for you.'

'Call it even.'

'Yeah. Anyway, the *why* didn't seem important. But now, what, twelve hours on? I want to know. All of it.'

'Fair enough.'

They sat in silence for a while, listening to the rumble of the engine and the coarse tyres on the road and the heat coming through the vents.

'So? Out with it, Walker. Why you? Why are you doing this for my cousin and why isn't it the Navy or Army or whoever?'

'The Army?' Walker looked at her sideways. 'What have they got to do with anything?'

'I don't know. I was just thinking, who looks after the Navy when they're in trouble? I mean, it can't be the Air Force.'

'Because we're all fags.'

Squeaker smiled. 'Right. Score two . . . But if not the Army,' she continued, crossing her arms over her chest, 'who does look after them? It should be the police or FBI, maybe even the Secret Service. So, why you? Why one lonely guy?'

'Who says I'm lonely?' Walker smiled. He saw that Squeaker was serious now, and wanted a serious answer. 'Okay. It's because . . .' Walker slowed for the bend and then powered out of it. 'My father was involved in this. Still is. And then I got involved in it, over a year ago. This attack that's coming, if we don't get to your cousin and see if he knows how to stop it?' Squeaker nodded. 'It's part of something bigger. It's the first of twelve.'

'Twelve? Twelve separate attacks?'

Walker nodded. 'That's it. We're looking at a worst-case doomsday type of scenario. Twelve separate attacks, all around the US. Each attack triggers the next. And none of them are connected with the others – so it's not like we can stop them all in one fell swoop. This is going to take time. It's got to be methodical.'

'And how were you and your father connected with it?'

Walker paused, said, 'You said you read the papers. You saw that attack on the Vice President, in New York?'

Squeaker thought a second, then nodded. 'At the Stock Exchange. He nearly got blown up.'

'That's it. That was the trigger that started all this.'

'You were there?'

'Yes.'

'Okay. And who's your dad?'

'Just a guy . . .'

'Ooh – I sense some history here.'

Walker shook his head to signify he wasn't playing a game. 'He's just an old dude. Out there somewhere. Doing something related to this Zodiac stuff.'

'Good or bad?'

'It's not that simple.'

'Okay. Is he trying to stop this as well?'

'I think so. Maybe.'

'You think? Maybe? He is or he isn't. He's either like you, some kind of lone hero, or he's what – a terrorist mastermind?'

'It's complicated. But I think he's trying to stop this too, in his own way.'

'And why you, Walker?' She held up her hand to the width of his face as though covering his eyes and said, 'Wait – are you Batman?'

Walker choked on a laugh. 'I was Air Force.'

'You said that.'

'Then I was CIA.'

'Cool.'

'Not really.'

'Did you have cool spy gadgets?'

'No.'

'What are you now?'

'I'm just a guy.'

'A lonely guy . . .'

'I'm not lonely.'

'An old dude . . .'

Walker smiled.

Then the speed sign up ahead signalled that the town of Mountain View was coming up. Walker slowed. Squeaker tensed.

'This is it,' she said. 'This is where we don't want to be.'

33

Walker didn't see what the big deal was. The town looked like the previous three. Similar size, similar layout, similar-looking people. Half the stores were empty or boarded and chained up by banks. And banks there were aplenty. For every other store, there was a bank.

'Hillfolk,' Walker said as he slowed to cruise through town. 'I can tell. By how they're walking. Less rickety up here. Hillfolk are the worst, am I right?'

Squeaker was silent.

Walker said, 'I was joking.'

'Ha ha.'

'You really don't like this place.'

'Nope.' She craned her neck to do a double-take at a guy who came out of a sports store carrying a heavy bag to his pick-up. She looked forward again. 'I don't like it, not one little bit. It's the wrong state, for one. And you're right. They're different people.'

'I thought the Ozarkeans didn't much care for state borders.'

'Everyone cares about state borders,' Squeaker said. 'What is this, the 1930s? We all gotta work, pay taxes. We all know what state we're in. We all know what counties we fall under.'

Walker nodded. 'You know Old Pelts Road?'

'Nope.'

'It's not on maps. I'll have to ask.'

'We could have asked that last barman,' Squeaker said as Walker slowed to pass a tavern.

'He wasn't the talkative type.'

'Right.' She looked at the note the barman had written. 'I wonder if there's a New Pelts Road?'

'Old Pelt is probably some old guy,' Walker said, passing a bar that could have been the last one that they'd been in, but he decided it looked too busy, too dark. Down the road he saw a sign that would surely be of use. He kept the Tahoe pointed at it, kept the speed on thirty. 'Or his hat. Made of the pelt of some critter that was road kill.'

Walker pulled up to the Sheriff's office, a yellow-brick building built in the sixties, the roof boasting an eighty-foot-tall antenna held upright by dozens of cables pulling it every which way. The device could probably pick up chatter from the moon landings. The car park was host to one cruiser and a big pick-up with chunky tyres and spotlights all over.

'Really?' Squeaker said to him.

'What? If anyone knows the roads around here, it'll be the cops.'

'Cops here aren't like in the cities.'

'What are they like in the cities?'

'All, like, helpful and stuff.'

'Yeah, that's exactly what they are,' Walker said, unclipping his seatbelt and leaving the engine running. 'You wait here. I'll go find out what I find out.'

Walker got out of the truck and headed for the door.

•

The United States Naval Criminal Investigative Service – NCIS – investigates criminal activities by or against United States Navy personnel. Half of the workforce are civilian Special Agents trained to carry out a wide variety of assignments at locations across the globe; they are the Navy's police and FBI all in one.

'Calling it early,' Hutchinson said as he walked to the NCIS office of the San Diego Naval Station. He was wearing an oversized jacket, so that he could pull the sleeve over his cast, which was still in a sling. He walked with the gait of a guy who'd played a lot of pick-up basketball as a scrappy player, given he was just pushing six feet, and he'd spent way too much of his adult years stuck behind a desk and adding weight around the middle. 'I don't like these guys.'

'Because they get paid more than we do?' Somerville asked.

'What? They don't, do they?'

Somerville announced their arrival to the Assistant Director's secretary, who picked up her phone, spoke for a moment and then pointed them to a door on which a plaque read: Assistant Director of Special Investigations Luke Grant.

Somerville made the introductions, and Grant didn't bother getting up from his desk or shaking their hands.

'I know why you're here,' Grant said.

'May we sit?' Hutchinson asked.

Grant shook his head. 'Like I said to McCorkell on the phone, this is a Navy issue. Compartmentalised. Sensitive. You've got no place here looking into it. So there's really nothing for us to talk about.'

'With due respect,' Somerville said, her hands on her hips, 'this is a Homeland Security issue, and we have the authority to track down terrorist activity. So, we'd appreciate any and all information you have on Charles Murphy.'

Assistant Director Grant stood and pointed at his door. He was a short man, his head around shoulder height for the two FBI agents.

Somerville and Hutchinson looked to each other.

'That means,' Grant said, 'meeting's over.'

34

Inside the Sheriff's office two deputies sat at desks behind the counter. One was reading a mess of newspapers and drinking coffee, the other was working on a computer that might have come with the building's original fit-out.

Walker waited. The cop reading the papers glanced at him, then went back to his article. The other cop typed, using only his index fingers. A solid brick wall ran down one side, to Walker's right. In the middle of the back wall was a steel door, leading either out the back of the building or to holding cells. Or maybe the bathroom. To Walker's left was a frosted-glass wall with timber framing that formed two offices. One was marked 'Sheriff', and Walker could make out two man-sized blurred forms inside. The other office was labelled 'Restricted' – probably the radio room, admin supplies and all kinds of stuff. Or the bathroom, and they didn't want outsiders using it.

Just when Walker considered tapping the brass bell on the counter, the door behind him opened. Squeaker, the Tahoe keys in her hand, joined him at the counter. She looked at him silently. Walker shrugged and turned to tap the bell—

'Help you?' The cop at the computer had slunk over, and he moved the bell from under Walker's falling palm, his eyes on Squeaker.

'Yep,' Walker said, and before continuing he waited for the cop to look at him. The gaze didn't last long. It was a measuring glance: Walker's eyes, then his bulk, then back to Squeaker. He looked her up and down, her scruffy hair pulled back in a ponytail, her pale skin rosy from the Tahoe's heater, her lips red and pouty now that she had warm blood and plenty of food and drink running through her.

'Well?' the deputy asked, looking directly at Walker. His name tag read 'Chester'.

'Old Pelts Road,' Walker said.

The cop watched him. Waited.

Walker waited.

The deputy behind had stopped sorting through newspapers and joined his colleague.

'What about it?' Chester asked. He had red hair, thick and curly, the kind that could only be inherited and never really bred out. He was tall and lanky, with freckled pale skin.

'I'm looking for it,' Walker said. 'Can't see it on a map. I heard it's out north, past here some place. Can you tell me how to get there?'

The deputy looked to the other.

This guy was short, with square shoulders and a barrel chest; ten years older, the kind of cop who would have been the watch sergeant in a big city. His name was Jones.

'Nothin' out there,' the senior deputy, Jones, said. 'Mud track, serious drivin'. Used by Land Management only.'

'It's a government road?' Walker asked.

'They're all government roads,' Jones replied. He held Walker's gaze, not bothering to look at Squeaker.

'Okay,' Walker said evenly. 'How do I get to it?'

'What for?' Jones asked.

'Sightseeing,' Walker replied.

'There's nothing there.'

'You said that.'

Jones was silent. Walker too. Just the hum of the fan heater behind the counter. The cops were in shirt sleeves. Walker was in his jacket, unzipped, and he was hot. He wanted to shrug it off, but he knew that moving in that way might antagonise the situation. Whatever the situation was. Small-town lawmen were a dangerous bunch: as unpredictable and easy to offend as the TSA at airports.

'Look, guys,' Walker said, 'I'm just asking for some directions here.'

Chester put his hands on his hips, on the top of his gun belt. He looked at Jones.

Jones looked like he was weighing up what to say, maybe even trying to dig out directions from the recesses of his brain. But he didn't get there. He didn't have to.

Because then a door opened to Walker's left. And the Sheriff came out of his office. And he looked pissed.

35

'We're good people, right?' Hutchinson said as they headed back towards the airport.

'Better than most,' Somerville replied as she drove. 'Fighting the good fight and all that.'

'Right. So why is it like this?'

'Like this?'

'We're getting nowhere.'

'Aw,' Somerville chided him. 'You wanna play in the sandbox with terrorists and Special Ops and you want, what – people to roll over like petty crooks doing a bit of financial crime?'

'That's not what I mean. I mean the Navy. Can't they see what's going on? I mean, McCorkell's got the Vice President in his pocket on this – so why isn't the Secretary of the Navy or the Joint Chief making some calls on our behalf?'

Somerville looked at him. 'Bureaucracy at work.'

'Glad to see 9/11 brought us all closer together is all I'm sayin'.' Hutchinson fell silent, watching the world pass by.

'Relax,' Somerville said. 'Right now Walker's probably got to Murphy and figured all this out. Hell, they've probably trussed up a bunch of terrorists and are now in some Navy bar getting free beers while they tell their tale.'

•

The Sheriff paused when he saw Walker and Squeaker and his deputies all standing at the counter, as though surprised that someone was there or that any work might be being done that morning. Clearly, he'd been stuck in his own conversation, his own worries. Walker then saw a second man exit the Sheriff's office.

A big guy. Huge. Bear of a man. Six-five, maybe 300 pounds, at least a hundred of it surplus fat in his stomach. The big guy headed for the door, red in the face, angry in his gait. He looked at Walker and Squeaker but it was a passing gaze on his way by, as though he had his own issues that were far bigger than a couple of strangers blowing through town.

The door to the station opened and slammed closed behind Walker, the big guy crunching off through the gravel car park out to the side.

The five of them stood there, accompanied by the whir of the fan heater. Jones shifted a little.

'What's this?' the Sheriff asked.

'These two,' Jones said, breaking his gaze from Walker and turning to his boss. 'They want to get to Old Pelts Road.'

The Sheriff looked at Squeaker, and then settled on Walker and said, 'That right?'

'Yes, Sheriff,' Walker said.

'Nothing out there,' the Sheriff said.

'That's what we hear,' Walker said. 'Still, if it's all the same, I'd like to drive through it.'

'Well,' the Sheriff said, walking over to the counter. He didn't wear a name tag. The red flush of his face faded with every moment, as though this new business was calming next to whatever he'd just had to go through in his office with the bear. 'Each to their own, my pa used to say. Skip, get the big map.'

'Right,' Chester said, going to the room labelled 'Restricted'.

'And you two are?' the Sheriff asked.

'Walker,' he said, his hand out. 'This is my niece, Susan. Thanks for your help.'

'Sheriff Lincoln,' he said, shaking Walker's hand. 'Old Pelts is only about fifteen miles up to the nor-east. It's not maintained, and it runs to a dead end after, what, ten miles? What car you got?'

'Tahoe,' Walker said. 'Jacked up, off-road tyres.'

The Sheriff paused, then said, 'That'd do it. Maybe. Winch?'

'Yep,' Walker said.

The Sheriff took the map from Chester and spread it on the counter. It was the size of a pool table, laminated and with numerous pinholes at the corners.

'Here,' the Sheriff said, putting a stubby finger on the map. 'That's us. Here's Old Pelts Road – see that faint line?'

'Sure,' Walker said, tracing the route from town. North for about five miles, then east for three, then a series of left and right turns through what must be private roads before getting to it.

The Sheriff said, 'It was a road, back in the twenties; the government put it there.'

'I hear,' Walker said, 'that the government puts all our roads in.'

'Yeah, well, this one was superseded when this town here formed,' the Sheriff said, tapping a spot about halfway along the middle of nowhere some ten miles west of the start of Old Pelts Road. 'They had a gold rush that lasted maybe four years. Towns emptied as quick as they started. Buildings taken down, rush moved on; towns go up, then they come down again.'

'America in action,' Squeaker said out of the side of her mouth to Walker, though loud enough for all to hear.

'What's that?' the Sheriff asked.

'Nothin'.'

Walker said, 'And the road just ends?'

'Yep. At this mountain pass,' the Sheriff said, looking back to Walker. 'It was gonna be a tunnel, I think, taking the road right on to the north-east and linking up with the highway. But they never bothered once the old town died. So, Old Pelts Road just ends. One way in, one way out. Hell of a track.'

'Okay,' Walker said, taking a final glance at the map. 'Thanks.'

The Sheriff nodded. 'We got a problem, though,' he said.

Walker paused. 'What's that?'

'You can't go there.'

36

Walker looked from Sheriff Lincoln's face to the two deputies. All watched him.

'The road's down; been that way near-on two days,' the Sheriff said. 'We've had mudslides all month.'

'The rains,' Jones said.

'And too much logging,' Chester added.

Jones looked at his counterpart like he was providing too much information.

Walker asked, 'Which road?'

'Here.' The Sheriff tapped it. It was the road running north. The other roads that flicked off it were the only way to Old Pelts. 'A crew's out there trying to get it all fixed up. Ain't easy work; the stuff's like quicksand. No way out there until tomorrow.'

'No other way?' Walker said.

'Unless you spend the day on back roads and go around the other side, about 400 miles all told.' Sheriff Lincoln shook his head. 'And believe me, Mister . . .'

'Walker.'

'Walker, right. You're the last of my concerns, you and your niece. I got thirty people out there, livin' on plots and ranches now cut off from those roads. And I've got truckers and foresters and miners here in my town who can't get to work or beyond. See? Problems. Up to it this high.'

Sheriff Lincoln made a show of putting his hand horizontal and at his neck.

Walker thought of the bear of a guy who'd left the Sheriff's office a few minutes earlier. He had the look of a trucker or logger. He'd likely been telling the Sheriff that he was losing money hand over fist because that road was down. Maybe he and his trucking or logging company supported the Sheriff's re-election. No wonder the Sheriff had been red-faced – he had problems stacking up and a town at bursting point with people complaining to him. That and then some.

'Tomorrow,' Walker said. 'You know what time?'

'When it's cleared, you'll know,' Sheriff Lincoln said.

'How will we know?' Squeaker asked.

Sheriff Lincoln looked at her as though seeing her properly for the first time. 'Half the guys in this town are waiting for it to be cleared, and they're stuck here,' he said. 'When you see the mass exodus, you'll know it got cleared. Right? 'Sides, word spreads real fast hereabouts.'

'Right,' Walker said. 'Thanks, Sheriff Lincoln. Deputies.'

Chester said, 'Here to serve.'

'Like the president,' Walker said to the Sheriff. 'Your name, I mean.'

Sheriff Lincoln paused. 'Like the car.'

Walker nodded, looked to Squeaker, then back to the cops.

'We'll find a place to stay the night.'

'Town's all full up,' Jones said. 'Half those guys stuck here are sleeping in their cabs.'

'We've only got three motels,' Chester added, his voice eager, as though he was adding something of use.

'We'll figure it out, thanks,' Walker said, looking out the window to the heavy grey sky.

'Here,' the Sheriff said, leaning down on the counter and writing something. He passed over a slip of paper with a name and address scrawled on it. 'She's a good lady, she'll put you up, give you breakfast too. You pay her, of course. Pensioner. War widow. It'll be helping ya'll out.'

•

'Got it,' Levine said, emerging from a trailer.

Woods was sitting on the hood of their Ford, flicking through his notebook, looking at a whole lot of nothing he'd got from the other neighbours over what felt like hours of standing on their porches, talking through flyscreen doors. 'What'd that be?' he asked.

'North. Over the border, in Missouri,' Levine said, walking towards him. 'Raytown, that's where they're headed.'

'How's she know that?' Woods asked, nodding to the trailer.

'She heard them say it when they came back for the body.'

'Body?'

'Walker killed a guy here, soon after midnight. Self-defence. Knife through his brain, that nice lady told me.'

Woods looked over Levine's shoulder to see the woman standing behind her screen door. Tall, stooped, as though her life had given her a body full of dull aches and pains.

Woods said, 'Do you think the Sheriff knows that?'

'Probably, but no cops have been here to check things out. Just the guy's co-workers, to pick him up, first light this morning.'

'Like that, hey?' Woods pocketed his notebook.

'Like that.'

'Who was the dead guy?' Woods asked, opening the passenger door as Levine went for the driver's side.

'Muscle,' Levine said over the car's roof.

'Who picked him up?'

'Guys that work for Barb Durrell.'

'Right – wait.' He flicked through his notes. 'I've got a Black Tahoe 2013 model registered to a Gus Durrell, right here in town, one of only four such vehicles registered in a hundred-mile radius.'

'Then that's our vehicle.'

'We go for Walker, though, right?'

'After. I want to talk to those guys first.'

Woods hesitated, then said, 'We've got a trail that's getting colder by the hour.'

'But those guys are now after Walker too,' Levine said, opening the driver's door. 'This is their turf, right? They're going to be pissed, and they're going to be chasing after Walker – so we can follow them. If they're some organised crew running or manufacturing drugs, then they've got eyes and ears all over, right? Besides, it won't take us an hour, you'll see. We'll make up time.'

Woods looked around the clearing, seeing it in a different light now: a murder scene. 'A buck says they've got the local Sheriff's department onside.'

'You're probably right, so keep your dollar in your pocket.' Levine climbed inside, started up the Taurus and was reversing into a U-turn before Woods had fully closed his door. 'And I want to know who they are and what their involvement is.'

'Do you want to get some back-up on this?' Woods asked as Levine put the car into drive. 'State police?'

'What, you got your period?' Levine stomped on the gas and tore out of the clearing.

37

Walker pulled to the kerb outside the little house of the war widow, Margaret. It was timber-clad, double-storey, with wide verandahs all around. Built when things were made to last. Painted the same dull grey as the sky. The garden was a neat clipped lawn but the flowerbeds and trees hadn't seen much attention in years. The rusted roof needed replacing. The chain-link fence was on iron posts that could have been reclaimed civil war canons.

'Could have been here since the Civil War,' Walker said, getting out.

'Probably has been,' Squeaker said, standing on the damp easement out the front. 'You sure you want to stay here?'

'Gotta stay someplace,' Walker said. 'What, you don't like houses, or little old ladies, or both?'

Squeaker hit him in the arm and climbed the brick steps.

The door creaked open as they approached.

Margaret stood in the doorway. Stooped and shrunken with age, she was smaller than Squeaker.

'So,' she said, 'you're the out-of-towners.'

'Sheriff rang you?' Walker said.

'Nope. Ain't got a phone.'

'Right,' Walker said.

'Only people I get callin' on my door is when the roads are down and the town's all full up. Come on in. Board is twenty a night – that's each.'

'Thank you. One night is all we need,' Walker said. He motioned for Squeaker to enter first.

Margaret stood at the door and waited for them both to pass, then closed it. She eyed them both, up close. Her eyes were cloudy.

'What's your name, girl?'

'Sq – Susan.'

'What's that?'

'Susan.'

'Susan. Where you from, Little Rock?'

'Near there.'

'Thought so. Your accent says it.' Margaret turned to Walker. 'East coast. Virginia maybe.'

'Philadelphia.'

'What's that?' Margaret said, her hand to her ear.

'Philadelphia,' Walker said, louder.

'I've been there, when I was a teenager,' she said, walking down the hall with the aid of a cane. 'You stand like a soldier.'

'Yes, ma'am,' Walker said, following the two women to the kitchen out back. The floorboards creaked under his weight. 'Air Force.'

'Air Force?' she said, looking at him. 'Hell, no soldiers in the Air Force. That's my husband there.'

Walker looked to where she was pointing with an age-gnarled finger. The mantle over the fireplace beyond the small kitchen table held a framed photo of a strong-looking square-jawed man; it reminded Walker of so many photos he'd seen of his grandfather's service in Germany.

'Airborne,' Walker said.

'Yes, that's right,' Margaret said, putting an aluminium kettle on the gas stove and lighting it with a match. 'He and my brother, both of them went. Neither came back.'

'Japan?'

'Okinawa.'

'I'm sorry for your loss,' Walker said.

'What's your name?'

'Jed.'

'Ted?'

'Jed. As in Josiah.'

'What kind of name is that?'

'Family name.'

'Right. I'll call you Mark. You look like Mark, my brother, rest his soul.'

Margaret went to a glass-fronted cupboard, removing some good china rather than the mugs that hung on hooks by the stove. Walker wondered if every guest got this treatment, or if it was just that he had the military connection.

'I'll help you,' Squeaker said, taking the cups and saucers from her.

'Help?' Margaret said. 'You can make it. Tea and coffee there. Milk and sugar there. I'll show Mark to your room.'

Squeaker nearly lost it with laughter as Margaret started up the corridor and let out a loud fart.

'Hear that?' Margaret said, not pausing her slow shuffle up the hall. 'Earthquake. Been getting them five times a day this year. Four times a day last year. Before that, near-on never, maybe once every couple of years.'

'What's causing it?' Walker said.

Margaret stopped and turned. 'Gas.'

Squeaker laughed.

Walker said, 'Sorry?'

'Gas. In the ground,' Margaret said. 'They dig it up, flush it out somehow.'

'Fracking.'

'What's that?' Margaret said.

'They call it fracking,' Walker said. 'I've heard about it wrecking underwater tables. You sure that's causing earthquakes?'

'Can't be nothing else,' Margaret said, continuing her slow stroll up the hall. 'The whole Ozarks are full of caves and whatnot. Government built whole cities underground around here in that Cold War.'

'Yeah, I've heard rumours.'

'Not rumours, young Mark,' Margaret said, pausing at a closed door leading off the hall, opposite the sitting room at the front of the house. 'I've seen it, when I could see good. As young'uns we used to play in the caves. In the fifties they started sealing them all up. Building things. The Air Force even sent down some monster drill – a tunnel maker, biggest machine I ever saw. I heard it tunnelled from here to Ozark – that's the town, near Springfield – then it goes all the way up to St Louis.'

'That'd be a hell of a tunnel,' Walker said. 'Hundreds of miles.'

'Country was crazy then,' Margaret said. 'Building things we'd never need, preparing for a war against the communists – a war that never came.'

She opened the door. The curtain was drawn, leaving the room in darkness, but Walker could make out a double bed with a quilt, and dust-covered side tables. Cobwebs collected in the corners of the ceiling, but the room was dry and warm, and that's what Walker looked forward to most.

Margaret let out another fart. 'Aftershock,' she said, shuffling off. 'Damn gas.'

38

Margaret offered them dinner of beef pot stew but Walker and Squeaker headed out. It was early for dinner, just on five, but the sun's glow in the grey sky was almost extinguished.

'Walk into town?' Walker asked.

'Hell no,' Squeaker said. 'I'll drive us.'

Walker tossed her the Tahoe keys. She gunned the engine and took off in a cloud of tyre smoke.

'Great,' Walker said, looking back at the twin lines of rubber she'd left out the front of Margaret's house. 'She'll think we're petrol heads with no respect.'

'It's how everyone with a pulse drives around here,' Squeaker said, slowing at the stop sign but putting her foot down when she saw it was clear, sliding the back of the Tahoe out as she pulled onto the street running behind Main Street. 'She was a character, no?'

'Yep.'

'You believe that, about the tunnels?'

'Maybe. Cold War they spent billions on stuff we won't ever know about, let alone find a use for.'

'So, you're a long way from Philly here, huh?'

'Yep. Have you been?'

'Nope. I haven't been north of Missouri.'

'I'm sorry for your loss.'

'Ha ha.'

She stopped at the next stop sign to let an eighteen-wheeler blast by, headed south.

'What are you going to say to him?' Squeaker asked, taking a sedate right turn, looking at storefronts as she motored. 'My cousin.'

'Just what I know.'

'That's he's in danger?'

'That. And that he has information that will help stop a catastrophic attack that's coming – only, he doesn't know that he knows.'

'Maybe the rest of the SEALs have already told whoever's protecting them about what's coming.'

'Maybe. Maybe not.'

Squeaker slowed past a bar flanked by rows of motorbikes, all Harleys and choppers.

'Maybe another time,' Walker said, not wanting to get into yet another bar fight. 'How about that place?'

He pointed up the road to a red neon sign that had a larger-than-life statue of a 1950s waitress in a short skirt and on roller-skates holding a tray that spun around.

Squeaker said, 'I usually don't eat at places with flashing lights and all.'

'Do you have many of those in Calico Rock?'

'Enough to know I don't like them.'

'What's not to like?' Walker said as she pulled the Tahoe next to a near-identical vehicle in the diner's car park. 'They'll have cold beer and hot food.'

'*That*, for a start,' she said, pointing to one of the Sheriff's squad cars.

'Cops need to eat someplace. And in my experience, they usually know where the good simple food is at.'

'Yeah,' she said, sitting with the engine running, her little shoulders slumped forward. 'But you didn't grow up where I did, did you, mister?'

She looked at him, her big eyes somewhere between playful and tired. He remembered her in the shower, her body firm and pressed tightly against his. He shook off the thought. One more night, find her cousin, and she'll be on her way home.

39

The diner was packed. They sat at the counter, all the booths and tables full up. Men, mostly, either passing through town and stuck or cut off from where they lived out near the mining or logging operations.

Walker had a burger with fries and onion rings and a pitcher of beer.

Squeaker had a huge rib-eye steak, rare, with mashed potato and peas and lashings of gravy. When she'd cleared her plate, she picked up the bone and gnawed at the bits of meat she couldn't cut off.

'What are you going to do, after we find him?' she asked. 'After you stop whatever this thing is, I mean. After all this. What's next?'

'I'll move on,' Walker said, wiping his mouth and balling the napkin on his empty plate and pushing it forward. 'To the next job.'

'The next attack.'

Walker drained his beer, nodded. 'There's more to be done.'

Squeaker watched him and drank her seltzer before she continued. 'I could come with you.'

'Come with me?'

'After this. After we find Murphy, I mean. I could help out.'

Walker smiled. 'You could drive me around?'

'Yep. And I can shoot.'

'I know, I've seen you do both.'

'I'm tough.'

'I believe it.'

The waitress cleared their plates. Squeaker ordered a whisky, double.

'Want one?' she said to Walker.

He saw the single brand that they had and shook his head. 'I'll stick with beer.'

The waitress nodded.

A ruckus erupted in the corner behind Walker. Two table-loads were arguing. A guy stood. A big guy, with one of the thickest beards Walker had ever seen. He had his fists forming.

'Hey,' a voice called. Walker saw Chester, sitting alone at the counter, shaking his head at the guys. They seemed to get the message.

Walker felt a hand on his shoulder. Heavy. He turned, slowly, prepared for action, shifting his weight on the vinyl-topped stool, keeping his arms loose.

Sheriff Lincoln. His right hand rested on the butt of his service pistol. The clasp was undone. Jones was a few paces to one side of him, between them and the door. The diner quietened.

'Jed Walker,' Lincoln said.

Walker didn't react.

'You're under arrest for murder.'

40

Levine walked out of Barb Durrell's house. Woods could tell she was pissed. Even with his woollen overcoat and gloves, he was freezing. The house was full of activity. The Sheriff's car was parked out in the driveway, along with a dozen others, all shiny new pick-ups, American makes. The house was a veritable palace of bad taste. Levine's breath was fogging.

'How'd that go?' Woods asked her.

Levine shook her head and moved to the passenger side of their car.

'Told you,' Woods said. 'They're not going to talk around here. Badges just make these folk clam up tighter than a fish's butt.'

'Mixed metaphor much?'

'Well, a leopard can't change his stripes.'

'What?'

'I'm tired.' Woods said, throwing his coat onto the back seat before settling behind the steering wheel. 'And I'm just saying, around here, they don't even know the outside world exists. They don't care about it. They don't give a shit beyond what's happening in their lives right now.'

'You make them sound like they're all backwards yokels,' Levine said, unclipping her holstered Sig and putting it into the centre console before buckling up and raking her seat back. 'Head north. Fast.'

'Got it,' Woods said, taking off, watching the house in the rearview mirror before heading towards Route 63. 'Nope. They're smart. They've got what they need and aren't putting their hands out to get any more.' Woods was silent a moment, then added, 'It's the kind of quiet life we all wish we had.'

'You reckon?'

'Damn straight.'

'Well, I'm going to disrupt their quiet little lives right now. The next people we question, no more Good Agent.'

'You're the good agent?'

•

'Are you sure you don't want to talk about this?' Walker said.

Lincoln said nothing as he locked the cell door.

Walker was right about the cells being out the back of the station. There were three of them, eight-by-eight-by-eight cubes made up of half-inch steel bars. He was the only guest. Each had a single cot bed bolted to the concrete floor, and a stainless-steel toilet with a faucet and basin set into the top of the cistern. At the end of the room was another door, which led to a kitchenette and staff toilets.

'Cuffs,' Lincoln said, holding his keys out.

Walker put his cuffed hands through a gap in the bars and Lincoln undid them. Jones watched from two paces away, his hands on his hips and a shit-eating grin on his face. Chester emerged from the kitchenette with a cup of coffee.

'We knew you was trouble,' Jones said.

'*Was*, past tense,' Walker said. 'I'm all grown up now, no trouble to no-one.'

'Save it, smart guy,' Chester said.

Lincoln looked at his deputy as he squared his cuffs away on his belt.

'Sheriff, it was self-defence,' Walker said to Lincoln's back as the Sheriff headed for the door to the main station. 'He drew a knife on me. A big one.'

'Witness says otherwise,' Lincoln said. 'Same witness whose car you stole. That's another charge right there.'

Walker rubbed his wrists, said, 'You spoke to him? Gus?'

'Yep. He's headed up here right now, with some business associates,' Sheriff Lincoln said. 'As a matter of fact they're going to be staying the night. I'll be taking their statements first thing in the morning, unless you wanna just confess, save me some paperwork?'

'Okay, I confess. I borrowed that truck to save a life.'

'And the guy you killed?'

'Self-defence.'

Lincoln smiled, said, 'Save it for court.'

'Court?'

'Jones will take you to Springfield tomorrow, soon as the road is clear,' Lincoln said, turning away again and heading for the door.

Walker said, 'What about Squeaker?'

Lincoln paused, turning once more.

'Chester's dropping her at Margaret's. She'll find her own way home, whenever.'

Walker said, 'She won't be safe if she goes back there or home.'

'She's a big girl,' Lincoln said with a smile. 'She knows how things work themselves out around here.'

Lincoln departed.

Jones went to the kitchen, made himself a coffee.

Walker watched them, his mind elsewhere. *She knows how things work themselves out around here.* And he knew that Barb and Gus wouldn't ordinarily involve the law like this – *why would they? That would just bring a world of hurt down on them and their business operations. Something was wrong here. Business associates? Does that mean Lincoln knows what business Barb and Gus are in – and does he condone it? A guy like that, on the take, no-one around to call him out on it . . .*

'I need to make a phone call,' Walker called to Jones as he was nearing with two coffees, one for him and one for his boss. 'Andrew Hutchinson. FBI. I'm working with him.'

Jones walked by without stopping. He put the coffees in the other room and came back to close the door.

'FBI?' Jones said, his head in the cold cell block. 'Hell, why would we want to involve them in a little thing like this?'

•

'Walker's phone's switched off,' Hutchinson said to Somerville as she drove them into San Diego Airport. He was about to board a flight to DC, and she was headed for St Louis.

'Might be out of reception,' Somerville said. 'All those hills and mountains and whatnot out there.'

'Maybe,' Hutchinson said. He dialled McCorkell.

41

Walker was tired but he couldn't rest, let alone sleep. It wasn't the lumpy plastic-covered mattress nor the damp cold sucking through the concrete floor. It wasn't even the thought of his overarching mission, nor the fact that every minute he stayed here kept him a step away from finding Murphy.

It was Squeaker.

She was there, by his side, an accessory to murder, and they didn't arrest her.

She knows how things work themselves out around here.

So, Walker paced. He checked the cell. The cage was sturdy, at least in the case of man against steel. The welds were tight and true, as were the bolts into the concrete floor and ceiling. The lock and hinges on the door were strong. There was some wriggle and wobble to them, but there was no way he was going to bust out of here by hand.

He'd need help.

The closest help was the police. Either the Sheriff or his deputies. One of them would do.

He started to bang the bars.

It took five minutes.

'What?' Chester said.

'Hungry prisoner,' Walker said.

'Breakfast's a long way off.'

'How about a coffee?'

Chester hesitated, then got him a paper cup of coffee from a percolator in the kitchenette and put it on the floor just outside the bars. Walker bent down to pick it up. Warm, not hot. He drained it in a gulp.

'You're in luck, Walker,' Chester said. 'The road's gonna be closed another day. That means no court tomorrow.'

'How do you know that?'

'Crew working from the other side just updated us,' Chester said.

'How big is this mudslide?'

'Quarter-mile, in two spots,' Jones replied. 'It'll take them a day and a half with heavy equipment to clear it all out.'

'The town can't rally from this side with backhoes and snow ploughs?'

'Tried that, before my time. Takes a week. Relax. A day or so's nothing here. Enjoy your cell time.' Chester smirked and turned to leave.

'Wait.'

'What?'

'Is Squeaker still in town?'

Chester hesitated. 'Yeah.'

'You're sure?'

'Yes.'

Walker saw something in the way the deputy was behaving. 'Why – what's happened to her?'

Chester looked to the door to the station, hesitant to share information. Walker could see the wheels turning in the deputy's head as he was getting to the thought that, what the hell, this guy's in a cell and going to be shunted to court the day after tomorrow, why not.

'She made hell outside the station here an hour ago, demanding you be released,' Chester said. 'And same again twenty minutes ago, saying that the world would end if you weren't released. Sheriff cuffed her and drove her back, both times, to Mrs Coulter's.'

'Margaret's?'

'Yeah.'

'You have to look out for her. She's not safe. Not if those guys from Arkansas are headed there.'

'And why would that be?' Chester asked.

'She's in danger. She was there when I had to defend us.'

'You mean when you murdered that man.'

'Semantics.'

'She'll be fine,' Chester said. 'Susan ain't there no more.'

'Ain't where?'

'Mrs Coulter's. She made another ruckus. Neighbours called us, so Sheriff Lincoln went out and picked her up.'

Something in Chester's tone made Walker watch him carefully. 'Where is she?' he asked, slowly.

'Safe.'

'Nowhere's safe.'

'Yeah? How about the Sheriff's own house?' Chester said, then smiled. 'Yeah, that's right. She'll be looked after real good. I'll probably head out there later on, look after her for the morning shift.'

Walker said in a low voice, 'You have no idea what you're doing.'

Chester walked closer. 'Is this part of your mission – to save the world or something?'

'Yeah, about that,' Walker said, his voice quieter. 'Listen, it's up to you now, Chester. You hear?'

'What?'

'You have to be the hero here,' Walker said. He turned from the bars and looked away, whispered, 'I guess you'll get all the accolades, not me. They're gonna give you awards, medals. Might even get a handshake from the President.'

'What's that?' Chester asked, leaning on the gate, his hands through it. 'What'd you say?'

Walker moved faster than Chester could react. One pivot, one step, and he had the deputy's wrists. The next second he pulled, hard. Chester's head hit the steel bars. A loud clang rang out. Chester slumped. Lights out; two vertical dints in his forehead. But his weight was held by Walker against the bars.

Walker stripped the deputy of everything of use – all of it in his utility belt. Gun. Cuffs. Keys to the station. He let the unconscious man fall backwards and then unlocked the cell and dragged him into it.

He locked it, Beretta in hand, and headed for the door.

42

'Who's the guy?' he asked Squeaker. The barn off Sheriff Lincoln's house had been converted to a garage. An old 1970s Corvette sat in the middle half-rebuilt. It was cold in the barn, and the concrete floor was damp where she sat. A couple of powerful light bulbs hung overhead.

'He's just a guy.' Squeaker looked up at them. Two of Barb's guys. She'd seen them around before but didn't know their names. One was young but already bald. The other had hair down to his butt. Barb was in the house with the Sheriff. They'd be back soon. Squeaker knew that her chance of escape was now or never. She was handcuffed to a block-and-tackle that was built to lift engines out of cars. It was on wheels, castors, which meant she could move around, push it, but not far, and not fast.

Baldy came over and slapped her. 'Who is Walker?' he demanded. 'Who's he work for?'

Squeaker was quiet.

'Is he DEA?'

No answer.

'He's definitely government, we know that much.' Baldy moved away.

Squeaker said, 'He was Air Force.'

'Air Force?' Hairy said.

'Was?' Baldy added.

Squeaker nodded. Spat out blood. 'Then CIA.'

The two men looked at each other.

'Aw, look at you two,' Squeaker said. 'Looking at each other like that. Mr Bald Man, does your hairy friend here complete you?'

Baldy said, 'Huh?'

Hairy said, 'CIA? Like, spies and shit?'

'Yep,' Squeaker said. 'And he's got all kinds of gadgets.'

Baldy said, 'Gadgets?'

Hairy said, 'All kinds?'

Squeaker nodded, said, 'Yep. You should see them. His watch – with his watch he can track me.'

Baldy said, 'Track me?'

'*Me*,' Squeaker said. 'Maybe you too, though, you never know.'

'How?' Hairy said, sceptical but still intrigued.

Squeaker hung her head and shook it. 'Flu shot.'

Hairy said, 'What?'

'I got a flu shot, you know?' Squeaker said. 'A needle, an injection, at the doctor's, two years back.'

'What?' They looked at each other.

'This guy, Walker? He's bigger than you, stronger than you. Hell, he might be part government robot. I saw him wipe out Barb's guys unarmed. How's one guy do that? They had guns and knives. That's Gus's truck he's driving around in.' Squeaker leaned forward in her binds, spoke in a low voice. 'And soon he's gonna be here, smashing down your door, because he can track me, find my location, with his gadgets.'

Hairy said, also in a quiet voice, 'Because of a flu shot?'

'They track the nanomites in it. With satellites. Some kind of Cold War invention, when they were spending billions of dollars on things you'd never know about. It's science.' Squeaker stared them down.

One guy talked to the other, then Baldy said, 'Shit. I went and got a flu shot once.'

'What? Idiot! He's gonna track us!'

'What do we do?' They looked to each other and then to Squeaker as though she might have the answer.

'If I were you guys?' she said. 'I'd just cut me loose and run. Fast as you can. Get away. At least five hundred miles. That's the range, see?'

The guys nodded. One drew a knife, took a step to cut her free—

Then the door opened. Gus came in. He looked at his guys, at the knife, and gave them a look that turned them to stone. And Squeaker knew that her chance of escape was gone.

•

Deputy Jones was unconscious and stripped of his utility belt, cuffed to Chester in the cell. Walker headed outside. It was dark. The stars

142 of JAMES PHELAN

and moon were nowhere to be seen. It was close to freezing and
the damp made it colder. Every now and then a fat wet snowflake
fluttered to earth.

Walker took a patrol car and turned onto the main road, following
it north-west towards the Sheriff's house; the address had come
courtesy of Jones, who'd proved, with nothing more than a tap on
the nose, that he was talkative after all. Then, as Walker drove by the
biker bar they'd seen coming in, a low concrete-block building with
no windows and a neon beer sign buzzing on the roof, he knew he
should make a detour first.

43

There were fourteen of them, in colours and embroidery and patches on their leather jackets. A few others lingered nearby, but they didn't concern or interest him.

Walker headed for the group at the end of the bar. A guy was holding court, but he wasn't their leader. Too insignificant. The leader had a greying beard and bulging eyes, was short and stocky and fat, like he was under pressure inside and could burst at any point.

Walker stood close by them. Close enough to be noticed, close enough to irritate, close enough to elicit an immediate reaction. The group fell silent, their drinks left on the tables as they sat and waited.

'There's another crew here,' Walker said. He watched for reactions, for an indication of who would speak first.

'Crew?' asked a man with a trimmed goatee and a smooth shaved head. 'What the fuck does that mean, *crew*?'

'A crystal crew, meth runners,' Walker said. A bar stool slid back on the floor and a regular punter made to leave the bar but goatee made eye contact with him and he stopped by the door, head down, then returned to his seat. 'From Arkansas.'

Silence from the men, but the music played on. A 1990s track, Pearl Jam. Walker thought he would've been about Squeaker's age when he first heard it.

'I'm on the clock here, boys,' Walker said. 'You want what I know or not?'

Eventually goatee said, 'Maybe go tell the law your little story.'

'Yeah,' the guy closest to Walker said. He was the biggest, easily six foot eight and 350 pounds, sitting across two chairs. Next to him was a lanky guy with long greasy blond hair and a scar across his cheek and mouth that gave him crooked lips. 'Go get your bitch ass outta here.'

Walker tossed two sets of handcuff keys into the big guy's lap. 'The deputies are preoccupied,' he said. 'And the Sheriff is going to be dead soon. And you've got a crew from down south on your turf.'

Silence. The big guy looked to goatee, either seeking permission or questioning whether they were to keep listening to Walker at all.

'Surely you boys are the muscle here in town? Making sure things are kept running just so? Well, I'm telling you, right now, and it's the only warning you're gonna get – you're getting fucked in your own home and you don't even know it.'

Goatee's bug-eyes glanced to the big guy, who gave the slightest nod.

'You get up off of those chairs,' Walker said to the 350-pounder, 'and I'll break your legs. Then I'll push your girlfriend here head-first up your ass so you can use her legs to walk you around.'

The guy didn't move as he watched Walker. He took the comment in a way that showed he hadn't been spoken to in an offensive manner since he was ten years old and knocking out grown men. He looked to goatee, who was flushed red in the face.

'They're the muscle,' a voice said behind Walker.

Walker turned around and zeroed in on the speaker, who sat at the far corner of the bar.

'*My* muscle.' The man stood and walked over. It was the guy Walker had seen in the Sheriff's office, the bear-like one he'd thought was a trucker trying to get through town. 'This is *my* town, and the Sheriff's *my* guy. These here, they are *my* guys. So, if you or anyone else is fucking with them, with me, with my business, you'd best tell me, right now, all of it you know. You've got two minutes to impress me.'

Walker raked his eyes over the crew. 'I hope they put up more of a fight than the deputies did,' he said.

The leader was silent but he checked his watch.

'I don't need two minutes,' Walker said. 'I've told you all you need. So, are you in or out? If you're in, this is over, fast. We help each other get rid of these Arkansas guys. If you're out, then I'll deal with it on my own, which will take me longer, but I'll get it done. The thing is, if I do it that way, there might just be no town left for you and your girl scouts here to play in anymore.'

The music had stopped. Walker could almost hear the light-as-air snowflakes landing on the roof.

'Take him outside, dump him in the woodchipper,' the bear said to his guys. 'Then go get the Sheriff and bring him here and get me some straight answers. If anyone from down south is here, I want them strung up fast and sent home in a meat truck.'

44

Menzil looked out his window.

The team had been late, having done some op that his boss had sent them on, something in Little Rock. He didn't like that. He'd brought these guys in, and he wanted to be their only level of command. But as soon as this all started, he'd been removed from several decisions. The SEAL hits, months in the planning, had been executed with exacting precision. All had gone well. But they hadn't found Murphy, yet they'd had to act then, on those they had located. Menzil wondered why – *why that day? Why not wait until they'd got Murphy too?* He'd asked his boss and the answer had been because the opportunity to hit the other eight was there and needed to be taken. But Menzil wondered about that. *They'd outsourced the overseas hits, which could have been coordinated with the home ones on almost any given day – so why not wait another week or so, until they'd located Murphy?*

But it was not for him to wonder, for the wondering and the waiting were almost completely over. He'd be on the other side of this and get out of it exactly what he desired for his brother, and himself. Revenge for past wrongs, and restitution to secure a comfortable future. He could live with all that.

•

Walker knew that the 350-pounder would be the first to get up, that he'd make a good show of punishing Walker to reinstate his dominance. And Walker also knew that the guy's buddies would no doubt sit and watch the show, drinking their beers and moonshine while enjoying the entertainment.

The thing was, this wasn't about a bigger guy fighting someone he saw as smaller and less capable. Far from it. Walker had spent his entire adult life at the pointy ends of the military and intelligence worlds. His life had been one long period of high operational tempo, where every movement and action was so honed that it was second nature to destroy an enemy at every given chance.

These guys – even the 350-pounder – spent their days sitting around drinking and eating and looking tough, using their numbers to intimidate, occasionally employing a knife or gun or bat or fist to do some stand-over work. But they would always have that safety in numbers, knowing that regardless of who they were threatening or running out of town, there were more than a dozen comrades at arms standing next to them, a wall of beef not to be messed with.

Walker didn't want to destroy this guy, because he might well prove useful. But he needed to send a strong message to all in the room.

The guy took off his jacket. His arms were heavily tattooed skin over the kind of bulk that only came with steroids and protein. He cracked his knuckles, grinned, and lunged forward.

Walker parried the blow and grabbed a wrist, using the 350 pounds of momentum to turn the man back to his table, where he twisted the arm around, forcing him to counteract and turn his back to Walker to move away from the bone-shearing pain. Walker then grabbed the other wrist, put his knees into the guy's back, and pulled the arms out and then back, fast.

A double pop rang out as each shoulder dislocated. The guy let out a whimper as Walker rested him face down on the table, bent at the waist.

'Ready to play your part?' Walker said to the biker with the long greasy hair, pointing at the 350-pounder's butt. The guy was wide-eyed and silent. 'Hope you can hold your breath.'

'Enough,' the leader said.

Walker turned to him.

'Who *are* you?' the bear asked.

'I'm the guy trying to save a friend who's here, in town, from that Arkansas crew,' Walker said. 'If we do this together, it works out well for all of us.'

The bear looked at his enforcer, who hadn't moved from the table.

'Can you fix him first?' the leader asked.

'As quick as I broke him,' Walker said. 'And it ain't gonna tickle.'

45

The leader's name, the bear Walker had seen in the Sheriff's office, was Hogan, Hogan Copper. And among his business interests he did indeed have a logging-truck operation. He was losing money while he thought the Sheriff wasn't doing all he could to clear the roads.

'You sure they're in town?'

'I heard the Sheriff say so,' Walker said. 'Said he was meeting him at his place, to talk business.'

'Son of a bitch,' Copper said. 'He's a dead man.'

'That's what I said.'

'This friend of yours?'

'A girl. Susan. From south of here.'

'She's your girl?'

'She's a friend.'

'What do the Arkansas crew want with her?'

'They want me,' Walker said. 'I started this. That's why they're meeting with the Sheriff in the first place, to discuss what to do with me. He's no doubt talking to them now, figuring out what's the best deal for him to hand me over.'

'What'd you do to these guys?'

'Killed a couple of them. Stole a truck.'

'Why?'

'Why not?'

Hogan nodded. 'Okay,' he said. 'This is how we're going to do this.'

•

'What does Walker want with Murphy?' Barb said.

Squeaker was silent.

'Girl, I'm giving you a chance to talk,' Sheriff Lincoln said. 'Tell it all, to me, or I just leave you with your kin here.'

Squeaker didn't look at Barb. But she did stare at the Sheriff. Kept him in her gaze, her little world. He was maybe her best hope in it.

She knew that she could buy time with this guy, by talking to him, spin a story, draw him in.

'She ain't talkin',' Barb said. 'Give her over to us now. We'll get her hummin'. Then we'll get this Walker guy. We'll get him out of your town, for good.'

Barb looked at the Sheriff, waiting for a reply.

'The way I see it,' Lincoln said, 'she's my prisoner here. So, until we work out what's in all of our interests, she's mine and mine alone. Walker too.'

Barb was silent. Then, she gave a slim smile, the web of creases around her lifetime-smoker's mouth forming into a grimace.

'Keep your eyes on her,' she said to one of her guys. 'Me and the Sheriff here are going to work out what's what.'

•

Walker rode in the back seat of Copper's twin-cab truck. The rest of the crew took to their bikes. They wound out of town in a convoy, headed for the Sheriff's house. Copper drove; the big guy was next to him, still massaging where his shoulders had gone back in. Walker was behind on the passenger side, and beside him was a guy with a sawn-off pump-action shotgun across his lap.

'Point that the other way,' Walker told him.

The guy stared into Walker's eyes, unflinching, but after about a minute he gave in and placed the gun the other way, so that if it went off it'd blast the door instead of turning Walker into a sausage creature.

It was a five-minute drive out of town, where the land was cleared and formed a small valley of fields surrounded by treed hills. Copper pulled to a stop at the corner of the turn-off from the road, an intersection populated with a tall pine and several mailboxes, a mile-long lane that fed off to long driveways. Behind, the crew aligned their bikes into a row, all pointed back to town, then killed engines and headlights.

'His house is at the end of the third dirt track,' Copper said over his shoulder. 'To the right. See?'

Walker saw the dotted lights of a squat house in a small clearing closely surrounded by a ring of birch, their leaves red-orange and fluttering from the branches in the breeze, the scene lit by a couple of floodlights on the barn. It had cleared acreages to the front and sides, forest to the rear. Light caught the windshield of the Sheriff's patrol car parked by the steps that led up to the porch, and there were three pick-ups parked in a row.

The Arkansas crew.

Now that Walker could see the terrain and layout, he saw the sense in what Hogan had proposed. This guy wasn't dumb. He might have done service once; he'd certainly done time, judging by the prison tatts that showed at his cuffs.

Walker had the two police-issue Berettas tucked into the back of his belt, two spare clips in each pocket.

The 350-pounder sat still in the front passenger seat. He looked somewhere between sheepish and furious, his only movements during the drive the occasional rolling and rubbing of his shoulders, the joints no doubt inflamed where they'd been popped back in. In the truck's tray two men were lying down, out of sight, each armed with an AR-15, the civilian equivalent of the military's M4 assault rifle. Each had a high-capacity barrel-shaped mag that held 120 rounds.

'Like I said, Walker,' Copper said, looking at him in the rear-view mirror. 'I'm gonna drive up there and see what's what. This Sheriff understands that he serves at my pleasure. If things are as you say, then you'll hear my signal and move with my men. Not before. Got me?'

'Yep,' Walker said, getting out of the cab and joining the guys from the bikes. Each sported a firearm of some sort, sawn-off shotguns a favourite, and a couple of pistols, nickel-plated showy things.

'If he tries anything before or after,' Copper said to his crew, nodding towards Walker, 'cap him.'

•

Walker set off on foot with twelve of Copper's men. They walked through the field, approaching the house from the east. It was dark, the moon a thin sliver in a night sky filled with low clouds. They moved in single file. Walker was second, behind the long-haired guy, who carried a sawn-off shotgun. It would take them ten minutes to make it across the grassy terrain to the tree line, at which time Hogan would start up his truck and drive up the track to the house.

With every step, Walker thought of Squeaker.

The twelve men split into four groups, each trio headed for a different corner of the house. They stopped out beyond the ring of birch trees, just twenty yards short of their objective. They moved heavily in their boots and leathers, some wheezing from whatever they smoked. But there were no sentries outside, so the infiltration went unnoticed. In his three-man team was the guy with the sawn-off, watching him. Walker had eyes for the situation before him.

They waited. Walker watched the house. The southern and eastern sides had three windows, all lit up. One was the lounge room; he saw the forms of two people standing in there, their positions suggesting they were standing over someone, letting their presence be felt.

His grip tightened on one of the Berettas. He started to think of an escape plan, once he had Squeaker in the clear. He could shoot the three crew members next to him faster than they could turn to react. But there were four separate teams of them, plus Hogan and his three guys, which gave him a problem to solve. Quickly.

He could lay cover fire while he took one of the trucks or the Sheriff's car, with Squeaker driving. But the other vehicles would soon be in pursuit.

All that, because he'd made a temporary deal with the devil to help him get his friend.

He started thinking up a story that might give Hogan pause, when the two guys in the lounge room moved out of sight.

'They've noticed the truck's coming,' Walker said to his three companions.

One of them grunted in reply. Another raked his pump-action shotgun, the sound cutting through the mountain air and making Walker wince. If shooting started, he could take these guys, and the three to the south-west corner that he could see, before the others reacted. Six down, six more out here.

But then Hogan and 350-pounder would be in the house, possibly with Squeaker. And his two guys with the assault rifles in the back of the truck's tray would start lighting up the night.

He would have to get to them fast. Walker felt confident that he could snipe off those men outside armed with short-range weapons of shotguns and 9-millimetre pistols, but then it would be a siege situation, with a host of unknown forces inside holding Squeaker as a bargaining chip.

Then he'd be back to square one.

Shit.

Walker saw Hogan's truck start up, the bright headlights coming up the lane. He started to move, slowly, settling the pistol in his hands. He liked the Beretta; it was a fine pistol. The M9, the US military called them. Side-arm of the greater portion of the DoD for many years. Reliable. Relatively accurate. It was the first pistol he'd trained on, and holding one was like an extension of his arm. Point and shoot. Fifteen rounds.

Suddenly, gunshots, from the house. Two of them, from a .357 revolver. Sheriff Lincoln.

Then they all heard the tinny-sounding pop-pop-pop of a 9-millimetre as it was emptied.

The crew members around Walker started to rush the house. They were the second group to climb the front stairs. He heard the back door being broken down, and then he saw the two guys standing in the back of Hogan's truck, their AR-15s rested on the roof, their eyes looking through scopes, waiting for clear shots should anyone they didn't like appear at a door or window.

As Walker approached the house, he saw through glass balcony doors that Sheriff Lincoln was spread out on the floor, a 9-millimetre gunshot wound to the head. The 350-pounder was also dead, two neat .357 holes in his chest.

Hogan held a compact Glock, the slide raked back as it had emptied the mag.

Two other men were dead on the floor, and four had been rounded up by the crew coming from the back door and were now sitting lined up at the kitchen table.

Barb's husband, Gus, had caught a round through the throat and was clutching at the wound, arterial blood oozing through his fingers. Slumped on the couch, he would bleed out or drown in less than thirty seconds.

Next to him, Squeaker. She had a bruised eye and fat lip. She was wrapped in a ball, her arms pulling her legs up tightly to her chest. She was pale and in shock, but when she saw Walker standing in the doorway, filling that space, she opened up and ran to him and wrapped her arms around him. She felt tiny, cold, tense. Walker hung onto her.

'Tie them to the dining chairs,' Hogan told his men. The Arkansas crew were shoved roughly into 1970s vinyl chairs, their wrists and ankles soon shackled with plastic cable ties. 'We're going to get everything they know, and we've got all night to do it.'

The Arkansas four looked wild-eyed and spooked. One pissed his pants. Walker figured that within an hour, Hogan would get everything he could from these guys and then he'd sanitise this place; maybe make it look like the Arkansas crew had taken out Sheriff Lincoln.

'Come on,' Walker whispered into Squeaker's ear, and took a step back, keeping his eyes on all in the room.

Hogan gave a tilt of his head in Walker's direction and he felt a sawn-off barrel press against the back of his head as he raised his Berettas.

'Put those two in the barn, tie them up,' Hogan said.

'We had a deal,' Walker said. He knew that even if he got by the guy behind him, the snipers out in the truck had a clear line of fire at him with their scoped rifles.

Hogan shrugged. 'I still got to decide what kind of future you and your little friend here have.'

46

'Some rescue,' Squeaker said, a tiny smile on her face, the movement making her wince against the pain in her lip. They'd injected her with something, and by her pupils Walker guessed it was some kind of barbiturate. 'You're trained at this sort of thing, right? Oh, yeah, Air Force, I forgot.'

'Ye of little faith,' Walker said. They sat on the concrete floor, dusty old hay forming a loose ground cover, the Sheriff's old ride-on mower, the half-rebuilt Corvette the only machinery in there. The two side walls held workbenches and tools in varying states of disarray and rust, as if the Sheriff had bought the place like this and never ventured inside except to get the mower.

One of the biker crew watched over them. He was armed with a pistol, a nickel-plated thing in his belt. He also had Walker's – the deputies' – two Berettas.

Squeaker asked, 'You're not worried?'

Walker said, 'Why would I be worried?'

'Ah, five minutes ago it was just me prisoner. Now it's the both of us. That's a worry.'

'That's not worth worrying about.'

'Why?' She looked to the biker at the door, who'd put the Berettas on the dusty boot of the Corvette. 'That guy has your guns. And his own. And a dozen friends.'

'Yeah, but I don't really rate them.'

'And we're tied up.'

'Not really.' Walker watched their watcher light up a smoke, turn his back to them and lean against the open doorway, looking out to the night sky and towards the house. Then he looked to Squeaker and spoke quietly. 'Who hurt you in there?'

'Gus.'

'Well, at least I don't have to worry about going into the house to break his arms.'

'He's dead, right?'

'You didn't see?'

'I closed my eyes when the shooting started, and covered my ears too. When I opened them, I just saw you. And in that moment I forgot everything else.'

'Aw, shucks, that's sweet.'

'How are you so calm right now? We're trapped here.'

'No, we're not,' Walker said, getting up. He pushed his arms up, then drew them in hard and fast towards his butt, pulling them outwards as he connected. Snap. 'Cable ties are for pussies.'

He crept up behind the smoking biker. The guy was on sentry, thinking that he and his armed buddies had everyone and everything covered, maybe even that their turf was about to double overnight after what had gone down here. That they'd won tonight and that was that.

Wrong.

Walker wrapped an arm around the guy's throat and pulled him in, hard, squeezing. When he couldn't squeeze any tighter, he flexed his bicep against the front and slightly to the right-hand side of the biker's thorax. He heard cartilage shatter. The guy's breathing was almost ending. His smoke-stained hands stopped grappling at Walker's arm, and then his legs gave out. Walker dropped him to the ground.

'Is he . . .'

'Unconscious, for now.' Walker took the guy's pistol and tossed it out into the field. He then used the guy's knife to cut Squeaker free.

Squeaker looked to their former captor. 'For now?'

'Well . . .' Walker looked down at the knife in his hand.

'Don't.'

'It'll be one less guy at our back. You think he'd hesitate to kill us?'

'But we don't need to kill him, do we?'

Walker looked down into her eyes. The toughness was all gone out of them, replaced by a young woman full of hope.

Squeaker said, 'Let's just get out of here. Okay?'

'Okay. Follow me.' He paused a moment, knelt at the biker, patted down his pockets and took his bike keys. Then he took the knife, the three-inch blade shiny under the light, and sliced the guy's boot at the back, deep, through the Achilles. 'One less guy at our back.'

•

Levine rang the bell again at the Sheriff's counter. No answer. No sign of anybody. But the place was open, and two squad cars were out front. The frosted-glass office marked 'Sheriff' was empty, lights off. Lamps were switched on at two desks out of six; one held a half-eaten sandwich and a cup of coffee.

'A town like this, how many cops?'

'Five, maybe six,' Woods said. 'About one per thousand population seems about right around here. Not much crime that doesn't get sorted out in their own Ozarkean way.'

'Ozarkean? I'm not sure that's a word,' Levine said, stepping around the counter and walking to a deputy's desk.

'It shouldn't be a word, if you ask me.'

'Don't be a hater of my southern kin,' Levine said.

'You're from New Orleans,' Woods said, checking the Sheriff's door – it was locked. 'That's different. Good people. Here's just weird.'

'Says the whitest man in America.'

'Ouch.'

Levine felt the cardboard coffee cup. 'It's cold.'

'Maybe they got called out. That sometimes happens to cops; they have to work.'

'Leaving their cars out the front?'

Woods shrugged.

Levine heard noise, like a TV or radio was on. 'Hear that?'

'What?' Woods said. They were quiet. 'I hear nothing. Come on, let's split.'

Then they both heard it. Noise, coming from out back.

47

Squeaker leaned on him. 'Thanks . . .'

'You're my partner in this,' Walker said. 'We're a team, and this is what teammates do.'

'Yeah . . .' she said, dazed, drugged. 'You're really tall.'

'Taller than most.'

'You're nice.'

'Thanks. You too.'

'Think I can see Philadelphia some day?' Squeaker said, her eyes out of focus. 'I want to – with you. Yes? I mean, you can take me there, show me around . . .'

'Sure.'

'City of brotherly love, right?'

'Yep.'

'So gay, am I right?'

Walker smiled.

'I want to see it!'

'You will,' Walker said, helping her to the bike. 'I'll take you there.'

'Promise?'

'Promise.'

'They signed the Declaration of Independence there.'

'They did.'

'And the Constitution.'

'Yep.'

'And the first White House was there.'

'That's right.'

'Philly cheese steak . . . what is that, exactly?'

'It's like a sandwich, a grinder of meat and cheese; they're good.'

'Grinder?'

'In Philly they call a hot sandwich a grinder and a cold sandwich a hoagie.'

'Okay. Well, I want a grinder. No. I want two.'

'Sure. My treat.'

'And a city-wide special – they have that, right?'

'Three bucks for a beer and a whisky. Helps dull the pain when the Eagles lose.'

'I want that. I want lots of that. With you.'

'Okay. Come on, let's go,' Walker said, picking her up and carrying her the remainder of the way.

'They're good, these grinders?'

'They're great. They taste like home.'

'Where're you from?'

'South Philly.'

'Tell me about it . . .'

Walker looked around at the cluster of bikes and then at the keys in his hand: two worn silver keys on a rabbit-tail keychain. 'Plenty of Italians.'

'I like Italians. I like their food.'

'My mother is half-Italian. Such a good cook.'

'Can she cook for us?'

'Sure, Squeaker.' Walker paused, then saw a bike with a rabbit foot hanging off a handlebar and headed for it. 'Come on,' he said. 'Time now to sit behind me and hang on tight – we're getting out of here.'

•

Levine went to the door set into the back wall.

'Maybe they're busy?' Woods said before she opened it. 'Could be a couple – a male and female deputy, you know, going at it. Could even be two guys. Either way, maybe you don't want to just burst it open – knock first.'

'When have you known me to knock?'

'Or two cousins? Think about that. That shit'll be burned into your retinas for years.'

Levine shook her head and opened the door. Past a kitchen space and storage area she saw another long back wall with internal door. And the noise was louder in here. Not a radio or TV. People. Two. Men. Calling out. This door was stencilled with small lettering: 'Holding Cells'.

Prisoners?

She opened the door and saw two uniformed deputies, locked up in their own cells, calling out for help.

48

'Where are we going?' Squeaker shouted into Walker's ear.

They rode the Harley Electra Glide west on Highway 60. Then they'd head north around the town of Willow Springs, arcing around and then coming north-east. A good 500 miles to cover to Old Pelts Road.

'Where we should have gone this morning,' Walker replied over his shoulder. He held the bike on the yellow line down the centre of the deserted road, keeping a decent screw on the throttle, easing off only over crests and through bends. It was a bike designed for a good cruise on the wide open American roads. Here, Walker made it do what he needed. 'We're getting to your cousin the long way.'

'Do you know how to get there?'

'Yes.'

'How?'

'The map at the Sheriff's.'

Squeaker yelled into his ear, 'You remember it?'

'I never forget a map.'

'Okay.'

Squeaker rested her face side-on against his back. Her hands were slipped under his zipped-up jacket, wrapped around his stomach. Clinging to him kept her warm, and the seat too was warm against the cold night from the heat of the engine. The Harley's headlight was fat and powerful, and the ride on the open road was like sitting back on a comfortable recliner.

Walker wound the engine out on the long straights, cruising at ninety miles an hour. It felt like it could sit on 200 without breaking a sweat. The gas gauge was three-quarters full, but he had no idea how far that would take them. There were plenty of towns along the way. With stops, and with slower riding through the smaller or twistier roads, it would take them six hours. They'd be at Old Pelts Road by sunrise.

•

'That's it, we swear,' Deputy Chester said. He was at his desk, his co-worker Jones next to him, the latter unable to talk after Walker's goodbye tap. Levine sat on the end of the opposite desk, while Woods leaned on the counter, watching and listening.

'Bullshit,' Levine said.

'I – we – promise!' Chester said. 'We just did what the Sheriff told us. Go ask him.'

'We will,' Levine replied.

Woods said, 'He's not answering his phone or radio.'

'Maybe that Walker guy got him – he's crazy!' Chester said.

Jones nodded, holding a bloodied rag to his face.

'No,' Levine said. 'You guys were crazy to lock him up.'

'And lucky to be alive, if you ask me,' Woods said.

'Old Pelts Road!' Chester said in a moment of clarity. 'That's where they asked to go, right?'

Jones nodded.

'Right. Right!' Chester said. 'That's where he'll be headed, for sure. Road's down, though, you'll have to go around, through Willow Springs and all. Take a few hours.'

'We can show you on a map,' Jones said.

'Do it,' Levine said, getting up. 'Show us. And then show us where the Sheriff lives, because we're going to have a talk with him before we leave.'

Chester looked to Jones. The latter shrugged.

'But – but you just want this Walker guy,' Chester said, 'and he's on the loose.'

'With our side-arms,' Jones managed to say through his wrecked nose and mouth. 'He's armed and dangerous.'

'He could have killed you two with a look,' Woods said.

'He's not travelling alone,' Levine added. 'He's with a young woman by the name of Susan Orlean. And you've not mentioned her once. So, I'm thinking that maybe the Sheriff knows something about her whereabouts, and that Walker broke out and locked you two idiots up and has gone to get her before continuing on. Right?'

Chester looked to Jones again, and they shared a look of defeat.

'That's right,' Levine said, satisfied. 'If you two don't give up all you know and help us until we're satisfied, you'll be impeding a federal investigation. You know what the Patriot Act allows us to do to guys like you who stand in our way? Hmm? Woods?'

'I hear Afghanistan's nice this time of year,' Woods said. 'We've got plenty of shit-hole black sites over there where these unpatriotic guys can be looked after real good. The boys in there would love some fresh meat. I mean, look at Jones here, he's a knockout with that red hair.'

'The Sheriff took her to his place,' Jones said.

'We can take you there,' Chester said.

Levine stood and tossed them keys to a cruiser. 'We'll follow you.'

49

Walker filled the gas tank at Willow Springs. Squeaker was steadier on her feet and made her way to the bathroom. He wondered what they'd given her. A hit of meth? Just a small taste? By the time she came back, Walker had bought them strong coffees and a bag of doughnuts, as well as a packet of jerky and bottles of water for the road ahead. He'd also purchased two woollen hats and two pairs of lined gloves made of some kind of animal hide. The coffee was hot, and the doughnuts gave him a sugar rush, waking him up against the night. He stashed their supplies into the cargo panniers on top of the twin Berettas.

Walker asked, 'Feeling better?'

'Yes,' Squeaker said, pleased with her new hat and gloves. 'And thanks.'

'For the coffee?'

'For saving me, dumb-ass.'

'Oh, that, it was nothing.'

'Seriously. You didn't have to come get me. You could have left me there, gone on without me.'

'No, I couldn't.'

Squeaker smiled. 'You don't need me to help you in any way. You have to see Dylan on Old Pelts, right? That's it, that's all we've got.'

'We've got each other.'

'I'm being serious.' She punched him playfully on the arm.

'Okay, well, first up, you're welcome,' Walker said, eating another doughnut in one bite. 'Second up, no, I couldn't leave you there.'

'Why not? There was nothing in it for you but danger – you could have been killed.'

'It'd take more than some greasy-haired middle-aged men to kill me.'

'Stop being a jerk about it,' Squeaker said, punching his arm.

'I'm not,' Walker said. 'And at any rate, you punch harder than any of those guys ever could.'

'Grrr!' Squeaker said, walking around the bike, stomping the stiffness and frustration out of her legs. 'I was being serious and nice and all.'

Walker gave her a second to cool, then said, his tone softer, 'I know. And I'm saying I *had* to. I brought you into this. And I let you tag along. And sooner or later I might need to leave you behind, but I promise you that it's not going to be in the custody of a group of depraved men, okay?'

'Okay.'

'Good.'

'I could have got away on my own, though.'

'I'm sure you could have.'

'I'm being serious!'

'Me, too. You're a strong young woman, Susan.'

'I'm not *that* young,' she said. 'And don't call me that.'

'You're stronger than you think you are, Squeaker. A spirit like yours – you could do anything you set your mind to. Don't ever forget that.'

'Yes, Ma.'

'And here *I* was being serious.'

Squeaker cut off her laugh and said, 'Yeah, I know. Thanks.'

'Come on, then,' Walker said, getting on board the Harley.

'Onwards we go?' Squeaker said.

'Yep,' Walker replied. He paused as a police cruiser went past the truck stop. It rode slowly, observing the cars and trucks parked in the car park, but then continued on its ride through town. 'The quicker we get there the better, for a whole bunch of reasons.'

•

'Sorry to wake you,' Levine said into her cell phone. She looked over to where Woods was walking a line with the deputies, their flashlights sweeping the grounds around the Sheriff's house. 'We've got a mess here.'

A moment passed before Grant responded. 'Is it Murphy – is he dead?'

'What? No,' Levine said. 'We're not quite there yet.'

'Not quite there?'

She could hear him shuffling out of bed, and then came the sound of coffee pouring into a cup. It was now 4.30am local time, which meant 2.30am back in San Diego. He'd be wearing his shorts. The house would be dark.

'As of yesterday we learned that there's another party looking for our man.'

There was a long pause, but Levine could hear Grant's breathing and could almost perceive an elevated heartbeat.

'Who?' Levine said. 'Who is it?'

'That guy. The lone wolf. Jed Walker. He's working with a UN investigative team.'

'Damn.'

'I went through his file. Ex-Air Force Spec Ops, and later a decade at Langley. Something strange happened after that – seems he recently dropped off the face of the earth for more than a year. I think he's going to be trouble.'

'Okay. I'll organise local law enforcement from my end, see that they hold Walker up.'

'Thanks.'

'So, what's the mess?'

'Walker is leaving a hell of a carnage in his wake. I think we need more boots on the ground here. And he may have a hostage, a young local woman.'

'Why would he have a hostage?'

'She's Murphy's cousin. We think he's using her to find Murphy, to flush him out.'

'Jesus.'

'More hands would help, boss. Walker is at least four hours on the road ahead of us.'

'And you think he can get to Murphy?'

'Yes.' Levine looked at the cut and snapped cable ties in the barn, and the scuff marks and half-pint of congealed blood on the ground. 'From what I've heard and seen, Walker's as capable as any man our armed forces has fielded. We've got reports and evidence of at least two dead local criminal types, along with the body of the local Sheriff.'

'Jesus,' Grant said again. 'Do you know where he's headed?'

'A place called Old Pelts Road, out in the boonies somewhere.'

'All right. This is what we're going to do. Start with putting out an APB on Walker. Have every cop in Missouri looking out for him. Our team of heavy hitters is in the state and will be en route. We've got to stop him, fast.'

50

They were pulled over on a side road in southern Missouri, for a pit stop and awaiting a call about directions. Menzil watched the sat-nav system in their rented Suburban, the blinking dot on Old Pelts Road. Estimated travel time was four hours.

'Okay, let's move,' Menzil said from the driver's seat.

He watched the four of them prep and repack their weapons. They were efficient. Well drilled. Hard men who'd never go soft. Killers.

•

Walker stopped the bike at the junction. The sign was pocked with bullet holes.

Old Pelts Road.

The middle of nowhere and none, Old Pelts was a single-lane gravel track winding up into forest that had a deep ravine at its centre, a river running through it. The sun was aglow beyond the mountains. The motorbike had just under half a tank of gas.

Walker put it into neutral and said, 'Quick pit stop.'

Squeaker climbed off, and then he did. His legs and arms were stiff, but the gloves and hat helped keep the warmth of his body heat in. It was coldest in the early mornings here, and it was that same cold that seemed to cut with a damp knife into his joints. He patted his face to get the blood flowing.

'So, this is the road,' Squeaker said. 'Now how are we going to find a guy called Dylan?'

'We stop at the first house we see and ask.'

'Okay,' Squeaker said. 'Jerky?'

'Sure.' He took a strap and chewed at it. The taste took him back to USO care packages they'd received in Afghanistan. And that reminded his senses of so much. The smell of sweat and fear and gunpowder and the funk of his unwashed buddies as they trekked through the mountains on long-range patrols. Of the deep, deep dark of cave systems and the crystal-clear cold nights with impossibly big skies. Of designating targets and calling in air strikes and the feel of percussion of the high explosives as they went off. Of mountains being reduced to little more than mounds of gravel. He'd heard a MOAB go off once. The Mother of All Bombs, the biggest thing that went boom in any nation's arsenal short of a nuclear device. He'd been a little over twelve miles away, and felt the force of the blast vibrate through him and ring in his ears for an hour after. He and his team watched and cheered as the B52 had flown in over the drop site. They'd sat around in silence after, as though they'd nearly witnessed the end of the world in the mushroom cloud that stayed in the air all day. Three miles closer to ground zero and they'd have all been permanently deaf. Three miles closer than that and the shockwave would have blasted off limbs and ruptured internal organs and membranes. Any closer and they would have simply ceased to be, just a grease spot on the ground.

'You okay?' Squeaker asked, passing him an open bottle of water.

'Yeah,' Walker said, drinking. The water was warm from where it had been stowed in the panniers near the bike's exhaust. 'Just thinking of another time and place.'

'The war?'

'Yeah.'

'Which one?'

'They're all the same.'

'Which place?'

'Hell.'

Squeaker paused, then asked, 'You think we did good over there?'

'Afghanistan? Sure. The Taliban were bad news, but the world should have acted a lot sooner. Iraq – well, that's a work in progress.'

'But we lost in Afghanistan, right?'

'It wasn't a win-or-lose scenario; it was never about that,' Walker said. 'We went in to change the system, and we achieved that. We got the worst of the despots and women-haters out; killed a lot of them in the process.'

'You killed over there?'

Walker nodded.

'How do you feel about that?'

'Just fine.'

'Fine?'

'Every Taliban I dispatched wanted to meet his maker, so I obliged.'

'How about Iraq?'

'I was there, for a while,' Walker said, pacing around and stretching his legs, then taking a Beretta from the stowage and checking it over. 'That was different.'

'About how we went in – all the WMD lies?'

'Yeah, that, and the rush to get in and do it. It just felt wrong. Sure, Saddam was a war criminal who got what was coming, and it was long overdue, but here at home the country got all whipped up thinking that we were there because they had some kind of hand in 9/11.'

'Not because we suspected he had WMDs?' Squeaker started in on a doughnut she'd saved, eating the pink icing off the top.

'He had WMDs. He used them, many times, against his own people. And the world didn't act then. We went in for oil and money and all that bullshit.'

'If he used the WMDs in the past, why didn't we find any – did he use them all?'

'Used them, sold them, destroyed them, who knows? A lot of them were moved out of the country when our government here was building a case for the world to go in there.'

Squeaker finished her doughnut and licked her fingers. 'Do you think Murphy thinks like you?'

'About what?'

'About how they were different wars and all that?'

Walker nodded, said, 'Yeah. All soldiers who served in both theatres think about the same. They were different wars, very different, in lots of ways. The only similarity was that there were guys wanting to kill you every day you woke up.'

Squeaker watched him for a moment before she spoke. 'Why'd you choose that kind of life?'

'Because . . .' Walker said, stowing the water bottle and tucking the Beretta into the back waistband of his jeans as he climbed onto the bike. He thought about his father. And his grandfather. And the stories they'd told him growing up. How that imprinted on him. 'My whole life I've had this thing where I can't just stand by idly and watch shit go down. It's in my blood.'

51

It turned out that it wasn't hard to find Dylan on Old Pelts Road, because the first and only house they came to, ten winding and climbing miles up the corrugated gravel track, was Dylan's. Walker pulled the bike to a stop and kicked out the stand. It was dead quiet but for a dog barking. He came round from the backyard. Doberman. Male. Bukowski-sized balls. He stood halfway between the arrivals and the house, barking and dribbling.

'What can I do for you?' Dylan asked, eyeing Walker and Squeaker and their hog of a ride parked out front of her timber house.

Dylan was a strong-looking woman, easily Walker's size, with square shoulders and thick forearms, and calloused hands showing beneath her rolled-up flannel shirt sleeves. She had a two-ton truck parked under a lean-to cover, dozens of four-foot gas bottles lined up and a huge industrial-sized gas tank next to the garage. Alongside that were smaller tanks labelled 'Gasoline' and 'Diesel'. Beyond the garage hundreds of rectangular hay bales, some wrapped as silage, were squared away under a long metal roof two storeys high and covering a half-acre. Stacked at the end of the clearing next to the tree line out back were enough foot-and-a-half lengths of firewood to burn until the end of days.

'My name's Walker. This here is Squeaker,' he said. 'We're looking for a guy, Squeaker's cousin, lives up hereabouts. Charles Murphy.'

Dylan looked at them, the legs of their jeans soiled and wet from the road leading up here.

'You said Charles Murphy?'

Walker nodded. 'Yep.'

Dylan looked to Squeaker. 'Your cousin?'

'That's right.'

Dylan was quiet a second, then asked Squeaker, 'What happened to your face?'

'It's nothing I couldn't handle,' Squeaker said, licking at the swollen and cut lip, the whole left side expanding in a welt.

'Can you be more specific about that?' Dylan asked, looking from her to Walker as though she might have to straighten out some kind of domestic-violence situation this morning before breakfast, and it'd make her day.

'Some bikers back in Mountain View,' Squeaker said. 'But we licked them good. But what's comin' for my cousin, if we don't get word to him fast? It's going to be a lot worse.'

'Right. Why don't you come in?' Dylan said, standing aside at her open door. 'Get warm, have a coffee, and we can talk some more.'

'Thanks,' Walker said, standing still. 'We're actually in a hurry.'

Dylan looked at him and her face didn't flinch at all when she said, 'You may be, Walker, but up here there's no hurrying. Especially no hurrying where *you* want to be going. Ain't no fast way to it, and ain't no quick way back. So, the least you can be is warm and fed before all that trekkin'.'

Walker asked, 'How far from here?'

'It's not the miles, it's the time,' Dylan said. 'Crow flies? Maybe twelve miles, though it could be fifteen or so. Call it half a day on the road, but.'

'This road?'

'Yep. I run supplies up for him and his clan, four times a year,' Dylan said. 'Takes the best part of a day there and back. I can only drive half the way, then I take the four-wheeler off the truck for as far as I can, then I dump it where I can't drive no more and he somehow hauls his supplies the rest of the way. I don't really know how, to be honest.'

'Doesn't sound too bad,' Walker said. 'We should get most of that way on our bike. We might buy some gasoline off you first, if we can.'

Dylan nodded and came down onto the porch. She was nearly eye level with Walker, maybe six foot two. She looked from Walker to Squeaker. 'Where you from, girl?'

Squeaker answered with her arms folded across her chest. 'Calico Rock.'

Dylan nodded. 'Murphy's from there. He's a good man. Good

family. Wants to be left alone. No other reason for him to be out there like that. His choice, you see.'

There was silence on the porch for a moment.

'We need to warn him,' Walker said. 'There's trouble headed his way, and it's the kind that will keep coming until they're sure there's not a breath left inside the man.'

Dylan asked, 'Who's his trouble?'

'It's a long story,' Walker said.

Squeaker added, 'The short answer, Dylan, is that we don't know.'

'Well, like I said,' Dylan said, standing to the side of her doorway, 'why don't you come inside and tell me. At least what you know.'

Walker smiled. 'I'm guessing that Murphy told you, if the day ever came that someone came to your door looking for him, that you had to screen whoever it was – and what? Send them off in the wrong direction?'

Dylan smiled. 'If I don't like what I hear.'

'You ever had anyone look for him?'

'No.'

Walker nodded. Silence again. He looked around at the forest. Wondered when they'd be coming. How many. How capable.

Squeaker moved closer to Dylan. She was at least a full foot shorter than the mountain woman and half her weight. She looked up and brushed the hair from her face, tucking it under her woollen cap.

'You see my face?' Squeaker said. Then she held out her wrists. 'And see here? The marks? This man here, Walker, he saved me from a group of men who thought nothing of tying me up, roughing me up – and worse. They were talkin' about what they'd do to me. And he came and got me and saved me – and he didn't have to do that. And he's going to do the same for Murphy, because there's a group out there, far, far worse than the ones who took me, who are going to get to him. And this mister doesn't have to do that, either.'

'Murphy's tough.'

'But as tough as he is?' Squeaker said. 'It's gonna be bad, real bad, because they'll sneak up on him and wait and maybe who knows? Like you said and like I know, he's got a good family up there in the forest. Murphy can protect himself but not all of them, not from what's comin'. This is my cousin, my blood, you get that? I've *got* to warn him.'

Dylan looked from her to Walker.

'Walker is as tough and crazy as Murphy ever was,' Squeaker said. 'He'll warn him and protect his family, I promise you that.'

'How'd you two get my name?' Dylan asked.

'O'Halloran's,' Squeaker said. 'The owner wrote it down for us long after we'd asked. He trusted us but not others in the room, and he was right about them too.'

'What'd this barman look like?'

'Ex-Navy,' Walker said. 'Girl riding an anchor tattooed on his arm.'

Dylan nodded. 'Yeah. Okay. That'd be Brian. He knows Murphy. And I know Brian too.'

'Please, Dylan,' Squeaker said. 'This ain't for us nor you, it's all for Murphy and his family. He doesn't know it and I'm sure won't accept it easily, but he needs our help, and at the very least, he needs our warning.'

'You tell me one thing, and you be right honest now,' Dylan said, distaste evident on her face. 'This thing, this threat of killin' a man and his family – has it got anything to do with drugs?'

'No,' Walker said. 'Nothing to do with drugs.'

Dylan looked at him. Then at Squeaker.

'I'll gas your bike,' Dylan said. 'And draw you a map. And you'll need to take some food, too, a blanket and tarp, and some matches and fire-starters to make camp, in case you get lost and I gotta go in tomorrow or the next day and rescue your sorry arses.'

52

Grant answered his phone on the second ring.

'AD Grant.'

'Grant,' Levine said. 'We're closing in on Murphy, and Walker, fast. We're headed for . . . what's it called, Woods?'

'Old Pelts Road.'

'Old Pelts Road,' Levine repeated. 'Should be there within a couple hours.'

'Send me GPS coordinates once you're there,' Grant said. 'I'll get that help I mentioned to you asap. They're already mobile.'

'Who've you got coming, boss?' Woods asked. 'Staties?'

'A good crew, don't you worry,' Grant replied. 'Just check in every half-hour, and when you're closing on Walker or Murphy, hang way back and let me know, and I'll have my team of heavy hitters go in and do their thing, copy?'

'Copy that,' Levine said.

'Good job, the both of you,' Grant said. 'You've done in a few days what other agents couldn't do these past couple of weeks.'

'What can I say?' Levine said. 'When you need the job done, you need a couple of agents with decent pairs of eyes to see what others can't.'

'Yeah, decent pairs,' Woods added. 'Big hairy ones.'

Grant said, 'Keep me posted.'

The call ended.

Levine shot her partner a look.

•

Walker and Squeaker followed the road for eleven easy but slippery miles, the hardest part being that the bike's tyres were made for sealed roads – and that was nowhere near what they were driving on. He got the bike up to third gear only once, and that lasted about ten seconds. Old Pelts Road was originally topped with gravel, now in most places washed smooth to the dirt, a type of clay that turned to sticky glue in the damp bends and gullies while the uphill climbs were corrugated and torn to shreds by the rains and whatever trucks used it.

Walker pulled up the Harley where the road stopped. An old abandoned mine shaft was boarded up. Some long-ago-rusted machinery stood forlorn. Hardwood timber stumps were all that remained of whatever buildings had been here up until fifty or so years ago. There was a clearing amid the old wreckage and newer growth, big enough for Dylan to turn her truck around. Splitting off to the east through the forest ran a track that could accommodate her four-wheeler or a serious off-roader, twin grooves of chunky tyres having worn through the foliage.

'Can we take the bike up there?' Squeaker asked.

'Yep,' Walker said. 'Hang on tight. I'll have to take it as fast as I can and keep it that way, so that we don't get bogged down and never get going again.'

'Good luck with that,' she said.

'If it tips over, go with it,' Walker said. 'Don't put out a leg or arm to try and stop it – this hog will snap your bones.'

'What am I, stupid?'

Walker felt her thighs tighten against his, and her grip on his hips moved so that she wrapped her arms around his waist. He tapped his toes to put the bike into first and gave it juice as he let out the clutch. Soon they were in second and he held it there, keeping the engine revs between five and six thousand RPM, the back wheel zigging and zagging over the broken and slimy track of mud and mossy ground cover.

The bumps and twists ran through the front shocks and handles and up his arms. The forest around them was quiet but for their bike and the sounds of birds. The bike was loud, the throaty roar pure and genuine. His father had had a similar road bike once, which he'd restored over several years in the garage. Walker smiled at the thought, wondered what had become of it, with his mother having been in assisted living for a few years and his father's 'death'. *Should I tell her about him?* Walker had not visited his mother, who had dementia, for a year. She had her sister, he knew, who still visited every day. But with every visit he'd managed before he had to leave the country, there was less and less of her present, which he'd never thought possible, for how do you lose more of something that's already lost?

Maybe David visits her. She'd be none the wiser. At the funeral, she thought she was just sitting in a park for an hour. He had to take her from the wake early, because she had started to fret and panic.

Meanwhile, his father had been out there, doing something that Walker himself would do soon after. Fake a death, because of Zodiac.

He knows about Zodiac because he was there, in its inception. He's implicated in it all the way.

But which side will he be on, in the end?

Then, Walker stopped thinking about anything but riding and applying the brakes. Ahead, the track ended.

53

'Can we stop?' Squeaker said, slightly out of breath. 'Toilet break.'

'Sure,' Walker replied. He was tired too, but not from the hike, which had been near-on an hour.

It was the tracking.

Murphy was smart. He'd taken many routes from the spot where the off-road-vehicle track ended and Dylan left the supplies. At least four distinct routes set off from that point. Those four soon split into several more, leaving maybe thirty paths in the realm of possibility.

It was tiring work to keep up, identifying which track seemed the freshest.

Assuming it was just Murphy making these tracks. For all Walker knew, there could be a few families out here, living in log cabins away from the grind of mortgages and microwaves and the American way, trekking it for that waypoint. Or hunting parties. Or scouts for logging companies. Or Parks people. Or conservationists. Walker did what he could – he took what seemed the freshest, reading signs from the tracks on the forest floor and the occasional broken branch and flattened plant here and there, the wrecked foliage not yet dried up or dying off. Whoever made this track had worn military-style boots, a couple of sizes smaller than Walker's, but they were deep, the wearer heavy, as he or she walked with a fully laden pack.

'We're going to get lost in here,' Squeaker said, having relieved herself behind a tall pine. She crashed down to the ground with a thump onto her butt, chewed a piece of jerky and drank from a water bottle. 'Dylan never saw Murphy's house. Never went beyond that point back there where her four-wheeler and our bike had to stop.'

'Yep.' Walker hadn't taken her hand-drawn map, just glanced at it and burned it in front of her. It had a vague indication of when she *thought* it might be.

'Yep. We're going to get lost.'

'Lost, no.'

'You really think you can find it? Out here?'

Walker nodded.

'Okay,' Squeaker said.

'Okay?' Walker asked her.

She nodded. 'I trust you.'

As he helped her to her feet, she fell against him. She looked up into his eyes. 'Walker?'

'Yes.'

'Jed?'

'Yes, Squeaker?'

'Do you think I'm pretty?'

'Sure.'

'But?'

'But nothing. You're cute.'

'Cute?'

Walker nodded. 'I've told you. You're too small and too young for me.'

'I mean after all this,' Squeaker said. 'I could come with you, to Philadelphia.'

Walker smiled. 'I don't live there anymore. Haven't for nearly twenty years.'

'Oh. Where do you live?'

'Nowhere, really.'

'Everyone lives someplace.'

'True,' Walker said. 'So, I guess I live in whatever place I'm at.'

'So, where are you now?'

'Some forest in Missouri.'

'Don't be a prick.'

'I'm being honest. I've not lived in the same place since I joined the Air Force. Since then, at least every year, sometimes several times a year, I've been in a different place, a different country, living out of a pack.'

'Sounds . . . awful. A person's got to have roots. Some place to settle.'

'You sound like my wife.'

'Wait – you're married?'

'Separated. Some people have no interest in that kind of life.'

'Marriage?'

'Moving around without much notice. Never being home.'

'What was her name?'

'Her name is Eve.'

'Is she pretty?'

'Yeah. Look, besides, you get used to it. The moving around. And doing the job I was in, I never had time to think about it.'

'Special Operations, for the Air Force.'

'Yep.'

'Then the CIA.'

'Yep,' Walker said, leading the way, following the tracks in the damp ground.

'And you still travelled a lot,' Squeaker said, 'with that job?'

'Yep.'

'Doing?'

'You could say that I specialised in wrecking things.'

'Like Casey did from his bathtub?'

Walker laughed hard and loud. 'Not really,' he said. 'I was working to make our country a safer place, at any cost.'

'Sounds . . . glamorous.'

'Sometimes it was, nice hotels and all that,' Walker said, pausing to crouch down, picking up the track again as it turned a hard left. 'Other times it was far, far worse than whatever the worst thing is that you can imagine.'

'Being in the bare mountains of Afghanistan,' Squeaker said. 'Hot summer days and sub-zero winter nights.'

'Yep. That and then some.'

'I've read a bit about it. And Murphy told me some stories. It sounded like an awful place.'

'It's not so bad. Though I've got to say, sometimes it's the funk that's the worst of it – yours and your buddies'. None of you showered or washed in weeks, hiking with hundred-pound packs day in and day out, feet so blistered you get blisters on your bones. And the worst? MREs.'

'Huh?'

'Military food. Ration packs. MREs – Meal, Ready to Eat. We'd often trade with another country's troops – it was more a novelty for them, getting what's loosely described as mac-and-cheese, or a hot dog, or apple pie.'

'I like apple pie.'

'This wasn't apple pie.'

'What was it?'

'Old Chinese newspapers was a popular guess.'

They walked in silence for another twenty minutes, Squeaker's footfalls crashing behind him, her breathing a constant rhythm. Walker knew that she'd be valuable, when they got there. That Murphy would be the hardest of all to win over, for an outsider – that it was then she'd prove invaluable. He just hoped she wouldn't feel used. Meeting her had been a gift, and he had realised straightaway what her later value would be: an instant in with Murphy. A guy like this, choosing to live out here, was going to take some persuading.

'Tell me about Eve,' Squeaker said, her tone too casual, as if she hadn't been thinking about this for the past twenty minutes. She dragged her feet a little as she walked, making a ruckus. 'Did you marry her young, before she knew your shitty job, then she divorced your ass while you were overseas?'

'Something like that.'

'Something like that?'

'We got married young,' Walker called over his shoulder. 'Separated a while back, when she got sick of my shitty job.'

'You never settled down, tried to have a family?'

'That was the idea we had. We bought a place in Texas, where she was from, where I was born.'

'What happened to that idea?'

'Zodiac happened. Something went down on an op, then I was forced to live off the grid trying to figure out why it happened.'

'It?'

'They tried to kill me, so I played along. I died for a year.'

'Oh. Right. That makes sense.' Squeaker trudged on behind him. 'I mean, no, it makes no sense at all. You *died*? For a *year*?'

'Shh!' Walker said.

He crouched to a stop. Squeaker did too, behind him. The loudest noise was her breathing through her swollen face. He calmed his heart rate. Closed his eyes. Listened. Movement, through the undergrowth, to his three o'clock.

54

Walker listened, hard. It was there, then it stopped. Then it started again. And stopped. Twenty yards away. Something or someone moving across their path, deliberately being cautious, brushing by branches and ferns and snapping the occasional small twig. Not coming near. Not moving further away. Parallel to their course.

Walker turned silently to Squeaker, his finger to his lips. She nodded, then he motioned with that same finger for her to stay put in that spot. She nodded again. Walker shrugged off his pack and put it down, gently, quietly. He took the Beretta from the back of his waistband and thumbed off the safety, then got to his feet but hunched over, keeping low, under the cover of the thickest of the forest undergrowth.

Moving as quietly as he could he left the path he was tracking and headed to his five o'clock, to go out and get behind the noise. He stopped three times to get his bearings, making his way closer with every cautious step. Every eight or nine paces he stopped completely. Watched. Listened.

The sound exploded around him. Fast, frantic movement.

Something fleeing.

He caught a glimpse of white tail. Deer. A doe and her fawn.

Walker stood to safety the pistol, then headed back to Squeaker. He found her sitting cross-legged on the near-invisible track, eating a ham-and-cheese sandwich that Dylan had packed for them.

'Nice,' Walker said, holding out a hand to help her to her feet. 'What if that was a bunch of bad guys and shooting started up and things got crazy?'

'At least I would have died with a full stomach,' Squeaker said, taking his hand and letting herself be lifted to her feet. 'Want some? Ain't no MRE apple pie, but it's good.'

Walker took the offered half-sandwich, shouldered his pack and ate as they walked.

Squeaker asked, 'What was it?'

'Deer.'

'Yum.'

Squeaker was silent behind him but for her footfalls and her jacket catching on branches. Then she bumped into him, because he stopped. He crouched down. She followed suit. Whispered, 'Another deer?'

'No.'

'What?'

'The track,' Walker said. 'It stops here.'

•

Menzil told his four-man team to stay in the car. There was another vehicle on scene, and he knew who they were.

He climbed out and approached the house, a timber-boarded thing that got plenty of upkeep from its owner, one of the more impressive women he'd ever seen: blonde hair cut as short as a businessman's, over six foot, broad shouldered. Standing up there on her porch, looking down at the Federal Agents standing by their Ford, she looked for all the world like some kind of Amazonian statue.

Menzil walked over to the two NCIS agents.

'You must be Levine,' Menzil said to her. 'And Woods. I'm Grant's point man on this. My team's in the truck, ready to roll.'

Hands shook. Levine appeared nervous. Woods looked hopeful.

'Where are we at?' Menzil asked them.

'We just got here ten minutes ago,' Levine said.

'This woman refuses to talk to us,' Woods said, not lowering his voice as Dylan watched on. 'We've asked her all kinds of ways about Murphy and Walker.'

'She's said nothing to you?' Menzil said, looking up at Dylan.

'Nothing,' Woods replied.

'But she knows something,' Levine said.

'She may know nothing,' Woods said.

Menzil looked to Woods. There was something there, he decided, in his eyes, in his demeanour. Woods was trouble. He was the type of agent who would grab hold of something and not let it go. He could be a problem. But Menzil had enough problems right now, and he knew that Woods might still prove useful if this Dylan woman refused to cooperate. It would be good to know that he had these two NCIS agents on hand if he needed them later.

'Okay,' Menzil said. 'We'll take things from here and close in on Walker, who's clearly closing in on Murphy.'

'Is Walker our man?' Woods asked. 'Is he the guy who's been killing all these SEALs?'

'I'm not at liberty to say anything about that,' Menzil said. He turned to his vehicle and motioned to the others. The four ex-US Army piled out, the SUV riding higher without the 900 or so pounds of flesh and bone weighing down the chassis. The four of them stood around the vehicle, their arms folded, their sunglasses on despite the dull overcast day, their combat boots and black tactical outfits – as well as their shoulder span and chest bulk – displaying that they were a Spec Ops outfit.

'What unit are you guys with?' Woods asked.

'Can't answer that either,' Menzil said. 'You know how it is.'

'No,' Levine said, challenging. 'How is it?'

Menzil smiled at her, then looked to the gravel ground.

'See that track in the mud?' Menzil said, pointing. 'Motorbike. Heavy. A couple of passengers. We know that Walker and Murphy's cousin were on just such a bike.'

'That doesn't mean that this woman spoke to them,' Woods said, looking up at Dylan, who seemed the same size and bulk as the four guys by the Chevy.

'See there?' Menzil said. 'The bike stopped there. There's the indent from the stand. And then the deeper groove as the tyre dug in. And it's not full of water, as the truck tracks are here, from yesterday's rain, so it was today. Walker was here, today, and he stopped the bike and got off it and then got back on and left. Headed up Old Pelts Road.' He stopped, looked from the NCIS agents up to Dylan. 'How am I doing so far, sweetheart?'

Dylan didn't reply.

'You two can go now,' Menzil said, looking back to Woods and Levine. 'We've got this from here. Thanks for your work.'

55

The track stopped at a round clearing the size of a large bedroom. The compacted ground was covered in a thick blanket of fallen leaves and pine needles. It was slightly elevated from the forest around it, and had a huge towering pine standing sentry at one edge. The bark of the pine to chest height was worn and scarred from buck deer rubbing their antlers on it. There were also a couple of deep scratches high up, from a bear's claws.

'There's other tracks here, on the ground, see?' Squeaker said, pointing to two distinct paths that cut through the small clearing. 'One of them could be Murphy headed to his place?'

'They're runs,' Walker said. 'Deer, rabbits, and whatever else calls this forest home. Not Murphy. Not any human. They're the tracks of little critters scurrying along the same path, again and again, generation for generation. It's their highway, their interstate. There's a lot of good eating to be had for anyone who cares to put a snare along these runs.'

'So, you're saying that whoever came in here on the track that we've been following,' Squeaker said, waving a hand around the clearing, 'that they, what – only had that one way in and out, the one that we just used?'

'Yes,' Walker said.

'Why?'

'Because this is a good hunting spot. It's elevated. And it's central to animal traffic – at dawn and just before, it'd be like Times Square here.'

Squeaker nodded. 'So, someone would hike all the way from that crappy off-road path to here, and then back there again?'

'Yes. I think so.' Walker looked into the forest. Nothing showing, though he knew that a log cabin out here would blend in and could be just fifty yards away and he'd not see it.

'So, we go back?' Squeaker said. 'Find another way?'

'Maybe,' Walker replied, still scanning their surroundings, taking it all in.

'Maybe?'

Walker made his decision. 'We've got about three hours of daylight left. There's plenty of dead wood here . . . It's as good a place as any to make a camp.'

'But what about finding Murph—'

'There's a quicker way to find your cousin than trying out more of these tracks through the forest,' Walker said, putting his pack against the tall pine. He chose a spot in the centre of the clearing and brushed it free of leaves with the side of his boot. 'We'll make camp here. Set a fire in the centre, here, lace the tarp up against that tree to sleep under.'

'Really?' Squeaker said, looking around and wrapping her arms around herself as though the prospect of sleeping out in the cold, even for an Ozarkean like her, was a step too far.

'You'll be grateful for the tarp when the morning frost and dew settles. We'll be dry, and I'll put a big log on the fire at night so that we're kept warm.'

'I meant, do you really think that we should make a camp out here?' Squeaker said. 'We could go back to the bike, camp there, set off again on a different path at first light?'

'No, this is better,' Walker said, already with an armful of kindling. 'You wait and see – I'll get us a fire going that will heat through to your bones.'

'It'll be seen, the fire,' she said.

'No, it won't, not in a forest like this, not unless you're right up close to it,' Walker said, now loading up with larger twigs and sticks. 'But it will be smelled, for miles, because this dead wood will burn fast and hot but with all this lichen it's going to smoke like crazy.'

Squeaker looked to the growing pile of wood and said, 'You want us to be found?'

'Yep.'

Squeaker cottoned-on, said, 'You want Murphy to come to us.'

'Yep,' Walker said, setting alight a ball of stringy bark fibres in the centre of a teepee shape of dry twigs. He blew at the glowing bark and the sparks climbed and the oxygen fed it to flames. The kindling took fast. 'I figure a guy like him will come looking, for peace of mind. And then he'll see us.'

'He'll see *me*.'

'Yep,' Walker said, standing and setting off to collect bigger firewood. 'And that should be enough for him to talk to us. My bet is he'll go out at or before first light, to check snares and maybe do a little shooting.'

'Well, just as long as he doesn't shoot *us*.'

•

'Who do you figure those guys were?' Woods asked.

'Who cares. It's their op now,' Levine replied.

Woods was taking a turn to drive and was averaging about forty miles per hour on the B-road. They were headed north-west, where they'd take a right onto the interstate and go all the way up to St Louis. From there they'd get a flight back home and be assigned to a new case. 'I'm looking forward to getting the hell out of here to someplace warm. I miss California weather. This shit's cut deep into my bones. My knees have been locked up all week.'

Levine was silent, watching the scene out her window but not really seeing it. 'I'm thinking we should stay on in a hotel in St Louis for the night,' she said. 'In case there's something we need to help wrap up.'

'Really? Like what?'

'We'll call Grant when we get there,' Levine said. 'See where that team is at. They may come up with nothing. We may be needed still.'

'Those guys have got this,' Woods said. 'If you ask me, they're SEALs, or recently retired SEALs, and Grant's got the NCIS using them to do all this protection work. They'll find Murphy and take him to safety. Nothing surer. Our work is done. We'll get a pat on the back for this, you know that? Probably get a few days off. I'm gonna get drunk and remain that way as long as I can. Poolside at some swank hotel where the chicks wear bikinis all day.'

'Walker's still out there,' Levine said, detached from her partner's dreams of a happier time and place. 'And Murphy's cousin, Susan.'

'A couple of civilians, working their way blind through the forest. So what? Forget them. They'll be in there all week, looking for a ghost.

Or if Walker *is* part of this, some kind of assassin, he's no match for those guys we just saw. No match. Those guys we just met – they'll track and find Murphy tonight. Maybe sooner. Probably have him and his family squirrelled away in some resort in Orlando by the morning, where he and the kids can stand in queues and sit on rides until all this bullshit blows over.'

Levine looked at him. 'You really think that?'

'Sure, why not?' He looked to his senior partner. 'Those guys are going in to protect one of their own from some terrorist scum. Hell, they've probably found the Murphys already, calling in a helo or Osprey to pluck them all out fast.'

Levine turned back and watched out her window, seemingly unconvinced. 'You really think Walker could be behind all this killing?'

'Maybe. It's not our brief,' Woods said. 'The boss will have that covered, you know that. It's probably being handled by the FBI, right? Terrorists, on US soil – that's their turf. They've probably got a hundred Homeland Security field agents in this state alone looking for the bad guys. So, relax a little, okay? We've earned it.'

'Turn the car around,' Levine said.

Woods glanced at her. 'What?'

'Go back. To Old Pelts Road.' Levine waited before going on, as Woods slowed the car to the shoulder of the road. 'That woman, Dylan. I want to be sure that whoever is tracking these bad guys is aware that she's the conduit between them and Murphy. Right? She needs to be protected until we know we've got Murphy.'

'She can take care of herself,' Woods said. He kept the car sitting there, pointed away, waiting. 'I mean, she could snap the two of us in half as soon as spit. We've done our job, and our orders were to hand over—'

'Tom, do I need to tell you again?' Levine stared at him. 'And don't you want to see who walks out of that forest for yourself?'

Woods's wise-ass antics were replaced by a reluctant respect for his superior. He checked the mirrors and made a U-turn, then headed back the way they'd come.

56

They had left their SUV behind the parked Harley, the motorbike's engine manifold still warm to the touch. After an hour's trek, the point man stopped and raised his hand, and they all came to a halt.

Menzil was in the middle, with two men ahead and two behind him. He had a Sig pistol in a hip-holster. The four men carried HK416s. Short-barrelled assault rifles, carbines really, reliable and rated extremely accurate to 330 yards.

Initially they had debated whether they would be more effective splitting into two teams, but they'd stuck together. After ten minutes on the first track they had stopped and turned back. A discussion among the four men had ended when one of them walked off down another track and two minutes later waved them to follow.

He'd found the tracks of Walker and Susan.

The point man had his hand raised, and soon the other four men knew why.

They could smell it.

Smoke.

•

Walker dragged the big log onto the fire. It was at least as heavy as he was, and one end had been hollowed out aeons ago and used as an owl's nest. It spat and crackled as the flames wrapped around its girth and consumed it, first searing the lichen and making it hiss all over as the remaining water vapour bubbled and steamed into the night. It was dark now, and the forest was beginning to wake around them. Bats had flown at dusk hunting the bugs in the air, and critters worked their way through the undergrowth, chasing each other in a death race in which the biggest was often the survivor.

'Should we sleep?' Squeaker asked, sitting close by the fire and watching as the huge log started to ignite through its hollow core, the fire sucking at the oxygen.

'You should,' Walker said. 'Under the tarp. I'll sit up, right here, keep watch.'

'Watch?' Squeaker said. 'For what – creepy-crawlies?'

'It's more what hunts them that I'm concerned about. Well, that, and whatever it is that hunts Navy SEALs.'

'Yeah, well, I think I'm safe with you watching out for us against men,' Squeaker said. 'But the meat-eaters that roam this forest? With those little popguns you've got? I'm not so sure. I'm talking red wolves, feral hogs, mountain lions and black bears. You sure you're up for the night watch?'

Walker smiled. 'You go sleep. Wrap yourself in the blanket. I'll keep the fire going – that'll keep away most of the wildlife. Except maybe the bears.'

He got up and put all their food trash into the fire. The packaging curled and disappeared in the blue flames of the hot coals. Squeaker shuffled over to the lean-to tarpaulin tent and wrapped herself in the heavy blanket. Walker kept close to her, a slightly offset line between her and the fire. He laid out the two police-issue Berettas, checking again that they were each chambered with a round. Nine-millimetre Hydra-Shoks. Good rounds for killing, Walker knew; the expanding notched jacket and hollow cores made a real mess of internal organs and created at least one big bleed-out wound. Nothing like what the military were allowed to use in international warfare, which was governed by the Hague Convention of 1899. Pistols in the military were a secondary firearm, a next-to-last resort in case the primary weapon, usually an M4 assault rifle, became jammed or ran out of juice and there was no time to reload as an enemy came within twenty-five yards. That's all a pistol was really good for, as far as Walker was concerned, and even then most soldiers and operators had little regard for the 9-millimetre Parabellum rounds that the military supplied.

Still, as a secondary weapon, it was better to go for a pistol with regular 9-millimetre ammunition than the tertiary option: the combat knife. Walker had never been a fan, and had never drawn a knife in a combat zone with the intent to kill. He'd used them against those who had brought them to hand-to-hand combat – like Seabass – but never by choice.

Walker thumbed the safety off the closest Beretta and placed it next to his hip. From his pack he took the small bottle of unlabelled whisky that Dylan had packed for them, and took a pull. It was a dark caramel colour, smooth but strong, well over the regular proof. He replaced the lid and settled in. He'd not had a decent sleep for a long time but felt he had this sentry duty covered. The thought of a black bear sniffing around their camp was enough to keep his eyes open until sunrise. The 9-millimetre would be like a mosquito biting a fully grown bear.

But Walker was wrong; he didn't need to stay awake all night.

Because what was hunting them did not wait until sunrise. It preferred to do its hunting at Zero-Dark-Thirty.

57

Menzil's team waited until the time of night was perfect for the task ahead. They didn't all have night-vision equipment, just two sets between them, but just enough light penetrated the forest from the fire and their eyes had long since adjusted to the scene. The four men worked in pairs, right in close, just behind the foliage of the clearing, from where Menzil hung back twenty yards. This was their end of the op. The pointy end. The grunt work. It had taken them over two hours to get this close, edging their way forward on their stomachs, brushing their paths clear of any twigs that might be dry enough to make a snapping noise.

In position, they waited until 3am to make their final move.

•

Walker's eyelids were heavy. He wished he had coffee, hot and strong. He ate the last strap of jerky at midnight, then another of Dylan's sandwiches at 2am. The bread was homemade, the outer crust chewy and hard, and the inside dense with rye and grains. At 02.30 he went for a leak, behind the big pine tree. At 3am he was standing by the fire, stoking the flames to ensure that oxygen made its way to the brightly glowing coals.

That's when it happened, and Walker heard the movement only *just* before he saw it.

•

Levine headed out of Dylan's house in a hurry and bent over the rail of the front porch to empty herself of all she had eaten that day. She kept retching until her throat was sore and dry and her eyes watered.

Woods had gone around the back of the house, after they'd been unable to rouse Dylan. Levine heard him make the discovery about a minute after she did; she heard him let out what she'd describe as a whelp and then he trudged through the place, the wooden boards creaking under his heavy forlorn footfalls.

He joined her at the rail.

'Jesus,' he said, over and over again, hyperventilating in the dead-cold mountain air.

Silence fell between them. Night had long set in by the time they'd arrived here and used their flashlights to illuminate the scene, along with the headlights.

'I guess we now know why the power was out,' he said. 'They must have cut it, before going in and . . . attacking her.'

Levine was silent.

'Walker, right?' Woods said. 'It must have been. He's probably got this Susan girl tied up on the back of the bike he stole; comes here, Dylan won't talk, won't say boo about Murphy or his location . . . so Walker does *that* . . . to make her talk.'

Levine remained silent.

'I mean, she was telling us the truth, then, when we drove through here before, right?' Woods said. 'That she'd not seen Walker? Somehow we got here before him. That track Menzil pointed out could have been made by anyone, right?'

Levine's hands were tight on the handrail, her knuckles white from the pressure.

'I've read Walker's file,' she said. Her voice was shaky. 'This isn't him.'

'You think this is some random coincidence? Some insane murderer passed through in the last few hours, since we first showed up?'

Levine was silent again.

'Who, then? The kill team that are after Murphy – you think they're on scene now?'

'We've seen who did this,' Levine said, standing upright, something resolving in her that made the shock and revulsion make way for professionalism born out of exposure to the worst. Yet nothing could have prepared her for that sight. 'We saw them. Five men. They got here and we handed this woman, Dylan, right on over to them.'

'What . . .'

'They did this, Woods,' Levine said, looking him in the eye. 'Those five guys who were here. You saw them. Four were killers. And the Menzil guy. They did this.'

'They're working for Grant. No way would they do *that*.'

'Maybe. How do we know that for sure? Maybe those guys killed Grant's real crew. Maybe they're in a ditch somewhere off the road, looking just like Dylan.' Levine watched Woods. 'And now they're out there, after Murphy.'

Woods said, 'And Walker?'

'He's involved in this too, until we learn otherwise.'

Woods's shoulders were hunched, his arms loose by his sides, his face lax. 'What do we do?'

'I'm calling Grant.'

58

McCorkell left the meeting at the FBI's Counterterrorism Centre and met Hutchinson at the kerb.

The FBI man said, 'How'd it go?'

'Good news and bad,' McCorkell said.

'Start with the good,' Hutchinson said, walking beside his boss.

'You and Somerville are stuck with me for the duration of this investigation into Zodiac.'

'That could be forever.'

'Told you it was good news,' McCorkell said, hitting the walk button and waiting at the crossing of Pennsylvania Avenue outside the Hoover Building. He looked at Hutchinson, the Special Agent near-on forty years old and as good an investigator as the Bureau had. 'What, you'd rather be stuck here in DC, behind a desk, looking into corrupt bankers and insider trading and sexting crimes?'

'Sexting crimes?'

'Feds don't look into that?' McCorkell said. He grinned, added, 'What about if it's a member of the House sending some junior staffer pictures of his, ahem, undercarriage?'

'Undercarriage?'

The walk signal changed. They crossed the road. McCorkell was fit for a man his age and he clipped along at a decent rate. Hutchinson was full of recent war wounds, and a swollen knee slowed the pace.

Hutchinson said, 'And the bad news?'

McCorkell shook his head, said, 'No-one back there believes in Zodiac. They think we're chasing shadows. Until we or Walker get some kind of proof of a pending terror attack, you and Somerville are all the resources that we're going to get from the Bureau.'

'Gee, well, shucks . . . that makes me feel real wanted. By them, and you.'

'Chin up,' McCorkell said, slowing for his colleague. 'Day's not over.'

•

Walker saw the movement coming from two directions at once: the north-east and south-east. Crashing through the foliage, within ten yards. Even with the darkness that spread from their position, he knew danger was coming in fast.

He dropped down to the Berettas, picking up one in each hand. The possibilities raced through his mind as he stayed on a knee and raised the pistols, applying pressure to the trigger of the unsafed left-hand weapon and thumbing the safety off the other. It wasn't bears – they didn't hunt in pairs. Unless it was a mother and cub, and this was some kind of tutorial in how to disembowel campers. Maybe mountain lions. He doubted wolves, not with the fire and all the easier prey that would be here. Unless they'd decided to camp in the middle of their territory. *Damn . . .*

He realised as the pistols came up in his straight arms that it could well be anything crashing towards them. And that their campsite, while elevated and clear, had those two critter tracks converging through it – it was a virtual smorgasbord.

An amateur mistake.

And what unfolded happened within three quick beats.

In the first second, Walker saw the form of the first man emerging from the north-east into the glow of the firelight.

Walker sighted his left-handed weapon on the guy's centre mass.

He spent the third second calculating whether or not to shoot. What if it was Murphy? At the end of that third second, the form of a man appeared to the south-east, rushing in.

Walker's right-handed weapon tracked the form.

Murphy was out here alone, wasn't he? Just him and his family – a wife and two or three kids.

Walker wasn't sure enough, with the light close in to him, to fire blindly at these apparitions. So, even as his fingers tightened on the triggers, he hesitated. Each Beretta with its safety off and the single-action pull required five-and-a-half pounds of pressure to engage the trigger mechanism and release the firing pin. As the pressure increased, he knew he could not afford to shoot Murphy.

And so, by the end of the fourth second, Walker was full of regret, for then two more men appeared, one behind each of the rushing figures. Their firearms became clear – HK416s. Serious military weapons. And commands were shouted from all angles:

'Down-down-down!'

Four barrels pointed down at Walker. The men were now in the small clearing, within five yards. None would miss. Their stance and demeanour showed they were men of considerable training, Special Ops of some sort. And American, by their accents. *Maybe this was the NCIS team headed in to help out Murphy? Maybe they're the good guys, and this will soon blow over as a misunderstanding, and by sunrise they'd all be on their way, together, to get to the rescue of the final SEAL.*

Walker held his hands up and out, the Berettas loose in his grips. Five seconds, beginning to end.

One of the operators came in close, his HK held just by the pistol grip, pointed close at Walker's face as he took the pistols in his hand.

'Clear!' the guy said.

Another rushed to Squeaker, who was sitting up and wide-eyed at the sight of four big men covering them with automatic weapons.

'Relax, guys,' Walker said to them, his hands raised, one knee remaining on the ground. 'I think you'll find we're on the same team here.'

'I doubt that,' a voice said. Menzil entered the clearing.

Walker's hopes faded fast on seeing the guy. This was no NCIS outfit. Ex-military led by an ex-cop. The kill team.

Menzil said, 'Tie them up, and be wary of *him*.'

The first operator passed the Berettas to another crew member and then took flexicuffs – proper riot-control ones – from a pouch in his combat pants.

'I take it you're not with NCIS,' Walker said as his hands were secured behind his back in a second. The guy didn't answer, just moved on to Squeaker and did the same with her wrists, then he patted them both down for weapons. Walker turned his attention to Menzil. 'They've got a team headed out here. You know that?'

Menzil was quiet. He took a cell phone out, and watched the screen while walking around and checking for a signal. Clearly he got none, for there were no towers in these dense, unpopulated mountains, and he put the cell phone away. He then approached Walker.

'You know where Murphy is?' Menzil said.

Confirmation: the kill team.

'Sure,' Walker lied. These were the guys who had gone after the other SEALs. Trained American ex-Special Ops, turned mercenary to hunt their own. Walker looked forward to hearing the final breaths emanate from each. 'It's just a couple hours' hike from here.'

Menzil looked at the campfire, then back to Walker. 'Then why'd you make a fire and set camp?' he asked.

'We didn't want to sneak up on a trained killer at night,' Walker said. He couldn't get a read on Menzil. He wasn't dressed in the uniform manner of the others, nor was he as fit and muscled. He was ten years older, mid-forties, and his skin tone and features were a mix of Central American. He had the look of a hard man turned office guy. Definitely a former cop. He dressed that way. He was in boots, but not combat boots. He wore outdoorsy clothing, not considered optimal for close-quarters combat. But Walker couldn't shake for the hundredth percentile that this crew wasn't the NCIS team. *Maybe Menzil was an ex-cop turned desk agent for the Navy, tasked with finding Murphy, and his men were some kind of ex-Spec Ops types who formed the paramilitary arm of the NCIS . . .*

Then, in a simple sentence, Walker knew that he was wrong. Very wrong. These guys weren't with the Navy. Nor any other branch of the US Government.

The sentence was spoken by the man behind Walker, the one who had taken the Berettas and then cuffed the two of them.

He stood next to Walker, looked to the leader, Menzil, and said, 'Menzil, you want me to kill the girl, or the guy?'

59

'No ifs or buts,' Grant said over Levine's cell phone, which was on speaker function and resting on the porch railing of Dylan's house. 'My guys have got this. You two move on.'

'Boss,' Woods said, 'I don't think you understand what we've just seen in—'

'Agent Woods,' Grant said, a little louder. 'Get yourself together. We're dealing with hardened terrorists here, remember? They've killed SEALs, and done only god knows what to civilians like what you've just seen there. So, listen up: Levine, Woods, get your asses back to St Louis, as planned. *Now.*'

Levine paused, the scene from inside the house still reeling through her head.

'We've got a crime scene here,' Woods said into the still night. 'Murder, at its worst. We need to wait until state police show up. That's procedure. Sir.'

'Have you called the state police yet?' Grant asked.

'No, you're our first call,' Levine said, getting herself together.

'Good, leave it to me,' Grant replied. 'Local PDs will make a mess of this. I'll have the FBI out of St Louis get there. Hell, I'll get their whole St Louis Field Office down there, soon as possible.'

Woods said, 'This scene needs to be preserved until then.'

'I'll arrange a deputy to sit on the porch and wait for the Feds,' Grant said. 'But I need two of my best field agents back on the road. You read me, Agent Woods? Levine?'

'Get to St Louis,' Levine said, looking to Woods. 'We hear you.'

'That's right,' Grant said, his tone consoling. 'You need to be there when we bring Murphy's family in. That's what you can do. Meanwhile, trust in our team. They'll beat this Walker to the Murphys.'

'Where in St Louis?' Woods asked.

'I can't say yet,' Grant said, his voice now optimistic. 'Just get back through to St Louis, rest up and then be ready to fly back to base by nightfall.'

'Copy that,' Levine said.

'I know this has been hard, but you're both doing a fine job,' Grant said.

Woods said, 'But, I mean, what if there's another force out here that we've yet to even know about, torturing, killing—'

'Walker did that, in that house,' Grant said. 'You read that same file I did. The guy was a killer for our government for nearly twenty years. One of the best we had. Think about it. You think he now just does needlepoint? *He's* got to be the one who's been hunting these SEALs.'

Woods looked to Levine, said, 'But that crew you sent in, they might be in—'

'Agent Woods, those guys are doing their duty, as sanctioned under the Patriot Act, to defend this country at all costs and against all threats, foreign and domestic. They'll get Walker, don't you worry.'

'What if . . .' Woods looked to Levine. She looked hard, like she knew what was coming, what he was going to say, and that he shouldn't say it, but he did, anyway. 'I was maybe thinking that those guys we saw might not be who you think—'

'Agent Woods, I'm going to stop you right there,' Grant said. 'Do you seriously think we're in the business of killing US civilians?'

•

'Kill the girl,' Menzil said. 'We might need this guy to lead us there.'

'She's too valuable, you idiots,' Walker said, his hands on his head while he rested on his knees by the fire, at gunpoint. 'She's Murphy's *cousin*.'

'So?' Menzil said.

'So,' Walker said. 'You lose her, you lose Murphy. If I take you to Murphy and something goes wrong, you'll *need* her.'

Menzil said, 'How do you figure?'

'How do I figure?' Walker said, looking from Menzil to the others, his expression as though Menzil was not seeing what was obvious. 'Without her, you're screwed.'

'Why?' Menzil asked.

'She's a *bargaining* chip,' Walker said. He evaluated the guys: Menzil had ex-cop written all over him; the four with the HKs were ex-military. 'Murphy will die in a fight out here to protect his family, killing his share in the process – but he won't jeopardise Susan's life if he can help it. Hell, why do you think I've brought the kid along for the ride?'

Walker looked to Squeaker. She looked at him, all kinds of betrayal written on her face. *Good* . . .

Menzil shrugged. 'Fine. Then we kill you,' he said. 'And she takes us to her cousin. Easier that way. We can hold a gun to her head and have him come out of whatever hidey-hole he might be in.'

Walker shook his head. 'That's just dumb in about five different ways.'

'Oh?' Menzil said, his hand rested on the butt of a Sig automatic in a thigh holster.

'Firstly,' Walker said, '*I* know where Murphy's cabin is – *she* doesn't.'

'Is that right?' Menzil said, looking at Squeaker.

She nodded.

'And do you really think you're going to sneak up on Murphy – get in such close range that he can either see or hear that you have a hostage?' Walker said. 'Forget it.'

'But you could?' the guy behind Walker said. 'Why you and not us?'

'You bet I could, bud,' Walker replied. 'Murphy's got more traps and defences set up than you could ever find, all five of you, in broad daylight, all day long. Nope. You'll be triggering them while he's out hunting you down from behind, slitting throats one by one until there's just your point man to get sight of the cabin from a quarter-mile out, at which point a round from Murphy's M110 will delaminate your skull.'

Walker looked at the faces of the four operators standing around him. He could see they were messy and grubby from where they'd lain prone and shimmied their way in towards the camp over a matter of hours. Professionals. Well trained. But they had – especially the questioner behind him, he knew from a glance – something written on their faces now that they didn't a minute ago: *doubt*.

'You know that's what happens when a jacketed seven-six-two round from the one-ten hits your head, right?' Walker said, keeping the fear and doubt rolling. 'Close range like that, the kinetic energy takes the bullet right through, small entry and exit; the bullet doesn't even get the resistance to de-form. But the sheer force of the shot? It sucks the skin right off your face and pulls it through the entry hole and drags it out the back. Completely skins the skull down to muscle and bone. *Delaminates* it. I've even seen an insurgent in Iraq survive that, sure – for a few hours, with immediate medical care. How long do you think you'll survive like that out here?'

Walker could see that he'd got to them now. Three of the operators were looking behind them, all of a sudden aware that they were prone and standing in a clearing that was well lit, the forest around them deep and dark and holding all kinds of secrets. The guy with the cuffs looked to Menzil for direction.

Menzil looked at Squeaker. He still had murder in his eyes.

60

'I'm going to ask you again,' Menzil said to Squeaker, then his voice raised as he said, 'Do you know where Murphy's cabin is?'

Squeaker shook her head.

'What's that?' Menzil asked. He held her chin in his fleshy hand. 'Answer me!'

'No!' Squeaker said. 'I don't know where it is!' She calmed a moment, looked to Walker, settled. 'I've never been out here.'

Menzil watched her face for a lie and found none.

'Okay, Reece?' Menzil said, leaving Squeaker alone. 'We keep them both, alive, for now. But we're not taking two prisoners to a potential gunfight. Steve, you keep the girl here, as insurance.'

Steve nodded. Reece looked uneasy.

'How far to the cabin?' Menzil asked Walker.

'Two hours,' Walker said. 'In daylight. It's insane terrain. I have to follow the track, and it's impossible in the dark. So we have to wait for sunrise.'

Menzil took the two night-vision devices from Steve's pack and thrust one pair against Walker's chest.

'We go now,' Menzil said. 'You'll lead, Walker. And you know what? Reece is *right* behind you – you try anything, it won't be a bullet peeling off your face, you understand me?'

'Sure,' Walker said, standing up. He was more than a head taller than Menzil, but Reece had Walker's measure, maybe with another thirty pounds of muscle through the neck and shoulders, the kind of bulging build that only came with lifting serious amounts of iron and injecting disastrous amounts of steroids and human growth hormone.

Walker took the night-vision goggles. They were civilian spec, which confirmed that these guys were not *currently* on the government's dime, despite their fancy guns. And good as they might be, they weren't the best – only the government threw money at the best. That was a small consolation. On the down side? The four guys under Menzil's command had started to look uneasy.

'If we're not back in five hours,' Menzil said to Steve, 'kill the girl, then follow our tracks.'

Steve nodded.

'Quick word?' Reece said to Menzil, and they moved over to the tree. When they spoke, it wasn't hushed; the space was merely a show of respect for the chain of command.

'We're due in St Louis later today,' Reece said. 'We have to be ready and prepped by 17.00 for the demonstration at 17.30.'

'If Walker's telling the truth, we'll be in and out of here in four hours,' Menzil said. 'Right?'

'Maybe, but only *if* he's telling the truth about a two-hour hike,' Reece said.

Menzil looked over.

'Two hours?' Menzil said.

'Two hours,' Walker replied. He could feel Squeaker looking at him. 'In daylight.'

'Okay,' Menzil said, looking back to Reece. 'How long will you need at Murphy's cabin?'

'Ten minutes should do it.'

'Good,' Menzil said. 'So, five hours should cover it, round trip with some fat built in. We hustle. We head back via here.' He looked to Steve. 'Remember, if we don't show in five hours, kill her. Then follow our trail and meet up with us. You'll either find us coming back or you'll help us out.'

Steve nodded.

Menzil said, 'Gives us time to get back to the car.'

Reece looked to his guys, then to Menzil, and nodded.

'Let's roll,' Menzil said, looking at Walker.

Walker mouthed a 'don't worry' to Squeaker. It wasn't ideal, leaving her alone like this, but he figured she was safe with this guy as long as she had some perceived value, as long as Murphy remained unfound.

Already, Walker had got the four capable men down to three, leaving one with Squeaker. Three against one was better than four against one. Escape was do-able with those odds. Four capable men against one unarmed was near-on impossible. And as for Menzil – well, Walker had no doubt he was a threat as long as he had time to draw the silenced Sig from his thigh holder. But barring that, he knew he had him cold – Menzil was the type of soft-target guy who maybe dreamed as a teen of being a Special Forces operator but didn't have the mental or physical toughness to do what it took to get there.

And Walker had one of only two sets of night-vision goggles. And that meant he had just over three hours of darkness that he could use to his advantage.

Now he just had to find a way to Murphy's cabin in the woods. And somewhere along the way he had to figure out what to do about these three capable guys.

61

'Agent Woods,' Assistant Director Grant said over the agent's phone. 'How are you holding up?'

'Nothing some therapy can't fix,' he replied. They were stopped at a roadside diner while Levine used the restroom. 'And maybe a paid holiday. Somewhere sunny and warm. With nothing bloody in sight.'

'Okay, I think we can sort that out,' Grant said, a smile evident in his voice.

'You texted me to call when I was alone?'

'That's right,' Grant replied. 'Now, Tom, I want you to listen to me very carefully, and keep this to yourself, because I believe that your senior partner may now be operationally compromised. You read me, Agent Woods?'

'Yes, sir . . .'

'Good. Now, here's what I want you to do: get Levine to St Louis at all costs, and keep her there, as focused and stress-free as you can, until I give you further instructions.'

'Got it, boss.'

•

Walker decided that Reece had to go first. It was nothing personal, but he had the other set of night-vision goggles, and he was closest in behind Walker. There was another operator right after him, Stokes, following close for the limited visibility in the dark night, moving more through hearing his teammate ahead than seeing him. Menzil was fourth in line, and then the third of the ex-military operators, Duncan, took up the rear. The last man carried a backpack, the sheathed barrel of a sniper's rifle poking out one end.

The track that Walker took them along was man-made, but it did not feel as fresh as the track that had led to the clearing. It was an offshoot of that track, fifty yards back towards the spot they'd all come from. Walker hadn't bothered with it when he and Squeaker had headed for the clearing, because it was obvious that it had not been used in at least a week. There was the occasional footprint and broken branch, but nothing worn into the ground that would show it to be a path used more than once or twice. But he followed it. It headed along a ridge in the hillside, the ground underfoot turning to bare loose rock in places where small landslides caused by heavy rainwater and fallen old trees had cleared paths down to a creek in the gorge below.

Walker moved at a comfortable pace. Reece was never more than three steps behind him; he slowed when Walker slowed, stopped when he stopped, moved as he moved. Clearly he had done this before, plenty of times, probably in the mountains of Afghanistan, which weren't so different from the feeling here except that the air there was thinner and the cold was different. There, the cold stung your lungs and cracked your lips and burned your eyes dry. Here, it seeped into your joints and ached away at old injuries and wrapped around your spine like a slow-moving glacier.

'Pit stop,' Walker called, halting.

Reece pulled up without a word.

They'd been moving for an hour, and although Walker didn't need the break he did need to take every opportunity he could find. He turned his back to Reece and took a few paces to the edge of a drop-off and pissed with the breeze that flowed down the mountainside.

He heard Reece unzip. He saw with his night-vision goggles that the guy was in more urgent need of this break than he was. Walker had maybe six, seven seconds of Reece being distracted, his mind on the task of relieving himself, his attention and hands elsewhere. Stokes was five yards back, stopped and taking a water flask from his pack. The path was too narrow for Walker to see past him. Stokes was near-blind in the dark, and his eyes glowed wide in the iridescent green of Walker's night-vision.

Walker didn't zip up his pants or take his hands from the region. He simply turned to Reece, took one backwards side-step to close the distance and planted a boot into his back. Reece flew off the edge of the mountain pass and was turning through the air to face them and yell and bring up his HK on its shoulder strap as though to fire at Walker while he fell through the air – when he hit a branch of a sturdy pine. It was a mid-back impact and Reece never saw it coming. It had been a sixty-five foot drop. The sound was a heavy thud; the big branch held, but Reece's spine didn't. Walker saw him, through the green vision, fall from the branch, head-first, slowly, his feet disappearing in a whipping motion as his legs cartwheeled over the branch. That was the last he saw of Reece.

But not the last he heard. The sound of the guy smashing down through another sixty or so feet of intersecting branches was incredible, as loud as a rock concert in the still mountain air.

One down. Three to go.

62

Stokes charged at Walker, HK raised at where he imagined his head to be. Menzil and Duncan were right behind him.

'Hands!' Stokes screamed at Walker.

'Okay,' Walker said, zipping up his jeans and raising his hands above his head.

'Where's Reece?' Menzil demanded.

'He went over!' Stokes said. The guy was pointing animatedly over the ravine.

Menzil looked down into the black fall.

'He's over the fucking edge!' Duncan said.

'Reece!' Menzil yelled over the edge of the ravine. '*Reece!*'

The sound echoed through the gorge and Walker could see that Menzil regretted it as soon as the sound escaped his lips. When no response came from their disappeared cohort, Menzil shoved by Stokes with his firearm raised and closed on Walker.

'What did you do?' Menzil said.

'Nothing,' Walker said. 'I was taking a leak. Reece was too, and he must have lost his footing – he fell, hit a tree on the way down. *All* the way down. Surely you heard it. Boom, boom, boom, all the way down.'

'Bullshit!' Menzil said.

'Your buddy here can vouch. He saw,' Walker said.

Menzil turned to Stokes and asked if it was true. For a second Walker thought that this was a chance to take down the three of them – charge them, shove them off the path to meet a similar fate to Reece's, using the opportunity while they were shocked and preoccupied, all while they were forced into a position of one man across and three deep. But it was that depth that made Walker wait. Duncan, who carried the large pack and the sniper's rifle, was a good eight paces away, and he'd have plenty of time to back-step, draw his pistol, aim and fire as Walker dealt with the first two.

So, not now.

Soon.

One down, two to go, and then Menzil.

'I – I saw Walker was takin' a leak when I got here,' Stokes said.

'You really think Reece would have slipped?' Menzil asked.

'I – no, but – maybe.' Stokes looked from Walker to the ground underfoot. 'It's real loose here. Crumbling. It's possible.'

'Shit.' Menzil looked from Stokes to Walker, and then over the ravine, which to him by the thin moonlight must have looked like a bottomless black abyss. 'We've got ropes, right?'

'Right,' Stokes replied.

'Go down, check on him,' Menzil said. 'If he's gone, take the night-vision.'

'Do we have time for that?' Duncan, at the rear, asked.

Menzil was silent.

'If he's not dead,' Walker said, 'he's got a broken back. I turned when I heard him slip – I saw him hit the first branch, hard, back-first. That branch was big, nearly a foot in diameter, and it held. His back took the force of that impact. And it's a hell of a drop.'

Menzil stared in Walker's general direction, then turned to Stokes.

'You're going down there,' he said.

'It's a long way, in the dark,' Stokes replied. 'And we're on the clock.'

'Take Walker's goggles,' Menzil answered.

'It'll chew up time,' Stokes countered. 'Maybe a couple of hours. Then we'll have lost our tactical advantage of being in place at the cabin by sunrise.'

'Who's leading this?' Menzil said.

'With due respect, we were hired by your boss to do a job, and to get it done on time,' Stokes replied. 'Reece knew the risk; it came with all those zeros on the pay cheque. And besides, that'd leave just the two of you up here, in the dark, with him. You want that?'

I want that, Walker thought. But he could see the wheels in Menzil's mind turning over.

Menzil turned to Walker. 'How far from here?'

'We're a quarter of the way,' Walker said. *And I'm a quarter of the way through your guys.*

'Okay,' Menzil said. 'Lead on. And not too fast. We stay close. No more than a few feet apart. And if you do anything stupid, Stokes will drill a round through your arm. And that's just the start. We'll shoot bits off you, piece by piece, until Murphy hears your screams and comes looking, right into Duncan's scope. Got that, Walker?'

'Got it,' Walker said. 'Follow me. And watch your step.'

63

Squeaker knew that against this captor, she had little to no hope of escape. He'd bound her moments after the others had left and had been silent the whole time since, alert, ready to respond to any threat he heard or saw. He kept the fire going at low-light embers, little more than immediate heating. Her only hope, she knew, was of Walker returning before deadline. She watched the guy, waiting for that moment. If he came at her then, with a gun or knife or whatever, she'd do what she could to survive. Until then, she knew, she had to wait. And hope.

•

Twenty minutes later Walker lost the track and stopped.

'What is it?' Menzil called out.

'Okay,' Walker said, facing those behind them, his voice as quiet as the breeze. 'First thing, you can't call out like that, because we're getting close to Murphy and the mountain air is thin and sound travels like a bitch, okay? I'm saying that because as good as your two boys here may be, Murphy's better – and we're playing in *his* sandbox.'

Menzil was silent. Stokes and Duncan too.

'Secondly,' Walker went on, 'you're moving too loudly, Menzil. Not you, Duncan – you're light on your feet, careful with how you use your body through the bush. Same goes for your retarded buddy – Stokes, was it?'

'Fuck you, pal,' Stokes said, his voice just above a whisper.

'Great, glad you're all listening to my suggestions,' Walker said. 'And last thing, we have to double back. About five minutes.'

'What?' Menzil said, his voice quieter this time.

'Five minutes back,' Walker said. 'There was a branch of this track that led to the left; we were meant to take it.'

'This is crap,' Duncan said. 'I've been watching Walker close; he doesn't know where he's going.'

'Is that true?' Menzil said to Walker.

Silence for a while.

It was darker where they were now, and Walker could see that Menzil had a heavy flashlight in his hand. He'd not used it yet for illumination, but it would make a decent club, and it could also temporarily blind Walker through his night-vision goggles if it was switched on and turned his way.

'Is that true?' Menzil repeated.

'What do you think?' Walker whispered. 'Maybe I *don't* know where we're going. Then again, maybe I know exactly where we're going, and I've walked you around in a circle and you're about to be gang raped by a family of hogs that live near here.'

'How do you know?' Duncan asked Walker. 'How do you know where Murphy lives? If his own cousin doesn't know, how is it that *you* know?'

'I've been there before,' Walker said. 'I helped him build the place. Log by log. Steel sheetroof – even doubled up on the roofing screws, so guys like you can't pry through the ceiling.'

'I'm calling bullshit,' Duncan said. 'He's lying. We should cap him here and now, for Reece. Then we track back to the clearing and wait for first light and find the path to Murphy ourselves. Hell, we could start on his cousin, get her squealing real loud, set a trap for Murphy, then – *blam.*'

'How *do* you know where Murphy is?' Menzil said to Walker. 'Time to be truthful, or these boys will get their wish.'

No-one spoke for near-on a minute. Stokes raised his HK at Walker's forehead.

'Okay,' Walker said. 'Someone told me. Someone who runs supplies to him and his family.'

Stokes lowered his weapon.

'Dylan,' Menzil said. The corners of his mouth moved to a grin, misshapen, sinister in the green glow of Walker's vision. 'She ran supplies to Murphy. But only to the end of the off-road track.'

Menzil paused. Walker felt a weight in his stomach. *These guys had found their way here because they'd paid a visit to Dylan too. That was the only way. How did they get to her? Not from a note passed at a bar. Maybe they got information somewhere along the way that pointed to Old Pelts Road and then called in to the first place that they came upon. It may have been blind luck.*

'Oh yeah, Dylan,' Menzil said. 'She put up a fight, that one. Tough. Tough as a man. Fragile as a man too, when it comes to flesh meeting a knife.'

Menzil pulled a black anodised combat knife from a sheath next to the holstered Sig. Only the thin sliver of the sharpened edge caught the light of the moon through the tree canopy above.

Something settled in Walker. The anger that came from knowing that these guys had cut Dylan, killed her for what she knew, steeled his thoughts and actions. The next hour was the last hour that any of these men would breathe the same mountain air as he, and their screams would be heard interstate.

'Well, she was tough,' Walker said. 'Tougher than any of you, because clearly she went to her grave keeping the location of Murphy's cabin a secret. You idiots were too dumb to get it out of her. Really? Killing her, with a knife? Before you got what you needed? Dickheads. And you know what? I'm no different from her, so take your best shot with that blade. I can promise you that you and your buddy here'll be dead before your screams end. And the guy up the back might get off a shot, he might bring me down, but then it'll just be him and Murphy, all alone in the forest. Oh yeah, boy, you'll have one of the most decorated Navy SEALs known to history hunting you down, chasing the echoes of your buddies' screams.'

Menzil looked at the knife in his hand.

'What's it going to be, office man?' Walker said. 'You want me to give you a colonoscopy with that knife, or you want to backtrack five minutes and get on with the job?'

Menzil re-sheathed the knife. 'Keep a gun on him,' he said to Duncan. 'If he even thinks about something smart, delaminate *his* skull.'

'The five-five-six round doesn't do that, fool,' Walker said, pushing past the three men and heading back the way they'd come. He wasn't a fan of knives for combat, not at all, but given the images screaming in his mind of what had happened to Dylan, he looked forward to becoming a little more accustomed to using one.

64

'How long do we give him?' Woods said.

They sat in the car, out front of Dylan's dark, lifeless house. The Ford Taurus's engine pinged and hummed, the heater on low, chasing the heat to the outer layer of the windows in a battle of nature versus Detroit engineering.

'St Louis,' Woods said. 'That's what Grant said. Get to St Louis.'

'Give it some time. See who comes walking out of the forest,' Levine said.

'But how long? That could take hours,' Woods said. 'The Feds will arrive first thing in the morning to go through this crime scene.'

'Murder scene,' Levine said, her voice detached, as though the images were unshakable in her mind. 'Torture scene. What happened here . . . it wasn't necessary.'

Woods looked at her. She appeared tired as hell, as though the past twenty-four hours of chasing a ghost across the country had hit her all at once. 'This place is going nowhere, Levine. Let's split. Get to St Louis. Rest a few hours. See what's what in the morning.'

Levine watched him, thought about it, looked around the dark cold night. Finally she said, 'Okay. You drive.'

●

'Sh!' Walker said.

The three men behind him stopped.

'Listen,' he said, noting the sound of falling water.

'It's been just over two hours,' Duncan said to his boss. 'We should be there by now. The sun's just an hour away.'

'Where is it, Walker?' Menzil said.

'About ten minutes beyond the water,' Walker said, as he crouched down. He saw footprints beneath the loose leaf litter leading off the main path but he stood quickly, not letting on that he had found a path that Murphy – or someone else – used regularly. If it was

Murphy, they were close now – the path was well used and no care had been taken to conceal the footprints or disturbed foliage; as if the user presumed that no-one would track him this far; as if the user was close to home.

'That way?' Menzil said, pointing.

'Yes,' Walker said, hoping that he was not leading three armed brutal killers towards an unsuspecting family.

'Ten minutes?'

'Yep. We're close.'

'Okay,' Menzil said, looking at Duncan but gesturing towards Walker. 'Kill him. Make it quiet. And don't damage those night-vision glasses.'

Duncan pulled out a HK pistol and screwed in a long silencer.

65

Levine had said nothing on the ride so far, a good hundred miles. Woods was behind the wheel, keeping the Ford about five over the speed limit at all times.

'What'd he say to you?' Levine asked Woods.

'What's that?'

Levine looked across to him. 'What did Grant say to you, about me?'

Woods looked uneasy. 'He said to watch out for you.'

'Watch out for me?'

Woods nodded.

'What's that mean?'

'Don't really know,' Woods said. 'Maybe he thought seeing what we'd seen back there might trigger some kind of trauma.'

'Trauma?'

'Yeah . . .'

'What?'

'Nothing.'

'Something.'

Woods squirmed a little, said, 'A while back, I heard that you found your father's body.'

Levine was silent.

Woods glanced at her. 'I'm sorry.'

Levine remained silent. Woods watched the road ahead. 'Grant said we should bug out, fast, to get you home, via St Louis.'

Levine watched Woods. After another few miles, she said, 'Did he tell you to keep that to yourself?'

'Not as such. Just to persuade you back to St Louis fast as I could. Make sure you got some rest. Wait there for further instructions.'

'But you told me,' Levine said. 'Why?'

'Because,' Woods said. 'I . . . I've never seen anything like what happened here. And, well, if you want to talk about it, or what you saw, then we can. We've got the whole drive ahead of us. I can listen. It might help.'

'I really don't think it will,' Levine said.

'They say it helps, talking stuff through.'

'No,' Levine said, looking out her window. 'I've got my own ways of dealing.'

•

'Good luck, guys,' Walker said as Duncan brought the pistol up. It was a .45, a serious weapon, made for the sole purpose of killing a man. No manual safety like on the Beretta, just the double-action trigger pull: about twelve pounds of pressure needed on the first shot, then the pressure needed to fire again dropped to five so that the engagement could continue as quickly as the shooter could pull the trigger.

'Even as you're about to die,' Menzil said, 'you're a wise-ass.'

'Not at all,' Walker said. 'It's just I know something that you don't.'

Duncan sighted the pistol at the centre of Walker's chest. 'What would that be?' he asked.

'You don't think Murphy put all kinds of traps and trip-wires and kill zones around his house?' Walker said, focusing on the man with the gun. 'You really want to go tumbling through there blind? Menzil here, sure, he might. But not you two. You're smarter than that. You've trained for assaults on urban scenarios, I can see that. You know that intel is critical. And this place has been set up by the best there was at attacking these kinds of places. And you know, if I were you guys, I'd want every bit of intel I could get. Because you're on the clock, to be in St Louis all set up by 17.00 for a 17.30 demonstration, and you going in there blind will mean that, if you're somehow still out here and still alive by 17.00, it's just a matter of time before Murphy finds another way for you guys to die.'

Duncan looked to Menzil.

'You need what I know,' Walker said. 'What Dylan told me.'

'Fine,' Menzil said. 'He lives another ten minutes. But we don't need what you know, Walker. You're going to do the hard work for us. You walk in front, ten feet out this time. If there's a trap of any kind, you're the sucker that's going to trigger it. And, so you know? Duncan here will shoot you in the arse the first time it looks like you're doing something stupid, got that?'

Walker didn't reply. He just looked from Menzil's eyes to the silenced HK in Duncan's hand and then turned and followed the tracks to the stream.

It was a fast-flowing brook, one foot deep and six wide, the riverbed all round pebbles of various sizes. The water was near freezing, pouring from the tops of the mountains, where snow and ice were forming ahead of winter.

Walker didn't break stride as he crossed the brook, climbed the bank and picked up the tracks again, some hundred yards upstream. He heard Menzil curse as he slipped over on the slimy leaf litter.

Beyond the stream at that point the forest opened up to a clearing. It was old work, the forest reclaiming it by half its original space, the rest of it either too polluted or too full of rocks to make it habitable terrain for trees of any substantial size. Some rusted machinery for logging and splitting lumber was scattered about, along with some old railcar tracks that led into a boarded-up mine shaft in the mountain's side. Maybe it was for coal, or gold, or gemstones, all of it once plentiful in these parts.

Walker followed the tracks that ran around the edge of the clearing. The four men were underneath the head-height shrubbery and would have been hard to see at any time of day, let alone night, but the night-vision's green glow acted to pick out the small indents of the sides of boots that shuffled through here many times.

He knew even before he was through the clearing and heading over a small ridge that he was close to Murphy's home.

And then it came into view: a squat log cabin in the woods.

66

Walker looked at the log cabin, 150 yards ahead. It was a handsome design, from another time – as solid and reliable a construction as any – slightly elevated from the ground on stumps. The logs of the walls were local, maybe taken from this very clearing, close to a ton each. The roof was iron, the double screws twinkling as little bumps through the night-vision lenses. It added up to a lot of painstaking work. Walker remembered Dylan, and her size and strength and disposition – she may well have helped Murphy build this place. And she died with that secret, at the hands of these men. A good woman.

Justice will be served on her behalf this morning.

The cabin was dark; no lights or candles from within. A front door, a front porch, a window each side, curtains drawn. The smell of woodfire hung in the air, but no smoke rose from the chimney. It was just after 5 am. Maybe the fire had gone out in the night, the smoke settling in the sleepy hollow that formed around the perimeter of the house.

'Give me the glasses,' Menzil said to Walker.

Walker passed them over.

'Okay,' he said, sliding them on. 'I'll wait here. You two, follow Walker in. All the way, to the front door.'

'Negative. We're splitting up,' Duncan whispered, handing Stokes his pack. 'I'll head around the back. Stokes, set up the rifle and cover Walker and the front.'

'On it,' Stokes said, heading off to a raised area to their right. Walker saw him settle low on the ground, using the pack as a gun-rest, assembling the rifle. It was an M40 bolt-action – fielded with success by the US Marine Corps for a long time. And Stokes looked proficient in using it. Even by the dull light of the thin moon Walker could see that the guy checked over the bolt mechanism and wiped down the rounds before loading them. He settled into a shooting position, lying prone.

He would be hard to get.

'You head north, fifty yards or so, to get a cross-fire position,' Duncan said to Menzil.

Menzil looked up at the sky. 'Which way's north?'

'There,' Duncan said, pointing to the tree line at the edge of the clearing where a row of vegetable garden beds were laid out. Walker saw potatoes, yams, gourds, beans. He was surprised to see corn growing as tall and thick as head-high weeds; it must have been some hardy heirloom variety, this place at this time of year. There was a child's toy tipped on its side, a small tractor. Walker clenched his fists as he watched Menzil head over to his position.

'Go,' Duncan said, nudging him in the back with the HK. 'All the way to the front door and knock. You try something, I cut you down and then turn this house to sawdust with a couple-thousand rounds.'

Walker looked from him to the house. Then across to the vegetable garden. He couldn't see where Menzil had concealed himself behind the corn, but he saw the child's toy again, and knew he had to do something before he got to that front door, because whatever happened then, it was the end of things for some of them out there in this night.

67

Lights cut the darkness up ahead. Red-and-blue strobes, bright headlights neared, fast, and flashed by them at speed, the wake rocking their Ford.

'That'd be the state trooper,' Woods said. 'They've just turned on to the interstate.'

Levine was silent. She watched ahead, a blank stare fixed.

'You okay?' he asked her.

'Yep. Keep on, to St Louis.'

Within a minute Woods said, 'What if those guys we saw back there aren't who they seemed?'

'Who would they be?'

'They just seemed a little . . . I don't know.'

'They knew Grant. They'll get to Murphy.'

'But what about this Walker guy?' Woods continued, looking across to her. 'What if he's already got to Murphy?'

Levine looked to him, then said, 'Just keep your eyes on the road and get us to St Louis.'

'But what if Walker *could* take down those guys?' Woods said. 'He may be laying in wait for them, snipe them off or something. Or what if—'

'All I hear is a bunch of *what if*s and *maybe*s,' Levine said.

'Yeah, well . . .'

'Well?' Levine watched him.

Woods eased off the gas a little, said, 'I think we're better off at Old Pelts, hanging with the Statie. See who comes back *down* Old Pelts, just to be sure. Because to me, there's too many *what if*s about this whole thing.'

Levine was quiet as she looked at him.

'Call me old-fashioned, partner,' Woods said, 'but I prefer to see something with my own eyes to believe it. And right now, I feel that we've got the time. So, why not turn back and see what's what?'

Levine rubbed a hand over her neck, then said, 'Shit. Turn around. Go back.'

Woods slowed to a stop and twisted the wheel, heading the Taurus back in the direction of Old Pelts Road, fast.

•

Walker headed forward, towards the cabin. The ground underfoot made for quiet progress, the earth sodden and covered in a thick carpet of mossy ground cover. He wished for some kind of trap, even something that could sound a ruckus, but realised that with three small kids running about out here during the day, Murphy wouldn't risk it; it would be too easy to stray into a trip-wire or trigger a claymore.

With every step Walker ran through scenarios. This wasn't like being picked up by the cops. And this wasn't like Squeaker being handed over to the bikers. This was the A League, or close to it. Walker could feel the sights of the rifle watching over him. He glanced over his shoulder – Duncan was five paces behind. Too far for him to turn and charge; that assault rifle would cut him to shreds before he got halfway.

And these guys weren't some Al Qaeda types, which is what he had expected, if getting Murphy was some kind of vendetta or reprisal for killing bin Laden, or part of a campaign to keep the SEALs quiet on something that they'd seen. That was curious. Did they outsource, to a local crew? Or were these converts to a cause?

Fifty paces to the front door.

Then another possibility, a new thought, cut through Walker's mind. That this kill squad, and all those dead SEALs, had nothing to do with bin Laden's death whatsoever.

68

A shiver crept around Walker's spine. He glanced back – Duncan was there, but he was now eight or nine paces back. Cautious, expecting Walker to head up the steps and cross the porch and knock on the door – and then have all kinds of hell break loose.

The ground underfoot changed. It was drier now, rising on a slight incline up to the house. Three timber steps up to the porch. There was no handrail, no furniture to duck around or behind – just six turned wooden posts holding up the verandah.

Two raised earthen berms came into view. They were carpeted in the same dense ground cover, so Walker had not made them out. One each side, small earthen walls just above knee-height, about the same level as the floor of the front deck. The path cut through them. Maybe they were there to form a barrier against the rolling frosts that were starting to settle before sunrise. Walker was six paces from stepping through the gap.

He looked back over his shoulder. Duncan had halted twelve paces behind, the HK nestled tightly into his shoulder and the barrel pointed at the ground somewhere behind Walker's feet, a stance that meant he would be ready to raise, aim and fire within the same second.

The berms were three paces ahead. It seemed the only chance he had was to duck behind one and use the surprise of suddenly dropping from view to then roll under the house, which was now five yards beyond.

Walker settled, keeping his pace steady. Two paces. Move to the right or the left? One pace. He was through the gap in the berms and dove to his left, turning through the air as he flew, landing hard on his right shoulder and keeping the rolling momentum going, turning across the ground and under the deck.

No gunshots rang out. Clearly Duncan wanted to keep his element of surprise. He should have kept his silenced HK pistol – not the assault rifle – but Walker knew that operators the world over always preferred their primary weapon, in this case an assault rifle with impressive accuracy and firepower.

But firing it would be akin to setting off fireworks on a clear night.

Walker edged back under the cabin. Still no sound from Menzil, and Walker couldn't see him from his position.

Then he looked up to the underside of the floor. He touched the thick wooden boards between the floor joists. They were warm – very warm. A fire, probably in a steel pot-belly stove sitting on a base of bricks on the floor, had been raging, until recently. But no smoke came from the chimney, so it had either just gone out or been deliberately extinguished . . .

Murphy had been expecting them.

A bright light shone in Walker's face. A flashlight, the brilliant white of expensive LEDs and powerful batteries. Menzil's large flashlight. It came from next to the stairs at the front.

'Get out,' a voice said. 'Now.'

It was not Menzil's voice.

69

Walker shielded his face from the beam of the flashlight. He rolled out to the side of the stairs that led up to the deck. He lay on his back looking up, wary of Stokes and the sniper's rifle, but no shots came. He saw the form of Duncan, lifeless, on the ground, and looked up at the face of the man before him. It was made up of bright white eyes and seemingly nothing more – the face, like the man's body, was almost invisible in the dark. He wore woodlands camouflage fatigues and his face was painted in blacks and dark greens.

Charles Murphy.

As Walker's eyesight adjusted, more detail emerged.

Murphy held a silenced HK pistol in his hands.

Duncan's silenced HK pistol.

Slung across his chest was the strap of a rifle, an AR-15, and he had a Colt .45 in a hip-holster. A large hunting knife was sheathed in a scabbard against his thigh.

'Where's the third guy?' Murphy asked.

'The sniper?'

'Down. The other guy – the non-soldier.'

'That way.' Walker pointed to the high screen of corn.

Walker started to stand but was dropped to the ground by a sucker punch to the stomach.

Murphy shone the powerful flashlight in that direction – Menzil was gone.

'Talk, fast,' Murphy said, the silenced HK pointed at Walker's forehead. 'Who are you?'

'Jed Walker, ex-24th Tac, and, right now, the only friend you've got out here.' Walker wiped blood from his lip as he got to his feet.

'24th?' Murphy said.

Walker nodded. He saw that earned some respect from the SEAL.

'What about this little friend here?' Murphy said, motioning with the pistol.

'I'm here to save you, jackass,' Walker said, ignoring Murphy and looking around.

Murphy was silent.

Walker looked directly at the Navy SEAL he'd been searching for all week. 'You don't know, do you?'

'Know what?' Murphy said.

'You haven't heard,' Walker said, 'because you're out here, completely off the grid.'

'Know *what*?'

'Your old DEVGRU team that hit Abbottabad. They're being hunted.'

Murphy was silent.

Walker said, 'They're being killed.'

'Huh? Right. Good luck.'

'Eight down in a day.'

'What did you say?'

'Eight of your team killed in one day.'

'In 'Stan?'

'No,' Walker said. 'All over the place. Including here, at home.'

'Bullshit.'

'True.'

'Who – by those guys?' he said, gesturing impatiently towards the two men he had silently killed.

'Maybe.'

'Why?'

'I'm hoping you might know.'

'Me? I'm just learning about this now.'

'Well, now you know. Now you know that every SEAL from the Abbottabad raid is being hunted down. And these guys came out here to kill you.'

'Who they working for? Al Qaeda?'

'They could be. Revenge hits. We should get going—'

'Not yet,' Murphy said. He gave Walker a no-nonsense stare, the silenced HK loose in his hands. 'How are you involved?'

'I was CIA. I've been working on this while no-one else would.'

'Was?'

'Retired, like you.'

'Great. So what, you're a retired spook, and just humping around the Ozarks trying to save an ex-SEAL?'

'It's more complicated than that.'

'Okay, ex-24th Tac, ex-spook. Why do you think my team's being hunted?'

'Maybe you guys saw something in that house in Abbottabad.'

Murphy paused, considered it, said, 'We saw plenty, but no-one went through anything we found – we were on the clock, right? We bagged everything that looked important and took it with us and handed it over to command and CIA when we touched down in Bagram. Hundreds of pounds of intel, computers and hard drives and tapes and discs and files. Everything we could carry.'

'Well, now someone's after you all, because your team saw something in that house that's worth killing for.'

'We saw something that we don't even know we saw?'

'You might remember.'

'If someone saw something important, they'd have said. Hell, it'd be in someone's autobiography by now.'

'They'll keep coming for you. Safe as you think you are out here. That's gone now, and whoever is doing this has the reach to hit eight guys in a twenty-four-hour window.'

'When was this?'

'We should go.'

Murphy said, his voice hard, 'When did my eight teammates get hit?'

'A week ago.'

'Nothing since?'

'The Navy hit the panic button as they started putting the names together. NCIS scooped up the rest of the guys from all over the world and are holding them at secure sites.'

'Secure sites?'

'Yeah. I don't know where. It's being handled out of the San Diego NCIS. They're all under guard. Their locations safe, compartmentalised. It's like witness protection.'

'Do you know the names?'

'Names?'

'Of those eight guys from my team.'

'No.'

'Damn.' Murphy looked around in the darkness. 'Really? This is real?'

Walker nodded.

Murphy said, 'What do I do?'

'You join the line of protection.'

Murphy nodded. 'My family?'

'Navy will protect them too.'

Murphy paused, then nodded again.

'But before we get to that,' Walker said. 'We've got two things to do.'

'What's that?'

'We have to save someone out here, and then we have to save a whole bunch of people in St Louis.'

70

Murphy listened to a minute's run-down of how Walker had found him, then said, 'They have a hostage out here?'

'Yep.' Walker said. 'The third guy out here, Menzil? He'll be headed back, to the fourth guy, and their hostage.'

'He'll get lost,' Murphy said, then stopped Walker from starting to backtrack. He said, 'Who's the hostage?'

'Your cousin,' Walker said to him. 'Squeaker – Susan. She's out there.'

'She's a *hostage*?'

Walker nodded.

'Shit. I thought she must have stayed back.'

'What?' It was Walker's turn to be confused.

'Dylan radioed me. Told me you two were coming.'

Walker paused, thinking of the woman and what had become of her if those guys were to be believed. 'She radioed you?'

'What, you think this is the dark ages? I've got an antenna, up one of these trees,' Murphy said, pointing up, 'set just lower than a lightning rod I got in another.'

'You knew we were coming.'

'Since last night.'

'And you went on a hunt? Leaving your family?'

'My eldest daughter could shoot you from a half-mile away,' Murphy said. He looked at the corn. 'Besides, Dylan vouched for you. So, where's Squeaker?'

'Back out there, on the track we came in on. And there's a clock.'

'How long?'

Walker checked his watch – iridescent in the night.

'An hour thirty remaining,' he said. 'After that the guy has instructions to kill her and head here, following our track.'

'Shit.' Murphy looked again towards the corn. 'She's a good kid.'

'The best,' Walker said. 'Look, the third guy here, Menzil, he's got night-vision. He'd have seen what you did to his two best guys and he'll be running.'

'He won't be far. A few hundred yards. Probably headed the wrong way. I can catch him.'

'Right. Well, you've got to choose: you can either track him down now or save your cousin.'

'Shit. Yeah. I know.'

'Hell, we can probably get to her and then double back here and track him before he gets any place out of this forest, right?'

'That's possible.'

'He's not like the other four, he's civilian.'

'I noticed that.'

Walker pointed to the house. 'Your family – they're out of here now? They're safe?'

'Yes. Soon as I figured you were heading my way, I doubled back and got them out.'

'Good. Let's get Squeaker.' Walker set off. 'And along the way we figure out what you know. Somewhere in that squid brain of yours is something that you've seen that's worth killing for, and it's going to save lives, and we're going to rattle it out.'

'You think?' Murphy said, moving ahead of him on the track, the SEAL silent as he ran.

'It's got to be that. Think about it. This isn't just a reprisal for taking out bin Laden.'

'I don't know anything. Hell, this could be *about* anything.'

'It's in there, somewhere – at the back of your brain; you just don't know it yet.'

They headed the way that Walker had just come, and he picked up Duncan's HK416 as they passed the corpse.

'What about the other SEALs – in protection?' Murphy asked.

'What about them?'

'Ask them. Maybe one of the other guys knows exactly what this is about. You said yourself they're in protection, have been for up to a week. Ask them.'

'We're working on that.'

'Working on it?'

'Navy is putting your team's safety front and centre. We're getting stonewalled in regards to questioning them.'

'Who? Who's getting stonewalled?'

'My guys.'

'Who are they?'

'Good people.'

Murphy let the comment pass as he moved. After a few minutes he said, 'I heard what you did, with the guy out on the pass – I heard the scream. How'd you do it?'

'It was a tight section of the mountain pass,' Walker said. 'I gave him a little bump.'

Again, Murphy let it go. Walker ran next to the guy who was a few years younger and a hell of a lot fitter, wondering with every step about Squeaker, and Murphy's family, and St Louis, and what could possibly be coming.

71

As they approached the original campsite, Walker checked his watch and his heart skipped a beat; it was two minutes past the deadline. If this fourth guy, Steve, was punctual, then Squeaker would be dead by now. And after all that she had been through and done to help save her cousin and his family . . . to miss by two minutes . . .

Murphy stopped. The smell of the campfire was thick in the air. The two men edged forwards, off the path, around the western side. In the glow of the fire a figure sat.

Squeaker. She was still. Unmoving.

We're too late.

An image flashed through Walker's mind: Squeaker sitting there, hunched forward, a bullet hole neatly drilled through her forehead.

Then he saw movement. The fourth guy, Steve, coming back from around the big tree, zipping up his pants. He'd been taking a leak, in the same place as Walker had earlier, as though there was some primordial part of the brain that knew where best to do such things, even in the middle of a forest.

Walker caught Murphy's arm and motioned him to shoot Steve in the kneecaps, then signalled with his hand like a sock puppet talking, and Murphy got it: they needed this guy alive, so he could talk.

Murphy gestured for Walker to curve around the clearing and held up one finger; they would strike a minute from now.

Walker headed off, continually glancing from Steve to his footing so that he would move quietly. He got to the three o'clock position, all the while counting down from sixty, then turned and signalled Murphy.

Murphy waved him forward.

Walker didn't hesitate. He emerged from the thick scrub at the edge of the clearing just as Steve checked his watch and picked up his rifle.

Steve looked up and saw Walker – too late.

A twin PAT! PAT! sounded to Walker's left.

Murphy fired as he emerged from the shrubbery, a ghostly apparition in his combat fatigues and camouflage face-paint.

Steve let out a whelp and collapsed as Walker rushed him, taking the rifle and the holstered side-arm and the sheathed knife. Steve's right knee was now a ragged mess of flesh and bone splinters. It was different from the wounds Walker had seen on the battlefield, where hollow-point and expanding ammunition was banned. The devastation caused by the first silenced .45 Hydra-Shok round was irreparable. The other round had gone a little high, maybe because that was the second shot and by then the guy was already collapsing, and maybe because of a little muzzle climb.

'You right, Squeak?' Murphy asked, cutting her loose and helping her to her feet.

Walker could see that she was only just now registering what had happened and who had done it. Her eyes went from the fallen guy who'd held her captive to Walker, then to the painted face before her, and finally she recognised those eyes that reflected the firelight.

Walker turned his attention to Steve, who was now breathing hard and fast, in deep shock, his body responding to the flood of pain by releasing huge amounts of chemical compensation.

'Who sent you?' Walker asked.

No answer.

'They're all dead,' Walker said to him. 'Your buddies. Gone.'

No answer, but the reaction was there, a slight twitch in the eyes, the final realisation in the lizard part of the guy's brain that said: *if you didn't know your life was over already, you know it now*.

'What's happening in St Louis this afternoon?' Walker asked him. Nothing.

Walker leaned over and took a burning branch from the fire, a thick stump about a foot long with red-glowing embers at one end. He held it out in front of Steve's face. 'St Louis. At 5.30. Tell me!'

Nothing. The guy was starting to shake and shiver, the colour gone from his face.

Walker looked down. The shot that went high had torn out a chunk of the thigh and shredded an artery. He had seconds to live.

'Tell me!' Walker said, tossing the stick and hefting Steve up by the lapels. 'What's the attack? Why St Louis? What's the demonstration of? Where is it?'

Steve's face relaxed as he died, his mouth slackening into a loose smile.

72

'I should go track that last guy,' Murphy said. 'The non-soldier with the night-vision. Get him to talk.'

Walker looked up. The stars that blanketed the night sky were going out one by one. Already the sky was lightening with dawn. Some people claimed that it was darkest before dawn. It was so said in movies and novels and songs – and it was bullshit. It was always darkest in the halfway point between dusk and dawn, in the moment the sun was most hidden to the observer.

'That might take too long,' Walker said, checking through the dead guy's pockets and backpack. 'It's been an hour and a half. And you need to double back all that way. The quickest you could find him might be three hours. The *quickest*. It might take all day.'

'Who was he?' Murphy asked, using the moment to check over his weapons and reload.

'I don't know, but he was their leader. He was different from these guys,' he said, indicating the dead body of Steve.

'They were Army,' Murphy said.

'You sure?'

'Certain. The way they stood, the way the sniper reacted when he made me three paces out and stood to fight. The Modern Army Combatives method. They were US Army.'

Murphy crouched down to Steve's body and used his knife to cut away at the guy's sleeves, all the way from the wrist to the shoulder, revealing the arm. Nothing. He did the same with the left arm – and found a tattoo on the triceps: a shield with an eagle's claw, talons extended.

'See?' Murphy said, pointing at it with the knife. 'He was 502 Parachute Infantry. Judging by the length of his hair, he's been out of the game for at least three months.'

'Minimum,' Walker agreed, nodding. 'Maybe more. Maybe years.'

'I said *at least*,' Murphy said, standing and sheathing his knife.

Squeaker was sitting by the fire, a bottle of water in her hands, rocking gently back and forth.

'You're sure your family is someplace safe?' Walker asked.

'They're getting there,' Murphy said, unscrewing the silencer of the HK pistol. The silencer went in his pocket and the pistol was holstered in a new thigh holster taken from the dead guy, on the opposite thigh to his Colt .45. He checked his watch. 'They're walking a fire-trail that'll lead them around to the back of Dylan's house. Should be there any minute.'

'We should head there too,' Walker said. He held out a hand and helped Squeaker to her feet. 'You okay?'

She smiled, said, 'What took you so long?'

Walker allowed a smile, but he thought of Murphy's family, of what they might find when they got to Dylan's.

'I'll lead,' Murphy said. 'Keep up. Right, little cuz?'

'I'm faster than you,' Squeaker said.

Walker was relieved to see the fighting spirit still burning in her. She looked tired and worn out, but she'd be okay; nothing some rest and food and a hot shower wouldn't fix.

'And while we go, Walker,' Murphy said, 'tell me how it is that you knew of these fuckers coming after me.'

Murphy led at a light run. Squeaker followed, light on her feet. Walker kept thinking about what might be coming at five-thirty this afternoon.

•

Grant checked and rechecked his mental list for what would happen the day after tomorrow.

He had a car with two new sets of IDs and documents waiting in a car park here in San Diego. American sedan, ten years old, two previous owners, silver duco. About as average and inconspicuous as you could get. The boot held bags, two of them, packed for two people, the contents of which looked for all the world like a couple going on vacation, with maps and brochures on Mexico. They'd stick to the west coast, with the goal of winding their way down to Chile.

There, a bank account waited with enough in it to last a lifetime. *A good lifetime, in a place like that . . .*

Grant's next movements were dependent on word from the field. Despite others looking into this, he had no worries. Not with the crew he had.

He considered the money in the bank account. How it had come. Along with the money he got for Menzil to facilitate all this. All of it, several million all told, came from the information that had led to a site in South Dakota, which he'd used to help a fellow NCIS agent crack a cold case. That had proved to be a mutually beneficial situation all round, in ways far beyond the financial. What they'd found hidden away there he'd divided up and partially on-sold to a group in Syria. Benefit of being a Federal Agent with tentacles that stretched internationally: all that he had access to, plus a list a mile long of cashed-up bad guys who wanted to buy it.

Now, he just needed things to settle and fall into place. And so far, so good.

But then along came some guy named Walker.

73

Dylan's house was dark. The sun was rising. It had taken them two hours to get there, and they found Murphy's family in the hay barn out the back, rugged up under a couple of heavy blankets.

Murphy hugged his wife, Jane. His two daughters were asleep on a stack of hay. His son was at Jane's breast.

'You didn't go inside?' Murphy asked.

Jane shook her head, Walker was relieved to see.

'There was no answer at the back,' Jane said, 'and when I went around the side, I saw a police car parked out front. There's a deputy sitting in it. I figured maybe they pulled Dylan in for questioning. I wasn't sure what to do, so I just stayed here, waiting for you.'

'I'll check it out,' Walker said, and Murphy nodded.

'I'll come,' Squeaker said.

'No.' Walker put a hand on her shoulder. 'Stay here with your family. I'll see what's what.'

Squeaker didn't look pleased, but then the oldest of the kids stirred and made a grizzling sound, so she lay next to her on the hay under the blanket and soothed her back to sleep.

Walker asked Jane, 'Do you have a cell phone?'

She passed one over. A basic thing, pre-paid, probably lived in a bottom drawer at their house and used when they went out to town. Walker punched in Somerville's number. She answered on the third ring, her voice tired.

'It's Walker,' he said. 'I've got Murphy, and we're headed to St Louis.'

'St Louis?' Somerville said.

Walker spent two minutes explaining what had gone down in the woods.

'Okay. Okay, I'll let McCorkell know,' Somerville said, her voice animated. 'I'll get on the first flight to St Louis and meet you there with FBI back-up.'

'Thanks.' Walker ended the call, handed the phone and the Berettas to Murphy, not wanting a shootout with a cop, and headed for Dylan's back door. Murphy had listened the whole way as they'd hiked back here. He'd had questions, mostly about which of his team members had been killed – questions Walker couldn't answer because he simply didn't know. Murphy's response was of disbelief. *Eight guys? From DEVGRU? Murdered? Assassinated? By those four Army guys? No way. Not the guys from my unit.*

They would work out the how and why soon, Walker hoped. Answers would be in St Louis.

And another answer would be waiting for him on the other side of this door.

Walker tried the back door to Dylan's house. It was unlocked. He crept inside, through the kitchen. They'd sat in there yesterday, with Dylan. And although there was nothing showing, he knew why that deputy was sitting in his car out front. Menzil wasn't lying or bragging about Dylan. This was a crime scene. A murder scene. He could smell it. The blood. The body fluids. The funk of death that even on a cold night had emanated from a corpse and filled the air of the house.

He considered going out the back door, walking around the house and approaching the deputy and getting him to call for back-up. But Walker had to know, to see for himself. There was the slim possibility that it was not Dylan who had met her end in here, but he knew as he padded quietly up the hallway to the living room, following the smell, that it was her, for that was how Menzil and his men had tracked down Murphy's location. They would have come here, asking about Murphy, and seen some kind of resilience, defiance, of a protector not giving away anything. Her friendship with the Murphys had been her death sentence. If she'd known nothing, they probably would have read as much and moved on to the next house they found. But they had come up against her, and sensed that she'd been stonewalling, and it would have escalated from there.

Walker could imagine her holding out.

Then he saw it. Dylan. What had become of her. And he wondered how she could have held out. There was no easy way. He fought the compulsion to find a blanket and cover her. He wanted whatever forensic evidence there was to be preserved so that if that fifth guy, Menzil, was apprehended, he'd get the electric chair for his involvement in this. Did they have the chair in Missouri? Or an injection? Either way it was a safety net – in case Walker failed to find the guy first, at least there was a chance he'd be killed by the state. But Walker hoped otherwise. Either in the course of the day, or another day after, he hoped that he would be the one to catch that killer and exact justice.

He heard a vehicle approaching. Headlights beamed into the front windows and a dark sedan pulled up next to the police cruiser.

•

McCorkell received a call from Somerville, and then he rang Assistant Director Grant.

'You've got nerve,' Grant said.

'Excuse me?' McCorkell replied.

'Your guy Walker has been causing hell across two states,' Grant said. 'I had a specialist team headed to the Murphys – he's compromised that.'

'The Murphy family are fine.'

Grant paused, catching up to what that meant: Walker got the Murphys out.

'You sure about that?'

'They were too late,' McCorkell said. 'Don't worry about the Murphys, they're safe.'

Grant said, 'Where are they?'

'With my people.'

'Where?'

'Headed to New Orleans,' McCorkell said, selling the lie to see where it led.

'New Orleans?'

'They're safe.'

'I need the address,' Grant said. 'I'll take them from there, put them into protection with the others.'

'I need something first.'

'Excuse me?'

'A list.'

'Maybe you don't understand what's happening here,' Grant said. 'The Navy's finest are being hunted down. I'm tasked with their protection.'

'Right, well, with due respect, the Murphy family would have been no more if it wasn't for my guy there.'

'Walker.'

'That's right.'

'He's with the Murphy family?'

'They're safe.'

'Safe?'

'Two things,' McCorkell said. 'We have an open investigation. We're trying to prevent a major terrorist attack. And you're looking in the wrong—'

'Terrorist attack?' Grant said, urgency in his voice. 'What are you talking about?'

'This is about Team Six, but it has nothing to do with killing them just for participating in Abbottabad,' McCorkell said. 'It's about what's happening next.'

Grant was silent, then he said, 'What's happening next?'

'We're hoping Murphy will know.'

'Where's Murphy?' Grant said. 'More to the point, where's what is left of my team? How did Walker beat them to Murphy?'

'Secure.'

'Headed to New Orleans?'

'That's right.'

'Bullshit,' Grant said. 'Why would anyone take a family there for protection, from where they were? It's a zoo. Either you're lying, or you and your staff are complete idiots.'

Grant hung up. He had a battle on his hands and his involvement was about to get a lot more hands-on.

74

Walker opened the front door and stood on the porch.

Three figures looked up at him: a man and a woman from the car that had just arrived, and the state trooper.

'Hands!' the state trooper shouted. By the silhouette of the headlights Walker could make out the officer's side-arm, aimed directly at him.

'On the ground, now!' the state trooper shouted.

Walker stood still. The other two figures, each wearing a dark suit, also had pistols drawn and pointed at Walker.

'On the ground!' the state trooper yelled. 'On your knees! Now!'

For a moment the thought ran through Walker's mind that maybe this wasn't a state trooper here to protect a crime scene but another one of the deputies from Mountain View, here to exact some kind of revenge or silence Walker. Maybe he was here to clean up, to shoot him dead. Or maybe arrest him for murdering those back at the Sheriff's house.

Walker took two paces closer, slowly raising his hands as he moved. He squinted against the headlights and then made out the uniform of a state trooper; it was unfamiliar, definitely. The two in suits may have been plain-clothes homicide cops, but they seemed dressed too sharply and built too lean. Some kind of Feds, then, but it was hard to properly make them out with the bright headlights behind them.

'Last chance!' the state trooper yelled, taking a step towards Walker, his service pistol pointed in a double-handed grip. 'On the ground!'

Then Walker smiled. The state trooper had frozen, and by the illumination of the headlights and the breaking dawn, Walker could see that his eyes had gone wide, and that the front of his tan trousers had spread with a dark smudge of wetness.

The barrel of a submachine gun to the back of the head will do that to a man.

'Firearms on the hood of the Taurus,' Murphy said.

The two suited figures looked across to Murphy, cutting a mean look in his military garb and face-paint and weaponry. For a brief moment it was like they had entered his world, and they understood that he was in total command of it.

Walker made his way down the steps. They were definitely Feds, he surmised as he closed the distance. The woman was around forty and looked like she'd been in the game a while. Tall, long-limbed, the kind of handsome facial features that said she probably looked more like her father than her mother. The guy was an average white male in most ways, and his hair was grown over his collar at the back.

The state trooper slowly put his pistol on the hood. He looked like he was going to be sick or pass out, or both. He was young. He'd probably seen a couple of car wrecks in his time, some domestic violence, some trespassing and theft, and plenty of traffic violations – but it seems he had never been held at gunpoint at a murder scene.

'Chief Petty Officer Charles Murphy,' the woman said, her voice calm and relaxed, putting her Sig on the hood of her car and motioning for her partner to follow suit; he did so, reluctantly. 'I'm Special Agent Levine of NCIS. Sailor, we're here to protect you and your family.'

•

Bill McCorkell pulled through the security gate of Marine Corps Base Quantico. The population on any given day was around 20,000, on federal land covering over 55,000 acres of Virginia, the Potomac slicing through it. Sprawling parade grounds. All the amenities of a mid-sized city. They drove past a Marine Corps Memorial, a replica of the statue of the second flag-raising on Iwo Jima.

'Feels like coming home,' Hutchinson said.

'When were you at the Academy?' McCorkell asked.

'A lifetime ago,' Hutchinson said, looking in the direction of the adjoining FBI Academy. 'Have you met this Director before?'

'No,' McCorkell said, taking a ramp for the visitors' car park near the Russell Knox administration building and pulling into the first spot he saw. 'Career administrator, brought over a couple of years back from the Secret Service.'

'Sounds all right,' Hutchinson said, getting out the car awkwardly, reaching across his body to pull the handle with his free left hand.

'He's from financial crimes,' McCorkell said. 'A bean-counter from way back.'

'Sounds like a fun guy,' Hutchinson said. He took a pen from his breast pocket and itched inside his arm cast as they walked.

'Bet you can't wait to get that off.'

'I'm just looking forward to being able to jerk off properly again,' Hutchinson said, deadpan. 'I mean, don't get me wrong, I'm not holding back. But the left just ain't the same – it's like a stranger's going at it.'

'Seriously,' McCorkell said, chuckling and holding his chest as they entered the lobby and walked to the security desk. 'I'm too old for jokes like that. You'll give me a heart attack.'

Hutchinson showed his FBI credentials and they asked for NCIS Director Bruce Trotter. They were ushered through and escorted to an elevator.

Hutchinson said to McCorkell out the corner of his mouth, 'I tell you about the one where this guy is driving his car in the desert? He notices this guy jumping along the road. The guy's buck naked and his hands and feet are tied with rope . . .'

75

The stand-off lasted for ten seconds, as Murphy looked from Levine to Walker, then back to the NCIS duo, then he lowered his HK submachine gun from the state trooper's head.

'No hard feelings,' Murphy said to the guy. He passed the officer his police-issue Glock pistol. 'You go around back, to the hay shed; you'll see my family. You stand guard over them, now. If you see so much as a squirrel coming near them, you take its head off, do you hear? Can I count on you to do that until you're, well . . .' Murphy looked down at the trooper's pants, 'until you're properly relieved?'

The state trooper swallowed hard and looked from the face-painted killing machine in front of him to the two NCIS agents, and Levine nodded to him.

'Got that, yes, sir,' the state trooper said to Murphy and moved off at a jog around the house.

'You're Jed Walker,' Levine said, turning to him.

Walker remained silent. He nodded. Had they heard of him through Somerville and the others? Whatever. He saw these two as a roadblock – they'd want to take Murphy in, hide him away someplace where he couldn't communicate with the outside world, and Walker couldn't let that happen.

'We need to talk,' she said.

'No, we don't,' Walker said. 'Murphy and his family need to be protected. That's first.'

'That's why we're here,' Woods said. 'Why are *you* here? To do – to do *that*?' He motioned towards the house.

Walker knew that these guys had either seen or heard about what was inside. Seen, he decided, reading their looks. A sight like that didn't leave you in a hurry. It took plenty of nightmares and drinks – or therapy – to be rid of it, if it ever truly left.

'What happened?' Murphy said.

'What do you think?' Walker said to Woods evenly. 'You think I could do that?'

'Walker?' Woods said. 'Dylan – she's – did those guys . . .'

Walker looked to him and gave the slightest confirmation, then he looked to Levine.

Levine stared him right in the eye as she answered. 'Walker, *I* think that you did that in there.'

'The men who did that are dead,' Murphy said simply. The SEAL stood in close to the two NCIS agents. His HK was on a strap over his shoulder and held across his chest, pointed at the ground, his gloved hands resting on the stock. 'We got them. They were after me and my family.'

'Dead?' Levine said. 'The whole team?'

'Dead. They were ex-US Army,' Murphy said.

'They gloated to me about the killing,' Walker said. 'And I just saw it, for myself.' He turned to Murphy. 'Don't go in there. Remember her how she was.'

Murphy nodded.

'How did you . . .' Woods said, '*get* them?'

'How do you think?' Murphy said. 'And if it hadn't been for Walker, it might have gone bad – really bad – the other way.'

The two agents were silent for a beat.

'There's one out there still,' Walker said to the agents. 'The leader. Non-Army, at least not pointy end, ex-Army like the other four. He looked like an ex-cop. They called him Menzil. Five-ten, one-seventy, tanned skin, dark hair, about forty-five. He'll be headed for St Louis.'

Neither agent spoke. Levine's eyes darted from Walker to Murphy and back again. Woods glanced around in the early morning light, as though he might spot Menzil in the shadows.

'You got that?' Walker said to them. He took a step closer into the group. He towered over all of them, none over five-eleven. 'What are you two going to do about it?'

'We'll inform the local PD and the staties, search the forest and close the roads,' Woods said, looking to his senior agent. 'And tell them to bring K9 units.'

Levine remained silent.

Woods walked away, took out his phone and started dialling.

Levine, getting back on task, said, 'We're taking the Murphys to a secure site.'

'How can you protect Murphy's family?' Walker asked.

Levine said, 'We've got a lot of resources on this—'

'Clearly,' Murphy said. There was anger in him now, as though he was putting the deaths of Dylan and his teammates at the agent's feet. 'Shit – you and the Navy couldn't find me when this one guy and my little cousin and then a bunch of ex-Army could. That doesn't instil much confidence.'

'You'll all be safe,' Levine said. 'We've got the rest of the team in safe houses out west, guarded round the clock. The threat is against all your old team.'

'I know, Walker briefed me,' Murphy said.

Levine looked to Walker.

'They don't have to go with you,' Walker said to her. 'This is just a courtesy, from Uncle Sam, and a late one at that, right?'

'Late?' Levine said. She took a step closer and crossed her arms.

'Eight dead and *then* you act?' Murphy challenged.

'I agree on that,' Levine said. 'But this isn't my case.'

'You're just following orders?' Murphy said.

'Yes,' Levine replied. 'To find you and your family, get you to safety.'

'Where's safety?' Walker asked.

'Via St Louis,' Levine said. 'Then we fly. West. California. We drop you at San Diego. That's all I know – you'll then be handed over to another team of agents and taken to a site. You'll be moved again, maybe two or three times, each occasion by a different crew, until you're at the off-base site with the rest of the DEVGRU operators and their families.'

'They're all together?' Murphy said.

Levine nodded. 'All those who were on the bin Laden hit are there.'

'That's a big target,' Murphy said. 'Putting them all together like that.'

'Safety in numbers,' Levine said.

'Let's do it,' Walker said.

Levine seemed a little taken aback.

'Really?' Murphy replied. He looked to Walker, surprised.

'I'm not finished,' Walker said. 'We go to St Louis, sure. Then we meet up with my guys from the UN. Then we talk some more.'

'Talk?' Levine said. 'The *UN*? You're joking, right?'

'Agent Levine, you've got this whole thing ass-end backwards, or, at least, you don't know the half of it,' Walker said. 'Because this isn't about retribution for the bin Laden hit. It's about something that the team has *seen*. And it's about a terrorist attack that will happen this afternoon, in St Louis, at 5.30.'

76

NCIS Director Trotter was a large man. McCorkell was like a mini-me version of the guy, a good foot and a half shorter and near-on half his weight. Hutchinson was somewhere in the middle. After introductions the three men sat in Trotter's office. It was on the third floor and looked out at the line of flags and parade ground.

'That happened in New York?' Trotter said, motioning to Hutchinson's arm.

'It was part of that, yeah,' Hutchinson said, giving McCorkell a brief sideways look that said this guy had checked up on them before the meeting.

'Director Trotter,' McCorkell said, 'we're not going to beat around the bush.'

'A man with your background, I'd expect not,' Trotter said. 'What can I do for you?'

'It's about the SEAL protection operation that is occurring right now,' McCorkell said.

'That's being handled out of San Diego,' Trotter replied. 'Assistant Director Grant of Special Investigations is leading it. Would you like his details?'

'We have them,' McCorkell said. 'And we spoke to him and got nowhere, so we thought we'd check in with you.'

'Right,' Trotter said. He leaned back and his plush leather executive chair creaked under his shifting mass. 'Well, it's his op, and I trust him implicitly to run a tight ship, so what he says goes.'

McCorkell nodded, then looked to Hutchinson.

Hutchinson asked Trotter, 'Can we meet with the SEALs?'

'Did you ask Grant?'

'Yes.'

'What'd he say?'

'No.'

'Well, there's your answer, I'm afraid.'

Hutchinson fell silent.

'This is a sensitive operation,' Trotter said. 'I'm sure you both appreciate that.'

'Can we talk to them remotely?' McCorkell said. 'On a video call, from here?'

'Not if Grant said no. There are people out there who want those boys in the ground. That's our priority – protecting them. They're owed that and then some, agreed?'

'They knew what they signed up for,' McCorkell said. 'And they signed up to protect their country, and they need to do that, right now.'

Trotter said, 'How do you figure that?'

'These assassinations are about another terrorist attack,' replied McCorkell. 'Something that's coming – soon.'

Trotter leaned back, the information settling. 'I've heard nothing about anything like that. Says who?'

'Says us – we're telling you now,' Hutchinson said.

Trotter crossed his hands over his belly. 'And it's related to the SEALs how?'

'We're working to figure that out,' McCorkell said. 'And talking with the SEALs you have in protection is our best lead right now.'

'That's it?'

'That's it.'

Trotter's face had the look of a guy in senior command who, unless he had all the cards, didn't want to play a hand. 'Well, gentlemen, when you have something more to share, come back and let's see what's what,' he said, 'shall we?'

Hutchinson looked across to McCorkell. The national security specialist just stared at the Director.

'I'm sorry, but my hands are tied on this,' Trotter said, leaning forward and putting his half-glasses on his nose, making a show of sorting through papers.

'Director Trotter,' McCorkell said, his voice reasonable. 'We're asking for something that will help save lives. American lives. Civilians.'

'No is no, I'm afraid. This is an operational matter, and I sure don't answer to you, a civilian.' Trotter looked up at McCorkell over his glasses. 'But, like I said, quid pro quo and all that. You get me more, maybe I can do something. Until then . . .'

•

Levine said, 'We just want Murphy.'

'I *need* Murphy,' Walker replied, matching her determined tone. 'And you're not going to get in my way.'

Levine shook her head. 'Oh? You're saying that you want us to look the other way, to fail at our mission, for . . . what? Something you think will happen this afternoon?'

'It's not failing, it's delaying,' Walker said. 'Twelve hours, tops. We all get what we want.'

'Why? As a helping hand to you?' Levine said. 'So you can prevent some terrorist attack that no-one else in the intel or law community are seeing?'

Walker shrugged. 'However you want to look at it.'

'That's what it is. How else is there to look at it?'

'Okay, fine.'

Levine said, 'Fine? What's fine?'

'That's what it is. Look the other way. Just for a day. Not even a day. Twelve hours, tops.'

Levine said, 'No.'

'Really?'

'No.'

'Then I'm sorry.'

'For what?'

'For you,' Walker said. 'For failing in your mission. Because it will take more than the two of you to get me to leave the side of this man and his family.'

'Look,' Woods said, trying to defuse the situation. 'Let's just all of us get to St Louis, okay? We can figure it out on the way or once we're there.'

Walker stared at Levine. She got into her car without a word.

77

Walker and Murphy rode in the back of the NCIS sedan. Woods drove. Levine sat in the front passenger seat. St Louis was 150 miles away, and they were a third of the way in. They'd recounted what happened in the forest. They'd speculated over the providence of the ex-Army crew. They'd received confirmation that the state patrol had blocked roads fifty miles out to the south-east of the forest, and an APB had been put out for Menzil. Forensics teams from the St Louis federal building – a mix of FBI, DEA and Homeland Security – were en route to recover the four bodies of the dead assailants, along with that of Dylan.

Murphy looked behind them out the back window every five minutes or so.

Behind, Squeaker drove the Murphy family in Dylan's SUV, a big old Jeep.

Woods's cell phone rang. The caller ID came up on the centre console as AD Grant.

Assistant Director Grant, Walker assumed, and he knew he was right when instead of opting to answer the call on the wheel-mounted Bluetooth button, Woods passed his phone to Levine.

'Levine,' she said. 'No, he's driving. We're headed to St Louis – you didn't get our messages. Oh, right. Yes, that's right – we've got Murphy here, and his family.' She paused, Grant clearly speaking, then she said, 'Walker helped out, saved him with a heads-up. We've got four dead bad guys in the woods, one on the run. A guy named Menzil. Staties will have the place locked down in a couple hours. So, you can sleep easy, boss – this might now be over, if that was the only kill crew. And our final SEAL is with us. Job nearly done, right?'

Levine listened for a while.

'Yes, we'll get the Murphys to safety,' she said. 'First flight from St Louis, got it.'

She ended the call and passed the phone to her partner.

'Congrats and good job all round,' Levine said.

'That's what he said?' Woods asked.

Levine looked at him. 'Yeah. And next time, answer your own phone.'

The two agents rode in silence for the next twenty minutes. Murphy continued to look over his shoulder. Walker wondered what was next. There was no way he could let Murphy go when they got to St Louis – the guy might be the best chance of stopping whatever was coming later today.

'So,' Walker said as they passed a marker for St Louis: 80 miles. 'We get to the part where I tell you guys why I'm here, and why saving Murphy is so vital.'

●

Grant allowed himself a quiet moment to make decisions. He closed his eyes. After Levine had told him of the deaths of the four men in the forest and advised him that she and Woods were now with Murphy – and Walker – he needed to think.

One man got away. Menzil. How did he survive where the others did not? Maybe he ran and hid, while the others stood up to fight. Where would Menzil go?

Options.

Option one was to let them get the Murphys to San Diego. By the time they got there, and debriefed, and moved about, it'd be too late. And in that time, he could orchestrate another crew.

But what was Levine's state of mind? What was Woods's? And what was this Jed Walker doing, tagging along?

Option two was looking easier: use the asset he had on hand to clean things up before or at St Louis.

Flip of a coin . . .

Grant opened his eyes.

Option three: get to St Louis himself. Make sure the job was done right. Finish things himself.

78

'That was you, at the Stock Exchange,' Levine said, looking on the diagonal to Walker, who sat behind Woods. 'You saved the Vice President.'

'Yes,' Walker said. 'And that was when we got confirmation of Zodiac.'

'Twelve linked terrorist attacks?' Woods said.

'That's right,' Walker said. 'The attack on the VP was the trigger event. It was big and public, put on to make a show, to be sure that the next link in the chain saw it and started to act.'

'But you stopped it,' Levine said. 'So why would it still trigger something else?'

Walker replied, 'It was a close call. There was shooting and an explosion – the VP was lucky. *We* got lucky. But it was enough to set in motion the next cut-out cell in the Zodiac program. But it's vague – more just a reference that makes sense when we start seeing ripple events leading to an attack.'

'Like my old team being hunted down,' Murphy said.

Walker nodded.

'Walker, who exactly are you working for?' Woods asked, eyeballing him in the rear-vision mirror. 'UN doesn't have sanctioned field operatives working here in the US.'

'I work for no-one,' Walker said. 'But I'm helping out where I can.'

'So, what, you're some vigilante?' Woods said.

'No, it's nothing like that,' Walker said. 'I'm part of this because my previous work in the CIA and then the State Department led directly to Zodiac. Then New York happened, and I learned that not only were some in the CIA a part of this, but that my father was part of the original think-tank that put Zodiac together as a worst-case scenario.'

'Your father,' Levine said slowly, watching Walker, 'is a part of this?'

'He's connected to it,' Walker said, giving a short version of what he knew. Then, he added, 'He was there when Zodiac was spit-balled.'

'You really think all this started in some government think-tank?' Levine said.

'Yep,' Walker said.

'Separate lone-wolf-type terrorist groups,' Murphy said. 'Not known or affiliated with each other – just acting as triggers to the next attack . . . Jesus, that's scary.'

'And you feel some responsibility about this because your father was there, somehow thinking it up?'

'He didn't let the genie out of the bottle,' Walker said, 'but he put it in there.'

'And so here you are,' Levine said, looking at him.

'Here I am.'

'And your father, brainstorming up bad shit that could be used against us?' Levine said. 'That's some help.'

'It happens all the time,' Walker said. 'We plan and prepare for the worst, right?'

'And this worst-case scenario fell into the wrong hands,' Murphy said, looking back over his shoulder again. 'That's just great.'

'And what's this got to do with the SEAL team that hit bin Laden?' Levine asked, watching Walker.

'Maybe nothing,' Walker said.

'Nothing?' Levine looked at him, all kinds of questions in her eyes.

'Maybe the hits on the SEALs aren't about bin Laden,' Walker said. 'I mean, who said they were?'

There was silence in the car, then Levine said, 'It's definitely that op. Those killed were on that op. I can confirm that.'

'I need a list of those names,' Murphy said. 'I want to see it, the names of the guys who are down. When I see the list, I'll know for certain that it was that op.'

'He's right,' Walker said. 'We need that list.'

'We can't get you that,' Woods said.

'Bullshit,' Murphy replied.

'We can't,' Levine said. 'We've never even seen it. This is all compartmentalised way up high, because you're special operators, and that op was, obviously, one of this country's most notorious.'

'Who's got the list?' Walker asked.

'Our Assistant Director would have that info. He's the one who sent us here,' Woods said. 'Him, and some people over at JSOC, right, Levine?'

Levine shrugged.

'You do what you have to do to get us that list,' Murphy said, 'or you can pull over now and let us out.'

Walker waited for the answer. The two NCIS agents shared a look. A truck stop with a fast-food chain attached loomed on the highway up ahead.

And then an answer came. Not in the form of one of the agents making a decision, but from behind them. Squeaker, in the Jeep, flashing her headlights and putting on her indicator to turn off the highway.

79

The two older Murphy kids needed the bathroom, and both vehicles were gassed up while there was time to kill.

Walker stood and watched over proceedings. The sun was up and the day promised clear skies. Squeaker's face was turning black and blue, one of her eyes closing up and puffy, but she was doing a good job of playing surrogate nanny and goofball to keep the kids occupied.

As Levine walked towards the store to pay, she took out her cell phone and either made or took a call; Walker couldn't be sure which, but he could see that she was annoyed by what she heard.

'You think these NCIS will help out today?' Murphy asked Walker after he'd put his kids back into the car, passed Squeaker a bag of hot greasy food and made his way back to the NCIS sedan. His face was mostly cleaned of the camouflage paint thanks to copious amounts of hand soap and warm water and paper towels. If his combat outfit startled anyone inside the place, it was hard to tell; the locals probably just thought he was another national guardsman, a survivalist nut-job, or maybe a soldier from Fort Leonard Wood. 'Since we're all headed to St Louis, maybe they can help?'

'Maybe. But probably not. It's going to take some persuading,' Walker said. 'These guys are concerned with your safety only – when I mentioned a potential attack, right at the start when we met, their eyes glazed over. They want to get you someplace a long way from here, and I might need you to hang around and help me out later today. At the very least, I definitely need to go through that list of names with you. And we need some time to talk about what you may or may not have seen.'

'You want me to turn down what they're offering?' Murphy said as Woods came out the petrol station. Levine was a few steps from the driver's door of the Taurus. 'The protection?'

'Like they said,' Walker replied, 'this may be over now that we got those guys back in the forest.'

'You think it's over?'

'No.'

Murphy looked to the Jeep, to his family. Squeaker was at the wheel, eating, alert, ready. Walker could see that Murphy's mind went from his family to the car and then its owner, Dylan, and what those men had done to her to get to him. And what she had done to protect him and his family. 'You can count on me, Walker. One way or another, this thing will be over today.'

•

Grant leaned back in his chair. No sooner had he hung up a call from his Director, saying that McCorkell was mentioning a terror attack at 17.30 in St Louis, than Levine rang from a gas station some sixty miles south of St Louis.

Option three was a go.

'Okay,' he'd said to Levine. 'It's the only option. I'm on my way.'

80

St Louis loomed up ahead. The Lou. Gateway to the West. Some good family memories. Walker wasn't going to let anything happen to it, not at 17.30 today, not any other day.

'Where you headed?' Walker asked.

'Airport for us,' Woods said. 'We've got flights to San Diego booked for the five Murphys, departing 11.45.'

'Slight change,' Levine said. Woods looked to her. 'Our boss is headed here, to St Louis.'

'When?' Walker asked.

'He's probably in the air right now.'

'Why?' Walker asked.

'I didn't ask him,' Levine said.

'Yeah, about that,' Murphy said, glancing sideways at Walker. 'Have you guys asked up the chain for that list yet?'

'List?' Woods said. 'Oh, yeah. They're on it.'

'On it? They're my teammates,' Murphy said. 'You know, the ones who've been assassinated? The ones you couldn't protect?'

'Right,' Woods said, looking uneasy. 'I asked about—'

'We're getting out at St Louis,' Murphy said firmly. 'And sitting tight, until I get that list.'

'Excuse me?' Woods replied.

'You can't hear right?' Murphy said.

Woods looked at him, then turned away.

'Fine. Okay,' Levine said. 'I'll get you the list. And we can wait in St Louis, if that's what you really want. Does that suit *you*, Walker?'

Walker nodded.

'Then you can see that this is a reprisal attack for bin Laden's death, just like Grant said from the get-go,' Levine said. 'And then you'll realise that you need to get the hell out of Dodge and someplace safe, until we're sure there's no more threats out there against you and what's left of your team.'

'Okay,' Murphy said. 'I see this list, with Walker, before we go any place other than St Louis. Then we talk again.'

Levine's phone rang. The number came up on the centre console's screen. It wasn't stored in the phone's memory under a name, but Walker recognised it. It was Bill McCorkell.

'That'll be for me,' Walker said.

'Here,' Levine said, taking her phone from where it was plugged in charging near the armrest.

'No,' Walker said. 'Put it on the speaker.'

Levine hit the call-answer button. 'This is Special Agent Levine, you're on speaker.'

'Hey, Bill,' Walker said loudly. 'We're just entering St Louis, and you're on speaker phone in the car with the two NCIS agents, Levine and Woods, and with Murphy.'

'Okay,' McCorkell said. 'Murphy, how's the family holding up?'

'They're all good, sir,' Murphy replied. 'Little cousin's a bit worse for wear, but she'll come good.'

'Good to hear. Now, you know who I am, son?' McCorkell said. 'Who I was?'

'Yes, sir,' Murphy said.

'Right,' McCorkell said. 'And I assume that Walker has briefed you all on Zodiac?'

'They're as caught up as we can get,' Walker said.

'Right,' McCorkell said. 'And you mentioned the intel on St Louis, from those men in the forest?'

'It's a demonstration,' Walker said. 'At 17.30.'

'But why here, sir?' Woods said. 'In St Louis?'

'Walker, what's your read?' McCorkell asked.

'Opportunistic,' Walker answered from the back seat. 'They're doing it here because they were already here in the area, taking care of business, so to speak, in eliminating Murphy. So while they're in town, they're demonstrating what they can do.'

'This sounds far-fetched,' Levine said. 'A massive conspiracy of linked terrorist attacks and there just happens to be one occurring today, in the very city that we're passing through?'

'The very city that a group of hit-men-cum-terrorists were due to pass through having just dispatched the remaining SEAL,' McCorkell said. 'And for all we know, there's more of this group, in the city, plotting and planning and getting ready for what's coming.'

'What is it you want from us, sir?' Woods said.

Levine shot him a look. He ignored her.

'I have Special Agent Fiona Somerville, FBI, in St Louis, just checked into the Hyatt,' McCorkell said. 'Head to her. Murphy, we have three rooms, adjoining, and she has agents from the local Field Office there, standing watch and kitted out to protect you and your family. There are three local PD cruisers out front, six officers providing perimeter security. Murphy, your family will be safe there; it's a bubble of security.'

'Copy that, sir, thank you,' Murphy said.

'Look, Mr McCorkell,' Levine said. 'With due respect, we have orders from our—'

'I have the Secretary of the Navy on the other line, Agent Levine,' McCorkell said. 'He's been waiting all this time that I've been talking, listening to Bach. He's in Hawaii at the moment. You know the time in Hawaii right now? Early. And he's waiting with a phone to his ear, listening to the Bach waiting music – waiting, because he respects me, and he takes what I say seriously. Would you like me to patch him through to you?'

'Sir,' Levine said, 'our immediate superior, Assistant Director—'

'Grant is fully aware of this,' McCorkell said. 'I briefed him not twenty minutes ago. He has orders from the Secretary, along with Admiral Thompson of the Joint Chiefs, to follow my every instruction on this matter. Do you need me to have him patched through to you too? Or you'll only listen to Grant on this? The Secretary may be a little pissed, I've got to say, with your need for someone about a hundred and fifty titles below him to give you new orders.'

'No, sir,' Levine said after a pause. 'We're fine. We're headed for the Hyatt now.' She punched the hotel into the car's sat-nav system. 'We'll be there in fifteen minutes.'

'Good,' McCorkell said.

'Thanks, Bill,' Walker said from the back seat. 'Let's talk again from the hotel. And get that list of Team Six names to us.'

'Somerville will be waiting for you at the hotel,' McCorkell said. 'By the time you're there, that list will be too.'

•

Grant boarded the first plane to St Louis. It was 09.45 in San Diego, which made it 11.45 in Missouri. At 17.30 the country was going to witness a show that would put everything in perspective. He looked at the *Washington Post* carried by the guy ahead of him, its front page screaming out a landmark deal to bring Ukraine into NATO. For Grant, that was code for letting Europe do the work that the United States should be doing. Grant was not one of those pundits who thought that US foreign policy should go back to pre-World War Two thinking, all about internal and regional matters. Far, far from it.

The way he saw it, the United States was a power *because* of its power, and because it wasn't afraid to use it. Interventionists be damned. He was going to make a cause that would have the whole country rallying to arms. Debts would be paid today, and this event would become what 9/11 should have been: a rallying cry, not just of this nation but of the world behind it.

81

Walker liked St Louis. He had been here once, as a kid, a road trip with family. He'd been seven or eight. They'd gone to the top of the Gateway Arch and looked out at the view. The people below had looked like ants. The Mississippi had seemed impossibly big – they'd taken a boat ride that had included lunch on the way south and dinner on the way north back to their hotel. They'd been to a Cardinals game, against the Eagles. Philadelphia won that day. It was a good day.

He saw the Hyatt up ahead. It bordered onto the Jefferson Memorial Park, flanked by the Old Courthouse and wide green avenue that led down to the Gateway Arch on the banks of the Mississippi.

Somerville was waiting outside, with three suited FBI agents who wore dark sunglasses and in-ear radio sets. She looked a world away from him and the crew pulling up – she may have been up through the night too, but she'd not been through and seen what they'd all seen. Levine parked away from the valet station, and Squeaker pulled in next to them. The FBI agents formed a loose perimeter, looking out.

'Walker,' Somerville said, looking first at his muddied outfit and then his tired face. 'You look like death warmed up.'

'Thanks, Fi, right back at ya,' Walker said. Fact was, she was clean and made up and he could smell her perfume. 'This is Charles Murphy.'

The two shook hands.

'And his family,' Walker said, pointing to the sleeping kids; Murphy, his wife and Squeaker each carried one.

'And our two NCIS agents, Levine and Woods,' Walker said.

'Hey,' Somerville said. Levine shook her hand. Woods gave a half-hearted wave as he checked his phone for messages. 'Okay, follow me.'

Walker stayed next to Somerville at the start of the procession. They went through the revolving glass doors and across the granite lobby. Probably local granite. He hoped so; there was nice granite in these parts. That said, the 1970s-looking brick hotel had clearly undergone a recent refurb, and it was probably cheaper by a significant margin to import granite from China. Progress. Back in the day, this city, as a gateway to the west of the nation, had been a major trading hub as a port on the mighty Mississippi. It had been the backbone of the growth of America, right from the start. What was it now? What would it become if they failed today?

'Where do we start?' Somerville asked as they neared the elevators.

Walker said, 'McCorkell told us you had decent security assets here?'

'For protection of the Murphys, five agents,' Somerville said. 'These three will stay in the lobby and security room. This place is a secure building, it's why I chose it. The other two will be in the hallway. And there's St Louis PD in the street, and they have SWAT on a ready-go and can be here in ten minutes flat.'

'Okay,' Walker said.

Somerville hit the lift-call button. The door pinged open immediately.

Walker stood back to allow Somerville and the Murphys and Squeaker and the NCIS agents in first, then he squeezed in, eyeballing the concierge at the desk who looked down his nose at the sight of Walker and Murphy, all mucked up from their antics in the forests. The doors shut, and Somerville hit the sixth-floor button.

'Murphy and I both need a change of clothes; Squeaker too,' Walker said.

'Sizes?' Somerville asked.

Walker looked at the two of them, each carrying a sleeping child. 'Extra large, large and small should do it. Casual, muted tones.'

'Got it,' Somerville said.

'And breakfast.'

Walker looked at Levine, who was facing him in the cramped elevator, no more than a foot between them. For the first time he saw her front on, in the light. She was prettier than he'd thought in the dawn light, and younger: late thirties, dark hair, dark eyes, olive skin. Her eyes were tired – she'd worked through the night, like he had. The top of her head was at Walker's mouth level, which made her about five foot eight. She wore a black suit over a charcoal fine-knit turtleneck, no jewellery. Maybe this was just her work uniform. She'd look great in a dress, Walker thought.

'So,' Woods interrupted Walker's thoughts. He was behind Levine, her back to him. 'What kind of ex-Air Force and CIA guy gives orders like this to an FBI agent? I mean, am I the only one in here who thinks this is more than a little odd? Levine?' She turned to face him. 'I mean, we've got to talk to Grant about this. For all we know, that McCorkell guy was bluffing about the Secretary of the Navy thing before. I mean, really? He was waiting on the phone, for twenty minutes, from Hawaii, listening to Bach? Like, *really*?'

The elevator pinged at the sixth floor. The doors opened. No-one got out, though – for that to happen, the 230-pound mass that was Jed Walker would have to alight first.

'Stay in the hallway,' Walker said to Woods. 'Call your boss. Call whoever you need to. But I'm telling you: if you get in the way today, Somerville here is going to arrest you under some kind of Patriot Act clause, and you'll get to enjoy the most thorough cavity search this side of the Mississippi. Gloves, lube, cameras and clamps, all the trimmings.'

'Is that right?' Woods said, his tone trying to make light of the threat. He looked to Somerville, saw something harder, then dropped his eyes.

Walker led the way out of the elevator and headed up the hall towards the two waiting FBI agents.

82

The Murphy family were squared away in a two-bedroom suite, each bedroom containing two large beds and opening onto an en suite. As soon as Jane and the baby were settled in a bed, safe and warm, Murphy went to shower. Squeaker was in the other en suite, putting the two older kids in a bubble bath. Walker could hear the laughter spilling out from the room. To them, this was an adventure. The eldest would remember it; probably the three-and-a-half year old too. Walker had memories from that age, a trip with his father to New York City: mainly about food – eating a chocolate ice-cream while on a ferry going around the Statue of Liberty; a parmigiana in the Empire State Building cafe. The view from up top, looking down, his face pressed against the bars, seeing cars below and tiny dots that were streams of people. That view had all changed now, he'd heard – it was glassed in, and you couldn't get as close to the edge.

'Ten minutes to freshen up, then we shake what we can out of Murphy,' Walker said.

'Agreed,' Somerville said.

'What are you thinking?'

'We're not staying here long,' Somerville whispered to Walker. 'We'll move the family to a more remote site in a few hours. Out of the city limits, to be safe.'

Walker nodded.

Room service arrived. Two hotel staff stood in the hallway outside, each with a cart loaded with trays of plated food covered in silver cloches. The agents tipped the staff and they left the carts behind. One agent clattered a cart inside the Murphys' suite. Somerville had ordered for everyone: cheeseburgers, fries, salads and sodas, cakes and coffee.

Somerville motioned to Walker and they both left the room. In the hall she pointed to a door opposite, and they entered via a plastic keycard. The NCIS agents remained behind in the Murphys' room, leaning against the bench in the small kitchenette, sipping coffees and looking momentarily helpless.

Walker saw that this room was exactly the same but in a mirrored layout. They had their own room-service tray waiting for them, and Walker poured himself a coffee from the insulated pot. It wasn't a great brew, but it was hot and it was strong. Somerville settled onto one of the two large couches with a burger. Walker looked through the overpriced minibar and then, with the thought that the UN was picking up this tab in mind, helped himself to a miniature bottle of Johnnie Black, pouring it into his coffee.

Somerville looked at him; no judgement, nothing really. Just a look. Walker liked her. She was mid-forties and a career Fed with a pedigree to match, her father a legendary agent who'd spent his time busting mobsters back in the day when the Kennedys were in the White House. Walker would be happy to work with her any time, anywhere, as long as they were in or near civilisation. There were a couple of places, such as those lonely mountains of Afghanistan and the mean streets of Iraqi cities, where he'd prefer someone like Murphy standing next to him. A different kind of animal.

'You know,' Somerville said, eating the pickle that came with the burger, 'I remember a time when I used to think minibar prices were expensive.'

'They are.'

'They *were*,' she said, picking up a handful of fries. 'But they've hardly changed. Think about it. Ten years ago that might have been what, eight bucks instead of ten? Maybe eight-fifty?'

'And?' Walker took a burger. It had looked big on the plate, and huge in Somerville's hands, but in Walker's it was tiny. The bun was dry and the patty was disappointing, but it was protein and fat and sugar, and he knew he'd need all those things today.

'You go to a bar, it's similar prices,' she said. 'But ten years ago? Bar prices were probably half what they are now.'

'Progress?' Walker said.

'Something. I'm not sure.'

'It's probably the rising rents on bars,' Walker said. 'Wages. Maybe liquor licence fees went up a lot. Utilities. Public liability insurance.'

Somerville shrugged.

'Maybe we'll spend some time trying to figure it out after we've prevented this terrorist attack?' Walker said with a mock-sarcastic tone, then ate half his burger in one bite.

Somerville raised an eyebrow and smiled. 'So, we're here. Murphys are safe. Now what?'

'I need to spend more time with Murphy, as soon as he's done powdering his nose,' Walker said.

'You could do with the same,' Somerville said, gesturing to his jeans and boots, covered in mud and muck, and his jacket and shirt, stained with the blood of several men.

'Where are Hutchinson and McCorkell?' Walker asked, the only reaction to Somerville's comment being that he sat on the edge of a couch and undid his boots. They were caked in mud and moss from the Ozarks. His socks were soaked through, and he pulled them off and stood. The carpet was soothing underfoot, plush but firm. Every step and movement massaged and dried his waterlogged skin.

'McCorkell got stonewalled on the list, so he's in DC to see a man about a thing.'

'We need that list.'

'He's working on it.'

'Time's ticking.'

'He knows that too.'

'Okay. And where's Andy at?'

'Hutchinson's there too.'

'Holding McCorkell's hand?'

'Probably the other way around, given that Hutch is the one in the arm cast,' Somerville said. 'And once the list is with us, they're going into the Homeland Security HQ to quarterback our actions here.'

Walker checked his watch. Six and a half hours to go.

83

'Tell me, beat for beat, by the numbers,' Walker said, sipping his drink and adding more coffee. 'If we make something, what assets do we have in play here today?'

'Fourteen in total from the Bureau,' Somerville replied, 'and up to – *up to*, there's no guarantee until the time we need them – twenty uniformed from St Louis PD, and that was a nightmare because they're stretched to a thin blue line right now. Then – best case – I can call in maybe ten from the DEA out of Kansas City if we need them.'

'That's it?'

'Maybe twelve. But that's it. Remember, Walker, in their eyes? This afternoon's attack is still just a theory, based on something you overheard in the forest,' Somerville said. 'If we somehow get a credible threat, then I can press a button and things will go nuclear at Homeland Security and we'll get all kinds of boots on the ground.'

'Right. Hence we need that list.'

'McCorkell's working on it. Your NCIS buddies too.'

'We should have had it days ago. Right from the start.'

'Maybe you haven't met the military?' Somerville said. 'They're a part of the government? You know, bureaucracy and all that?'

Walker let a tired smile break through. 'I'm familiar with the concept.'

'Look, we've also got a Homeland Security office five minutes' walk from here. It's more like a mothballed operations centre, and it gets staffed from Kansas City in the event of an emergency, so I've had it activated.'

'With what? Desk jockeys?'

'Yeah.' Somerville checked her watch. 'They should be set up within the hour. I figure I'll set up over there and be your eyes and ears as needed – they're linked in to every CCTV camera and security service in town and then some.'

'Okay, fine. Sounds good. I guess.'

'It's the best we can do with what we've got, Walker.'

'And prep those DEA guys,' Walker said. 'We'll need them. The more boots on the ground, the better.'

'It'll take a few hours for them to get here.'

'Then get them moving.'

'Sure thing, boss – you want the National Guard activated?'

'That might help.'

'I was being facetious. On both counts – the boss thing, and the Guard.'

'I know. And even if we could, we can't have a battalion of uniformed grunts in Humvees roaming the streets – you know this can't be visible. We've got to let these guys show their hand.'

'Because of Zodiac.'

Walker nodded. 'Any news on my father?'

'The elephant in the room.'

'You say so.'

'No, nothing. Disappeared again.' Somerville watched him for a moment before she continued. 'Are you really sure about this attack here, today?'

'You got any intel that points to any other threat?'

'Nothing other than dead SEALs.'

'Exactly,' Walker said. 'Look, with this kind of cut-out cell, we need this attack to be something like what went down in New York.'

'So, close enough to make the news,' Somerville said, 'but not so close that we can't stop it in time to save lives.'

Walker nodded.

'That's beyond dangerous.'

'Welcome to the major league.'

'Eagles got beat by the Pats last night.'

'Why do you want to hurt me like that?'

'Look, Walker, if we let anyone in the Bureau or Homeland know your intention – about how close a call you want to make this attack – hell, they'd lock us up, thinking we're nuts, or that we're part of the attack.'

'It's the only way we keep this rolling, keep the chain unbroken.'

'Yeah, well, have you thought that this time you're so far behind the eight ball it'll play out to the end and you'll be too late?'

'We'll get them.'

'You're confident.'

'We'll get them,' Walker repeated.

'When you get that list.'

Walker nodded.

'What's that,' Somerville asked, 'a hunch?'

Walker shrugged.

'I like your enthusiasm, Walker. But it's odd. Dangerous. You're playing with fire if you let them get close enough for the media to report it as an attempted terrorist attack.'

'It is what it is,' Walker said. He went to the window. The sky was blue and clear, the kind of day that was crisp and cold but warm in the sun. What was the demonstration? Of something bigger to come? A small-scale explosion, to prove something bigger was in the works? Would they have demands? Would they reveal themselves?

After a minute's silence, Somerville spoke. 'So, you really took down four armed guys in the forest?'

'One. Murph got three. One got away.'

'How good were they?'

'Good. The four we got were the muscle. Well trained. Hell, good enough to kill the other SEALs, right?'

'But I just don't get it. They were all-American, you know? The 502nd? They're a part of the 101st Airborne, right? They're a patriotic bunch. Don't strike me as the "killing their own" types.'

'It's often those you least expect, right,' Walker said, turning to face Somerville. She was halfway through her burger. 'And, yes, as a rule, 101st are good eggs. I've learned that first hand, serving alongside them. But every unit has its bad apples. Remember the Mahmudiyah killings?'

'I'm still thinking of eggs and apples.'

'Mahmudiyah killings . . .'

Somerville sighed. 'Iraq, 2006. The FBI handled the investigation into those soldiers and the atrocities they committed.'

'Right,' Walker said. 'The thing is, those guys in the forest were a near-perfect hit team for this kind of op. I mean, not just their capabilities, but their pedigree. The 502nd, part of the 101st, seen plenty of combat. They probably used their stories to get close to the other members of Team Six. You know, approaching them in a bar or something, trading war tales. Getting the SEALs onside, getting close, and then – *bam*. A shot to the back of the head.'

'Hutchinson did say that five of the guys were hit close range with a HK pistol, fitted with a suppressor, a shot to the back of the head.'

'And that'll be matched to the HK just there,' Walker said, pointing to the weapon wrapped in a clear plastic evidence bag among others on the desk in the hotel room.

'We'll have them to Quantico by nightfall,' Somerville said. 'They'll work it fast.'

Walker was silent as he turned back to the window. *Not fast enough. Not if this is happening today.*

'Jed,' Somerville said. 'Do you have any idea what's coming?'

Walker shook his head. 'Short, scary answer: no. But it's something public. Shock and awe. A "demonstration", they said.' He was silent for a while, just looking down at the street below. 'Let's get Murphy in here, debrief him. He knows something about what's coming, I'm sure of it. It's why he's a liability for these guys, as long as he's alive.'

'He just doesn't know that he knows?'

'Exactly.'

'Great.' Somerville put down what remained of her burger, wiped her mouth and hands with a napkin and bunched it up on the plate. 'That old chestnut.'

There was a rap at the door. Walker opened it to see an agent standing next to a bellboy, the latter holding hangers of clothing, presumably from a nearby store that stocked outfits for people who frequented country clubs. Walker took the offered stack of size XLs, fished a five-dollar tip from his jeans pocket and closed the door.

'I'm going to go shower and change into a douche bag,' he said to Somerville, the clothes in one hand and the remainder of her burger in the other. 'Five minutes. Then we talk to Murphy.'

But Walker didn't get five minutes to take a shower, because there was another knock at the door.

84

The door to the suite was opened by the FBI agent standing sentry in the hallway. As the two NCIS agents entered, Walker could tell from the way they carried themselves that they were here for a fight. Some kind of show was coming, about who was running things in terms of the Murphy family's safety.

'Heads up. Our boss is on his way here,' Woods said to them. 'We just spoke to the office. They think he'll be here in about two hours.'

Walker nodded.

'Then we'll see what's what,' Woods said, looking to Walker and Somerville.

'Levine?' Walker said, looking to her for anything helpful.

She held up her hands. 'What can I say? Agent Woods here is his own man. The thing is,' she said, looking from Walker to Somerville, 'this is a Navy operation. Beginning to end. And we have to protect our people, all the way.'

'Safety first,' Walker said.

Woods smiled.

'You've done a great job of it so far,' Somerville said.

'You've got the lead, for now,' Levine said, ignoring Somerville's remark. 'We'll see where we all stand in two hours.'

'This ends one of two ways,' Walker said to them, without missing a beat.

'Oh, what's that?' Levine replied.

'You help us out,' Walker said, 'and I let you walk away with a pat on the back from your superiors and a note in your file stating that you did a good job. Or, you don't, and you end up working against us – well, then I'll have to treat you like all the others who have been in my way over the past twenty-four hours.'

'I don't think you know who you're talking to,' Woods said. 'You're a goddamned civilian.'

'Like you two are in uniforms,' countered Walker.

'We've got guns and badges,' Woods spat. 'You want to see them, up close?'

'My gun's bigger,' Walker said, motioning to the HK416 on the desk. 'You decide.'

Woods looked furious. Levine was cool.

'Make the choice,' Walker said. 'Help or move on. And be grateful I'm allowing you that, because frankly I don't think you're worth much to us.'

Silence.

'Last chance,' Somerville said. 'Tick-tock.'

'Okay, say we help you,' Woods said, and Levine gave him a look that said *leave-me-the-fuck-out-of-it-I'm-helping-already*. 'What's the help, and what's in it for us?'

Somerville said, 'You will be on the right side of history.'

'Wow.'

'Not ancient history, dickhead,' Walker said. 'You will have played a role in helping to stop a major terrorist attack on US soil.'

Woods merely stared at Walker, his disdain clear on his face.

'You really think something's going to happen, related to these SEAL hits?' Levine said.

Somerville nodded. 'It's happening this afternoon.'

'And how do you know that?' Woods said. 'Because some supposed terrorist hit man you claim to have killed in the forest in the Ozarks just happened to mention it in passing?'

'Because I've been doing this for longer than you have,' Walker said.

'What help are you asking for, exactly?' Levine said.

'You can help protect the Murphys,' Somerville said.

Walker said, 'And you can expedite us getting the list of the SEALs who've been killed.'

'We're here to protect Murphy and his family, it's as simple as that,' Levine said. 'And you're getting in the way of that.'

'And I'm not going to let myself take a fall,' Woods said. 'Levine, think about it for a sec. The way I see it, this guy here wants to get Murphy out of the picture, away from us. Why? Why would he want to do that? Because he's part of this?'

'Sorry, this is *me* you're talking about?' Walker said.

'I mean,' Woods went on, his attention all pointed towards his senior partner, 'where's our confirmation otherwise? Hell, have we even seen *Agent* Somerville's FBI ID? Or those of the guys out in the hall?'

Somerville had had enough. In one swift movement she flipped Woods around, put him into an arm lock, took his service pistol and ejected the mag and field-stripped it with one hand, letting the pieces thud to the carpet, and then, as she held him face-first against the wall of the hotel room, she flashed her ID. All of it inside two seconds.

Levine didn't move. Didn't even watch. She just stared at Walker, and he stared right back.

'One more word,' Somerville said into Woods's ear, her face flushed with frustration and adrenaline and plain anger at incompetence and petulance. 'And what Walker said before, in the lift, is happening – only you can forget the lube, and the clamps and the colonoscopy camera; it's going to be my foot, all the way up to my knee. You got that?'

Woods nodded.

'Say it,' Somerville said.

'I got it.'

Somerville let him go. Woods shook out the ache in his arm, picked up his dismantled pistol and headed over to a chair to sit in solace.

'Stay out of our way,' Somerville said, to both of them. 'I don't give a rat's what your boss has to say about anything. From here on in you're out of the loop. You can go out and stand in the hallway, protect your ex-Navy guy from there.'

Woods stood, holstered his reassembled side-arm and left the room without a word, but before closing the door he looked back to Levine, who was standing there, next to Walker.

'Really?' Woods said to her.

Levine shrugged.

Woods departed, closing the door behind him.

'Sorry,' Levine said to Somerville and Walker. 'He's a by-the-book guy. So, tell me everything you suspect might be happening today, and what I can do to help.'

'We really need that list,' Walker said.

Levine nodded. 'My boss will have it. So, worst case, in two hours, when he gets here, you'll have it.'

85

'You look better,' Walker said to Squeaker.

They were alone in the second bedroom of the Murphys' suite, the kids with their mother next door. She'd just had a shower. Walker was about to take one. She was wearing a thick white bathrobe, her hair wet and wrapped in a towel. She appeared tired, worn out, but there was a wise strength there that belied her size and age.

'You like this?' she said, touching her head-wrap just so. 'I saw it on an old TV show. Thought I'd try it out.'

'Very becoming,' Walker said. 'It's certainly old school.'

The smile left Squeaker's face. 'I heard you guys arguing before.'

'Just a pissing contest between Federal Agents.'

'Right,' Squeaker said, padding over to the minibar in the cabinet below the huge TV that faced the bed. 'Drink?'

'I'm good,' Walker said, seeing that she'd emptied two small bottles of Johnnie Black into a glass, neat. She sat on the end of the bed and sipped at it. The swelling in her face had gone down, and her cut lip was now washed of blood and didn't look so bad, apart from the swelling.

Walker sighed. 'Ah, who am I kidding?' He took a Heineken from the minibar and popped the top.

'I'm taking this into the shower,' he said, indicating his beer and picking up his new clothes. 'And don't you even think about doing what you did last time.'

'What'd I do last time?' Squeaker said. She leaned back on her bed. The tie on her robe was loose, the neckline showed her cleavage, and the front opened to reveal her crossed legs and inner thigh all the way up to where the robe hung low. Still, Walker felt his heart race a little.

'Susan,' he said, crouching down to face her at her eye level.

'Squeaker.'

'Right,' he said. 'Another place and time, sure. But I'm an old man compared to you.'

'You're not that much older,' she said. 'Besides, I like you. And I think you like me. You're attracted to me. And I want you.'

'Look . . .'

She leaned forward and kissed him, and Walker couldn't help but kiss her back, hard enough for her to know that the attraction was mutual, but then he broke away. She looked at him, her eyes telling him exactly what she wanted and how she wanted it.

'Squeaker . . .'

'Yes.'

'Can I tell you something?' he said.

'Sure,' she replied, moving her robe across her chest so that the view left nothing to Walker's imagination.

'I'm not going to over-analyse it,' Walker said, 'but I do think that part of your attraction to me is that I'm different from guys you've met. Simple as that.'

'You think?' She sipped her drink, flinching at the pain of the alcohol hitting her cut lip.

'You're a strong, capable woman,' Walker said to her. 'I know you know that. You're smarter than most people I've met. Street smart; it's ingrained in you. You're resilient and tough. And I know you know that too, but I'm telling you that you're even tougher than you think you are – I can see that, because I've seen toughness, and resilience, and smarts, many times. You've got them all licked.'

'Speaking of licking—'

'All else aside,' Walker said, standing and heading for the shower, 'we don't have time.'

'Fine! Live with regrets, old man,' Squeaker called out, sounding not so much disappointed as merely prepared to allow him to win round two of her advances, as though it was just a matter of time before he came around and saw things for how they should be.

Walker smiled to himself as he turned the shower on full, pulled off his mud- and blood-stained clothing and stepped into the steam. He was tired but he embraced it. His mind and body had been in this type of situation plenty of times. He knew how to work through it. To channel it. Use it. Tiredness was like anything else – fear or longing or hunger – and he had long ago learned how to deal with all those. The military had taught him that. War had reinforced it. Hardened it. Honed it to something that had become an advantage.

It was one of those aspects that allowed men like Walker, when at the coal-face, to slow down time. But in this case time was not on his side. And while he was used to deadlines and time being an enemy, it never got any easier.

86

As Walker stepped into the shower, Menzil was hitching a ride in a truck entering St Louis. The driver picked him up on the Interstate 44 outside Rolla, bitching about how he'd been stuck south of Mountain View for two days waiting for the road to open after a major mudslide, and about how he'd not be making a dime after figuring in the lost time and what he'd spent on food and booze while in town. The cabin stank, like the guy regularly slept in the bunk-like space behind the rear seats and never washed the sheets nor his clothes nor cleaned the interior of the truck. But that was no concern, just an irritant.

Menzil's trouble was that the 502nd guys were now gone. They were to be his protection, should he need it, this afternoon. That was a problem, although he'd been assured over the phone at the truck stop that a contingency was in place and the mission would go ahead as planned. On the one hand, Menzil thought, at least he didn't have to pay the four guys the second half of their instalment for completing the job, a cool hundred grand apiece. On the downside, he knew that Murphy was still out there, with that Walker guy, and while they lived, there was jeopardy for him. Probably not in preventing the attack today – that was a long, long shot – but after the fact, once the country and the world had witnessed the devastation, after Homeland Security and the FBI and the military had done their tests, then Murphy would make the connection. He alone would know who and what was behind the attack.

But Menzil was confident that Murphy, along with Walker, would not live to see another sunset.

•

Walker let the hot water wash away the sweat and blood and dirt and grit. He soaped up and leaned against the wall with a forearm against the tiles, the shower pouring over his head and down his back. He needed sleep, and might well allow himself a nap, he thought, if he could rattle something loose from Murphy fast. They just needed that start of a thread to tug on and the whole thing would unravel. A twenty-minute power nap would be a fine thing right now. He'd mastered them in training, and honed the skill operating in Afghanistan. He knew that he could close his eyes any time, anywhere, and twenty minutes later he'd open them and feel that the world was a better place. He also knew that if needed he could then go on for another six hours at full speed without any sustenance other than water and the adrenaline of the fight.

But he had too many doubts right now to afford that luxury. Serious ones. About what Murphy knew, and whether he could figure it out in time. About this city. *How many people in Greater St Louis? Two million? Three?* He didn't know the city well. *A terrorist attack here could be anything. They'll go for symbolism. There's nothing more symbolic here than the Mississippi. Maybe they're planning to blow up a passenger ferry, some kind of tourist cruise ship. Or maybe a water bus, a public-transport thing. The Greater St Louis area, all the surrounding suburbia, is wrapped around the river, and people have to commute somehow; 17.30 is a busy time – peak hour for people leaving work en masse.*

He'd ask Somerville to get her people to check all that. And other mass-transit systems: trains, buses, the interstate, the airport, anywhere there'd be a mass of people to make whatever this was as big as possible.

A demonstration . . .

It'll be public. They'll want their smoking-towers moment, something to be played again and again on the news. Maybe it'll be an incendiary attack, so that the boat – or whatever it is – will be ablaze, maybe for hours, the kind of magnesium or phosphate fire that can't be extinguished, so that it will literally burn into the eyes and minds of the Americans who view the atrocity on the news channels.

Americans. His people. Those guys in the forest, the ex-Army personnel and Menzil, they were Americans. Not some Saudi-born or Pakistan-trained or Afghanistan-bred terrorists hell bent on revenge. They were Americans, attacking their own.

It was the Stock Exchange all over again.

That's what Zodiac was. Twelve attacks, each as unpredictable in outcome as in pedigree. Its ultimate outcome was to create as much chaos as possible. *How do you fight an enemy whose homeland is the very one that they are destroying?*

The hot water ran over his body and the steam filled the bathroom. The more Walker thought about it, the more he feared two things: the unknown, and the impossible.

The unknown, in that Murphy may well prove to be a dead end in terms of a lead, because the more Walker thought about this, the less it seemed that it was something to do with bin Laden.

And the impossible. Because they were in the dark, with just a city and a time and the general provenance of perpetrators as leads; that was it. Without the target, without the method, without the suspects, there was very little to go on.

He scrubbed himself with soap and rinsed, then towelled off and dressed, all in under three minutes.

Time was ticking.

87

Bill McCorkell said to Bruce Trotter, 'We'll share what we know, and you'll be part of the investigation.'

'No.'

'Not even an hour?' McCorkell said.

'No.'

'Are you not a jerk?' Hutchinson said.

'N— what?' Trotter's face turned a deeper shade of red.

'We're here to help,' McCorkell said. 'Your man Grant doesn't know what he's protecting, and what he's unwittingly let happen by keeping those SEALs off the grid.'

Trotter said, 'You can leave now.'

Hutchinson stood and walked around the room, then turned to look at Trotter. 'No.'

Nothing but silence came from this senior official, clearly not used to being spoken to in this way. Probably not for over ten years. McCorkell watched him.

'Listen, Bruce – can I call you Bruce?' McCorkell said. 'We don't want to embarrass you. We're going to talk to the SEALs regardless. But we want it to be because you facilitated it. Not because I talk to the Secretary of the Navy as soon as I walk out of here.'

The Director of NCIS stared at them both.

'Come on now,' Hutchinson said, taking an expensive golf driver from a bag of clubs in the corner. 'Your guys and girls are good, but this – witness protection – it's a speciality, not a past-time. No disrespect. It's not your turf. We get that. So, save yourself some embarrassment here. Play ball.'

The red slowly flushed from Trotter's face. He sat upright. Straightened his tie.

'What's your lead?' Trotter asked.

'An NSA back door,' Hutchinson said quickly. 'Someone you're protecting broke protocol. One of the SEALs. They must have made a call and mentioned something that flagged a keyword that alerted our investigation. Oh, don't feel bad – that kind of thing, a protectee breaking the rules, it happens all the time with witness protection.'

'Grant runs a tight ship . . .' the Director said, but his tone was not so sure anymore. He stood. 'Let's go to the communications room.'

'Lead the way,' Hutchinson said, putting the club back.

Trotter nodded, then stood, got his jacket and briefcase, and told his secretary he'd be out for the day.

'NSA back door?' McCorkell said sideways to Hutchinson.

'Some bullshit that leads back to the Patriot Act,' he whispered as they followed the Director down the hall. 'Pretty much covers all bases.'

•

Walker sat in the suite with Murphy, Somerville and Levine. The coffee pot and cups were on the table between them. They sat in armchairs by the window, looking out to a sky that was still clear and a sun that remained bright as it burned through midday.

'I like St Louis,' Murphy said.

'Me too,' Walker replied.

'I mean,' Murphy said, 'if this was going down in, I don't know . . . Dallas? Or Phoenix? Hell, I might just walk the other way, let them get away with it.'

Walker and Somerville smiled.

'So, what do we do?' Murphy said. 'We can't stop something we know nothing about. And sitting around here isn't doing anything to stop it either.'

'It's not that we don't know anything about it,' Walker said. 'It's just we haven't yet connected all the dots.'

'Hell, you can't see the dots, let alone connect them up,' Levine said. 'You should just drop this. Let the pros handle it.'

'Homeland Security doesn't even classify it as a credible threat,' Somerville said.

'Well then, there you go,' Levine replied. 'A whole lot of worry for nothing. The Murphys are safe now. Let this be. Nothing more is coming.'

Walker shook his head.

'We don't even have a place to start,' Murphy said.

'Yes, we do,' Walker replied. 'We start with you.'

Murphy didn't look sold.

'Or you could walk away from this,' Levine said. 'Leave it up to the FBI and their Counterterrorism taskforce. Or Homeland Security – they probably need something to do. And if none of them have had any peep of a threat, then take the hint and pack up and go home.'

'As we speak, good people at the FBI's CTD are looking at it from all angles,' Somerville said. 'But we're having trouble getting a credible threat warning on this afternoon's attack.'

'Do you even think it's credible?' Levine said. 'I mean, really? Because of what you heard, Walker, way out in the boonies? From some armed thugs? Hell – I can see the Homeland's point. I mean: a) who the hell are you, Walker, and b) what actually went down out there? Are you really trying to convince us that four ex-Army guys were sent on a kill mission against Murphy – and Walker dispatched them? *Really*?'

Murphy picked up his fatigues from a pile in the corner and pointedly showed Levine the dried blood on the left arm. It was a decent stain, Walker saw; arterial explosion, probably from Stokes, the sniper. Walker ran through the scenario in his mind's eye: Murphy had snuck up behind him and used his left hand to lift the guy's head from behind and expose the neck, while the right hand used a knife to slice across the carotid artery. Death via rapid bleed-out.

'This ain't from no hog, I'll tell you that,' he said. Then he indicated the silenced HK pistol and the two 416 assault rifles, field-stripped and bagged in FBI plastic evidence bags. 'And they're not toys we got from the local Walmart either. So, if you or your friend out there question my bona fides again, you can go and get—'

A sound cut him off. A cell phone, ringing loud, close up.

Levine reached for her BlackBerry, clipped next to her holstered Glock. Walker saw the caller ID on the screen: Assistant Director Grant. That meant he'd landed.

Levine smiled.

88

'He wants to talk to you,' Levine said, passing her cell phone to Walker.

'Yes?' Walker said into the phone.

'Walker?'

'Grant?' Walker could tell that the NCIS man was in a car for all the white noise from the road at the other end of the connection.

'Right,' Grant said. 'I'm coming to your location now – about twenty minutes out by car. You're there with Murphy and his family?'

Walker looked to Murphy. 'Yes.'

'Right,' Grant said. 'Well, first up, let me just say, good work, saving him like that. You have our thanks – the entire Navy thanks you.'

Grant paused. Walker didn't speak. He felt that the NCIS Assistant Director was giving him the space to be gracious, to say something about how he just started the rescue and now here they were, all together, and that Murphy and his family wouldn't have been safe without the NCIS assistance that was now on hand. But that wouldn't be true. And Walker wasn't the type to resort to small and useless talk just for the sake of it – or, worse, for some kind of back-patting, congratulatory BS.

'So . . .' Grant said into his phone, the word carried with a deep exhale, as though the whole time waiting for Walker's reply had been spent breathless. 'Once I get there, we can do a handover on the Murphys.'

Walker was silent.

Grant said, 'Walker?'

'Yeah?'

'I said we can handle it from here on in,' Grant said. 'And, again, thanks for your assistance. Expect a letter of appreciation signed by the—'

Walker passed the phone back to Levine.

'I think it's a wrong number,' Walker said.

Levine hesitated but then took the phone, and Walker could

hear that Grant eventually stopped and said, after a pause, 'Walker? Walker, are you there?'

'It's me,' Levine said into her phone.

Walker moved away, joining Somerville, who stood by the window. Murphy followed.

'Her boss is spinning some kind of crap,' Walker said. He looked to Somerville. 'He's about fifteen minutes away. You might need to pull rank.'

'Got it,' she said to Walker, then turned to look Murphy in the eye. 'We'll move Grant and the others on, along with my agents here, and we'll escort your family to an FBI safe house just out of town. Is that okay with you?'

'You've got a safe house here?' Murphy said.

Somerville nodded.

'Why weren't we taken straight there?'

'It's a mothballed site, it takes a bit of time to clear and set up,' Somerville said. 'Besides, this is, well, a lot more luxurious. But I'll move them all on. It's safe there, with my agents and St Louis PD all around. All right?'

Murphy looked to Walker. Walker nodded.

'Okay,' Murphy said. 'Where is it?'

'About twenty-five miles north-east of town, off an old section of the interstate,' she replied. 'It's as secure as anywhere will be.'

'Right,' Murphy said. 'I'll tell Jane to get ready to move. Squeaker too.'

He left the room.

'Have your guys turned up anything in town classified as a threat yet?' Walker asked.

'This is the sum of it,' Somerville replied, passing over her cell phone, which showed an emailed list of possible targets. It was a long list, including transportation hubs, civic buildings, prominent people and any known gatherings of people.

'Who put this together?' Walker said.

'The CTD guys in Washington,' Somerville replied.

The FBI's Counterterrorism Division. They were a good unit,

Walker knew, with plenty of resources and plenty of wins that the population would never hear about.

Walker said, 'It's like they just rattled off every possible thing in town where there was a chance of there being more than five people. Hell, they've even listed burger chains.'

'I told them to go wide, given we've got nothing but the city and the time to go by in terms of leads.'

'It's not right,' Walker said, handing the phone back. 'Those guys were specific: a *demonstration at 5.30*. They're going to demonstrate the capabilities of whatever *it* is – a weapon, a strike, a method, whatever – at 5.30pm. They're not going to blow up a cinema or a flight or the mayor's office or any of those hundred or so targets. Certainly not a burger joint.'

'There is one demonstration there,' Somerville said.

'At a school?' Walker said, seeing it listed. 'Bunch of teachers' aides?'

'It's a demonstration. St Louis PD will be there in numbers.'

'It's listed for 3pm.'

'Still.'

'What about the energy grid, or the water infrastructure?' Murphy asked, rejoining them and scrolling through the list after taking the offered phone from Somerville. 'Bang for your buck, that'd generate a hell of a demonstration, right? Could be a bomb threat. Maybe a small detonation? Dirty even . . . Drop some contagion into a power station and it'd clear it out for days, big blackout across the city and beyond; it'd make for a hell of a national – international – news story, right? And the water supply – dump in there and you could be looking at hundreds sick and dead on day one, thousands by the end of the week by the time the authority tracked it to the water.'

'No,' Walker said. 'It's not that. It's specific to St Louis. You could attack any random target like that anywhere in the US and it'd make more of an impact. We're looking for something specific to this city.'

'What happened to it being opportunistic?'

'Doesn't feel right.'

'Another hunch?' asked Somerville.

Walker said, 'What's this city got that no other place has?'

'That's what we've got to figure out. It's something symbolic, and it happens at a specific time, a demonstration that would show what they're capable of . . .'

'They're the main landmarks,' Murphy said, passing the phone back to Somerville. 'What about airports?'

'We need to stop thinking of generic places,' Walker said. He was leaning against the thick glass of the large window, looking down at the pedestrians below. 'It's an event. Something that happens at 5.30. Somewhere there will be press, local and state and maybe some national TV news crews, beaming live satellite feeds from the site. This is for effect, and it's going to happen real-time, for the maximum shock-and-awe factor. That's what we need to look at first.'

'What happens at 5.30 in St Louis?' Somerville said. 'I mean, this isn't like New York, with the ringing of the bell at the Stock Exchange.'

'And it's not a demonstration for those perpetrating it . . .' Walker said, as though he hadn't heard Somerville. 'It's not proving to them that it's something that *they* can do. It's a demonstration – to the *rest* of us. It's proof of what they have, and of their intent to use it.'

89

The head of JSOC, Joint Special Operations Command, took the meeting because he and McCorkell went back a long way.

'I sent a four-man SEAL squad to Murphy's last known location,' the Admiral said.

'When was that?' McCorkell asked.

'Almost forty-eight hours ago,' the Admiral replied. 'I'll have them meet your man and Murphy in St Louis and protect them all the way into San Diego.'

He launched into a spiel about how those already in protection were being debriefed, as per McCorkell's request, by an FBI team, when there was a knock at the door. A junior officer appeared. The Admiral looked pissed at the interruption, but it was his private secretary, who stood inside the door looking flustered.

'A word, sir?'

The Admiral looked to McCorkell and Hutchinson as if weighing up whether to ask them to leave, but he saw the panic on his aide's face and he got up and left the room.

McCorkell was about to talk to Hutchinson when the door opened. The Admiral was paler than his white uniform.

'My audit crew,' the Admiral said. 'They're dead.'

•

'I'm tasked with your security,' Grant said to Murphy.

'My daughter's bigger and scarier than you,' Murphy said to the guy.

'I've had my Director talk to the head of DEVGRU,' Grant said, unflustered, 'and the latter's going to be there at the San Diego safe house by tonight, debriefing you and the rest of the Team Six guys from the bin Laden op.'

'This has nothing to do with Abbottabad,' Murphy said. He looked to Walker. 'Nothing.'

'You sound pretty sure about that,' Grant said.

'We are pretty sure,' Walker said.

'How do you figure that?' Grant said, his eyes darting from Murphy to Walker. 'What crap have you been peddling, Walker? What kind of Kool-Aid are you serving up here, hmm?'

'Murph and I talked it through all morning,' Walker said evenly. 'We're looking at other possibilities. Those guys operate together in units all the time, so we thought, who's to say that this has to be about the bin Laden op?'

'And the more I think about it,' Murphy said, 'the more I think he's right. I mean, we've seen nothing that confirms it—'

'Okay, say you're right, somehow,' Grant interrupted. 'Maybe it's not to do with that op per se. Though, I have to say, you're wrong, because I've matched the dead to those who were there.'

'I need to see that list of names,' Murphy said. 'That will prove it either way.'

'I'm sorry, Chief Murphy,' Grant said. 'I understand what you're saying, and that you knew these guys. All I can confirm is that all eight guys were there, in Abbottabad—'

'That's bullshit,' Murphy said. 'Total A-grade—'

'And you're the final SEAL from that op that we need to get to safety,' Grant finished.

Murphy was shaking his head. 'What's it hurt for me to see a list of my dead buddies? I mean, are you going to stop me from going to their funerals?'

'When you're back in San Diego, then moved off the grid, with dozens of armed guards on hand, then you'll find out,' Grant said. 'You can be united with your teammates by this evening. And then it will become obvious who the eight were – because they won't be there. Until then, it's operationally secure information. There might still be kill teams out there. We've got surveillance at all the SEALs' last postings and homes, looking out for the perps. We're taking no risks.'

'There's more at play here,' Walker said to Grant. 'They're not being killed in reprisal. It's because they *saw* something, in the field.'

'Something neither of you has any idea about?' Grant said.

Walker was silent.

'Say for a moment that you're right, Walker,' Grant said. 'That maybe killing these operators aims to lead some kind of resources or investigation somewhere else. We have thought about that – we're not idiots.'

'There's a terrorist attack coming,' Walker said firmly, his patience almost at an end.

'And what would that be?' Grant said. 'McCorkell mentioned it, but couldn't elaborate. Can you?'

'You're tasked with the safety of the Murphy family,' Walker said. 'So, I suggest you play a part in that. Here, in this city, for the day. Leave the rest up to those interested in stopping a terror attack.'

Grant didn't show annoyance but he said in a quiet dangerous voice, 'Excuse me?'

'Something is going down, here, in St Louis,' Murphy said. 'At 17.30 today.'

Walker watched for Grant's reaction. Nothing showing.

'Like I said, I've been briefed on that point,' he said coldly, 'but I'm not buying it. Are you really telling me that your intel is based on something you overheard from a group of guys *in a forest*? I mean, if they were so professional, why would they let you in on that?'

'They figured I wouldn't be seeing today's sunrise,' Walker said. 'That's why they spoke frankly.'

'And what happened, exactly, in that forest?'

'One guy tripped and fell. Then three of them met with Murphy.'

'Four?' Grant said, his eyebrows raised. 'All dead?'

Walker shrugged.

'What's that mean?' Grant asked.

'The guy who fell might be alive,' Walker said. 'But I doubt it. Regardless, he won't be moving from where he fell, so if he's not yet dead, he will be soon.'

'Jesus.' Grant looked at the two of them. 'You're civilians now – you can't go around killing people. I'm a Federal Agent, *do you understand*? Murphy, do you know that? What all this means?'

Murphy was silent.

'It is what it is,' Walker said. 'The Murphys are leaving now, with Somerville and her team, who will take them to a safe place.

Your guys too, and you, since it's your job – you're tasked with their security, right?'

'They're leaving the city?' Grant said. 'When?'

'Momentarily,' Walker replied.

'Okay, okay,' Grant said, looking at Murphy. 'Good. You should get out too, with your wife and kids.'

Murphy just stared at the NCIS guy.

Grant was silent for a beat, then said, 'None of your teammates were dumb enough to say no to our offer of protection. Nor did they stall. They all came back with the agents who went to collect them. Think of your family, for Christ's sake. You think they're safer around here, or with a bunch of SEALs in a secure facility guarded over by a platoon of heavily armed agents?'

Murphy looked to Walker and then back to Grant. 'My family is leaving, with Somerville and the FBI, to a secure site here. I'm staying around until this afternoon. Until at least 17.30. Then we'll see what's what. Fact is, I unknowingly had a hand in starting whatever this is, and I'm going to help Walker stop it.'

90

'They're chipped,' the JSOC Admiral said. 'All SEALs for the past year have been chipped with micro GPS markers, as part of a new program that allows us to locate them if they're captured or cut off from comms. DoD is looking to roll out the program across all frontline troops.'

'Congress will love that,' Hutchinson said.

McCorkell looked to Hutchinson then back to the Admiral. 'And?'

'They've just turned up. Dead. Murdered.'

'Where?' Hutchinson asked.

'We pulled them out of a lake in Little Rock.' He looked down at the brief report. 'They were in the water at least twenty-four hours.'

'Little Rock, Arkansas?' McCorkell asked.

The man with ultimate authority over the SEALs nodded, his mood heavy. 'They left for there two days ago, Navy flight, to then head on up to help NCIS look for Murphy. They were good men, as capable as any SEALs. They and a crew from the west coast have helped in bringing in all the Abbottabad Team Six guys over the past week, each time without incident. Until this.'

'How were they killed?' Hutchinson asked.

'Gunshot.' The Admiral looked down at his desk. 'Who would do this?'

'Single shot to the head?' Hutchinson asked.

The Admiral looked at the paper in his hands and nodded.

Hutchinson said, 'The same guys who killed the Team Six SEALs killed your men.'

'They didn't just kill them,' McCorkell added. 'They replaced them.'

'Replaced them?'

'Yes. There were four guys out there masquerading as your A Team, going after Murphy. And Murphy and my guy Walker got them early this morning.'

It took the Admiral a moment to catch up with that, then he said, 'Bill, what's going on here?'

'Something's coming, Admiral,' McCorkell said. 'Something catastrophic.'

•

Grant looked at those in the room. His two agents. The ex-SEAL. And the – the whatever Walker was. A giant. Grant had to look up to him.

Walker watched him in turn. He could have been a jockey, Walker thought. Or a flyweight boxer. He looked wiry, capable. His nose was a small flat bud, like it had been mashed a few times as a kid or teen. Probably from hard-scrabble fights, where he'd forged a reputation for being nothing like the pushover that he seemed. Walker had met plenty of short aggressive guys like that in the military. Napoleon complex, some called it. But Walker never underestimated people on their physical characteristics; it wasn't so much the size of the man in the fight, but the size of the fight in the man. He could see Grant had plenty of it in him.

'I'm sticking with you,' Grant said to Murphy. 'You're still a target here – in danger. Woods, you stick here too. Levine, you go with the Murphy family, take care of them. Until after 17.30, then we'll see what's what.'

'Negative,' Levine said, staring at Grant. 'I'm lead agent; this is *my* op. I'm with Murphy, all the way. Woods will go with the Feds to cover the babysitting duties. End of story.'

Grant looked at Levine, considered rebuking her, then shrugged. 'Fine,' he said. 'You stay with Murphy here. Woods, you will stick with his family.'

'Sir—'

'And I will accompany you all to the safe house,' Grant said, looking from Levine to his other agent, then to Walker. 'Until this blows over after 17.30 with nothing doing, and you, Walker, will look like the jackass you are.'

91

'Why NCIS?' Murphy asked.

Walker said, 'Because they're your cops.'

The two of them were in Somerville's room. The others had left to work out the logistics of their movements for the day. Walker was ready to crack this wide open, starting with more interrogation of the SEAL.

'But why are they the ones handling our protection?' Murphy said. 'I mean, I get that they would want to investigate the murder of SEALs, but some of us are retired and have been for years. Why not the FBI or US Marshals or someone like that?'

'Because it all goes back to one perp, one attacker, one case,' Walker said. 'And the Pentagon has far more money than anyone else, so they've taken charge.'

'I guess that sounds right.' Murphy stood by the window, looking down at St Louis. 'And then there's the whole secrecy thing.'

'Secrecy thing?' Walker said.

'We're not known outside SEAL land,' Murphy said. 'Our IDs, I mean, and that stands after we leave. In case of reprisals, just like this. But NCIS could get our details, if anyone could, right?'

'Yeah . . .' Walker was checking his email on his phone, but he stopped and looked up at Murphy. 'Did you see the shots in Abbottabad?'

'Bin Laden?'

Walker nodded.

'Nope.' Murphy shook his head. 'I heard them. I was on the ground floor. I got up there a few moments later.'

'How'd you feel?'

'At first? No different. A bit of jubilation I guess, a couple of days later. It was just an op. Our ROE stated that anyone at the target with or in reach of a weapon was to be put down, and that's what happened. Afterwards, when it sunk it, sure, it felt good, knowing that we were the ones who got him, finally.'

'You didn't think it was too quick an end for him?'

'Nope. He knew what was coming, the moment he heard the helos and then our breeching charges. But, really, he knew we were coming for him, and winning the war, for the best part of ten years. Al Qaeda is nothing now.'

'There's a hole in your record,' Walker said, looking back at Murphy's file, emailed through courtesy of McCorkell.

'There's plenty of holes.'

'We've got all your tours listed here,' Walker said, scrolling through the file. 'Three in 'Stan, three more in Iraq, a three-month training session, another tour of 'Stan, one aboard the *Zumwalt* in the Gulf of Aden doing anti-piracy—'

'The most boring time of my life.'

'Then back in 'Stan, a stint of close-protection work.'

'The second-most boring. No, maybe it was a tie. At least at sea we could get wet.'

''Stan once more as an advisor, and then almost as soon as you got there you and the team were pulled out to prep for Abbottabad.'

'Right. And where'd you get all that info?'

'My guy.'

'Your guy the President? Because SEAL files are sealed up tighter than a dolphin's butt – and that's watertight.'

Walker smiled, said, 'Tell me about the three months, listed as training.'

'It was R&R, put down as training because we deserved it.'

'Deserved it?'

'And then some. It's listed as overseas training so that we'd get paid overseas-duty pay.'

'But it was R&R?'

Murphy nodded. 'We had a good CO at JSOC.'

'What'd you do?' Walker asked.

'I rested. And relaxed.'

'Where?'

'Here and there.'

'Doing?'

'The usual.'

Walker nodded. 'I just wonder why it's listed as training instead of just being regular service as with all your other international training runs. I mean, I've been in that world – not as a SEAL, sure, but in 24th Tac – and we'd train more than we'd sleep. I've never seen anything listed like this, good CO or not.'

Murphy was silent.

'Did your whole team get this leave?' Walker asked.

'Lemme see.' Murphy took the phone and scrolled up and down, reading. 'Hmph. Yep . . . but it was no training. Nor R&R, to be honest.' Murphy looked up to Walker. 'At least, we got about ten days at the end. Made my second kid.'

'So, it *was* an op?'

Murphy nodded.

'It's listed in your official file as training. So, that means *very* off the books . . .'

'DEVGRU does stuff that's often not cited any place.'

'It will be recorded somewhere,' Walker said. 'This is the Pentagon we're talking about. Everything gets filed away. So, you might as well tell me, save us all time.'

'Well, maybe your guy has to get that file . . .'

'Murph, this might be relevant.'

'No, it can't be – this is about Abbottabad, you said so yourself, the guys who were there are those getting hit . . . you said it's because we saw something there, right?'

Walker paused, watching Murphy, who seemed to be thinking back to either that off-books op or Abbottabad, the guys he'd spent so many days and nights fighting side-by-side with, only to be assassinated.

Walker said, 'At least tell me where the op occurred.'

'I can't talk about it.'

'Ballpark.'

'It's unrelated.'

'You don't know that.'

'I know.'

'What was it?'

'Nothing related.'

Walker looked at the dates. 'Iraq was still hot then. Just pre the mission-accomplished appearance by Bush, which was about ten years premature.'

'Yep.'

''Stan was busy too.'

'You're getting colder.'

'Persian Gulf?'

'Nope.'

'Iraq.'

Murphy nodded.

Walker said, 'Close protection?'

'In a sense.'

'Of who?'

'No-one.'

Walker was confused, then he said, 'Something. Not someone. Your team were protecting some*thing*. An oil field?'

'I can't talk about it.'

'You're well out of your service now.'

'I signed a lot of papers when I became a SEAL, more when I went to DEVGRU to be part of Team Six. Another stack of them after this op. So, if I tell you what I did, it's federal prison for me – serious, long time.'

'Then don't tell me what *you* did,' Walker said. 'Tell me what your teammates did. Theoretically even. Broad brushstrokes. To rule it out.'

Murphy smiled.

'Fine,' Walker said. He looked again at the dates. 'You're *sure* this has nothing to do with it?'

'It can't. No reprisals would stem from it.'

'No-one was killed?'

'No-one important. No-one with family or friends with *this* kind of reach.'

'Yet it was big enough for SOCOM to not have a record of it, big enough for someone at DEVGRU command or higher up to falsify your location and list it as overseas training, technically breaking a law somewhere in the payroll department of the Pentagon.'

'Right.'

'Protection work, but not for a person . . .'

'Right.'

'Okay.' Walker tapped the list. 'We need the names, from my guy. If we get the names, it might jar something loose – about this op, Abbottabad, anything.'

'There's no jarring to be done, Walker,' Murphy said. 'You said it yourself, first up. Someone on the inside sold out the Team Six guys from Abbottabad and some AQ towel-heads are roaming the earth to snuff us out. Or paying ex-US Army pukes to do the dirty work for them. And you know what? They're going to fail, big time. Because I'm going to go hunting.'

92

'What you said before . . .' Walker said, turning from the hotel window.

'What?' Murphy asked.

Walker motioned with his head to the door of the hotel suite, through which the others had recently departed.

'About the NCIS,' Walker said. 'Before, you said that they, if anyone, could get SEAL IDs.'

'So?'

'*So*, how could these ex-Army guys or Menzil get your IDs?' Walker said. 'How could they know who was in DEVGRU at the time?'

Murphy thought about the question a while before answering. 'You think they have someone inside? In NCIS or JSOC?'

'Could be,' Walker said. 'We can't discount that.'

'I just don't get the *why*,' Murphy said. 'Why hit the team like this?'

'Because of what you saw in bin Laden's compound . . .'

'I've been thinking about it all morning. There was nothing there, nothing. All the intel was on hard drives. We saw nothing.'

'You think that's the case,' Walker said, looking back out the window to the Mississippi, as though clarity would be offered up from the muddy old girl in the form of some kind of solution. 'Hell, maybe you're right, Murph – maybe you didn't see it, but maybe the others did.'

'Maybe just one did . . .'

'Maybe.'

'Maybe one of the guys got all bent up over something, and he sold out.'

'You think that?'

'No. Never.'

'Okay.'

'I'm serious. No matter what, they'd never talk. They'd never jeopardise a teammate, let alone the teammate's family. They'd die first, however which way it was coming.'

Walker didn't press it. He just nodded, because he understood Murphy's sentiment. These guys were brothers and they covered each other's backs in such a way that it became an innate feeling. But he also knew that there were ways to make men talk, no matter how good and tough they were, no matter what kind of oath they'd forged in blood and sweat and tears. He let it slide, because it seemed the least likely of all, but he couldn't discount it fully. 'Maybe we're looking at this the wrong way.'

'How do you figure?'

'I'm not sure. But we're missing something.'

'We really need that list.'

'Damn straight,' Walker said, and picked up his cell phone.

•

McCorkell arrived at the White House and was ushered through security. The place smelled like home, as though the weight of the air was comforting. He made his way towards the administration area of the west wing, heading for his old office in the north-west corner, where he paused and knocked at the door.

'Hey, Ann,' McCorkell said after being summoned in. 'I like what you've done with the place.' He shook the National Security Advisor's hand, looking around his old office.

'If you say it has a feminine touch, I'll call the Secret Service,' Ann said with a grin.

'Me? Never,' McCorkell said. He took a seat opposite, the leather chair a modern design compared with those he'd had in here. It made him sit more upright, and feel uncomfortable because the seat was short and the armrests too low. A good ploy, probably, to leave the CIA or NSA or FBI briefers under no illusion as to who was the boss in here. 'So, you know about the SEAL hits?'

'You're cutting to it, as usual,' Ann said. 'Yes, I know about it. They're all safe now, bar one, who the Navy are having a hell of a time hunting down.'

'They found him.'

'Oh? When?'

'Early this morning, with the help of one of my investigators,' McCorkell said. 'Ann, this leads back to Zodiac.'

Ann raised her hand. 'Bill, I've looked at that every which way and been in all kinds of meetings with the Agencies and Cabinet about it. I have to tell you, there's nothing there but what you've brought me.'

'But?'

'But, you've got the Vice President in your pocket and you've convinced him otherwise, hence you're sitting here right now chewing up my time.'

'I just told you something you didn't yet know,' McCorkell said.

'About Murphy being found? That'll be in my inbox; I've been in meetings. Have you seen what's happening in Ukraine today? And in Pakistan? And Egypt? The Mid-East? The South China Sea? Hell, I've got a third of the world all lit up right now, flashing red on threat boards.'

'I just need a list,' McCorkell said. 'Names. The SEAL team on the UBL kill op.'

'Bill, I can't—'

'Ann, I need the list – not of all the operators. I understand that and will respect that,' McCorkell said. 'But give me the list of the dead. The hit list so far. That you can do – there's no more harm to be done to those men. Give me that list, eight names, and maybe I can drop by tomorrow and help out on the phone, put out some of these fires for you.'

Ann smiled.

'Okay,' she said, tapping away at her computer to bring up the file. 'The list of the dead I can do – it's in one of my Presidential Daily Briefings. I'll give you that, then you can set up a card table in the basement here and sort out the Middle East for me.'

'Deal,' McCorkell said with a smile, though he knew she was most the way serious about the workload owed.

93

'He's calling back asap,' Walker said.

'With the names?' Murphy replied.

'Yes.' Walker started tapping at the side table, then stood and started pacing the room. 'What if you didn't see anything in Abbottabad?'

'I didn't.'

'Right,' Walker said. 'But I'm saying, maybe no-one saw anything. Maybe it's this op listed as R&R?'

'That makes sense. No, wait, it doesn't make any sense at all.' Murphy leaned forward. 'You keep saying that we *saw something in Abbottabad*, now you're saying we *didn't* – make up your mind.'

'Exactly.'

'Huh? Look, we all saw plenty in there, okay?'

'Like?'

'Random crap,' Murphy said. 'Computers and files and pictures and tapes and scrapbooks and hard drives and maps and hair dye.'

'Hair dye?'

'For bin Laden's beard, we figured. He was a pretty vain guy, apparently. Probably comes with having multiple wives to keep interested. I mean, damn, he was housebound. The only time he'd go out was to pace around his vegetable garden. So, who else was he doing it for – either himself or for them, right? Probably dyed his beard in the mirror and then gave himself a selfie.' Murphy mimed jerking off.

Walker smiled, and then just as quickly his expression grew serious. 'Look, I'm saying . . . Murph, I gotta ask . . .'

Walker looked at him, expectant, as though an answer would rattle out, but Murphy just returned his stare.

'What?' Murphy said.

'Well,' Walker said, 'in the house, you boys really did . . . you know.'

'Really did . . . I seriously have no idea what you're getting at.'

'You really did get him, right? Just to be sure that this isn't some big conspiracy to stop the truth getting out—'

'Fuck – are you really asking me that?'

'Just in case. I've got to know. It's true, right?'

'Yes,' Murphy said, shaking his head, incredulous. 'Yes, Walker, we *killed* him. And then killed him *again*.'

'Okay. I had to ask.'

'Shit. Really? Look, we executed the op, fast and furious, then we flew back to Bagram in the Black Hawk loaded with the body and the intel, with most of the team riding out in the back-up Chinook. I was in the Hawk with five other guys. The two shooters sat on his body the whole way, grinning ear to ear; it looked all the world like some old-school photo of a couple of hunters who'd just brought down a lion or rhino. We touched down, then switched out to a couple of waiting V-22s and bugged straight out to the *Carl Vinson*, taking all intel – and the body – with us.'

'I know about the flights,' Walker said. 'A friend of mine's with 160th SOAR, he was one of the pilots of the other Black Hawk, the one that crashed on insertion. And I know the CIA guys who handled the intel after the fact.'

'They did good work, the 160th, that Black Hawk going down be damned. They got us in and got us out, undetected, deep in and out of Pakistan.'

'They're good flyers.'

'The best. So, what were you going to say?'

'What if what you guys saw wasn't there?'

'That makes sense,' Murphy said, then, even more sarcastic in tone, added, 'No it doesn't, yet again. You've lost me.'

'What if it was someplace else . . .' Walker looked back out the window, as if a thought was just out of reach somewhere out there. The day was still cold but the sun was out and it danced brightly on the chop on the Mississippi.

'What are you getting at, Walker?'

'Team Six,' Walker said. 'You guys worked all the time. High operational tempo, right?'

'The highest. Teams from DEVGRU were out there every night.'

'Exactly,' Walker said, looking to Murphy. 'So, maybe we're looking at the wrong op.'

'Well, who said it was the guys at Abbottabad?' Murphy said. 'I mean, in the first place, who made that connection, that statement?'

'I don't know where that started. NCIS maybe. Levine said so before, right – that Grant said it? Any rate, we were told it – it's the official line, from the Navy.'

'Well, they'd know,' Murphy said. 'It wouldn't be hard to deduce, right? I mean, eight killed; if all eight were on that op, that'd be it. Eight guys out of forty on that raid. It'd be rare for the same eight of us to be doing anything else but hunting bad guys, and bin Laden was the pinnacle – it's not like we'd get reprisals like this for shooting some Somali pirates, right?'

'Maybe. Maybe not. It could be another op you guys carried out. It could be this off-books thing or something like it.'

'Guys were in and out of Six all the time,' Murphy said. 'DEVGRU is a big unit. It'd be a hell of a coincidence if the eight guys down were on a different op. I won't know until I get that list of the guys killed. We need it.'

Walker checked his phone, waiting for McCorkell to call.

●

'Nice place,' Squeaker said as they pulled up to a decrepit group of buildings. It had been a motel, built in the 1960s, a cluster of twelve yellow-brick buildings with stained curtains and original fixtures and fittings. The office was connected to a diner, clearly abandoned years ago. 'But I think the train left this station a while ago.'

'It's safe,' Somerville said simply to her as they got out the car. She gave a set of keys to Woods and pointed to the third room, indicating that's where the Murphy family would be staying. 'The government has owned it for a long time. One road in, fences all around, nothing but farms and the old branch of the interstate that flashes through here. If anyone comes, we'll know about it well in advance.'

Squeaker nodded, then looked back at the diner. 'Have they got food here?'

'There's food,' Somerville said, handing her a key marked '2'. 'We stocked the rooms this morning. There's even running hot water and cable TV. Not just basic cable, either.'

'Tax money at work, hey?' Squeaker said.

Somerville smiled. 'That's about it. You go settle in with the Murphys; I'll set up out here and drop by in about ten.'

Squeaker nodded and helped Jane with the kids.

'You're sure this is secure?' Grant asked Somerville when it was just the two of them.

Somerville looked at him, then around the court. The empty road. The fields out back and to the sides. A couple of rows of old pines yellowing with neglect and age. The only other building visible was an abandoned petrol station a few hundred yards down the road. The sound of the interstate drifted in from half a mile to the west.

'You don't see what I see?' Somerville said.

'I see a field, a road, one way in, one way out,' Grant said, gesturing to each as he spoke. 'I see old buildings that have thin plate-glass windows and flimsy doors and locks that could probably be picked by my little sister. And you've got four guys here.'

'And I've got you and Woods,' Somerville said. 'And two unmarked highway cruisers parked further out on the interstate.'

Grant looked at her, then looked around again, squinting against the sun. 'I don't like it,' he said. 'I'm sticking close to the family.'

'You do that,' Somerville said, and passed him a key marked '4'. 'We'll keep our eyes out for bogeymen.'

Grant headed towards the Murphys' room. He could see through the lace curtains that Woods was inside, helping to settle one of the kids. Then Squeaker was in there too – her room next door had an interconnecting door. He looked up and down the road, and then back at the room full of life in front of him. There was nothing about this that he liked.

94

'It's been fifteen,' Murphy said, looking at his watch.

'He's onto it,' Walker replied, checking for new email on his phone. Nothing. He sat back in the armchair.

'Damn it to hell.' Murphy paced. 'The list, I mean. What will it show? Which of my friends is dead? Murdered. Back-of-the-head shots, right? Damn . . .'

'You'll get your revenge,' Walker said. The ex-SEAL looked at him. Seething anger there, just under the surface. The guy wanted to kill someone.

'I want more than that. I *need* more than that.'

'You can kill those responsible and then go dig up their ancestors and kill them too, all over again. How about that?'

'I'm serious.' Murphy stopped at the window and faced Walker. 'I need to know why. Why would they do this? Because they think we saw something that might stop a terrorist attack at 5.30 this afternoon?'

'It's a demonstration. The bigger attack will follow.'

'You know what I mean. We – the SEALs – weren't going to stop them, not today, not a month from now. If we'd seen a threat, in Abbottabad, you don't think we would have spoken up about it, stopped it before now?'

'Right.'

'So, I'm just saying, why the need to kill us? *Why?*'

Walker paused, looking up at the SEAL. 'You know we may not get the chance to ask that.'

'I'm calling bullshit on that,' Murphy said. 'This isn't war. This isn't sniping some towel-head off a mountain half a mile away. This is going to be up close and personal, right? I'm not going to use that .45 unless I have to. It's going to be this.' Murphy pulled out the hunting knife with which he'd dispatched Stokes and Duncan. 'This will get the truth out of them.'

'Torture will only get you the answers that you want to hear,' Walker said.

'You think?'

'I know.'

'You *know*?'

Walker nodded. 'Ten years in the CIA,' he said. 'Iraq and 'Stan were my sandbox. Later it became Syria and Lebanon, then Iran and Pakistan. You think I didn't see my share of so-called enhanced interrogation techniques?'

'They worked. We got the bad guy.'

'No, they didn't. We did that for over ten years to hunt bin Laden and we got nowhere.'

'We got him in the end.'

'Because of good old-fashioned detective work.'

Murphy scoffed. 'Now you're sounding soft.'

'Listen,' Walker said, getting closer to the SEAL. 'I want to know the *why* as much as you do. But you know what? I've been hunting these types of guys for a long, long time. Hell, I've been one of them, overthrowing governments and organising regime changes and assassinations and waging all kinds of economic warfare.' Walker took a moment, meeting Murphy square in the eye. 'I did it for my country. And some crazy people out there may well think that they're doing it for a similar purpose. Or, worse? They're doing it for a reason that we can't even fathom.'

'Like what? They *enjoy* it?'

'Maybe. You served with men like that. I know I did. There are a lot of guys who join the military because it's a legal way to kill. They're out there. We're paying them, arming them, giving them permission, indemnity.'

'Can you call your guy already?'

'He'll call. Any second now.'

'Damn it. I hate waiting.'

'Tell me about the op in Iraq.'

Murphy looked at Walker. Let out a sigh. Sat down. 'Okay . . .' he said. 'This can't leave the room.'

•

Somerville spoke with her FBI agents about protecting the Murphy family. The agents were decent guys, each around thirty, each had done the usual entry-level work in the Bureau and now had chosen St Louis to settle down a spell, raise families, put some time in. In that sense, they weren't about to go rocketing up the career scales, but then that was the vast bulk of her co-workers, and those at any other agency or institution, for that matter. Somerville knew that, as competent as many people were, they were content to hold down a job and pay the mortgage and not rock the boat. Dependable. You knew they weren't going to take risks or cut corners for the sake of getting ahead. In Somerville's law-enforcement experience, agents with outside-the-box initiative were just as dangerous – perhaps it was even more of a liability – as those who didn't have it.

And these four were those kind of dependable workhorses she needed right now.

They were in two vehicles, a couple of five-year-old Ford Crown Vics with tired old Detroit V8s thrumming under the hoods.

'I want you parked on the road in,' Somerville said into one car. 'Stay there until I say otherwise.'

'Yes, ma'am,' the agent at the passenger side replied out his open window.

Somerville turned to the car idling behind her and said to the driver, 'I want you guys to cruise the perimeter road, for the next hour.'

'Got it,' he said. 'Same circuit we did this morning?'

'Yep,' Somerville said. 'All of it. Every road, there and back. If you see so much as someone pulled over to change a flat, you check it out.'

'Got it,' he said again.

'On your way back,' she said, 'time the run from the state police station.'

'Eighteen minutes, at a decent pace,' he replied.

'Do it again in current traffic,' Somerville said. 'To be sure.'

'Okay,' he said, then added, 'Do you really think someone is going to go after the family? I mean, they're nothing, right? It's the Team Six guy they want dead.'

Somerville looked up and down the old road, which was cracked blacktop with bits of grass poking out here and there. The petrol station had a faded Shell sign, the kind that was a large raised shell of plastic, the yellow faded to an off-white. The motel was in a ghost town. The wind whispered in the weeds.

'I don't know what's coming,' Somerville said. 'And that scares me.'

95

'Like I said,' Murphy began, 'that three months wasn't training. Wasn't even R&R, aside from those few days at the end. It was an op, in Iraq, 2003. And there were sixteen of us involved. And if I'm right, and I'm pretty sure I am, nine of those, including me, were in the DEVGRU unit that later hit Abbottabad.'

Walker nodded slowly, checking his email. Nothing. 'So, what was it?'

'Well . . .'

Murphy suddenly looked sick, and Walker wondered what kind of an op would make a guy like this look like that; a secret so dark that, even now, with his family threatened and his ex-service mates murdered, it was still hard for him to talk about.

'After it, we were all given new papers to sign, the highest level of secrecy there is, apparently,' Murphy said. 'It carried the death sentence for treason, right in the first line on the page.'

'Go on,' Walker said. His mind imagined the worst. He'd seen and heard dark things in Iraq and Afghanistan. Soldiers and operators losing it, going out and raping and murdering civilians. He imagined that maybe this SEAL team did something like that, or was witness to it, or cleaned it up. Maybe some kind of My Lai-type massacre, and they were sent in to kill the US servicemen who perpetrated the attack. Walker knew that only the tip of the iceberg was ever reported, that all wars contained crimes. The bulk of them were handled internally, hushed up, wiped from the history books and cleaned from the face of the earth and all but the all-seeing eye of God and some General in the Pentagon.

So, Walker was completely thrown when Murphy said, 'We found WMDs. In Iraq. We *found* them.'

96

'We were on a long-range patrol in the north-west,' Murphy said. 'Sixteen of us. The place was sanitised, we owned it, but for a few towns where Republican Guard types were now in plain clothes and retraining in the art of making IEDs to wage asymmetric warfare on our asses.'

Walker poured more coffee and sat on the arm of a chair, cradling the steaming cup in his hands.

'We were sent out there to hunt down some brass motherfucker who headed up their chemical warfare division. One of those guys from the deck of cards. It turns out, we found the guy on the second day. We found him, expected to bring him back to the Green Zone and drop him to some CIA guys for a nice little debrief, but he started talking to us. Couldn't shut him up. The fucker spoke English better than half the guys in our team. Trained in the UK and US, sent off to study there by Saddam because his daddy was some Ba'ath party honcho. And so he talked to us and was all repentant, saying how he'd do anything not to be taken to a black site to be tortured until he disappeared. They were well known then, the CIA-run camps. Abu Ghraib was big in the news, the dog collars and naked pictures and shit. He just wanted to live out his years in this village in the desert with his family and his mud house. Said they had some date plantation that he wanted to retire into. Said he'd show us something that'd change our lives, if we let him go.'

Murphy looked briefly out the window, 'He said that he'd *show* us where the WMDs were. That there was a cache, a big one, about a hundred klicks north-west, in what was a depleted oil field near the Kurdish zone that'd been a no-fly zone since the first Gulf War, so it had been left all alone since then.'

'You checked it out?'

Murphy nodded. 'Yep. Our CO decided, since we'd been allocated three weeks to kill or capture this guy, that we had time to burn, and who knows – we might become national fucking heroes because of it. It'd make our careers and then some. Free beers and blow jobs for the rest of our lives. We all agreed. So, we bagged the dude and headed out to the site.'

Murphy paused, squinting at nothing in the distance as though he could see the dust roads and date plantations and craters and mountains of that region.

'It took us three days to get out there in a couple of trucks we borrowed from locals. The roads were out – we'd cut them regularly with B-1 Lancer strikes of 500-pound JDAMs to make sure they didn't become some version of a silk road from Syria pouring in weapons and ammo that'd do our boys there harm. So, we smashed and crashed our way along, and got to this site, and it was a mess, like nothing I'd seen – it could have been the surface of the moon. An old pockmarked runway that the Brits had cluster-bombed fifteen years earlier in the first Gulf War. The few buildings that had been made out of concrete were little more than rubble. What was left had been stripped and looted by the Kurds or whoever else had been there. We felt conned. The site was important, once, but long past useless now. Our CO nearly capped the fucker who took us there.

'But then he started talking and pointing and getting all crazy animated and walked out ahead of us, looking at landmarks and the footprints of the old buildings and roads and the runway and stood on a spot and said: "Dig. If you dig, you will find it." He just stood there, looking at our platoon, telling us to dig.'

'And?'

'And we unloaded our gear and started digging. Hard work. Hard ground. Shitty shovels. The second day we sent four guys north twenty klicks to get better picks and shovels. They came back with a fifty-year-old backhoe on the back of the truck. By that night we'd found it. The first one, at least.'

'What was it?'

'We didn't know. There were three trenches, each with a shipping container, the big forty-four-foot ones, buried about ten feet down under a good twenty tons of rocks and sand. We had two chem suits with us, so most of us cleared out, except for the two guys who drew the short straws.' Murphy smiled, almost laughed. 'Hell, we had a pissing contest. All twelve of us, in a line, six feet apart, pissing onto what was left of the runway. The two shortest streams were the lucky volunteers. Havock and Lobes. They suited up, went down and opened up the first container. It was chock full of artillery shells, fitted out for chemical payloads. The second container had drums of shit. Containers. Tubs. Canisters. Everything was labelled really neatly, military style. Mustard gas. Sarin. Anthrax. You name it. Then we got to the third.'

'And?'

'Lots of paperwork. Inventory of stock. Instructions for making up certain deadly cocktails and how best they could be deployed in the field. Supply invoices for chemical compounds. All of the chemists' notes and work, including their documentation of what they made from the base chemicals supplied and what the results were.'

'And?'

'And – and that third container was the worst of what we found. By far. That's when we knew we'd fucked the pooch. That this wouldn't make our careers. We stepped away, from the containers and from the Iraqi, and talked about what to do. All night. All through the night. Pros and cons. By sunrise we came up with two main options. Bury it all again, along with the Iraqi, and hope it never gets found; or if it does, it's someone else's problem. Or, second option, we go clean with command. We get someone at DEVGRU or SOCOM to send out the highest-ranking chemical-weapons specialist they could find and make the call on what to do.'

'And you did the latter.'

'Yep. We made a call, fairly vague, about intel that may have something to do with US-supplied WMDs to Iraq in the 1980s. Three days later a colonel from the Army arrived via helo. He looked over it all. We could tell he was going through the exact same process we'd gone through. He asked the Iraqi if this was it, if this was all he knew about. The guy replied in the affirmative – and that was his death sentence: a .45 through the frontal lobe by our CO, under orders from the colonel.'

Walker let out a deep breath. 'Shit. Okay. Then what happened?'

Murphy shook his head, and looked down as though he was ashamed. 'Then,' he said. 'We followed our orders. We shut up those containers, and we brought it all home.'

Walker stared at him. 'You secretly brought three shipping containers full of Iraqi WMDs home – onto US soil?'

Murphy nodded.

'Why?'

'Firstly, the how,' he said. 'We Chinooked it out to Basra, then put it onto an old Liberty ship, and we stayed with it the whole way, to Naval Station Norfolk. It took us near-on two months in that rust-bucket, via a roundabout clandestine route.'

'That was the time listed as a special training period.'

'You got it.' Murphy nodded, and Walker could see that unloading this story, recounting it, sharing it, was some kind of a relief. 'We then stayed with it as it was trucked to some disused Cold War site, a minuteman silo or something in South Dakota. Waiting for us was the JSOC Commander – you know the General in charge at the time?'

'Yep.'

'Well him, as well as that Army colonel, who had brought down a bunch of Army scientists from Fort Detrick. They were a small team – four, five guys, chemical and biological specialists – and they went through it all. Drum by drum, document by document. It was all legit. We'd found them. WMDs in Iraq. Enough product to kill maybe a million people every which way. And the instructions to synthesise about as much more as you'd ever want or need.'

'So, why no press release, no media, no fanfare?' Walker said. 'This would have galvanised the nation, the whole coalition of the willing, to keep fighting the good fight over there. It would have changed everything.'

'Yep.'

'But word never got out.'

'Clearly not.'

'Why?' Walker pressed again. 'It would have added some spice to Bush's mission-accomplished speech that year. Why would they cover this up?'

'I'll get to that,' Murphy said. 'Afterwards? After about four days there, we were sworn to secrecy, by the General from JSOC – he'd been with us the whole time too, just him, no support staff. All very weird. Political, right? Well, my team are shit-scared by this point. A few of them were convinced we'd be rubbed out, that some company of Rangers or some other hatchet-job guys would descend and kill us in our sleep. A couple of the boys actually thought the Detrick guys might do it; put some anthrax in our coffee or something.'

'Why – because of what you found?'

Murphy nodded. 'But instead, we signed a form. The treason clause if we blabbed; a military firing squad, no less. The guys signed fast and we were sent straight back to the Middle East, where we were split up and put into different teams. I went to DEVGRU soon after, and over the next couple of years half that old platoon joined me in that team that went into Abbottabad.'

'Eight, of the sixteen of you from Iraq,' Walker said.

Murphy nodded. 'Another four I know are dead. Chopper hit by an RPG in 'Stan in '05.'

'Operation Red Wings?'

'Yep. Then . . . Let's see. Of the other three, I know one bugged out and went private, to some kind of Blackwater-type outfit or whatever they call themselves these days; last I heard he was working in Africa. The other two, no idea. But we need to find out, to be sure. See if those three guys are dead or alive. That'd confirm this is all about that op, not bin Laden.'

'But you're sure. I can see it. You think it's this.'

Murphy nodded.

Walker asked, 'How's this been a secret for all this time?'

'Because it would be a national scandal,' Murphy said. 'It would have taken down the President, a bunch of old Senators and Congressmen, and it definitely would have fucked the then VP and Sec Def.'

'Because the latter were around in the 1980s, in government,' Walker said, the truth setting in. 'When we were real cosy with Saddam. Arming him, posing for pictures with him . . .'

'Yep. You got it.'

'You brought those WMDs and the paperwork – the inventory, the invoices, the instructions – home, to US soil,' Walker said, the truth now running through his body like a strong electric current. 'Because it's not that we found *their* WMDs – we found *ours* – it was coming home. This is where it was from. It was ours from the start. We made it, we supplied it, and we trained the chemists.'

'Yep,' Murphy said. 'We knew that Saddam had WMDs not simply because he used them against his own population, but because we'd sold them to him. We didn't use them as a pretext to go to war to stop him or find it – we went to war to *bury* it, to make sure that it remained a dirty little secret that'd be lost to time. And I played a part in it. A big part. And now I'm paying for it. I'm a final loose end.'

'No,' Walker said. 'It's worse than that, Murph. They're not just burying this – someone's going to use it. Whoever knows about this is going to use it – against the American people.'

97

'But why would they do that?' Murphy asked. 'And who?'

'That's what we have to figure out,' replied Walker. 'Who else knows about this?'

'Us. Me, I mean. My team. Sixteen of us at the time.' Murphy paused, added, 'And the colonel at Fort Detrick. The old General in charge of JSOC in '03. Maybe some other brass at the Pentagon. Certainly someone in the White House from then, you'd think. Probably a handful of Senators and Congress on some secret committee.'

'Damn.' Walker's mind went to McCorkell. *He was there then, wasn't he? No. That was part of the four-year gap when he wasn't working for the National Security team.*

'Right? We're fucked. If that's what this is all about, then this is a clean-up op, or maybe worse. The US *Government* against us. What are we going to do?'

'I've got to give my guy McCorkell a hurry along.' Walker started to dial.

'Is he the President?' Murphy said. 'Because I've got to tell you, anyone less ain't going to make any difference. Got it? If the government wants you dead, you're dead.'

'My guy will shake the world to get to the people he needs to,' Walker said. 'We've got to keep it together . . . And, this doesn't feel to me like the US Government is after you. This is different.'

'Oh? Speaking from experience?'

'Yes.'

Murphy nodded. 'You know what it's like, to lose guys like this?'

'Lost one of my best friends in 'Stan back in 2010,' Walker said, his ear to the phone as it started to ring through. 'We went to high school together. Played football together. Went camping as teens. Adventures. Girls. You name it.'

'Branch?'

'Army.'

Murphy nodded.

'I got the scars. I know what it's like.'

'Where?'

Walker said, 'Wrong place.'

'IED?'

Walker nodded.

'Fuck that,' Murphy said. 'They're the worst.'

'Right.'

Beat.

Murphy asked, 'Who was he with?'

'Delta.'

'Damn.'

'Distinguished Service Cross and a whole bunch of other decorations.'

'Shit.'

'Yep.' Walker looked out the window. McCorkell wasn't picking up – it went to voicemail. 'He'd been there and done that enough times to make wiping his ass seem a task he had to think about.'

'Can I ask something?'

'Shoot.'

'How'd it make you feel?'

'Sad. Angry. Full of vengeance.'

'Right. And? Ask me,' Murphy said, 'all I've seen and done? I wish we'd never put boots on the ground in that country. Just tell the Gen Pop, you got a week. Move on. Outta town. To the closest border refugee station. There's some fire and brimstone coming. And then just flatten the fuck outta the joint, then precision the fuck outta everything that stays behind. Toast it. All of it.'

Walker got that. He'd seen it. Heard it. Too many friends spent their lives for what was, in the end, a war on a word: terrorism.

'This is on our doorstep now,' Walker said. 'You got that, Chief Petty Officer Murphy?'

Murphy nodded.

'This? This is someone else getting access to that op in Iraq,' Walker said, redialling McCorkell. 'As secret as it was. They got into it, and they've got their hands on those WMDs.'

McCorkell answered. Walker spoke fast.

•

'Ann?' McCorkell said urgently into his phone as he drove. He'd just hung up the call from Walker, and what he had learned in that three minutes had rocked his world. 'I need another list. Personnel again. From an op in Iraq back in 2003. But it should pop up in a PDB from that time.'

There was a pause.

The President's National Security Advisor said, 'I can't get that. The dead SEALs was one thing.'

'You can get this.'

'No. The dead SEALs was the protection case that was in a PDB I delivered last week,' Ann said. 'What you're asking for now is old, and not on my watch. Hell, it was even before your time in the White House.'

'Not before. I did stints either side of that guy being president.'

'And you know the PDBs are all protected under Executive Orders.'

McCorkell knew the PDB – Presidential Daily Briefing; he'd given thousands of them. And he knew that they were technically compartmentalised Top Secret documents.

'I'm working on it from my end right now,' McCorkell said, 'and I need all the assistance I can get.'

'I can't help you, Bill. Try the Pentagon.'

'If you hear me out, you'll find that I'm helping *you*,' McCorkell said. 'You've been looking at this in the wrong light the whole time. Me too. This is going to be a big deal when you see it – it's going to shake some trees in the Navy and the Army, and you're going to come out of it with all kinds of accolades.'

The current National Security Advisor to the President was silent.

'Where are you?' she said finally.

'Me? I'm in DC.'

'But where?'

'Headed to the Pentagon, to see about this op in Iraq, in case you couldn't see any sense,' McCorkell said.

Ann allowed herself a small chuckle.

'That personnel list would be handy, if you can dig it up. That or the PDB,' McCorkell said. 'I could get the names off Murphy, go into a meeting with the Joint Chief of the Navy that way. But I thought it'd be easier coming from you, so I can confirm it with Murphy prior to me sitting down and selling this to the Rear Admiral.'

'This is Murphy's theory?'

'And Walker's. It's sound. It makes sense – more than Abbottabad. We just need to confirm the list against the members who have been killed.'

'Okay, Bill. Okay. Meet me. I've just left the office – I'll get the list sent to me and meet you. You can talk me through this new theory. If it sounds legit, I'll go back to the White House with you and get whatever you need.'

'Okay, where are you?'

'The Archer, a bar, off—'

'I'll meet you there soon.'

'You know it?'

'Know it? They've got a drink named after me.'

'The dog with a bone?'

'Close. See you there in ten minutes.'

98

Walker had ended the call with McCorkell and looked at the handwritten list on the hotel stationery. Eight guys. Half of the SEAL platoon. A quarter of the SEAL troop. A fraction of their DEVGRU team, known colloquially as Team Six. He passed the list to Murphy.

Murphy read the names in silence. He held the small notepad with reverence, as if it were the most precious piece of paper he'd ever come across, and to tip or tilt it would allow the names to fall right off the page and be forever lost.

'These were good men,' Murphy eventually said.

After a minute's silence had passed, Walker spoke. 'They were all in Abbottabad?'

'Yes. They were there. NCIS were right. But they were also all at Iraq, the WMDs.'

'You're sure?'

'Absolutely. Damn good men. Good, fine men . . .'

Walker looked out the window again. 'So, it *is* about reprisal and what you guys found there. A clean-up. Rubbing you all out so that whatever goes down later today can't be tracked back, that future attacks can't be prevented, at least not by any of you.'

Murphy watched him for a minute before he spoke. 'What's your plan, Walker? Use me as bait to flush out Menzil and whoever may be left?'

'Maybe. I'm not sure. Yet. I still think there's more to this. There's something bigger at play, beyond killing you all. It can't just be about revenge against the SEALs who found the WMDs.'

'Well, killing us would be a serious blow to the DoD. It's a powerful message, hunting the hunters, right? It'd say to every American, "No matter who you are, or where you are, we can get you. If you fuck with us, we will get you. It's just a matter of when." Right?'

Walker nodded.

Murphy said, 'But you're thinking there's more . . .'

Walker nodded.

Murphy looked again at the eight names of the dead.

'I could go to wherever NCIS have set up this witness protection of the Abbottabad team,' Murphy said. 'And I could talk to them. If you can't. I mean, NCIS ain't buying your theory, are they? So, use me that way – we call Grant, tell them I want to go in, join their protection, and once I'm in, I start asking around. Who knows?'

Walker thought about it. All of a second.

'No time, not yet,' he said. 'We do what we can to stop this demonstration event at 17.30 today, then we look at our next options.'

99

Levine worked on her laptop from the now-empty room of the Murphy family in the St Louis Hyatt. The Facebook page was connected to several other social media platforms, relaying the information to as many people as were connected, some ten thousand people. She was a well known user to the other members and followers, and they knew that what her alias said, her alias meant. She knew that not all the followers would respond, but maybe half would. She included news outlets to the feed. Levine knew that they'd show up.

•

Murphy hung up the hotel phone.

'Family?'

'All good,' Murphy said. 'They're plugged into the cable TV, watching some Disney channel. Somerville organised food for them before she left for the Homeland Security office. Sounds like they'll be fine out there until the youngest turns about fifteen.'

'You know what all that means,' Walker said. 'You'll have to get a bigger generator. And a satellite dish. Sixty-inch TV. Next thing you know, you'll be singing along to the tunes from the movies.'

'Nope,' Murphy said. 'It means that we'll be moving into a bigger town some place. I owe Jane that. She was happy where we were, but only so much. I took us there for safety, and that safety was shattered.'

'Once this is over, you'll be in the clear.'

Murphy shook his head. 'I can't hide away from everything,' he said. 'It's all right. We'll adapt.'

Walker nodded. He looked again at his phone: the screen showed an internet search for planned events not just in the city but elsewhere at 17.30. Somerville and Hutchinson had teams of agents doing the same, looking for one pattern or another as to whatever was coming. But, short of heading down to the street and looking around, Walker felt he had to do something.

'Anything big in town?' Murphy asked, drinking a coffee.

'Lots of nationwide stuff. There are a few colleges on the west coast marching for gay marriage,' Walker said. 'An anti-death-penalty rally in Oklahoma.'

'That'll be a small turnout.'

'Right . . .' Walker kept searching. 'The Tea Party are doing a thing in Minnesota.'

'Oh?'

'Yeah, it's this afternoon, six o'clock.'

'Have you tried Facebook pages?' Murphy said. 'There's probably all kinds of shit being organised on there.'

'Yep.'

'Twitter hashtags for protest?'

'Yep. Nothing serious. It'd take a billion hours to sift through it all.'

'Doesn't the NSA have programs for this via the Patriot Act?'

'They're probably busy spying on the rest of us.'

'There's something, somewhere . . .' Murphy leaned on the window and rapped his knuckles on the thick glass. 'Maybe it's been kept off the net, just a small closed group, no outsiders wanted.'

'That kind of defeats the purpose of a public protest, though, doesn't it?' Walker said.

'Yeah, I s'pose it does . . . What?' Murphy asked as Walker stared harder at the screen.

Walker showed him the screen. His phone rang: Hutchinson.

'Seeing this?' Hutchinson asked.

'Yep,' Walker replied. News of a rally in support of the government's response to the Ferguson unrest that happened here in St Louis. 'This legit?'

'Yep,' Hutchinson said. 'Already got about five thousand followers on social media responding to say they'll attend – at 17.50 today.'

'Where's this happening?' Walker said.

'Jefferson Memorial Park,' Hutchinson said. 'They'll be protesting . . . I'd call that a *demonstration* – wouldn't you?'

'Ferguson,' Murphy said. 'Those riots here in 2014.'

•

Grant went to his car, parked in front of Room 4. He opened the boot and scanned the bagged weapons from the dead guys in the forest: two HK carbines, one silenced Sig. He looked up and down the car park. At the far end one of the Crown Vics was pointed away from him, nearly half a mile out. The other one had departed the scene.

In Room 3 the lights were on but he could see that Squeaker was still in Room 2 with the Murphys. Two girls and an infant boy. *How old are the girls? Two and four? Maybe; it's hard to tell.* He didn't want them to have to witness this.

Grant checked his watch.

He took the silenced HK from the clear FBI evidence bag and checked the mag – it was loaded with six shots. The chamber was empty. He racked back the slide, then put the pistol into his belt on his left front hip, hidden under his suit jacket. He had to do what he had to do. Thankfully, Woods was here. It was always good to have a fall guy.

100

'So, the SEALs found WMDs in Iraq and are being killed for it?' Hutchinson said from the Homeland Security HQ.

'Yes,' McCorkell said, driving back from DC, where he'd met with Ann at the bar and got the list. 'That's the short answer.'

'Why haven't we ever heard from these guys?' Hutchinson asked. 'Why haven't they gone public? Finding *the* smoking gun – WMDs in Iraq? It's a hell of a story.'

'The war was still going strong and it was already unpopular,' McCorkell said. 'To say that these SEALs found what they found – well, that just wouldn't happen. And, the SEALs know what Uncle Sam would do,' McCorkell continued. 'If these guys ever pop up on the grid, they disappear. And it won't be a black-site prison; it'll be a burial at sea. Or incineration some place. Or a firing squad. There'll never be bodies to find to tell any tale.'

'We'd do that? Why?'

'To protect the realm you wouldn't believe what we're capable of.'

'Bill, I'm missing something here,' Hutchinson said. 'You're saying that the government is killing these guys because they found WMDs in Iraq? They should be heroes.'

'No, it's not that simple,' McCorkell said. 'We went to Iraq because we knew Saddam had WMDs. We knew he had them because he'd used them. We knew he had them because *we gave them to him*.'

Hutchinson was silent.

'Are you there?' McCorkell finally said. 'Are you sitting down?'

'I'm driving,' Hutchinson said. 'With one arm in a sling. But . . .'

Silence again.

'But what?'

'Are you telling me we made them? The weapons?'

'Exactly. Murphy says that they got a match on site in Iraq, by an Army colonel sent from Detrick, that was derived from the same bacterial strain used here in the anthrax attacks of 2001.'

'The Ames strain,' Hutchinson said. 'I was on the case for the FBI. Hell, half the Bureau worked that case.'

'They blamed it on a US Army guy at the time,' McCorkell said.

'Blamed? I worked on the periphery of mounting a case to arrest him. The evidence was there.'

'It never went to trial.'

'The guy checked out . . .' Hutchinson paused, then said, 'Wait – are you saying maybe the Iraqis did that?'

'Maybe. They had the same strain of anthrax. It's just that we gave it to them in the first place.'

'Jesus . . .'

'So, whatever the case, it's a precedent: a biological weapon made on US soil by the US Army was used against the US population. And it's going to happen again. Today.'

'So, where you want me?'

'Fort Detrick, Maryland,' McCorkell said. 'Get a driver to take you out there, quick smart. We need to see about the container-loads of anthrax and VX and whatever else it was that they brought back from Iraq. Go through the inventory. Find out about the colonel involved in 2003 – a Colonel Brandt.'

'You think they're just going to show all this to me?'

'No. I don't think they'll be able to.'

'You think it won't be there.'

'Yep.'

'Then why am I going?'

'Because it *should* be there.'

•

Walker always knew it was going to be a race against time. Now, he understood the stakes.

A WMD attack on US soil. At 17.30pm local time.

Three hours to go.

'There's one way to be sure,' Walker said.

'We find that Army chemical-weapons specialist,' Murphy said, coming to the same conclusion. 'The colonel. Brandt – that was his name. Colonel Brandt.'

Walker nodded as he dialled Hutchinson's cell and hit speaker.

'Hutch,' Walker said, 'we need to look at everyone who ever had anything to do with our chemical and biological program with Iraq.'

'Yeah, I just spoke to McCorkell. I'm headed to Detrick now,' Hutchinson said from his car. 'How about while I'm at it I just ask the Pentagon for any personnel files they have on those who supplied WMDs to Iraq pre-1989 so that we could later go to war against them, twice, to get the weapons back, in the process pumping trillions of dollars through the military industrial complex and Big Oil. Maybe give that Rumsfeld guy a call too, while I'm at it?'

'Excellent, run with that. Call us when you get answers,' Walker said, ending the call.

Murphy said, 'I think Hutchinson was being a smart ass.'

'He's always making out he's a good FBI agent,' Walker said, as he rechecked the two Berettas.

'Is he?'

'We'll soon find out.'

101

Menzil had changed and prepped and walked from the warehouse, following his local fixer. A big guy. Handy, having a guy like this on the payroll, given what Walker had done to the ex-Army pros. He adjusted the pack on his back and headed towards his target.

•

Walker answered his phone.

'We just got a hit on Menzil,' Somerville said from a tech suite in the Homeland Security office. 'A security camera outside a building on Chouteau Avenue and South 4th Street, fifteen minutes ago.'

'That's only seven blocks from here,' Walker said into the phone. He looked out the hotel window. 'Which way was he headed?'

There was a knock at their door – Murphy let Levine in. She looked flushed, like she'd raced back from wherever she'd been, maybe even taken the stairs up here at a run.

'Towards the Jefferson National Expansion Memorial,' Somerville replied. 'And the Gateway Arch.'

'That's a hell of a target.'

'It's symbolic. And Walker, he had a backpack. A big one, like those European backpackers wear at Penn Station. Big enough to be carrying an explosive.'

Walker said, 'Big enough to be a WMD delivery.'

'Yep. He was wearing a buttoned-up black coat and some kind of dark cap.'

'Right,' Walker said, remembering back to the first time he'd met Special Agent Andrew Hutchinson, at Penn Station, just last month. He could picture the type of backpack. 'And nothing since?'

'No, but I've – wait,' Somerville said. 'I've got Hutchinson on the other line. I'll bring him in.'

Walker heard the sound of background activity and then Hutchinson said, 'I'm nearly at Detrick – and just saw the ID hit on Menzil.'

'We got it,' Somerville said. 'I'm at the Homeland office here in St Louis, and I've activated all assets on hand. They're keeping their eyes out for him. It's a matter of time – a big backpack like that; he'll be spotted.'

'We're going mobile, walking the streets,' Walker said, looking to Murphy and Levine. 'Call me the second you get another visual. I want this guy tracked. We need to know what his endgame is here, or we may miss it – he may not be working alone.'

'Copy that, Walker,' Hutchinson said.

'And keep your head down,' Somerville added.

Walker ended the call and then went to his muddied leather jacket. On top of it, the two Berettas he had taken from the deputies in Mountain View. He tucked one in the back of the waistband of his jeans and offered the other to Murphy, who declined and tapped the butt of the .45 Colt on his hip. Walker offered the spare pistol to Levine, who shook her head and tapped her holstered Sig.

'If you want to do this,' Levine said, heading for the door, 'follow my lead.'

102

'You remember our SOP?' Murphy said.

Walker's silence was answer enough.

'You were Air Force, is all I'm saying,' said Murphy.

Walker smiled at that. As a member of the 24th Tactical Unit in the Air Force, he had accompanied plenty of SEAL missions. Their Standard Operating Procedure when engaging an enemy was basic and drilled in at training until it became an unconsciously competent mantra to be implemented in the field: how to acquire targets, to work through them, to shoot without thinking about it because that would chew up time and in a fire fight against overwhelming odds time was something that you did not have. Address all immediate threats. Be in the now. *Where am I? Where am I going? What do I need to do next?* What Murphy was really saying was: can you execute a plan, and how fast can you do it? And beyond that: have you got my back? The thing was, as all special operators in the US armed forces knew, no plan survives beyond first contact.

'Are you two done messing around?' Somerville said into his ear via a headphone plugged into his pocketed cell phone.

'We're on the ball,' Walker replied, scanning the crowd. 'Just a little friendly banter.'

'See,' Murphy said. 'Army thinks they're better than Navy. Navy thinks they're better than Marine Corps. Air Force doesn't really have a lot to say.'

'Right,' Somerville said. 'FYI, the DEA team just swept the scene at the warehouse. All they found was Menzil's clothes.'

'He's changed?'

'Yep.'

'Into what?' Walker wondered aloud, continuing to scan the crowd. 'Whatever it is, he's still got the backpack.'

'He may not be working alone,' Somerville said.

Walker considered. 'Maybe not. But if he's running this, he'll see it through.'

'I bet he's alone,' Murphy said as they started to hit the crowd leaving work for the day. 'His four ex-Army buddies are dead. If he'd had more guys at his disposal, he'd have taken them with him to kill me.'

'I think you're right,' Walker said. 'But we can't discount it.'

'Agreed,' Somerville said.

'Hang on,' Walker said, 'I'm getting another call.'

•

Grant entered Room 2 without knocking. He closed the door behind him.

The television was on, some repeat 1990s sit-com.

Woods sat in an armchair by the door. His jacket was off, over the arm of the chair, his service pistol visible at his right hip. It was a deep chair, tilted backwards in the seat, and to get up would take effort and time. And, with the high arms, Woods could not reach and draw the pistol without sitting forward, which would take about as much time as standing.

So, Woods was not an immediate concern.

Grant clocked Squeaker, on the nearest of the two single beds, reading the two older kids a picture book.

On the next bed Murphy's wife, Jane, was finishing changing and redressing the baby boy. He was red in the face and crying. Jane cooed, trying to console him. Behind her the bathroom door was open and the lights on. There was a tiny window in there, above the shower stall, the frosted glass barely a handspan high.

Grant checked his watch: 17.08.

He drew the silenced HK, turned to Woods and shot him in the gut.

•

'Did you get another sighting on Menzil?' Walker asked into the headphone mic as the people of St Louis streamed by.

'No,' Hutchinson said. 'But I've got news.'

'What's that?'

'The ex-Army boys you and Murphy managed to dispatch,' Hutchinson said. 'They've just arrived at the morgue there in St Louis, but the CSI team on scene sent through pictures of faces and identifying features into the system.'

Walker said, 'You got hits?'

'Yep. We've got IDs on all of them via the Homeland Security system here.'

'Something tells me you've found something more significant than IDs.'

'You can say that,' Hutchinson said. 'Are you alone right now?'

'No,' Walker said. 'I've got Murphy next to me and Levine behind, and hundreds of the good people of St Louis leaving work en masse.'

Hutchinson said carefully, 'Is Levine in earshot?'

'No.'

'Are you sure?'

Walker paused, just a slight beat, then said, 'I'm sure – you're in my ear.'

'Okay,' Hutchinson said. 'Listen up. The Army boys were busted out in 2002, the four of them, for going AWOL in Afghanistan – they deserted their posts.'

'I feel better for their fate.'

'There's more,' Hutchinson said. 'They were caught ten days later at the Pakistan border, trying to move a truckload of antiquities out. The load was worth around five million on the black market, and maybe four times that on the legitimate one.'

'Who caught them?'

'Pakistani military police at the checkpoint,' Hutchinson said. 'The Army boys figured that they could buy their way through, then fly the stuff to a broker in Odessa. After the drop-off at the airport, they were planning to return to post after a fortnight being AWOL, stating it was PTSD-related stress. And they very nearly pulled it off.'

'But they thought wrong?'

'Damn straight. They thought they could buy their way across with ten grand they'd put together. The Pakistani MPs love a cash graft as much as the next Pakistani soldier, but our 101st boys didn't bank on them having a bigger motivating factor.'

'They'd do anything to paint American servicemen in a bad light.'

'You betcha. Our boys were turned over to US Army MPs – and this is where things get interesting.'

'Okay . . .'

'One of them, a corporal, Duncan, has some second-cousin's uncle or something who's a well-connected colonel. All kinds of favours are called in and the four get spat out the system with their discharges and no records.'

Walker, scanning the crowd, said, 'A colonel did that?'

'Yep. At the time there was a barrage of bad press about drone strikes against Pakistani civilians, and the brass at the Pentagon wanted to avoid another scandal – the guys hadn't actually hurt anyone, and in the end the truckload of goods was, in a roundabout way, saved from being dispersed into smaller caches and sold abroad. It's all now in the museum in Kabul.'

'I sense that there's another element here.'

'Yep.'

'Well?'

'Our colonel?'

'Yeah?'

'Colonel Brandt,' Hutchinson said. 'Our guy from Fort Detrick.'

Walker paused mid-step, said, 'The one who went to the site in Iraq.'

'The same. And I just got to Detrick, and was informed that he's the same colonel who was then killed, get this, just a *week* after the WMDs arrived back in the US.'

Murphy stopped, looked to Walker.

'Brandt's dead?' Walker said.

Murphy raised his eyebrows at the news.

'Apparent suicide by firearm, according to the current CO here,' Hutchinson said.

'You think it was a hit?' Walker said. 'It's got to be, right?'

'There was nothing suspicious in what the CO just told me,' Hutchinson said. 'But I'm with you. But Walker? The guy's daughter looked into it. She was an attorney in DC. She was obsessed with it; it's all in the police file. She bugged them for near-on five years then seemed to go quiet. There's bio notes in here. They say her life came apart. She stopped going to work, got divorced, became fixated on her father's death being part of a DoD conspiracy. She went from being a high-paid lawyer in DC to becoming a Federal Agent.'

'Her father's recent death, her recent employment implosion, her recent divorce,' Walker said. 'None of that added up to a negative psych evaluation?'

'Pedigree and patriotism trumps all,' Hutchinson said. 'He was a colonel in the Army, third generation. Her joining up, and just a couple years after September 11, would have looked the patriotic thing to do. Recruiters probably figured that she needed the change, and aside from the turmoil in her private life she would have been seen as a star recruit.'

'Jesus.'

'And Walker,' Hutchinson said, 'you want to know the best bit?'

'I'm listening,' Walker said.

'Brandt's daughter. She married, and then divorced, but she kept her married name when she became a Federal Agent. She's a civilian agent, working for the Navy. And right now, she's a few paces behind you.'

103

Woods writhed in pain and squirmed from the armchair to thump to the floor.

Squeaker had stopped reading. The book fell to the floor.

The baby boy had stopped crying. Oblivious to the carnage, he just saw movement and action and was distracted.

Jane Murphy had stopped cooing. She started to shake, shock taking over her.

Grant stamped down on Woods's hand as the agent reached for his holstered automatic. He bent down and pocketed the gun, then transferred the silenced HK to his left hand and kept it trained on Squeaker. With his free right hand he took a cell phone from his pocket and tossed it to Squeaker.

'You're going to call Walker,' Grant said. 'His number's the last called.'

Squeaker shook her head. She wrapped both the children up in her arms.

Grant motioned with the silenced HK pistol to the form of Woods bleeding out on the 1960s brown carpet.

'You're going to call him, and tell him that Woods here has you at gunpoint, and that Walker needs to get here, with Murphy, as a trade-off.'

Squeaker said, in a quiet voice, 'Trade-off?'

'For your lives,' Grant said. He waved the gun at the Murphy children. 'Your lives, for theirs, if they get here fast enough.'

Squeaker looked over her shoulder to Murphy's wife. Jane was motionless, and she had her hand covering her infant's face.

'You don't want Walker to stop what's coming in St Louis,' Squeaker said.

Grant said, 'Make the call.'

'I'll do it,' she said, reaching forward, the children now in the crooks of her arms, their faces tight against her chest. 'But we do it my way.'

'I don't think you understand what's happening here,' Grant said, raising the pistol at Squeaker.

'I will do what you want,' Squeaker said, then motioned to Jane and the kids, 'but only if you let them go into the bathroom. They don't need to witness all this.'

Squeaker got to her feet, the children with her. The phone was in her hand; the pistol was aimed at her head. 'You've got me at gunpoint,' she said. 'And they'll be trapped in there.'

Grant looked to them.

'Tick-tock,' Squeaker said, something resolving in her. 'You've got what? Twenty minutes to your deadline? Less?'

'Go,' Grant said to Murphy's wife, and she ushered her two daughters into the bathroom while carrying her son.

Grant smiled at Squeaker. 'Now, make the call.'

Squeaker looked at the phone in her hand. She took a step closer, raised the screen towards Grant, took another step, and said, 'This number?'

'Yes.'

Squeaker threw the phone at his face and charged him, crashing her shoulder into his chest.

The pistol went off as they fell to the floor.

Squeaker didn't feel the first bullet for what it was. It felt like someone had punched her in her chest. The second passed through her arm. That felt like a hot poker had been seared onto her.

Her weight was on Grant. She screamed as he tried to push her off – she clawed at his face, pulled and struck with all of the life left in her.

Another hand appeared.

Woods. He grabbed onto Grant's neck with both his bloodied hands.

Grant dropped the pistol and tried to fend off the two attackers. Squeaker was a match for him, size for size. Her ferocity and determination were the deciding factor. As she drove a thumb into

Grant's eye, Woods scrambled for the Sig, put it under Grant's chin and pulled the trigger.

The sound of the back of the skull exploding out was louder than the report of the pistol.

Squeaker rolled off Grant. Woods dragged her to him. The chest wound was catastrophic – she'd bleed out faster than he would, and already bright red foam had formed at her mouth from a perforated lung.

Woods fumbled with his cell phone – his hands were thick with the blood from his stomach wound. He reached over, took his service pistol from Grant's pocket and fired two shots straight up into the ceiling.

The sound of the .40 calibre in the small hotel room was deafening. It would alert the agents outside as it carried across the distance. Squeaker's eyes were closing.

104

Police had set up bollards and roadblocks. They held the high ground, too, with snipers on rooftops. They all looked buzzed, jacked; this was a last-minute thing, all of them pulled out of regular duty and ordered here, told to expect the worst.

'What is this?' Walker asked a uniformed cop.

Levine showed him her ID.

'Some rally in support of the government and cops re the Ferguson unrest,' the cop said. 'But all we got so far are those against it. It's looking like becoming Ferguson all over again.'

Walker nodded and moved on with the crowd.

Near Walker, news crews did their thing. A dozen vans, a couple national, the rest city- and state-wide. Satellite dishes went up, cameramen shouldered their equipment, sound guys plugged in and hoisted booms. Newscasters added final touches to make-up, and checked notes and then image and sound. All of it happening fast.

So far, there was nothing to see.

Walker kept the headphone in his ear. Somerville said, 'I've had Homeland Security admit this as a credible security threat.'

Walker said, 'And you can't get the rest of the crowd dispersed?'

'Not without about a thousand cops,' Somerville said. 'The National Guard will take an hour to get deployed.'

Walker looked around. Buildings, and the Arch. 'This is about mass panic, mass hysteria. It won't be a repeat of New York. But have your agents checked the news camera trucks, just in case?'

Somerville replied, 'Three times.'

'And the crews?'

'All legit,' Somerville said. 'This is a small town, as far as cities go. This isn't about a demonstration – it's an unveiling.'

Walker nodded, still scanning the area. Then he looked up. The sun glinted on shiny stainless steel.

And then he knew. Symbolic. A demonstration: we can get you anywhere, anytime. The Gateway to the West. A delivery platform for a backpack full of chemical or biological agent.

'We're going up the Arch,' Walker said, and he started for it at a run, Murphy and Levine behind him. 'Double-check all security footage in and around the Gateway Arch.'

'You think it's being detonated from up there – not from in the crowd?' Murphy said, keeping pace with Walker.

'Maybe, but either way I think they'll be up there,' Walker said. 'Watching it. Filming it even.'

'They might drop it – if it's in a backpack?' Murphy said. 'It might have a GPS rigged to the trigger, set for detonation thirty feet from the ground.'

'That'd disperse it,' Walker said. 'Somerville, did you hear that?'

'Heard it,' she replied. 'We're re-scanning all footage from the Arch. Stay on the line.'

'Copy that,' Walker said.

They passed a couple of uniformed police. Levine flashed her badge, and after a quick explanation the police joined them as they continued to move faster than the crowd, pushing their way through. Walker felt a weight on his chest.

What is she up to? Is this reprisal, for her father's death? What's the connection to Zodiac? And what triggered it?

•

Squeaker was on the floor, flat, arms and legs out, like a kid making snow-angels on Christmas Day who had run out of energy. Woods fought the searing pain in his stomach as he pressed his hands against her chest. The blood flowed warm and sticky through his fingers. Arterial. Nothing to be done about it; she had seconds to live.

'I'm sorry,' Woods said.

'It's . . . okay . . .' she said to him. 'I saw my cousins, right? The kids are safe?'

'Yep, they're safe.'

'The . . . kids. Look after them.'

Woods, in a daze, said, 'Always.'

'Thank you.'

'I'm sorry.'

'Sh. It's okay, Walker . . . Tell me about Philly.'

'Walker? Philly?' Woods said, then saw she was delirious. 'Oh. Well . . . Shit. It's a good town. City. On the water. You've got all you need. It's got – it's got sports, and cool bars and places you can hang with friends. It's friendly. It – it kind of feels like your home town. Small. Everyone knows everyone who's important to them, you know?'

Squeaker smiled. 'I wish I saw it. With you.'

'Yeah, Squeak. I wish you did too.'

Squeaker fell silent. She never made another sound. Woods called out for Jane. She came out, leaving the two girls in the bathroom and holding her infant boy all swaddled up in her arms. She bent down to Squeaker and held her hand and cried.

105

'Menzil sighting,' Somerville said, her voice rushed. 'Headed towards the Arch, eight minutes old.'

'He's in the area, though,' replied Walker, eyes darting between faces in the crowd.

'Correct. Still wearing the black coat, cap and carrying the backpack. I've got ten plain-clothed DEA agents here. Where do you want them?'

Walker checked his watch: 17.12.

'Send two guys as back-up to the Murphys,' Walker said. 'And send the rest to the Arch, looking out for Menzil.'

'On it,' Somerville said, and he heard her relay the orders. 'There's almost thirty uniformed officers from St Louis PD around the Arch, and a few plain-clothed among the crowd. I've had their captain send out pics of Menzil.'

'Good,' Walker said as they started to slow for the crowd. 'Make sure they know to approach with care – we don't know what kind of detonation this guy will have. And get the Guard moving with chem suits.'

'He wouldn't blow himself up, would he?'

'I doubt it.' Walker did a double-take on a guy in a black cap – but it was a cop. 'But if he's got no way out and he knows it, he just might.'

'Do you have eyes on Levine?' Somerville asked. 'Hutch briefed me just after you. About her father.'

'Yes,' Walker said, watching the NCIS agent. 'I've got her.'

'How are you going to play it?'

'Still trying to figure that out,' Walker said quietly. 'I need her to show her hand.'

•

The nation's tallest monument, the Gateway Arch, gleamed in the setting sun. Built as a symbol of the westwards expansion of the United States, it was the centrepiece of the Jefferson National Expansion

Memorial, a ninety-one-acre site that sprawled along the Mississippi. The area immediately under the Arch and all the way to the river was already massed with more than five thousand people, most of them jeering at the police.

Levine showed her ID at the security checkpoint. The woman staffing the metal detector called for her supervisor, who ushered them around the device and towards the tram.

'Special Agent Somerville just called in advance,' he said to them. 'You sure we shouldn't close down the memorial?'

'Not yet,' Levine said, putting her slim ID wallet back in her inside breast pocket.

'Has anyone suspicious come through?' Walker asked him.

The supervisor gave a vague wave of his hand towards the security screening area. Tourists were lined up for the last tram ride of the day up to the top. Young and old and everything in-between. 'Everyone now looks suspicious to me,' he said, visibly shaken by the notion of a threat on his watch. 'Everyone who lines up here gets scanned. All bags get scanned.'

Walker saw that the two St Louis cops came around the scanner and were looking through the crowd. Alert, but not alarmed, as though they were doing a routine check.

'Just make sure you check every passenger,' Walker said.

The guy nodded.

'How many still up there at the top?' Levine asked the supervisor.

'I'm having my guy topside do a headcount now,' he replied, and then talked into a radio handset. Within a minute the reply came through. 'Forty-two.'

'That's not many,' Murphy said.

'Trams are running every five minutes, forty passengers per trip, so that's about 480 passengers up and back each hour,' the security supervisor said. 'We've got a full tram coming down right now.'

People started to stream out from a series of small doors.

'Last tram to the top!' an usher called out.

'That's your ride,' the supervisor said.

Levine headed for it, and Walker followed. He watched the outline of her body. Aside from the bulge of her Sig at her right hip, there was nothing showing beneath her dark suit. *What if it's as simple as a vial, dropped out a shot-out window up there? Or put into the ventilation system?*

Menzil had to be up there, with the WMDs, and an exit plan for them both. Maybe with another guy? Or more?

Walker followed Levine inside the elevator, with Murphy close behind them. He turned and gave the slightest hand gestures to Murphy – watch Levine. The SEAL nodded. He didn't yet know why to be suspect, but he trusted and respected Walker enough to do as instructed. The tram consisted of eight small connected cars, each with five seats, the journey taking just a few minutes. Levine sat next to the door on the left. Walker sat opposite her, and Murphy beside her. A mother came in next, followed by her son of about ten. Walker pulled his legs aside to let them through, and then the doors closed.

The tram car was a cylinder that turned on a gimbal to keep level as it followed the curve of the arch up and down. Levine looked from the civilian woman, who was wiping her protesting son's face with a licked handkerchief, to Walker. He held her gaze.

Walker's phone rang. As he listened, he looked from Levine to Murphy. And then his gaze dropped to the floor.

106

'Walker?' The man's voice over the phone was weak.

Walker said, 'Who is this?'

'Woods . . . NCIS.'

Walker's eyes shifted across to the front, but he still looked down, now at Levine's shoes. The tram car was making all kinds of whirring and mechanical clicking noises as it ascended.

'Yes?'

'Susan . . . she's – she's dead.'

Walker's hand tightened on the phone, his knuckles white. He kept his gaze focused on the floor as he felt his heart rate climb faster and higher than the tram car.

'Did you hear me?' Woods said.

The cell phone crackled.

'I heard you. How?'

'Grant. That son of a bitch . . .'

Walker closed his eyes for a moment. *Grant. In this, with Levine.* 'You sure that's what happened?'

'I saw him do it. With the silenced HK. After he shot me.'

'The others?' Walker asked.

'All fine. Just Susan. She stopped him before he could—' Walker heard the effort it was taking Woods to keep talking. 'He . . . he was going to hold the family at gunpoint, to get you and Murphy out of there. She stalled him. They grappled. The gun went off. She bled out fast.'

'You're sure?'

'Yes. And you're right, Walker, something's going down there. Grant wanted you guys out of the picture. You have to warn Levine – she's not answering my calls.'

'That end is compromised.' Walker opened his eyes. 'Copy that?'

Woods was silent, then he said, 'Okay. Okay. I get that. They – they were having an affair. Grant and Levine. For a year, or more. A few of us knew. But – but why? What is this?'

'Where's your suspect?' Walker asked.

'KIA.'

'Repeat last.'

'I shot him. But not before . . .'

Walker could hear commotion in the background: a door breaking down and loud voices – Somerville's FBI agents crashing the room.

'Get the help you need,' Walker said, and ended the call.

The tram slowed as it neared the top.

'All good?' Levine asked.

Walker looked up at her, meeting her eyes. Looking at Levine, all he could picture was Squeaker's face. Too young, too good to be gone. But she was. And Levine would pay for it.

'We there, Ma?' the boy asked.

'Almost, yep,' the mother replied.

Walker held Levine's gaze.

Murphy said, 'Walker.'

'All good,' he said.

'What was it?' Murphy asked.

Walker kept his eyes planted on Levine as he said, 'They sighted Menzil. He was near the Arch, headed for it, around ten minutes back.'

'Good,' Murphy said. 'We've got unfinished business, me and him.'

The tram car stopped with a heavy *thunk*. The doors pinged open.

'Let's go, Ma!' the boy said, stepping on Walker's feet as he pushed past.

'Sorry,' the mother said, brushing by.

Walker sat rock still.

'Let's see what we can see, shall we?' Levine said, still staring at Walker.

'Let's.'

A group disembarked and walked by the roped-off area where those waiting to head down were milling about. The usher waved the next group on to board. Walker watched Levine's back as she walked ahead.

Murphy caught the back of Walker's shirt sleeve, whispered, 'We all good?'

Walker didn't answer. He kept his right hand loose by his right hip, ready to reach under his shirt-back and pull out the Beretta. 'Work the crowd, start at the far end,' he said. 'And watch her.'

'Copy that,' Murphy said, pushing his way around eight people.

Walker kept his eyes on Levine.

107

Walker scanned the faces in the crowd while keeping a watch on Levine's movements. His hand was behind his back, touching on the grip of the Beretta.

About eighty tourists were on the viewing platform, most rubber-necking for a view outside. All had been vetted by security at the base of the arch, making their way through procedures similar to that at any domestic airport: walk-through metal detectors, wands and pat-downs for those who failed twice. All bags and packs and coats and boots were put through the X-ray machine.

So, Walker wondered, *if Menzil's up here, how'd he get a backpack through?*

Walker did a double-take at a guy who brushed by him – a St Louis cop, huge guy, black. Not Menzil. He was hustling towards the tram cars.

Walker got a bearing on Levine. She was at the centre of the viewing platform, looking out one of the windows that faced the Mississippi. He thought of Squeaker and his mind went to the last moments she would have had, grappling desperately against an armed man in an attempt to save her cousin's family. And she succeeded. And Walker had to succeed here today.

He approached Levine from behind.

He looked across at Murphy, who had reached the far end of the viewing platform. Walker, at six foot three, could see over most of the heads of the tourists. Murphy reached another uniformed cop at the end of the platform and then turned around to face back towards the crowd. Cops.

Walker looked towards the tram car from which they'd alighted just minutes before – the other cop was standing there, looking back at him.

Walker thought of the cops at the entrance at ground level, how they'd been looking among the crowd for Menzil – how they'd gone around the security without being checked.

The DEA agents had gone to the warehouse and found Menzil's clothes, nothing else.

He'd changed clothing.

And now Walker knew why.

Menzil was dressed as a cop.

Walker looked the other way.

Murphy was headed towards him. And the cop was close behind, closing in.

Menzil.

108

The pressure of something small applied to Walker's side. The barrel of a pistol. He looked over his shoulder. The other cop. Menzil had another man up here. Not military, maybe a local criminal, a fixer for whatever Menzil needed here in St Louis: stolen cars, a warehouse to store stuff in and operate from, police uniforms, weapons. He held a Glock pistol in one hand, and the other now tightly gripped Walker's arm.

Walker looked to Murphy, to the figure closing behind him. Menzil.

He had a knife. High-polished stainless steel, a filleting knife. The slice was quick.

'No!' Walker had never shouted so loud. The sound of it moved people. The guy holding him startled and his gun fired – the shot went wide but Walker felt the burn of powder against his back.

Murphy fell. Menzil behind him, knife in hand.

Screaming provided a soundtrack to the events.

Most of the visitors remaining upstairs were packed into the empty cars – all but twelve, who were now watched over by the other fake cop.

Walker looked up to the Glock in his hands, steady.

'Three base-jump glide suits,' Menzil said to Levine, tossing her a pack that the cop behind Walker kicked across the floor. 'You both follow my lead. You glide after me, pull your chutes a half-second after me, and we touch down on a rooftop across the river where the first car's waiting.'

'Good,' Levine said. She checked the contents of the big backpack.

Walker saw four canisters wrapped together, and sandwiched between them a block of C4 and a double-detonation trigger: a timer in the form of a small digital alarm clock, set for 17.30, and what Walker recognised as a proximity detonator fashioned from a hand-held GPS unit – which Levine set at thirty feet from the ground level below.

The pack would be launched out, and 620 feet down would come detonation level. Or, at 17.30 as a back-up. Whichever came first.

Walker checked his watch: 17.24.

He watched as Murphy struggled to keep pressure on the cut at his side. The SEAL was on the floor, flat, keeping as still as possible.

Levine pulled on the base-jump suit, then moved to a room marked 'RESTRICTED ACCESS'. As she pushed through the door, Walker saw an access ladder leading to a manhole in the roof. She climbed up, pushed the pack out before her and disappeared.

Walker moved fast. In less than a second he turned and pushed the Glock aside, causing it to fire again. He broke both the guy's arms before the pistol fell to the floor. By the time he spun his former captor around, Menzil had started firing his Glock – Hydra-Shok rounds, designed to expand inside a body and not pass through. Using the fake cop as a human shield, Walker dropped down, snatching up the fallen Glock as bullets shattered the viewing windows behind him.

Walker sighted and fired at Menzil, hitting him twice in the chest and then once in the chin.

The third bullet bored a hole through his head.

Walker rushed back to Murphy. He was bleeding fast.

The room went quiet but for the howl of wind blasting through shot-out windows and a few of the tourists who were screaming and falling to pieces.

'My family?' Murphy said. His face flushed red.

'I'm sorry,' Walker said. 'Susan didn't make it.'

'My family!?' Murphy shouted.

'They're fine,' Walker said. 'Jane and the kids, they're fine. Just Squeaker . . .'

'Shit. Who – who was it?'

'Grant. Woods killed him. But he got Squeaker. He was going to use her and your family to stop us. But they're safe now. Somerville's men are with them.'

'Go,' Murphy said, motioning in the direction they had last seen Levine. 'Get her. End this.'

109

'Don't,' Walker said to Levine.

She stood on the roof of the Gateway Arch, one of the arm slings of the backpack dangling in her hand. Her other hand held a gas mask, and she'd already looped a tethered safety harness around her forearm.

Walker said, 'You don't have to do this. You can get justice another way.'

She faced him. Something settling in her eyes. 'Justice?'

'That's why you're doing this, right?'

Levine dismissed him with a shake of her head, said, 'You have no idea why.'

'I know they killed your father, for what he knew.'

Levine paused. 'You just worked that out, did you?'

'It's easy to connect the dots when looking back,' Walker said. The wind buffeted them. 'I can see your reason. Revenge. Fair enough. But they're innocent down there.'

'It's more than that.'

'That's enough. I get it. The government had him killed to silence him. Revenge is understandable – but not like this.'

'You think he's the only one?'

'No. I know he's not. You've had the SEALs killed. All but one.'

'Because they're a part of this! They knew what they found and they kept their dirty little secret – it was men like those SEALs that ended him. I know it. Government-sanctioned murders. But now the whole world's going to know what happened. How that war was really fought, what it was about, what they covered up.'

'And then what do you think will happen?' Walker asked. He took a step closer. Then another. The wind was strong. 'They'll come out and prosecute the guys who hushed this up? The guys who killed your father?'

Levine was silent, staring him down.

'The SEALs found the WMDs, yes,' said Walker. 'They would have taken that knowledge to their graves, because to do anything else would have meant a firing squad. But the man who inspected the weapons, who verified them and their origins – hell, the man who *supplied* them to Saddam in the eighties and trained the Iraqis how to make the shit? That was *your father*. He's no innocent player in all this.'

'They killed him!' Levine said. 'He was killed by a DoD clean-up crew when all this stuff showed back up. I joined NCIS to investigate it. They were a DoD crew, Walker. DEVGRU, Team Six guys, right? US military – killing one of their own! *My father!*'

'If that's true, you could have come forward.'

Levine was silent.

'You can't prove it, can you.'

'It was them!'

'You can't *prove* it. You *suspect* it. Don't do this,' Walker said, pointing off the arch. 'They're innocent people down there.'

'No-one's innocent anymore, Walker,' Levine said. 'Don't be so precious. This here, today? It'll make a show – to bring the home front back here, to make every citizen feel a part of the war, and part of the response. To show them all what our government is capable of.'

'Just let this be.'

'*This*,' Levine retorted, holding up the backpack, 'this was made by the guys we've been fighting against in the Middle East all this time!'

'Your father made it,' Walker replied simply.

'He – he showed them how, but *they* made it,' Levine said. 'It's all politics, right? What's a few more deaths along the way! That will come out, all of it, after the event, when this contagion will be tracked back to Iraqi labs.'

'It'll be tracked back home. You know that,' Walker said. He took another step closer. The wind threatened to blow him off his feet. Levine held on tight to the tether. 'Those anthrax spores or whatever you've got there? They were cultured here. Sure, it may have been enhanced over there in Iraq, but it will point a finger back here. And that'll point to your father and his work. You really want that?'

'And what do you think our government will do about that fact?'
Walker paused. 'You want that to happen?'

Levine was silent.

'You know they'll cover it up – but it'll make waves,' Walker said.
'The military will know. They'll figure it out, make the connection.
It'll go back to your father. Ruin his reputation, if that's all that's left
of him.'

'It'll make them all see his death for what it was,' Levine said. 'And
it will raise questions all the way through the military, and intelligence,
and the government, about the truth of all this – the war, my father's
death, all of it.'

'They'll just cover it all up again,' Walker said, taking another
small step towards her.

'They might. But this – today – will get the country behind us.
Think about it. Weapons of Mass Destruction, from Iraq, used here on
American soil. They won't cover *that* part up. Quite the opposite. All
those hawks who sold the American people this war – the ones who
knew that there were WMDs there because they were the ones who
sold them to the Iraqis in the first place – they'll be clamouring for
another chance to go back there and get the job done right this time.'

'Who's your enemy here?' Walker said. 'The government that
went to war on a lie and then killed your father, or those in Iraq we
waged that war against?'

'They're all the same – governments all end up the same.'

'Is that how you sold this to those 101st boys?'

Levine paused, looked in the pack, at the timer, said, 'They had
their own reasons.'

'You're going to kill innocent people down there, for what?' Walker
asked, motioning over the side. Levine looked down at the crowd
and Walker shuffled a couple of steps closer. 'So you can restart a
war in the Middle East?'

'This will finish what we started,' Levine said. 'They're the ones
who brought the fight to us in the first place. They did 9/11. They
did London and Madrid and Bali. Let's put it back onto them. Al
Qaeda, ISIL, all of them. And while we're at it, let's get the whole
country, the whole world, behind us this time. It's a chance to stamp

out terrorism for good. Let's turn the Mid-East into glass – let's wipe the whole region off the map. Let's get our government and military and intel and police all focused in the same – in the right – direction.'

Walker stepped closer still, now just ten feet between them.

'Do you really think this will get the whole country behind another war over there?' Walker asked, looking over the edge. The view was spectacular. The sun glinted off the stainless steel arch and hit the city. The end of day. The beginning of night. The huge crowd was below, oblivious to what was unfolding above, energised by their own fury. Walker looked back to Levine and spoke simply. 'You don't have to do this.'

Levine laughed. 'So, what? Stop now? How do you think that would play out? I'd never see the inside of a court. You know that. They'd send me to some CIA black site and then I'd just disappear. You don't know these men and what they're capable of.'

'I do know. I was one of them. Tell me about Zodiac.'

'I'd never heard of it.'

'The attack on New York. The trigger.'

Levine smiled, said, 'You're trying to buy time, but there's none left.'

Walker took a step forward, seven feet between them. He said, 'Do you really want to die today?'

'Do *you*?' Levine countered. The wind whistled; it was hard to keep purchase. His stance was wide. Hers wasn't, but she was maybe half his weight. The pack was in her hand. 'Is this really something you're willing to put your life to?'

'Try me.' Walker checked his watch: 17.27. 'Time to decide.'

Levine smiled.

'Can you fly?' Walker asked.

Levine looked off the tower, then back at Walker – and they knew what was going to happen.

110

Levine reached her arm back and then launched the backpack over the edge. Walker dove right. His feet left the top of the arch, the hard steel of the memorial now behind him. He grabbed a handle of the backpack with his right hand, and now he was falling through empty space.

Below: 630 feet, five thousand people.

And in his hand, certain death, in the form of some kind of WMD, with a detonator and a timer. The explosives would be small scale but the blast would create a superfine disbursement, the resultant aerosolised mist deadly for those below – and then, in a secondary wave, for those who might rush in to attend the wounded and screaming and dying.

And it was in Walker's right hand. And he was falling . . .

He reached out with his left hand, his palm burning down on the sloping stainless-steel surface. It did little to suppress the pace of the slide, so he pushed hard with the tips of his boots, but they too couldn't halt the descent.

Walker slid on.

And on.

He brought up his right arm to let the pack's strap slip down his arm to his shoulder and allow himself to slam two hands flat against the polished-steel surface.

Still he fell; the slope and his 230-pound mass were too great.

He pressed his cheek against it, feeling the steel burn away at his skin as he slid.

Still not enough resistance.

He looked over his shoulder—

The arch disappeared—

And the surface under his feet changed. It didn't flatten out. There was no ridge.

Just a drop-off.

Six hundred and thirty feet. Five thousand innocent people.

First his feet went over, then his shins, then his knees, and as more of his body weight went over the edge and the resistance lessened, his fall quickened.

His waist went over, and he felt his legs dangle in midair as he kicked around for purchase.

Nothing.

Nothing but a 630-foot drop. He would be the delivery man of death.

At 17.28pm local time, Walker slid off the top of the Gateway Arch.

111

From the sloping top of the Gateway Arch to the lip where it ended was a sheer vertical drop.

Walker's fingertips found nothing but empty space.

Then caught a hold.

Nothing more than a finger-span deep, maybe three-quarters of an inch: a ledge of folded stainless steel.

Two hundred and thirty pounds, plus the loaded Beretta, plus his clothes, plus the backpack; a total closer to 280 pounds. Spread across eight fingers, hanging by fingertips.

Good news, for the smallest moment.

The tiny ledge was there just to block rain from the glass windows of the observation area inside. Those viewing windows faced the ground at a less than vertical angle – they were inverted, angling the other way from the sloped roof, and away from Walker, at around twenty degrees.

Walker forced his thoughts to calm, to slow. *Let go of this edge and it's straight down. Six hundred and thirty feet. Concrete paving below. Two hundred and eighty pounds falling at high speed and hitting a paved ground.*

Not going to happen.

Not today.

But before he could figure a way to get up, he had to get this backpack away.

How long to go? Two minutes? Less?

He let go with his right hand and slipped the pack off his shoulder, nearly falling as the weight slid down his arm, and then—

The weight caught. The forty-pound backpack hung from his right hand.

The tips of the fingers on his left hand screamed with pain. His left hand itself did not move – he had it shaped like a hook, and it would hold.

But for how long? Two minutes? Less?
And then what?

Walker closed his eyes, just for a second, and then he opened them. He could see into the window. Some tourists had gone to Murphy's aid.

First things first.

Walker glanced over his right shoulder. The afternoon sun glinted off the mighty Mississippi, the state of Illinois on the other side.

The river was close, but not that close.

Close enough?

Walker started to swing his body. Forwards and back in a huge arcing movement. Perhaps just enough to launch the pack into the Mississippi. Perhaps. As he brought his right arm to the zenith of the let-go of the pack, he thought of all the reasons he wished it to make the journey, of why he was here, doing this, right now: *the people below, the fallen SEALs, Zodiac, his father, Squeaker, Eve . . .*

He reached out.

And was stopped.

Murphy.

His arm reached out the shot-out window. He grabbed Walker's wrist and then went to work at the thick glass, which had shattered and held – laminated safety glass, the double panes held together by a film of plastic. He used his .45 to smash it out, making the opening bigger. Two men joined Murphy to help, using fire extinguishers to clear out the remainder of the shattered window.

Walker swung up with the pack, but he missed, and the top of it slammed against the window frame.

But the grip around his wrist held tight. Walker dangled, just for half a second, then he flung the pack through the window.

That done, he reached around on the next pendulum-like momentum and grabbed the window frame with his now spare hand.

'Check the time on the pack!' he yelled as he started to haul himself up.

'A minute twenty!' someone shouted back.

'Get me in!' Walker called.

Six hands grabbed at him, pulling him up until he came through the window frame and dropped to the floor.

Murphy was leaning against the wall, under the smashed-out window.

'Get . . . her . . .' Murphy said, shoving the pack Walker's way. The blood on his hand was dark and thick. 'Keep going. Let's see you move, Air Force!'

'On it,' Walker said, getting to his feet, shouldering the pack and racing towards the ladder up to the roof.

112

Walker moved quickly but carefully to the edge of the roof.

Levine was there, holding on to the clipped-in maintenance harness, looking over in the direction that Walker had flown, as if she were still waiting for him to splat onto the pavement.

Walker held his Beretta in one hand, and hefted the backpack from his shoulder and readied it in the other. The wind was strong and the last vestige of daylight was clear.

Walker neared his target.

Levine turned, her face working through a range of emotions and understanding. Her eyes dropped to the pack in his hand, and the gun.

'You won't shoot me,' she said, defiant.

'No. But you know what?' Walker said, tossing his Beretta to the roof and taking the backpack in two hands. 'It's the fall that's going to kill you.'

Keeping one hand to steady herself on the tethered harness, Levine dropped her gas mask and unholstered her Sig, then brought it up to aim at Walker's centre mass.

She sighted with one eye down the tritium sights—

Walker threw the backpack at her, a full-force pop-shot from his chest to hers. Before it connected, Levine fired.

Levine got two shots off before dropping the Sig and the harness to repel the backpack. Her eyes opened full and wide as the forty-pound mass of the pack hit her and took her off her feet.

Levine closed her eyes as she flew backwards.

Walker too went backwards – every action having an equal and opposite reaction. A proportion of the force of his throw travelled through his arms and down through his body to his legs, to where the soles of his boots met the roof of the arch. He steadied himself. The gunshots had gone wide but were close enough to ring in his right ear.

He ran to the ledge, grabbed the tethered harness, leaned out and looked over the side.

Levine wasn't falling down – she was falling through the air, away from the arch.

Walker had thrown the pack with all his strength, with such force as to shoot her off the arch and out in a curved trajectory – creating a new arch all of her own.

She was headed for the mighty Mississippi. If she hit the water before detonation, Levine and the WMD would be carried out to the Gulf of Mexico; one more substance added to the 12,500-mile dead zone out there.

If she makes it . . .

Walker watched Levine's flight. Rather, her fall.

He knew from high-school physics that for every second that an object falls the increase in velocity is the amount equal to the pull of gravity. In the first second Levine travelled at thirty-two feet per second. By the next second she was moving at sixty-four feet per second. And so on. The fastest a person will fall in normal atmosphere is 120 miles per hour, because the air resistance keeps the body from accelerating any more. Levine would not get to that point, because both the ground and the Mississippi were just 630 feet below.

First, Walker fixed on her face. She was only a second into her fall when her expression softened and realisation set in. She knew her fate and was resigned to it. He could see that she felt that she would be triumphant, in the end – that she would hit the ground at about the same time the backpack would detonate, and that she would give her life to her cause. She was doing it for her father, for all those she felt needed this. She closed her eyes, drifted towards success.

Walker saw differently.

He mapped her path. The arc was beautiful. Levine's trajectory formed the descending half of a catenary arch all on her own. She was being dragged to the ground by gravity but she was still headed out, away from the Gateway Arch, away from the ground and the masses of demonstrators down there, towards the river, a curve of physics and geometry in her wake.

Below, the mass of people had seen the falling body and panic had set in – the crowd split into two groups as though the person hurtling towards earth was some kind of contagion to be avoided at all costs.

113

There was nothing Walker – or anyone – could do but watch. Levine's gas mask was on the roof behind him but he didn't think much about putting it on. If the device detonated, and he masked up and went down to ground zero, saw the sum of his failure in the faces melting away, spewing the green bile or whatever hellish reaction to the WMD agent . . .

Six seconds later Levine hit the water. She was too far away for Walker to see her expression. He figured the fall would have killed her; from that height it would have been like hitting solid ground. Bones shatter. Vertebrae unlink. Internal organs rupture. The brain rattles around. The human body simply is not designed to stop suddenly from such a pace.

The water swallowed Levine up – and then threatened to spit her out.

The explosion was a muffled puff that made the water rise and fall. And that was it.

Walker saw the fire department arrive in their hazmat suits, rushing to the shoreline. He dragged himself back to the manhole and down the hatch. Murphy was pale, but by the look of it the bystanders had done a good job of patching him up. He gave Walker a questioning look. Walker gave him a thumbs-up and then helped him to his feet.

'Come on, sailor,' Walker said, slinging his arm under Murphy and wrapping Murphy's around his shoulder. 'Let's get you to your family.'

'Not hospital first?' Murphy asked as they climbed into a tram car.

'You Navy guys,' Walker said. 'A little scratch and you want your momma.'

As the tram car descended, Walker leaned back and closed his eyes. He was tired. He knew that with Zodiac he was closer to the beginning than the end. In his mind he heard the echoes of those two gunshots, back in New York. He could hear his heart beating in his ears, echoes of his father running through him. Progress.

Epilogue

'It doesn't matter. You can't stop this. Twelve attacks have been set in motion.'

'I can catch up.'

'No,' David Walker said to his son, shaking his head, 'you really can't.'

Walker stood in the hotel room. Watched. Listened. Waited.

The sun was rising. California sun. He was there for no other reason than he wanted to be somewhere warm.

The television was on. Muted. The news was reporting the terror attack. Hazmat-clad teams from the CDC and FBI were combing through the Mississippi for debris from the explosion. Traces of a weapons-grade biological agent were found, and each news outlet seemed to have their own experts giving different ideas on what that was and where it came from and who really did this. The tickers told barely half the truth.

His new cell phone rang. He let it ring. McCorkell's number. *A lead? Go-time on the next Zodiac target?*

The tone was incessant. He answered it.

'Where are you?' McCorkell asked.

Walker looked at the naked form of the woman in his bed. The white sheet covered her tanned back and was wrapped along a leg. Her long dark hair covered her face, fanned across the pillow. Beautiful. Enticing. Dangerous.

'R&R,' Walker said. 'What's up?'

There was a pause, then McCorkell said, 'It's Eve. She slipped away.'

'What?' Walker was awake now, alert.

'In the night. She left the safe house.'

'Where?'

'They'd just moved her to Boston. Somerville was going to talk to you and send her home, today, but she bugged out during the night, out her second-storey window. No sign of her since.'

'Why would she leave like that when she was being sent home the next day?'

'She spoke to Somerville late last night.'

Walker rubbed his eyes, remembered all the missed calls from Somerville that he'd seen when he got back into his room after 3 am.

'And?'

'We need you to get back to work.'

'What's happened?' Walker asked. He went to the coffee machine above the minibar, inserted a tiny capsule of coffee and hit the button. The hot brew bubbled into the cup below. The smell filled the room. The woman stirred in her sleep.

'Nothing. Yet.'

'Yet?' Walker took the coffee and went to the balcony. He stood outside and looked down at Sunset Boulevard. Cars streamed along. It was hot. The sun was bright. He squinted and looked at the sky.

'We've received a letter. From your father. Sending you a pic of it now.'

Walker's phone bleeped with the incoming message. He looked at the screen. Handwritten. Five words. His father's handwriting.

Jed – Barrow, Alaska. Five days.

'What's there?'

'Not much,' McCorkell said. 'Oil town. Closest government installation is an old ice-runway airbase, now some kind of NSA listening post, a relay station. Year-round crew of five.'

'Have you warned them?'

'Not yet. Thought you'd like to look around first, see what's what. Maybe there's something else. The oil rigs or pipeline.'

'Right.' Walker looked again at the image of his father's note. 'When did this letter get to you?'

'This morning. Not ten minutes ago.'

'How?'

'Found it in my pocket.'

'*In* your pocket?'

'Yep. I walked to work, went to take out my ID pass at the security checkpoint, and it was in my coat pocket.'

'Could have been there a while.'

'Pockets were empty when I left my apartment.'

'So my father's in Vienna?'

'Maybe. Though he wouldn't have done the drop, would he? He'd have used someone. Some pick-pocket, a local gypsy kid or something.'

'Maybe.' Walker thought about his father. Could imagine him doing the drop, the kind of sleight of hand he'd shown in magic tricks to Walker as a kid, and that he later learned had been part of his CIA tradecraft as a young intelligence officer in West Germany. A faceless man in a crowd. A ghost. Connecting people. Recruiting. Facilitating. 'So what's the plan?'

'You're getting on the next flight to Alaska.'

'Not Alaska Air. I hate those guys.'

There was a knock at the balcony door.

Walker turned. The woman stood there, wearing his shirt. She passed him an envelope, said it was just dropped at the door by the concierge. Walker gave her the remainder of his coffee and she took it and went back to bed. He'd thought that he could spend all day with her. He'd thought last night, looking into her eyes, that he could spend the rest of his life with her, someplace quiet and off the grid, with not a thought of the outside world. Similar to what he'd learned Levine and Grant had planned, with their arrangements to run down to Chile, new IDs and a suitcase of money to keep them anonymous.

That thought broke his fantasising.

He opened the envelope. Alaskan Air flight, LAX to Anchorage, leaving three hours from now.

'You knew I was here,' Walker said.

'Yeah. Patriot Act and all that, makes a place like LA a small town.'

'Three hours?' Walker said. He looked to the woman. She climbed into bed and gestured for him to return to her. He wanted to hang up the phone and go there and never leave.

'You can get a lot done in three hours,' McCorkell said.

Walker looked back out at the sky, as though looking for a drone that might be spying on him and relaying live video feed back to McCorkell. In truth, he thought, he was looking at his last blue sky for a while. 'You know what this means, though, right?'

'I think so.'

'My father.'

'Yep.'

'He knows more about Zodiac than he let on back in Hereford.'

'I'd say so.'

'He knows the next attack – how would he know that if he wasn't involved, right?'

'Involved or not, he knows more than he said,' McCorkell said. 'We're still looking for him, but he's a ghost.'

Walker glanced back to the bedroom, said, 'What did Somerville tell Eve?'

'She told her that she might need to be protected for a while longer.'

Walker was silent. The woman was lying on her side, watching, waiting.

'Hutchinson and Somerville are in DC, at Homeland Security,' McCorkell said. 'Got them their own office there, semi-permanent, fully staffed and resourced, until Zodiac is over. They'll be in touch, soon as you land in Prudhoe Bay.'

'Prudhoe?'

'Change at Anchorage. Prop flight to Prudhoe, then on another thousand or so klicks north-west, to Barrow. Weather permitting. It was the fastest way. Be there in twenty-four hours.'

'Great. Thanks. You know, that's almost in Russia.'

'Almost. Could probably see Russians from there.'

Walker looked out at LA. 'Weather permitting?'

'You've just been on the Ozarks. How much worse can the weather in Alaska be?'

'Speaking of, how's our SEAL?' Walker thought of Squeaker. He'd accompanied her body back to her home town, where she was put in a plot next to her mother. Murphy had cried. His kids didn't know what was happening.

'The Murphys say thanks. All the SEALs, actually. Say that they owe you one.'

'Great.'

'Handy thing, having a team of SEALs in your back pocket.'

'We'll see.'

'And Walker?'

'Yeah?'

'Good luck.'

Walker ended the call and headed inside. The woman got to her knees on the bed and held out her arms. Walker wrapped his arms around the woman he'd married and had somehow let go. He'd not make that mistake again. He closed his eyes and took in a deep breath against her neck, lost in her smell.

'I understand,' Eve said.

Walker remained silent.

If you enjoyed *The Hunted*, read on for the beginning
of the next book in the Jed Walker series . . .

KILL SWITCH

PROLOGUE

Fade in.

It's an interior shot. Dark. The camera finds a man on a seat. He is slightly to the left of frame. We see him head to toe. He is slouched. Not big, not small. Average. His hair is longer than short, blacker than brown. He wears wire-framed glasses. The scene is poorly lit. We cannot see his face in detail.

The scene changes. The lens or camera moves towards the seated man. It's centred on the figure, from the waist up. The lighting is better now, the focus too. He is in his thirties. Fine lines around his mouth and eyes. Two days' stubble. Sweat beads on his forehead, then slides down onto his nose. His glasses slip. A lip is swollen and cut.

The man pushes his glasses back to their position on the bridge of his nose. His nose is straight, never broken, but the viewers will not take much notice of that.

They won't, because they've just seen something else.

His hands. They moved together, as one, even though he only used one finger to push the glasses back.

They moved as one because they are connected at the wrist, by handcuffs.

It's then that the man's outfit makes more sense, and those watching will make the connection.

He is wearing an orange jumpsuit. A prisoner.

1

But this man is no prisoner of the law, and all of a sudden the audience gets it.

They have seen footage like this before. From Syria and Iraq and other places where nothing good comes of such an image.

This is a hostage situation. Propaganda. The audience will now know that the man seated is there not of his own volition. He is captive. But what will happen next? Should they look away? Will they see the captors? Will there be a beheading?

No. It's not like that.

This man? They're making him *do* something.

And he is about to talk, to the camera. There are unseen people around him, those who must be forcing him to do this, those who gave him that fat lip and the bruise coming up on his cheek. That's what the audience at home will think, that's what the world media will say: this poor guy has been worked over and they're playing with him.

But it's worse than that. It's worse because as bad as it seems for this man, it's going to be just as bad for those watching. What this scene is about today? It will take up all the air time for the next thirty-six hours.

Because what the captive man is about to say, what and who he is, will irrevocably change the world. All within the next day and a half. Forever.

Walker exhaled. *Inevitability . . .*

The CIA taught Jed Walker how to travel. How to remain inconspicuous. Avoid capture. Prior to that, military service taught Walker how to kill a man with nothing but his bare hands, and that's all he had at his disposal right now, having just passed through airport security at LAX. *Well, that's not exactly true*, he thought, in hindsight, watching the two men approach. He had his small backpack, which contained a change of clothes and toiletries. A few items would do. A toothbrush through the eye socket into the brain. The straps of the backpack could be used to choke a man. He had a paperback novel in there with an orange cover that he'd found in his hotel room that morning – and from the few pages he'd read during the cab ride to the airport, it could probably bore them to death.

A few decent options, but none was a good one right now.

He made a mental checklist of the possibilities around him. Steel-framed chairs. Laminated, sharp-edged tabletops. Metal stands in gift shops. Any number of items from said gift shops. The overpriced food from the restaurants. The fast food – he could force-feed these two guys a couple of foie-gras geese and watch them have coronaries. Gavage, it was called, but in France they used feeding tubes and corn and fattened the geese up for seventeen days then slaughtered them at four months. Funny how the Europeans had such strict laws for some things. At any

3

rate, Walker didn't have seventeen days, let alone four months. A glass beer bottle to the temple would be quicker. A twist of a neck.

But not now. Inevitability, and all that.

For Walker, a life on the outer had honed his thinking. Improvising. Making do. Surviving. To use what was at hand and to adapt on the fly and do whatever it took to see one more day.

He knew from the scene in front of him that he only had seconds of freedom remaining. Maybe thirty. He was trapped and he had little choice but to take what was coming.

Walker knew that none of his evasion training would come into play today. It would not help, because today he was a target. Not randomly selected. Not pulled aside for conspicuous behaviour. The men who came for him knew who he was. They had purpose. A singular goal.

His detention.

So. Cut and run, or stand and fight? Neither option good. Not here. Not against two uniformed TSA officers. One had his hand on his holstered Glock. The other had a taser drawn in his dominant hand, hanging by his side. They only had eyes for Walker.

It was inevitable.

2

The two men dressed as TSA officers found Walker with ease. They knew what he looked like because they had seen a photo of him. They knew what he was capable of because they had read a brief summary of his physicality and experience. They had both served in Special Forces units, but their target today had done that too – and then some. They knew it was him because he was six-three and 230 pounds and he moved with the physicality of a pro athlete. He was thirty-nine years old and in his physical prime; statistically, he'd never be faster or stronger than he was now. They knew he had about twenty years' experience with the military and CIA doing special ops work. Rated beyond excellent in hand-to-hand combat and the use of firearms. Capable. A man not to be underestimated. Which is why they had their weapons ready. Their orders were simple: apprehend and render him to another country.

•

Hands on holstered weapons made it clear to Walker that these guys were not here to chat. They were not sent to relay a message or warning about his mission. They were here to detain him.

And he had a plane to catch.

Walker was in LAX's terminal six. He had already passed security, so turning back wasn't an option. And there were cameras everywhere.

Locked doors and security up the wazoo. So, running for it was not an option either.

Damn.

But he remained calm, because that was his general disposition and because Buddha once observed that inward calm cannot be maintained unless physical strength is constantly and intelligently replenished. Walker had not read much of Buddha, and his mental image of the deity wasn't exactly the symbol of physical peak conditioning, but he'd heard that titbit from a member of the Gurkha Regiment, and they were among the toughest soldiers he had ever met. The remark had come after the soldier, serving in the British Army, had disarmed two insurgents trying to gain entry to Baghdad Airport. Neither insurgent survived the encounter, or kept their head. Walker learned never to pick a fight with a Buddhist.

With running ruled out, Walker was left with two choices.

The first was to fight. Put these two guys down and run; hope to get away. But these TSA officers were ready for him, and back-up would be on hand within seconds. LAPD and the TSA's own heavily armed response units would be minutes away, tops.

He could see the cafe just twenty paces ahead, where he had planned to wait for his boarding call over a couple of strong coffees, and maybe even read the newspaper. The paper could wait, but the caffeine he needed. Long night. Long week. Big days and weeks ahead.

Walker sighed. Relaxed his shoulders. Decision made. No point fighting.

Which left one option.

Give himself up to detention.

So, Walker relaxed and took what was coming. It was inevitable. He watched the two federal officers approach, a few yards apart and coming at him from the side. He put his backpack on the floor by his feet and kept his hands in clear view, his arms loose and hanging by his sides. One of the TSA guys, the one with a hand on a taser, kept approaching while the other, with his hand on the butt of his service-issue Glock, slowed and took a step to Walker's side.

Five seconds of freedom remained.

Whatever this was, Walker was certain that he would miss his flight, which was boarding in twenty minutes. How often were the flights to Alaska? He had no idea. Every couple of hours, he figured, tops. With oil and gas prices so low, he saw no good reason for workers to be flooding into the state. Lumber and fishing crews would be year-round or seasonal, not some kind of fly-in-fly-out types with any regularity. That left tourism and those visiting family and friends, and there couldn't be much call for that, especially just as winter had so recently ended.

Walker was confident that he could be out of here within two hours. Three, tops. He would phone a friend, and that friend would place a call, and then more phone calls would be made down the chain until word filtered down to these two front-line guys. The officers would apologise, he'd be issued a new plane ticket and retrieve his papers and backpack and be on his way. He'd board a flight to Alaska, where he had plans to avert a terrorist attack. Call it two to three hours, beginning to end.

But it still didn't feel right, and he still wanted coffee, and a good fight *would* wake him up good and proper, that's for sure.

The TSA officers slowed as they neared, watching Walker with intense curiosity. The one with the hand on the Glock looked around. No-one batted an eyelid as they passed, regular people wheeling their carry-on baggage, drinking coffee from styrofoam cups. In their eyes, just another random stop-and-search. Thank 9/11 and the Boston bombing and recent events in New York and St Louis for that. A couple of wars and the Patriot Act played a part too. Just another day at LAX.

The two uniformed officers stopped just short of arm's reach from Walker.

'Josiah Walker,' the taser wielder said. 'Place your hands on your head. We're bringing you in.'

3

Walker weighed it up.

Still no good option. These two guys had to be the cream of TSA officers, big and tough, near to zero body fat and muscles that bulked out their uniforms. Each was just the other side of thirty. Definitely ex-military. And that he'd been called Josiah, which was fine because it was on his passport and driver's licence, but no-one called him that, aside from his mother, and thinking of her made him a little sad, just for a half second, then that turned to anger and frustration at the delay, and that ticked him off.

Walker said, 'Can I at least get a coffee first?'

No answer.

Walker was led towards a blank door that simply stated: 'Unauthorised access prohibited'. He ran through a list in his mind, the CIA paper he'd helped draft a long time back for operatives being taken to security screening at airports – how to evade such scrutiny, and, when taken to secondary screening, how to get out with your cover identity intact.

Confirmed or suspected government or military affiliation almost certainly raises the traveller's profile. Walker's passport and papers had none of that – they were new, organised by the Vice President not long ago, replacing the counterfeit ones Walker had commissioned in Croatia. *Airport officials receive advance information on arriving passengers from airlines through an advance-passenger information system and passenger name records. APIS information, which enables an advance check against watch lists, includes passenger name, date of birth, sex, passport details and secondary contact information.*

Any red flag there and you would be in for closer scrutiny, secondary screening. Walker could see the door to those rooms, clearly marked, as they shepherded him away. *Referral to secondary screening could occur for concrete reasons, such as a watch-list match or discovery of contraband, because of random selection, or because the inspector suspects that something about the traveller is not right. Behaviour, dress and demeanour also factor into an inspector's decision . . .*

LAX is a major international airport, but Walker was in terminal six, Alaskan Air. Officials at US airports on average send about one in thirty foreign tourists and business travellers to secondary screening, although particular airports may impose higher percentages for certain groups. But he was travelling within the country, so he didn't have to declare any purpose for flying, he didn't have to pass any kind of immigration.

He knew how to avoid suspicion and close scrutiny because he had helped craft that version of the CIA's training manual on how to travel. He knew that and yet here he was . . .

Part of him wondered how quickly word got filtered through systems about watch lists; the kind of list maintained by security services that can also include names of confirmed or suspected intelligence officers, as well as people under surveillance or suspicion by security agencies.

Walker had been on such a watch list run by the Department of Homeland Security and Interpol until barely a month ago. A slight misunderstanding, it had eventually been ruled. He'd been on plenty of lists run by other nations, allies and others. The fact was, every nation on earth tried to keep tabs on each other's spies. He'd spent more than a year on the US watch list, when he'd been forced to go off the grid and work solo to bring down corruption within the

CIA, and it had forced him to avoid major transportation hubs and all legitimate airports.

He had since been cleared, though, his records cleaned up by the White House. But maybe these guys hadn't got word. Maybe their databases flagged watch-list people for a set period of time in case there was a stuff-up and a terrorist was let through. Better to err on the side of caution.

So, while this shouldn't be about his name ringing any alarm bells, he was prepared for that to be the case.

Maybe it wasn't that. Maybe they *were* getting a message to him, from Bill McCorkell, about the Alaska op.

No. This was not a message from McCorkell – he'd use a plain-clothed FBI agent from the LA Field Office.

This was something else.

Random selection? Not with the intent these officers were showing.

No. This was a problem.

He had no time for problems, but there was little chance of evasion now that he'd passed security. A dash for an exit, triggering a fire alarm, blending in with the masses . . .

No. He had to stay on mission. Which meant he had to bluff and lie his way out of whatever was coming.

Walker knew it the second he saw the glance between the TSA officers. It was brief, but it was definitely a look. He now had a big problem. Because he was on no watch list, and he knew how to travel. He knew TSA procedures. There was no reason for them to take him to secondary screening.

The ticket was booked via McCorkell's office. The national security expert's involvement would not raise concerns in internal travel within the United States.

As he was led towards the secondary-screening rooms, Walker ran through what he had on him. A backpack. No firearms, nothing that triggered security, though he had to pass through the scanner twice but there was nothing unusual about that. His pack held a phone charger, two sets of clothes, toothbrush and shaving kit. No computer, nothing for them to spend hours pulling apart.

His cell phone was near new, a pre-paid on which he could contact McCorkell, and be contacted. That's all he'd planned to use it for. That's who he'd need to call, once given the chance to make a phone call.

The combination of procedures available in secondary screening, a stressful experience for any traveller, may pose a significant strain on an operational traveller's ability to maintain cover . . . Not Walker. He could get out of anything these guys could dish out – but he couldn't afford to miss the next flight, or the one after.

This was a set-up. But to what end? Ordered by whom?

Ahead of him was a corridor. White walls and ceiling, grey tiled floor.

A TSA officer was before him, the other after. The one in front had Walker's pack over his shoulder and still kept a hand on his Glock.

They walked in silence, past the secondary-screening rooms. They then passed storage rooms and change rooms and doors and corridors that led to building services and plant rooms. Finally they got to a door that opened up to a staircase that led outside, onto the tarmac. A car was waiting; an airport-labelled Jeep.

Walker was shoved into the back seat and pushed across. The taser man climbed in next to him and pulled a black sack over Walker's head. His world went dark, but not just because of the material – the hypodermic needle that entered his neck had injected etorphine. He was out.

4

The hood was pulled off at the same time as a needle entered his arm.

Walker blinked away darkness and sucked in air. He was seated, cuffed to a chair, his arms behind his back. His head rolled about as he looked around, his equilibrium slowly returning as the drugs wore off, vertigo being a side effect of the cocktail of barbiturates. As his head tilted to the side it felt heavy, like a hundred-pound kettle bell atop his neck; his brain couldn't make sense of it and his neck muscles couldn't fight it, it was pulling him down and down, round and around, but he didn't fall over, he didn't tip, because his chair was bolted to the floor. His eyes could not find focus. He blinked. Wondered how he got here, but the concept of here and there was too abstract. For now it was all about survival. Of regaining his faculties. Of fading into the now. He closed his eyes and let the spinning and tugging just happen. There was nothing he could do about that, but he focused. The question *Where am I?* could not be answered, not like this, not now. There was a precursor to that question, and he felt that the answer to it was within grasp, if he could just manage to focus.

How did I get here . . .

•

Five past ten am Pacific Standard Time was five past one pm Eastern Standard Time.

An executive secretary, a second lieutenant in the Air Force, rapped his knuckles on his boss's door and entered. It was the first time he'd had to barge in quickly and to the point, and he didn't relish it. He was the General's fifth secretary in as many months. Her temper was legendary. But this couldn't wait.

'Ma'am, you've gotta watch,' the executive secretary said. He turned the TV on. 'It's on all news channels, live feed.'

General Susan Christie, US Army, head of US Cyber Command, looked up from her laptop. Her hair was a neat crop of silver-flecked red, and she had the poise of someone who always worked hard to keep fit and capable.

The television showed a man in an orange jumpsuit. The tagline was 'Breaking news – live'.

Christie said, 'Where is this?'

'No idea, ma'am.'

'Who is it?' Christie asked. She leaned forward, watching, listening as her aide turned up the volume. 'Have they identified him?'

He said, 'Just listen, ma'am.'

Acknowledgements

This book marks ten years of working with Hachette: ten years, ten novels, and I couldn't be happier. With *The Hunted* I owe a huge thank you to my publishing team: Vanessa Radnidge, Kate Stevens and Claire de Medici, for once again making the best of my work. Fiona, Louise, Justin and Anna have been by my side the whole way and very encouraging of this latest thriller. Big thanks to all others involved in the publishing process, especially those frontline sales staff who work tirelessly getting my work into readers' hands.

My thanks to my family and friends for the fun and friendship. The usual suspects, Emily (E Mac) and Tony W (Pa T), did an early read – thanks for being critical.

Gratitude is due to my agents for keeping things ticking along, particularly Pippa Masson and Laura Dunn.

This book is the product of a decade's worth of conversations with serving and former intelligence and military personnel across three continents, and I'm thankful for their time and candour.

Nicole, more than ever, has been my strongest advocate and biggest support.